THE
OLYMPUS
PROJECT

ZOË
ROUTH

For Leith

*Thanks for showing how leadership can
build a world worth living in*

PART ONE

THE CALL OUT

CHAPTER ONE

Humans evolve in their environment. If we can create environments that expand the human spirit, we have a chance of calling forward mankind's better nature.

THE WORLD DESIGNERS' MANIFESTO

Sydney: Xanthe

THE SPACESUIT PRESSED down on her like a lead blanket. The chair rattled and shook her violently. Xanthe felt the skin of her face grow taut and strained. Suddenly there was weightlessness. Relief. And the view of the world below: a soft, blue, mottled curve against the black forever of space. Awe swelled within her as it did every time she snuck in to the VR simulation hub for a joy ride.

All too soon, they re-entered the Earth's orbit, landed, and the lights burned bright, assaulting her senses. Back now in the VR room with its bland walls and disappointing reality. Xanthe trudged into the change room along with the other punters and stripped off her well-worn, hired sensor suit. She slipped out to the stinking hot streets of Sydney.

Poor Sydney. A pale version of its former glorious self. The city had survived the long years of COVID-19, the first pandemic. But then subsequent viruses had sent city dwellers scurrying for the country. Towering office blocks stood empty like soulless sentinels. The ground-floor windows, at first bright with hopeful 'For Lease' signs, were boarded up and smattered with graffiti. The 'For Sale' signs came next and fell, like autumn leaves, trodden underfoot. The tsunami washed out the rest, wrecking the beautiful harbour with a devastating backwash. It was only when the drought and the rising inland heat sent people back to the coast that Sydney experienced its latest renaissance. Old commercial properties were repurposed for inner-city living. New density requirements crammed people into renovated eco-buildings, brimming inside with vertical greenery, coated on the outside with plants to keep the structures cool. These often formed a hydroponic sleeve, feeding the building's inhabitants with a vertical farm.

Xanthe stopped on a corner and looked up. It was one of her prized projects. As chief designer, she had turned this old corporate tower into a family oasis. The entrance was resplendent with trees and tropical flowers. The exterior heaved with plant life and a few remaining birds grateful for a cool haven. Her smartest innovations were the network of clear plastic tunnel slides that allowed people to navigate quickly between floors, and habitat stations with ladders on the outside. She had managed to create a community where all food, entertainment and social interactions were self-contained. No one needed to brave the heat of the day ever again. She called it 'The Pantheon'. She smiled at the arrogance. Hell, she'd earned the right.

Xanthe took another moment and squinted up at The Pantheon, then pulled the sunshade over her brow. It was barely dawn, but the heat was baking already. It was late to be out, and Simon would be waiting.

Simon could always tell when she'd been to the VR Hub. Was it the longing she tried desperately to hide? The telltale stench of sweat from the overused VR suit still clinging to her? The disdain would crawl across his face. "Why do you bother? Falling into the crass, commercial claws of the Big Tech oligarchies. Such a betrayal…" and the lecture would continue, always the same, always bitter. He was an Earth Advocate, as she had been. Still was. Mostly.

Simon was committed to the salvation of the planet. He believed that technology should be deployed to rectify the climate disasters that ravaged Earth, not for some billionaire's folly to colonise other planets. He did appreciate the logic that life on Earth was ultimately doomed, since it would eventually boil dry as it approached the expanding sun. But that was still billions of years away. Life was happening *now*. Whichever philosophical or spiritual lens you put on it, Earth was humanity's home, and we should embrace our fate alongside it. Why poison other planets with our ineptitude? Better to get the management of this one right.

Xanthe heard his words echo from their last argument. She agreed with him on many points. Yes, Earth was sacred. Yes, it was beautiful and worth saving. But, she tried to add in spite of his eye rolling, consciousness was valuable too, and we had a moral obligation to help it survive our planet's eventual doom. That usually sparked a diatribe about the responsibilities of the wealthy and the outrageous waste of money on space tourism. She often backed down at this point. It was hard to argue about the money side of things.

Xanthe wasn't quite ready for another confrontation. She took the long way home and headed towards the harbour. It drew her there. The sea's siren songs plucked her heart strings, mournful. There on the harbour, the dawn licked the sky with a harsh red tongue. Xanthe remembered the rush of the tsunami once again. The dreadful roar and the incomprehensible power of the water that picked her up and threw her forward in a turbulence that choked all other sound. It was a moment, only a moment. The relief of breath. Then the awful realisation of loss. So much horrible loss.

As a paramedic, the despair was overwhelming. So many people she tried to save and couldn't. So many people lost. As the grief subsided, Xanthe found new purpose in the wake of the tsunami. She abandoned her job and dived into cleaning up the city. She worked first with the salvage crews, then trained with Gaia Enterprises to design new communities. She believed in resurrection, in renewal. The Phoenix, Lazarus and all those old tales. They would make something glorious of this wrecked, debris-strewn city. They would find beauty even as the world tore her heart in two. They would salvage what they could from the vengeful Earth and create something wonderful, beautiful and worth living for.

"I thought I'd find you here."

Xanthe jumped a little, startled from her reverie, and turned away from the water she had been staring over.

"Maja." Though she was surprised, her voice came out flat. "What are you doing here?"

Xanthe eyed the older woman with her impossibly smooth, brown skin, and noticed the trace of a few lines at the corner of her eyes, deeper now than when she had last seen her.

"I've come to see you." Maja's face was gentle, filled with love, her dark eyes deep.

You could swim in those eyes, thought Xanthe. Drown in them. She shuddered slightly.

"How are you, Xanthe?"

Xanthe considered Maja, then looked out again at the water. A wind stirred the surface. The hot wind rising already.

"I'm fine." They both knew it wasn't true. But true enough.

Maja took Xanthe's arm in hers and steered her along the shore that was one of the first areas they had repaired. People needed a place to go. To think. To breathe.

"Why are you here, Maja?" Xanthe knew Maja did not make house calls for former employees.

"We've got a new project to tender for," Maja said.

Xanthe frowned. Why not use the holocall? Since when did a project tender require in-person visits? Xanthe waited and let the silence draw Maja's words from her.

"It's something new for Gaia Enterprises. Something... audacious."

Xanthe found this surprising. "Audacious? Gaia has always been audacious, Maja. It's why I joined in the first place. Land reclamation communities that span the globe. Floating worlds. Rebuilding flood-ravaged cities. And what could be more audacious than the underwater worlds?"

Xanthe stopped to look Maja full in the face. What was she playing at? Gaia Enterprises had been one of the salvations of climate-change-ravaged Earth. After the droughts, the tsunamis, the rising sea levels, Gaia was helping humanity adapt to the devastation. It was creating new habitats. Although, not fast enough, thought Xanthe. Climate refugees were clinging to life, eking out an existence close to the water, living in the shadows during the day to stay out of the heat. Even now she could feel their eyes on her and Maja, hiding in the rubble of ruined buildings, in makeshift shanties. Xanthe and Maja were out too late in the day already. The sun burned the air around them. Xanthe felt the sweat soaking her thin cotton robe. Desert wear. In a city by the sea.

"What new project, Maja?"

Maja held her gaze, then looked away. "We are putting in a bid for the Moon."

Xanthe stared, aghast. "You're kidding!" she cried. "The Moon? Since when did Gaia abandon Earth?" This went against all Gaia principles. As its very name indicated, Gaia was about the Earth, not space.

"I know it sounds like a – a change."

"A change! This is sacrilege! Gaia Enterprises is about restoring human life on planet Earth! For years we've battled the Space Cowboys and their crazy quest to colonise Mars! All that money!

All those resources that could be saving lives – here – on Earth." Xanthe fumed. And she heard it too in her own words: *for years we've battled…* We. Even after all these years, she still felt the 'we'. The pull back to her designer origins.

Maja waited until Xanthe had vented her outrage.

"I thought the same. At first." Again, Maja hooked her arm through Xanthe's and guided her towards some shade at the corner of an old building. "But this is an opportunity to promote Gaia's work and vision here on Earth. A Moon project will show how beautiful Earth is. How it is worth preserving. Worth saving. There is no better view of the planet than from space. As you well know."

Xanthe froze. How did Maja know about her VR Hub visits? She kept it all a secret, except from Simon. Simon. Damn him. He must have told Maja. His own bitterness and frustration. The old wound between them, a heaviness like a scab on their relationship, big and ugly and misshapen even as it aimed to protect them both.

"Why are you telling me this, Maja? I'm not part of Gaia's pool of designers anymore."

"I know. But we're making a special callout. We need skills like yours. You've got the medical background and successful world design experience. Perfect for the complex designs needed for the Moon – and I personally appreciate your community focus." She paused and glanced at Xanthe. "I know you didn't like the direction Gaia was heading with its commercial decisions, but sometimes leadership means making choices that look bad in the short term, if the long term is served."

"Come on, Maja, I don't buy into the ends justifying the means. It looked like a sellout to me."

"I prefer to think of it as a 'borrow-in'."

"Really? Gaia Enterprises agreed to build a new Disneyland for crying out loud! Hardly helping climate refugees, as far as I can see."

Maja smiled at that. "There's always room for joy in the world,

Xanthe. Besides, that project allowed us to invest in terraforming technology. Not everything that looks like indulgence has no value.

"In any case, Gaia has gone from strength to strength. The worlds we've built are creating new hope for people around the planet. For its part, the Olympus Project is a little like the Disneyland one, except that the outcome isn't just joy rides. It's also asteroid mining and research. If we win the bid, it will give us another revenue stream that will advance our Earth salvage mission. And we'll take an ongoing management fee once the base is established. That fee will fund multiple projects we've been longing to launch here on Earth."

Xanthe was quiet as she considered Maja's elaborate business plans.

Maja continued. "We're opening up selection for the Olympus Project bid to applicants from other design companies. No more than one applicant per company to try and narrow the pool. We're expecting a huge amount of interest. Gaia has never opened its doors to other designers and we suspect there will be a few wanting to get a foot in the door. We're running a selection to put together a design and deliver team. The team will work the prototype as part of the project bid. If the bid is successful, that team will build the project together. On the Moon."

Xanthe gasped. Off-planet world building! It wasn't just about the design, it was the build too! But regardless of what Maja said, it was the antithesis of Gaia. Why were they abandoning their principles? If you can't beat 'em, join 'em? Selling the value of Earth, from space? Come on. There was more going on here aside from some possible future management fee.

The Moon. Against her will, Xanthe's heart pounded with excitement. The VR Hub had been her secret indulgence, a place to escape the pain that dogged her days on Earth. The chance to actually travel off-world, to space, to the Moon. Was she a hypocrite for wanting to experience the beauty of Earth from afar?

Maybe it would help her to find some peace again. Or maybe she just wanted to run away. And the Moon was about as far away as she could get. For now. The Mars plan was not quite in reach, in spite of the billions the Space Cowboys had thrown at it, not to mention the twenty-six lives already burnt in the pursuit.

"What do you want from me?" Xanthe asked finally.

"I want you to be part of the core design team. We need three lead designers, and then a pilot, mechanic and life support specialist to make up the team of six. Gaia would like you to be the third designer. We need you. You'd balance the team nicely."

"Wow. I'm honoured. Shocked, but honoured. I need some time to think about this, Maja."

"Of course. It's a big commitment."

"Just out of interest, who are the other two?"

"Troy Bruin and Xavier Consus."

"Oh my God! The superstars!"

Maja smiled. She was proud of these Gaia designers and was always delighted by the impression they made.

Xanthe took a deep breath. "Okay, tell me more," she said.

CHAPTER TWO

*Perspective is a matter of viewpoint. Change where
you stand, and the view changes too.*

ATHENA AI IN WISDOM OF THE AGES

Sydney: Xanthe

"YOU CAN'T BE serious." Simon leant against their apartment's kitchen counter. He clutched a mug of coffee, though its contents had soured for him. Everything tasted off with Xanthe's news.

"Maja says it's the best way forward for the future of Gaia Enterprises. For the Earth. People will want to invest when they see its beauty, its fragility."

"That's total bullshit, Xanthe, and you know it. They're selling out." He was more furious than she'd ever seen him. "You left Gaia years ago, remember? And why? You didn't like the direction, then – too much focus on commercial interests and not enough on design, on the human element. And now you want to *re-join* them? In space? Unbelievable!"

Xanthe let him fume. She didn't expect him to agree with her. His views on space tourism had been hardening year after year.

He protested along with the others every time there was a new space travel announcement. He was a dyed-in-the-wool Earthist. Xanthe's trips to the VR Hub and her joy in simulated space travel only widened the distance between them. Where they might once have leant into one another, nursing their aching hearts from the gaping wound the tsunami left, they now found themselves leaning elsewhere. Simon turned his gaze to the Earth, wanting to calm the fury that caused their loss, and make right the abuse of progress. As if by healing the planet, he might somehow heal his heart. Xanthe turned skyward: searching for meaning in the stars, away from the place that raked their lives with its claws. How could she reconcile nature and the pain that drowned her a little more each day?

This project was a chance to bridge the grief. A new colony on the Moon so that Earth's children might see it better, for the first time, and find some hope for a brighter future.

Or maybe, her secret heart whispered, it's a chance to escape.

CHAPTER THREE

A reputation is built brick by brick, moment
by moment, over a lifetime.

THE WORLD DESIGNERS' MANIFESTO

Sea Rover: Jonas

JONAS DROPPED THE heavy wrench, smashing the toes on his left foot.

"Bollocks!" he blasted into the steamy enclosed space of the engine room. He uncoiled himself from the awkward position around the engine and stretched his back while the throbbing eased in his foot. He wiped his greasy hands on his overalls then retrieved the wrench.

"Just one more nut, you bloody bastard, and we're out of here." Jonas was eager to go topside after the suffocating heat of the ship's engine room.

Ship. He knew he shouldn't call it that. It was the *Sea Rover*. A floating mass and home to 1,843 citizens of a semi-autonomous community. His parents, Don and Jenny Seaborn, were particular about that. They were proud of being the first world designers to create a movable world. Even if it was really just two cruise ships webbed together, thought Jonas. Otherwise, they wouldn't need him to service the damned engines.

He cranked the last nut in place, untangled himself, and inspected his work.

"She's a beauty!" he said to the empty room, and smiled. His parents were disappointed he did not enjoy the more grandiose aspects of world design, like they did. They found his interest in mechanical engineering pedestrian. Such snobs! They even changed their name to 'Seaborn' when news of the *Sea Rover*'s success went global. So pretentious. They rode that wave of fame high, taking credit for the 'groundbreaking' designs. How the media loved their stupid puns.

But it was Jonas's innovations with the engines and steering mechanisms that were the secret to the ship's manoeuvrability. And it was his damned designs that kept the webbing floor between the two hulls from ripping apart in heavy seas, maintaining the image of a landmass, rather than an oversized catamaran. They relied on his expertise more than ever now. Don and Jenny Seaborn had a lot to thank him for. But didn't.

He closed the engine room door behind him and took the narrow metal stairs two at a time until he reached the upper deck. He liked to test his fitness wherever he could. Good for martial arts training. He burst on to the deck with a nimble jump. The air was sweet after the confines of the engine room, but the sun seared his eyes, and he moved instinctively back towards the stairwell, into the shade. Even with the sea breeze, it was still damned hot. How the landlocked idiots coped he had no idea.

He went quickly to his own quarters to clean off the engine oil. "Neptune. Read the headlines." The AI responded:

"Twelve new corporations join the Earth Alliance. Green Economy policies gain momentum around the world. Pressure mounts against the United States to sign the Asteroid Mining Agreement…"

"Like that will ever happen," Jonas mumbled as he discarded his sweaty, stained overalls.

"...Earth First protests claim six lives in latest clash with European authorities. Mining heiress and Earth Alliance founder Aryanna Sharif rumoured to be behind the latest Moon Base bid—"

"Holy crap! Neptune, bring up the last headline report on the holodisplay."

The hologram story sprang to life as Jonas stood in his underwear, gaping. It showed the reclusive trillionaire with her trademark oversized sunglasses and white silk robes, on the steps of the Lunar Commission. Her bodyguards escorted her through the throngs of protesters to her waiting self-driving car.

Neptune continued: "Sharif refused to speak with reporters as Earth First protesters chanted 'Sellout'. Sharif's alleged tender for the controversial Moon Base is the third contender for the Lunar Commission's Olympus Project. Earth Alliance spokesperson Eli Heltay did not deny the rumour, stating, 'Earth Alliance remains resolute in its commitment to terraforming Earth and preserving habitat for humanity and all sentient beings. All projects remain committed to that end.'"

"Sounds like tap dancing to me. Neptune, bring up stories on the Olympus Project." Jonas scanned the article titles. 'Lunar Commission signs Moon Base contract as addendum to the Outer Space Treaty Moon Agreement', 'First Moon Base to be built within five years', Lunar Commission names the Moon Base "The Olympus Project" as protests continue'.

"Neptune, who is tendering for the Olympus Project?"

"The Olympus Project currently has three tender bids: Spaceward Bound, Human Habs and Gaia Enterprises."

"Hell's bloody bells! Gaia Enterprises?!" No way. Space tourism was not Gaia's thing; the Earth was Gaia's thing. Besides, Gaia didn't have that kind of money. Design and prototype with a twelve-month proof of concept would cost an absolute bomb.

Maybe there was truth to the Sharif rumour. She had the funds for it. But space tourism? Was it a sellout after all? Couldn't be. Sharif didn't need the money. She didn't have the ego either. Not like the other Space Cowboys. Jonas stared out the porthole window of his quarters to the vast shiny swell of the ocean.

"Neptune, bring up Gaia Enterprises." And there it was: 'Gaia Enterprises is pleased to announce its bid for the Olympus Project. The proposed Moon Base will be an exciting hub for space research, asteroid mining and human development. Gaia Enterprises sees this as important infrastructure and a stepping stone for its Earth terraforming and world design projects. We are seeking the best world designers, engineers, food scientists, life support specialists, medical technicians, mechanics and psychologists.'

"I'll be damned! They're opening the bloody gates!" Gaia had been a closed shop since its very beginning. They recruited and trained their own world designers, refusing graduates of other world design programs. Talk about elitism! But it had worked for them. They'd added terraforming to their design business, all along spruiking the future of Mother Earth as their main concern. They were the most successful world designers on the planet, with superstar designers like Troy Bruin in their midst. But not even Gaia had the funds to run a Moon Base tender without significant backing. Spaceward Bound had big tech giant Metasyn, Human Habs had the big pharma conglomerate Novartis Sun. And Gaia Enterprises had... Aryanna Sharif?

But now here was a chance to get in! Jonas had applied to Gaia Enterprises straight out of high school but had been knocked back due to his reputation as an unruly kid. Fair call, too, he thought. He was an arrogant and spoilt little shit. It was only when the Don kicked him off the *Sea Rover* and told him to 'shape up or ship out permanently' that he got his act together. He went to the Netherlands to study land reclamation world design. Hated it. He missed the freedom of movement of the *Sea Rover*. But he stuck with it and added ship engineering, waste management systems and enclosed ecosystems to his world design quiver. He consulted on a few world design projects before heading back to the *Sea Rover* for a stint. That stint turned into two years. Long enough in Mummy and Daddy's long, unappreciative shadow.

"Neptune, open up the Gaia Enterprises application form for the Olympus Project. For mechanics." Still in his underwear, shower now forgotten, Jonas Seaborn launched his own ship into uncharted waters.

CHAPTER FOUR

Ambition can be a useful tool. It can redirect
destructive energy for constructive ends.

MAJA GARCIA, THE JOURNALS

Los Angeles: Madison

"Damn! That was some shit-hot flyin', Mad Dog!"

Madison Floyd removed her helmet and smiled broadly at her colleague. They bumped knuckles. P.J. finished fuelling the plane and returned the bowser to its cradle.

"They don't call me Mad Dog for nothin', P.J.!" Madison thumped him on the shoulder, and he feigned pain. He followed her out of the hangar to the pilots' lockers. She peeled off her flying suit and folded it neatly. P.J. tried not to look at her long lean legs as she stood in her shorts and undershirt and applied deodorant.

"Those were some fancy turns up there. You teachin' those goons at Spaceward Bound those tricks?" he asked, staring into her face and working hard not to let his gaze wander.

"Not a chance! Those goons are barely passing the basics. Lord knows how they're going to put a bid in for the Olympus Project.

They think just because they change their name it qualifies them for something like space travel."

"What was their old name, again?"

"Tech Surf."

P.J. scoffed. "So lame. Who's runnin' the show over there anyhow?"

"It's still Lincoln Ellison."

"He's that woke surfie guy who made a ton of cash on NFTs and Bitcoin?"

"That's the one!" Madison pulled on her bomber jacket, put on her cap and aviator glasses. "Beer?" she asked.

"Sure." They headed to the pilots' lounge. "What's the deal with you and them anyhow? You're training their pilots, but they won't put you on the Olympus Project bid ticket?"

"That's right."

"Why are they jilting you, Mad Dog?"

"Why do you think?"

P.J.'s. face dropped in horror.

"Not because – not because – you're *black*, is it?"

"No, you idiot. Not this time. It's because Lincoln Ellison is banging some chick and he promised her a prime gig on the project. Turns out she's always wanted to fly, and so presto, they hire me to train her up, along with a few backups, just in case."

"Just in case – why?"

"Just in case she's not up to it. Just in case he gets bored of her. Who knows what goes through the mind of someone who is that drunk on money and power?"

"I hope you charged them a premium, Mad Dog."

"You better believe it. Top dollar. Plus 20 percent for pain and suffering – having to endure their ridiculous antics."

"What do you mean?"

"They're like a cult over there. Every morning Lincoln himself is there giving them a pep talk. He waves his arms all around like he's some kind of preacher. He gets them to huddle in a big group hug and chant stuff. He tells stories about space-faring heroes of yore. He has pictures of old spaceships on huge posters all around the hangar. You know the ones – they all look like giant dicks."

"Really?"

"No word of a lie. Who wants to fly a ship that looks like a giant penis for Chrissake? Except for maybe Mr Lincoln Ellison. Not sure what he's making up for or trying to express with that design. After about half an hour of this bullshit, they break up and all pat each other on the ass."

"Really?"

"Lincoln even tried to pat me on the ass."

"No!"

"Not one word of a lie."

"He didn't! What did you do?"

"I gave him the Mad Dog death stare and he backed off."

P.J. snorted at the thought of anyone trying to use an ass slap to get chummy with Madison "Mad Dog" Floyd. At the bar, he signalled the bartender for two beers. He handed one to Madison and they clinked bottles.

"To the wind beneath your wings!" she said.

"May it always be at your back!" he replied. They savoured a long pull on the bottle. P.J. picked at the label as it grew soggy with condensation.

"Hey Maddie… what about the Olympus Project? There is no better pilot for that project."

"Don't worry, P.J. I got it covered. Not all my eggs are in the Spaceward Bound basket."

"What's your plan?"

"I sent my application to Gaia Enterprises weeks ago."

"What? But they only just announced that this week!"

Madison tapped her nose. "It's who you know, P.J. A little

birdie gave me a heads up. Said they would put in a good word for me."

"Who's that?"

"Huw Chan." P.J.'s eyes widened. "I flew him and a few business buddies around all the disaster zones after the tsunami down in Australia. I told him about some land reclamation projects I'd heard about that would be well suited to solving the crisis."

P.J.'s face was incredulous. "You planted the seed of Gaia Enterprises in Australia?"

"I couldn't say for sure I was the one to give him the idea. But he did like my thinking. Told him the tsunami was a blessing in disguise. We could rebuild communities where everyone had a secure home. Where people didn't have to fight for scraps. Everyone had a place, something to contribute to, you know."

P.J. was quiet. He knew Madison was thinking of her mother. Gemma Floyd was a powerful campaigner for social justice. Until she turned militant and ended up in prison. Madison donned her mother's social justice mantle after that but hadn't really found a constructive outlet for her frustrations. Except to become the best damn pilot, in and out of the US military. Since she completed her service in the Air Force, Madison was a sought-after private trainer for all the big private corporations – especially the space tourism companies. She was an expert on suborbital flights.

"When do you hear about the gig?"

Madison shrugged as she sipped her beer. "Applications close this week. Selection is in about a month. So, anytime now."

P.J. nearly dropped his beer on the bar. "Damn! That's soon! Imagine that! Mad Dog on the MOON!"

They laughed and clinked their beers together.

CHAPTER FIVE

There is no deeper pain than that inflicted by families.

ATHENA AI IN WISDOM OF THE AGES

Helsinki: David

DAVID ERIKSSON SAT across from his husband, Sven. David's mood boiled along with the kettle as their daughter Sophia fussed over making the tea. David would do that: sit grim and silent, letting his thoughts work into an angry roll before they escaped in steamy frustration.

And it was always directed at the same person.

"Sven. You must stop taking her money. She's an adult for goodness sake. You must respect her rights, no? And this drinking is ridiculous. What did you get into this time? I thought we got rid of everything." David clenched his fists, punctuating his sentences with little angry thumps on the table.

"I only gave him a little money, Daddy," Sophia said. "He was desperate for coffee. And I forgot about the gin we got last Christmas as a gift. It was up in the top cupboard. He obviously found it. We should have hidden it better."

"Three hundred Euros buys a lot of coffee, Sophia. You've got to stop making excuses for him." He slapped a hand on the table, making them all jump. Hot water spilled from the kettle as she made the tea, burning Sophia's hand. She set it down quickly and twirled to run cold water over the burn.

Sven watched Sophia with bleary eyes as she dried her hand and inspected the injured area. Then she went to the cupboard, took a few mugs out and set them by the teapot.

"The tea will help, Sven," she said quietly.

"Thank you Sweetheart. Always such a help." Sven smiled and slobbered a little, flopping a hand over hers and squeezing.

David watched him as despair strangled his heart.

Get a grip! They don't write your story, you do. David fought to control his whirling thoughts. *You get to choose what happens next.*

"I'm stepping out for some air," he said. He opened the door to their small deck and breathed in the city night. Somewhere above the haze he knew there were stars. Sometimes you could see them, if the smog cleared a little.

He felt so stuck in this narrative. Always the same argument. Sven steals money from one of them, spends it at the casino, loses it all, drinks himself silly to blot out the remorse. It couldn't go on. Something needed to change.

He thought again of Gaia Enterprises and the call-out. Their promise of building better worlds. *Well, this one sure as hell can't get any worse, no?* Ever since he could remember, David had wanted to be a world designer. He fell in love with the legends: Troy Bruin and his crazy architecture that had both flair and environmental savvy; Xavier Consus and his family's innovations in vertical farming and seaweed products. He loved the idea that you could design communities that nurtured people's bodies and minds. Communities that were peaceful and equitable. Resourceful and sustainable.

It was a long shot, he knew. Very competitive. Plus, he loved the work he did with Archello in Helsinki. As a pilot, he had fantastic views of the archipelagos they built. He was proud of their designs. He always hoped to get into design school and saved carefully once he was a pilot. Then he met Sven. The gambling whittled away his savings and then raising a daughter... it kept them poor and struggling.

But Sophia was an adult now. She could strike out on her own, get away from this disastrous family triangle.

What they needed was a circuit-breaker. Maybe, just maybe, the Olympus Project could do that for them. If he was away on the project, then on the Moon, he couldn't fall for Sven's cycle of sin and repentance. His desperate, sincere apologies. The promises, broken again and again. He wouldn't need to forgive over and over. They could send Sophia away to university, like she desperately wanted. With the project's salary he could afford the tuition.

It would be a fresh start. For all of them. David dared to hope. He felt the flicker of freedom as he imagined contending for a spot on the Project. Something else stirred within him. A memory of who he once was, before Sven's gambling and booze and stress and endless debt. He remembered that man – he was fun, he was carefree, he enjoyed life. He enjoyed *living*.

It might just work. He resolved to review the application process again in the morning. What did he have to lose? *You can't win if you don't play, no?*

CHAPTER SIX

There is nothing that compares to the freedom of the sea.

DON AND JENNY SEABORN IN WORLD
DESIGNERS: PERSPECTIVE AND PRACTICE

Singapore: Pabi

PABI GUPTA LIT the incense stick and pressed his palms together in prayer. He murmured the words of the sutras over and over while the sickly sweet smoke coiled around him.

"*Beta!* Come now for dinner! Chana dhal is ready."

His mother's voice whined down the hall. Pabi wondered for the umpteenth time how everything she said could sound like a reprimand.

"Yes, Mummy-ji," he answered. He mumbled a few more prayers and steeled himself for the nightly ordeal.

At the table, his father sat like a bloated frog, all jowls and rubbery lips. His hands were already sticky with curry, and he snuffled his food with obvious pleasure. His mother stood with a pan and spatula, waiting to serve her son.

"Sit. Here. Chapati." She slid the bread on to the mountain

of dhal on his plate. Pabi reached for the salt. His mother slapped his hand with the spatula.

"No salt! You haven't even tried it yet! You think so little of my cooking, Pabi, you must smother it with salt?"

"Mummy-ji – you know I like salt."

"You like it too much. It will harden your arteries. And then you'll have high blood pressure like your Papa-ji."

Pabi glanced at his father. He knew it wasn't the salt that contributed to his father's high blood pressure, but the vats of ghee in his mother's cooking. That and the sweet gooey desserts his father snuck every night that his wife pretended not to notice. Pabi wisely kept his thoughts to himself.

His mother returned the pan and spatula to the kitchen and came back to the table. She watched Pabi tuck into his dinner. Then, satisfied he was eating enough and showing sufficient enjoyment, she served herself a small portion.

They ate in silence. His mother refilled Pabi's and his father's plates without asking, eyeing their consumption. *Fat husband, strong son, duty done.* Her mantra was laid out silently each night alongside the cutlery and jumble of dishes.

Pabi ate a little more than usual to make sure she was in a good mood for what he was about to say. He rarely spoke at the dinner table except when asked a question. He steadied his breath and began.

"Mummy-ji, Papa-ji. I have applied to Gaia Enterprises for the Olympus Project."

His father's jaw stopped moving, but his eyes remained fixed on his plate. He paused, swallowed, then wiped his mouth on his napkin and looked at his wife.

Her eyes caught her husband's and then she began to wail. "Pabi – not this nonsense again! When will you get married?! You are already thirty years old! I will be dead in my grave before I see my grandchildren! And Rechna – sweet Rechna – how long will she wait for you? First you disappear into the military and now this Moon story."

"Mummy-ji – I had to do military service. We have to in Singapore!"

"Don't interrupt your mother!" she scolded, waving a half-eaten chapati at him. "You make Rechna wait and wait. She is such a good girl – so smart, a *doctor, beta.* She is not getting any younger. She too is thirty. Her eggs are going mouldy. They will be useless soon. You go to the Moon, Rechna's eggs will shrivel, and your mother will die with a broken heart. No grandchildren and an ungrateful son…"

"Ishani! Enough." His father's bullfrog voice boomed across the table. She pursed her lips and threw down the chapati. She wiped her hands on her napkin and grimaced at Pabi.

"Pabi. Son. We have already discussed this. Our opinion has not changed. We need you at home. To contribute. To make a decent living. It is time to settle down." His father's tone was gentle after his outburst.

Pabi took a deep breath. He spoke quietly and looked at each of them in turn.

"Papa-ji. Mummy-ji. I honour you as my parents. I have tried to be a good son. I do not drink. I do not go out. I study. I work. I pray. I will marry Rechna – I promise. I do not forget. This one thing – this Olympus Project – is something I have dreamed of since I was a very little boy. You know it! You've seen the pictures on my walls and screensavers. Every school holiday I attended Space Camp. I have always wanted to be an astronaut, but I know we could not afford it as a family. Being a pilot in the army was one place closer to that dream. And now Gaia Enterprises – the company that built this island, that built this community – they want to build on the Moon. And they need pilots." His voice started to crack. "Papa-ji, Mummy-ji. I want to bring honour to the family. And wealth. If I win a place on the project, they will pay very, very well."

He felt his mother's eyes flash wider then resume their scowl.

"I will be a good son and provide for you. I will be a good provider for Rechna and for the army of children we will have. I will be able to pay for medical help if we need it, if we are not blessed naturally. It is only two years. And then a lifetime of fame and good fortune to follow. You see Mummy-ji, I have thought of everything." Pabi surprised himself with the depth of his feelings and the candour of his words. He never asked for anything from his parents. He rarely spoke of his space dreams. And finally, he'd laid it all out for them, desperately making a last stand for the only future he'd ever wanted.

"I see," his father said. Pabi's passionate pleading had tripped something in him. A snapshot perhaps of his own wistful youth, long since tucked and folded away in a drawer full of socks, underpants and an old man's memories. He looked again at his wife. She returned his gaze with the wordless exchange of a long-married couple. "I can see you are set on this direction. So much so you would defy your own parents' wishes." His voice had a hard edge. He did not want to appear to cave too easily – not in front of his wife, at any rate.

Pabi coloured and stared into his lap, crestfallen. He felt the door of opportunity closing. He knew that tone. Gone were his dreams. Gone was the reprieve from a loveless marriage with Rechna. Gone was his freedom. Gone was the chance to be his own man. The bright future of the Moon faded, and a grey tunnel of pre-destined drudgery loomed before him.

"I will discuss this matter again with your mother." Pabi looked up at his father. The eyes had softened. His heart dared to hope.

"We will see if my son becomes an astronaut."

CHAPTER SEVEN

*The best world designers are the ones who live fully
self-expressed. In their work, there are no hidden
corners, no sharp edges, only beauty and truth.*

MAJA GARCIA, THE JOURNALS

Terra Verdi: Xavier

XAVIER CONSUS HEARD the holocall's ring as he entered the management quarters at Terra Verdi. He hurried over and bashed his elbow on the couch as he leant over the comms unit.

"*Putain!*" he swore and rubbed his elbow.

"Call from Troy Bruin. Do you accept?"

Xavier beamed, forgetting the pain in his elbow. "Accept! Accept!" he said waiting for the projection to appear. Troy's image came to life in front of him.

"Troy! How are you, *mon vieux?*"

"Delighted to be speaking with you, my old froggy friend. How is life in the swamp?" he teased. Terra Verdi was a floating world for harvesting seaweed and hydroponic food production. It crawled with plant life, every surface green. Troy knew it grated on

Xavier to refer to it as the swamp, but for his old Gaia classmate and colleague, Xavier made allowances.

"Not bad, not bad at all. I am guessing you are calling about the Olympus Project, *oui*?"

"Of course! I wanted to see what my old chum was thinking. I take it Maja called you already?"

"She did, she did." Xavier poured himself a glass of water and wiped his brow. It was always so steamy in the Terra Verdi halls.

"And… you said 'yes'?" Troy's handsome face looked eagerly at his friend.

"I said, 'why would I want to spend all that time cooped up with an arrogant pretty boy like Troy Bruin'?" They laughed. "What do you think? Of course, I said yes! But first I have to clear it with Maryse."

"Ahh, the beautiful Maryse! How is she? How are the girls?"

"Maryse is good. The girls are good. Maryse runs the hospital in Naples and the girls are teenagers now. But I spend so much time here on Terra Verdi, I don't see them much, you know. The holo does not replace the touch of a fine woman." Xavier sat down on a lounge chair.

"That it does not!" Troy agreed with a knowing look.

"Seriously though, do you think you'll be able to commit?" Troy asked.

Xavier picked up his glass of water, sipped, and balanced it on his knee. He sighed. "It's a long time. It's a long way. My girls will be adults when – and if – we get back. I always said I wouldn't be like my papa – absent. But here I am. I am becoming him, you know?"

"You'll never be like François, Xavier." Troy's voice was cool and hard. His eyes narrowed. François Consus had built the family fortune through misdeeds and dodgy deals, and Xavier had worked his whole life to restore the family name and distance himself from scandal. Troy had seen up-front the sacrifices Xavier had made while they were students – and then colleagues – at Gaia Enterprises. "You're a good father. You're building a future for them, for communities around the world. And if we win the tender for the Olympus Project, you'll have a whole new market that will last generations."

"You make it sound very easy, *mon ami*. Generations mean nothing when you are hugging your own child, your wife, for what may be the last time." Xavier stared down at his glass, swirled the contents, and swallowed the last of the water.

"That's true. I don't have such considerations."

"Still the eternal bachelor, eh? Not even Sexiest Human Alive can win a sweetheart? How many times have you won that award, anyway?"

"More than you, my friend!" They laughed.

"Xavier, I would be honoured and would find it a privilege to work with you on the Olympus Project. I know it's a big decision for you and the family, but if it helps at all, I wanted you to know you were my first pick."

"That is very kind. I feel the same about you. *Santé*!" He raised his glass of water in a toast. Troy responded with a short bow.

"What about you? What did you say, Troy?"

"I said 'yes'. I can think of no finer canvas for a world designer than the Olympus Project. A place for humans to peer into space, to create new industry, to discover themselves. It will be the grandest place for a party in the whole Universe! And can you imagine looking back at the Earth with my Vision tea? Mind orgasm, my friend."

"Are you still making that stuff?"

"I have a whole new line of teas. Magnificent blends. One that has you dancing for hours. One that makes you sleep for days. One that makes you laugh like a kid. I'll send you some. I'll send you the French Tickler Tea – Maryse will love you on that!" Troy's smile was salacious.

Xavier blushed under his dark skin. He had never grown accustomed to Troy's openness about sex.

"*Merci.*" Xavier cleared his throat. "Seriously though – you are not reluctant? Not even a little bit?"

"Reluctant? No. Truth is Xavier, I'm a little bored. Caracalla has been my passion project, but I've found that in working so much on passion – and all the other human emotions – I need new… stimulation."

"Stimulation? I think you have had enough stimulation to last a thousand lifetimes, Troy. I think you might need something else. Maybe you need some love. Not just a piece of *cul.*" Troy looked confused. "*Cul.* It means 'arse'. You understand! Maybe you need the love of a good woman. Or a good man. *Mon Dieu* – maybe you need a heart, Tin Man?"

"And you think I might find one on the Moon?" Troy laughed.

"Not likely. There will only be six of us: three designers, a pilot, a mechanic and a life support tech. Not very sexy."

"Do you know who else they approached for the third design spot?" Troy asked.

"I thought they might pick Li Len, for her work in the Arctic. But *non, mon frère,* Maja flew out to Sydney to speak to Xanthe Waters."

"Xanthe? But she left Gaia years ago. And Maja flew out there?" Troy was incredulous.

"*Oui, mon ami.* Maja asked her personally. It seems there's been enough water under the bridge, as they say."

"Xanthe. Well, she's certainly a good designer. I liked her work on The Pantheon. Pretentious name, but good design."

"Oh and what are 'the New Baths of Caracalla', if not pretentious? You, *mon ami*, are the very definition of 'pretentious'. And ostentatious."

"And delicious. Don't forget 'delicious'." He posed a little for Xavier's benefit.

"You are too much, Prince Troy! 'Sexiest Human Alive' has gone to your head."

"Well?"

"Well what?"

"Well, what did Xanthe say?"

"Ahh. Madame Waters said she would 'think about it'."

"Truly? A personal visit from Maja Garcia and she's 'thinking about it'?"

"You know, she's an Earthist, like her husband, Simon. It's not just the Moon, it's her principles."

"Principles don't feed the starving."

"Neither do Moon missions, *mon ami!* I understand her reluctance. She left Gaia because Maja broadened our project scope. It wasn't just making new human habitats and rehabilitation of the planet anymore."

"Hmmm. I think it shows lack of imagination."

"*Au contraire.* I think it is because she *can* imagine that she does not jump to yes. She sees the dark tunnels we can go down. The Olympus Project needs to be 'human first', not just an ego playground."

Troy pondered this.

"Well, if she turns down the project because of 'principles' – even if they are misguided – that's one thing. But turning down the opportunity to work with *us*? Let me rephrase that: turning down the opportunity to work with *me*? That's sheer craziness." Troy winked.

"*Mon Dieu*, your ego is the size of the Moon. We won't need a spaceship to get there – we will just float up on all your hot air." They laughed again.

"Xavier, I've got to go. Let me know what you decide. And let me know if you hear anything more about Xanthe. And Gaia selection." He blew Xavier a kiss.

"Will do. Take care, *mon ami*."

CHAPTER EIGHT

Shadow and light: a world designer must allow
for the interplay. As within, so without.

Dubai: Gina

THE MOTORBIKE THRUMMED against her thighs, the heat radiating through her leather pants. Gina Casellatti tore open the throttle and the metal beast surged down the highway. She chased the bike's headlight through the black screen of the desert night. Stars winked as the engine noise filled her senses. There was nothing but her, the bike and the road.

Up the crest of the hill and down the long slope she rode until the surge of adrenaline left her and the voice in her head grew quiet. She released the throttle and let the bike drift to a stop. She pulled over, swung off the seat, kicked up the stand, and stood back, staring at the night sky. A puff of dust settled on her boots. She pulled off her helmet and shook out her long black curls; took a deep breath of petrol fumes and desert air. The smell calmed her.

Gina loved this relic of a bike. She'd salvaged it from a recycling yard. Pieced it together bit by bit in her friend Scott's garage. He let her crash there between her gigs at Space Adventures and her own travel escapades. Strictly speaking, these old bikes were outlawed. Only solar and electric were allowed these days. But here she was on the road to nowhere outside of Dubai, where things were a little more... flexible when it came to petroleum use. She had shipped her bike out of Rome under the pretence of it going to a museum, and paid a local Dubai kid handsomely to hide it for her in some underground storage unit.

Every chance she got she came down here and indulged herself in the late hours of the night. Revving the antique throttle and burning up the road, chasing emptiness and the quiet in the roar of an outlawed engine.

She looked up to the stars and felt the familiar longing fill her from head to toe.

What's out there?

The blackness between the stars had nothing to say to her.

The night sky was her puppet master. It dangled dreams just out of reach. She wanted to know. She wanted to understand the stars, the planets, the deep blackness of everything, the nothingness of space.

Perhaps in response to the despair she felt at never knowing, she took apart the world around her. As a kid she had dismantled household appliances to see how they worked. The first time she did it, her mother had appeared in the kitchen to find the espresso machine laid out with all its parts neatly in a row, down to the last bolt. Gina had received a thrashing and a sound education in Italian swearing. The pain of the beating had been cushioned by the shock of her mother's colourful language. After that, Gina had become skilled at taking things apart and putting them back together quickly – and in good working order. Once the kitchen appliances were mastered, she had moved on to electronics.

While she had deciphered the mysteries of the built world, the celestial ones had remained elusive. She had decided to get closer to the stars by working in the space tourism business. She felt she was in service to the Great Mystery in her work at Space Adventures. She was their prime mechanic, on call whenever they had a launch. She tinkered with all the tech, making improvements in everything from engine design to cabin layout to instrumentation panels. They had even let her up in one of the Space Balloons. She had one short and mesmerising journey to the edge of atmosphere, just so you could see the curve of the Earth and the Great Black Mystery that held them all in its cold, dark heart.

She felt the voice within start to kick in again. *What are you searching for?* it asked. She ignored it. *Why so alone?* She brushed the dust off her boots and inspected the bike to distract her. No nicks. Paintwork still good. Leather seat needed a bit of attention.

The holo in her jacket breast pocket hummed to life. She slapped at it, annoyed. She craved solitude. The desert night was a step closer to the heavens and she did not like to be disturbed.

Why so alone? the voice repeated.

"*Merda!*" she said. She dug into her pocket to turn the holo off as it vibrated persistently. She pulled it out and caught a glimpse of the message sender. Xavier Consus.

Xavier. She hadn't seen him in – what was it – three years? She had been on a break from Space Adventures, riding her solar bike – the one she'd pioneered for the motorcycle industry. She'd been down around to Sicily and was heading through Naples when she'd nearly run the man over. Xavier had been in a heated discussion with a man at the docks, arms akimbo. Gina had sped up to get around them just as Xavier had stepped back on to the street. She had had to do a broadie to miss him.

He had sworn at her emphatically in French and she had returned in kind in Italian. It could have got ugly. But he must have seen something of a kindred spirit in her. That, or he'd really liked the bike, she thought with a smile. In any case, he had invited her to Terra Verdi in exchange for a ride on her rig. She had spent a month there tinkering with his irrigation system, and re-designing the electronics for his seaweed processor and sensors. Xavier had been impressed. He'd offered her a job on the spot.

"Sorry Xavier," she'd said. "Unless you're growing seaweed in space, I'm not interested."

And now Xavier Consus was sending her a holo. "Okay, you crazy Frenchman, what have you got to say?"

"Gina! *Bongiorno*!" His dark face popped to life as she hit play. "Want to go the Moon?" He smiled broadly. "Gaia is putting in a bid for the Olympus Project and we need a good mechanic as part of the crew. You interested in getting a real astronaut ride? Applications close this week for selection. I'll be your referee. Would love to work with you again. Call me."

Damn. Gaia was entering the Olympus Project bid. She'd been following all the news about it, hoping Space Adventures would put their hand up. But they were keen to stay in their lane – 'tourism, not colonisation', they'd told her. But Gaia, now... this was a major turn of events.

And a major opportunity for Gina Casellatti, she thought. Mechanic, inventor, adventurist. And astronaut!

"*Grazie*!" she roared. Her voice sailed through the crisp air to the stars. She put her helmet back on, turned up the music full blast in her earpiece, and let the engine rip.

CHAPTER NINE

Loyalty is too often a trap built by the sticky strands of an
emotional web. We get caught in it, if we're not careful.

MAJA GARCIA, THE JOURNALS

Dubai: Dr Mohammad

DR MOHAMMAD RASHEED heard the drone of a motorcycle engine
cut through the dawn as he moved through his morning prayers.

"Idiot kids," he tutted to himself. How did they get onto the
Palms? Access was meant to be closely regulated. Where were the
guards? Sleeping? Incompetent fools.

Mohammad bowed his head to the mat. As he said his prayers,
his mind wandered to the letter that had been delivered by the
envoy the evening before. An actual letter, with the Sultan's seal.

Before the letter was handed over, the envoy, in full regalia,
expected a proper welcome. Mohammad bid him enter and hastily
arranged tea and sweets.

He poured the tea with dignity and grace befitting the envoy's
station, and with all the humility and honour of his own position.
He had served for thirty years as physician on the Sultan's special

project: the rehabilitated Palms. After nearly sinking, the original land reclamation project had been revitalised. The Sultan wanted the Palms to be the centre of longevity and health. Dr Mohammad Rasheed was his pick for life extension research, and trusted to treat the Sultan with the new therapies as he developed them. Mohammad gave praise to Allah every time he thought about the good fortune he had had. And for none of the treatments having caused any poor side effects.

Mohammad had toiled for long hours over many years to prove his loyalty and dedication. He was an acknowledged expert in his field, and he bristled with pride whenever he gained the attention of the Sultan.

The envoy sipped the tea in silence. He ate a few sweets. Mohammad offered the tray of temptations twice more, and twice he refused it. Mohammad knew it was now acceptable to inquire after the envoy's purpose.

"Honoured guest, how may I be of service, today?" he asked.

The envoy placed his teacup on the table beside him and retrieved a small, round object. A communication-jamming instrument. Mohammad recognised it instantly. Hard to come by, they were essential when meeting with the Sultan or any government official with sensitive information to be conveyed. The Sultan always activated one personally when he consulted with Mohammad.

The envoy leant forward and in a low voice, spoke earnestly. "Dr Mohammad Rasheed, greetings to you from His Excellency, the Sultan. His Excellency requires redeployment of your services in a new venture.

"You may recall an associate of the Sultan's, Madame Aryanna Sharif. The Sultan remembers the care and discretion with which you treated Madame Sharif on her visit to Dubai, some years ago. Madame Sharif is funding the Gaia Enterprises bid for the Olympus Project and has inquired after your availability. She would like a trusted physician to participate in the project."

Mohammad fought to contain his surprise. He remembered the interaction with Aryanna Sharif as if it were yesterday. The dark smooth skin, the thin long limbs, the sharp black eyes. She was not to be trifled with. At the Sultan's special request, he had administered Aryanna with some of his early longevity treatments. Knowing his reputation and career were on the line should there be any mishap, Mohammad took exquisite care of his patient for the few months that she underwent treatment.

"I am deeply honoured," Mohammad said, and bowed. "What does the position entail?"

"The position is as medical adviser and researcher to the Olympus Project, under the Gaia Enterprises tender bid. The position is not guaranteed, in spite of Madame Sharif's personal request. According to the terms of the sponsorship contract, Gaia retains full authority to select and train its crew for the project. You must apply and undertake their selection process – first at their James Bay training centre, and then their next round of training and selection at the New Baths of Caracalla and Terra Verdi. If successful, you will join the headquarters staff to monitor the health of the Project team as they build and live in the prototype for one year."

Mohammad let this settle in his jumbled mind for a moment. James Bay! He had never been to Canada. And he had heard so much about Terra Verdi. He had considered approaching them for joint research into nutrition and longevity experiments. The New Baths of Caracalla he *did* know about. He resisted the urge to scowl. They called it 'an emotional mastery centre'. All reports suggested it was a licentious pit of immoral activity. He shuddered inwardly at the tarnishing his reputation might receive if he attended any program there.

Then he asked, "Where is the location for the prototype?"

"That is top secret. However, I do know it will be in the desert."

The envoy slipped his hand into the inside pocket of his suit and retrieved an envelope. He leant over and handed it to Mohammad.

"The Sultan expects your answer shortly. Applications for the project at Gaia close soon."

Mohammad knew there was only one possible answer. One did not deny the Sultan a personal request.

After the envoy left, Mohammad stood holding the envelope, running his fingers over the golden embossed letters. Such an honour! From the Sultan's office!

He found a knife and carefully lifted the flap without tearing the precious paper. He opened the trifold and slowly smoothed out the letter. He could smell the quality of the paper. The ink was crisp against the thick page.

Dear Dr Mohammad Rasheed,

Thank you for your long service to His Excellency the Sultan of Dubai.

We look forward to your continued service.

We anticipate your successful application to the Gaia Enterprises Olympus Project bid. We know you will honour the Sultan with your efforts.

Yours faithfully,

The Office of His Excellency, the Sultan of Dubai

Mohammad savoured every line. He prayed with deep gratitude and fervour that evening, and now too, with the dawn prayers. He would serve the Sultan joyfully, be it in Dubai, Canada, the desert, or even on the Moon. The Sultan's glory would raise up his own.

CHAPTER TEN

The built world is more than a container for living.
The built world shapes the lives it contains.

THE WORLD DESIGNERS' MANIFESTO

Sydney: Serena

SERENA FOX STOOD at the top of the building reclamation site. She stared down into the dark abyss of the excavated foundations of a toppled building. She held a rescue knife above a taut abseil rope rigged around an old pillar.

"Give me one reason why I shouldn't cut these ropes, Devon," she yelled to her colleague dangling beneath her.

"C'mon, Serena! Don't be an arsehole!" Devon's voice echoed in the chamber below. She could see his head torch swing in looping circles in the darkness. Serena had him on belay and tied off so he could not descend any further to the cavern floor. He hung about twenty metres off the ground.

"You're the arsehole, Devon!" she hurled. "I trusted you, you son of a bitch! Those world designs were mine and you stole them!"

"I told you, I thought we were collaborating! I pitched the idea and Dan went for it. I didn't tell him it was my idea."

"You didn't tell him it was mine, either." Silence from the darkness below. After a few moments, Devon resumed his pleading.

"C'mon. This is crazy. Let's sort this out like adults. Stop messing around. Let me get down and finish the job."

"So you can take credit for that too?" Serena snapped. This whole project had been her initiative. While world designers everywhere were building vertical homes or out at sea, she'd focused on the opportunities below ground. These old buildings, wrecked by the tsunami, had great excavated foundations that were a whole lot easier to cool than those enormous towers. And at this site they'd discovered spectacular limestone caves. With careful design and management, they could incorporate some of the natural features into premium living spaces. And Devon was surfing her ideas right up the arse crack of their boss. He was firmly wedged up there. She'd be damned if she was going to let Devon screw her over.

"I'll tell you what. This is what you're going to do. You are going to march into Dan's office and tell him the designs were my idea. You will apologise for not making it clear from the outset. Then you're going to take the Project Captain role."

"What? What do you mean?" She could see Devon wriggling at the end of the rope, trying to get a look at her.

"You will take the Project Captain role, just as it's been offered to you."

"Why do you want me to do that? You just said you're pissed about me taking credit for the design. Which I didn't actually do, by the way."

"You're going to take the Captain role. In exchange, you are going to let me be the sole applicant from our company to the Gaia Enterprises call up."

"Ahhh. Shit, Serena! You can't be serious! Everyone wants that gig! That's not fair!"

"You should have thought of that when you took credit for my work, you wanker!"

"No way. I'm not doing it. I'm coming up now. Get me back on belay." She could see him secure his rope climbing jumars and start to shimmy his way back up.

She put her knife away and untied the rope to resume the belay. She watched him heave his way upwards, taking in slack as he climbed up. It was exhausting work, and she could see he was straining with the effort. Serves him right, she thought. She chewed her lip as she managed the rope, trying to keep her anger and sadness at bay.

When she met Devon at their first job site, he'd been cool towards her. She wasn't used to that. Women always prickled around her, intimidated by her looks and jealous of how she drew the admiration of the men. Blokes either hit on her or tripped over themselves for her attention. So she kept mostly to herself. Until Devon. He wasn't fazed by her and dealt her a straight hand. Or so she thought. She'd been a fool to let her guard down. Against her better instincts, they became friends. They traded banter on site and gossiped about the salvage operators. They even had beers together after work. Then she shared her ideas for designs, and it all went tits up.

Devon's helmet appeared at the top of the ledge. He extended his hand to get an assist up the last step, but Serena just glared at him. He heaved himself up, flapping like a fish at the edge until he had his body clear of danger. He stepped away from the hole, removed his helmet and eyed her warily.

"Look, I'm sorry I didn't make it clear to Dan about the design. I'm happy to turn down the promotion too. But no way will I give up an application to Gaia for the Moon project. That's the ultimate in world design – a brand new world! On another planet for Chrissake!"

"On the Moon. Not a planet. And I think you will," she said, her tone stony.

"C'mon Serena, I—"

"I know about you and Chantale."

He froze, eyes wide.

"What?"

"You and Chantale. You know, Dan's wife." Her grey eyes bright and flashing, a thin smile curling her lips.

"How in Hades do you know about that?" Devon ran his hand through his sweaty helmet hair.

"I have my sources. More importantly, I have proof."

"You're blackmailing me?" he asked, incredulous.

"Call it what you want. But here's the deal: you tell Dan the designs are mine, you take the Captain job, and I apply to Gaia, uncontested. It's a win-win."

"You're a real ball buster, you know that? When did you become such a hard-nosed bitch?"

"The day you stabbed me in the back."

Devon took a deep breath and kicked a stone. It tumbled over the edge. They listened to it bounce down the walls into the cavern. "You're a real piece of work, Serena."

"Thank you," she said.

CHAPTER ELEVEN

Even with all that we know, all we can access with our technology
and AI, we can still delude ourselves that we know what's going
on. The more certain we are, the more clouded our vision.

MAJA GARCIA, THE JOURNALS

Gaia Enterprises Headquarters: Maja

MAJA STARED AT the images on the table screen. This selection
process was tricky. Rather than the usual applicants for their World
Designers' training program, they were recruiting a team to pitch
to the Lunar Commission. This was the first off-Earth community
design project, and they were up against the huge space travel tech
companies. It was a hot, competitive bid.

Human Habs was the strongest contender, with their studies
on the impact of zero- and low-gravity on the human body. They
had established partnerships with many of the space stations and
even had their own shuttle system to carry medical research and
human physique conditioning equipment. In addition, they had
had a whole division dedicated to space tourism. Earth Rise Tours
they called it. According to Huw Chan, her fellow Director, who

had some contact at Earth Rise, the tours were incredibly profitable. So much so, they had funded their research.

Spaceward Bound was the surprise newcomer. Lincoln Ellison rebranded Tech Surf especially for the tender. Tech Surf was a conglomerate of startup tech companies in the Metaverse. Apparently, Lincoln Ellison had long been obsessed with space travel. With the success of his other ventures, and with the backing of tech giant Metasyn, he finally had the capital to sink into a space project. They just didn't have the experience. More money than sense, thought Maja. She allowed herself an indulgent moment of disdain. Fancy calling it 'Spaceward Bound'. It was a spin on the old outdoor experiential education school, Outward Bound. But in calling it 'Spaceward Bound' they missed the principle entirely. The real journeys are interior ones. Adventure is a journey for the mind.

Human Habs, with their medical focus and space tourism, and Spaceward Bound, with their resources and bravado: the other bidders were space jockeys. They had the space-based expertise but knew nothing about long-term community building. That was the Gaia specialty. But if they were to be successful in their pitch, they needed broader skills than what they currently possessed. Thus, the Olympus Project was the first tender they were opening to non-graduates.

So much was riding on this project. Finances were strained at Gaia. Thank goodness for Aryanna Sharif's backing! There was a lot of competition – and a lot of bad imitation. Builders and architects copied their designs but without their philosophical underpinning. This was Gaia's real chance at deliberately crafting social evolution. They had twenty years under their belt. Proven world design that fostered successful communities. Not that it had all gone smoothly, of course. That early experiment on Terra Blanca had been a disaster. Maja felt deeply ashamed in how she had misread human nature. And with lethal consequences. The cruelty that humans are capable of still horrified her.

But she had learnt from that early failure. It was the end of her naivety. She hoped. She had buckled down and revisited all the human development research. What would make a successful community truly work? The hippies had tried their experiments some hundred years ago. But they fell prey to excesses. They had their vision in the right place, but the successful delivery of a working community was lacking.

Maja had learnt too that the best of the human spirit required containers. Boundaries against which it could push. It was only with rules that people grew stronger. Rules were like a whetting stone: the human spirit needed its rough edges sloughed away. But with too many constraints, a community ground to a halt, stagnant. Stuck by its own processes. After twenty years of training world designers and tracking their work and communities, Maja felt Gaia was ready for the next developmental leap. They had to be. For humanity's sake. If they could not make communities work here on Earth, with all its abundant resources, then there was no way they were going to work on any other planet, especially not the Moon, or Mars, with all its challenges.

The Lunar Commission wasn't showing them any favours in spite of their experience. It had taken them years to get the Moon Agreement through. No one wanted to ruin the Moon the way Earth had been ruined. And no one wanted a repeat of what happened on Terra Blanca.

She looked again at the images of the applicants. A nice diverse range of faces, ages, life experiences. All hungry for growth, for contribution. So they said. The participant selection method would reveal those who were just talking the talk. She was proud of the process for its reliable sorting. They had fine-tuned the selection program over the years and she was pleased with the Gaia graduates. Most of them anyway.

Maja glanced at her fellow directors, also deep in thought, studying the candidate profiles. Claire Edwards had been one of their first students, brilliant at world design, and even more astute when it came to human development. Her observational skills were second to none, and her understanding of human drivers and patterns bordered on the supernatural; a more credulous person than Maja might call it psychic. Maja knew Claire had ambitions to take over as CEO. She'd spent the past seven years in dedicated service training designers, learning as much as she could from Maja, and challenging long-held conventions. Claire had visions of her own, Maja knew. But she wasn't so sure they were always grounded in the altruistic intentions she wished for in a successor.

Succession. It was the unspoken word, the elephant in the room. Maja was dying, she knew. No amount of med-tech could save her. They'd tried everything: stem cell therapy, nano technology, chemical rinsing of her cells, cellular redesign. She was getting old. Things were wearing out. And she did not want to live to 200 as others aspired to. Nor did she wish to jump on the cryo-freezing, eternal-life bandwagon. She just wanted to set Gaia Enterprises on the right trajectory: to support and steer humankind's evolution through environmental design that safely stepped citizens through developmental stages. After generations of rampant building for commerce and industry, finally humanity was ready for deliberate designs that developed head, heart and hands. Humans were ready to grow into their greatest potential. Especially as they needed to find solutions to the climate challenges of Earth, and the brave new horizons on the Moon, Mars and beyond.

Her business partner and co-founder Huw Chan was far more pragmatic. As a brilliant entrepreneur and forward-thinking businessman, he was ever attuned to the commercial savviness of applicants and students. He was no-nonsense, practical and ruthless. Maja could always rely on the small, stocky man to make the hard calls, unswayed by sentiment and unimpressed by pizzazz. He would just stand his ground, jut the bottom lip, harden his eyes, and speak the truth. It was refreshing. Maja was too prone to believe the best in people. She softened at the thought of their potential. And sometimes she had been wrong. Those realisations were always painful and full of regret.

This part of the recruitment process was always exciting: eager new applicants with a vision for the future. Maja enjoyed thinking about how they would interact with each other. Would they be able to rein in their competitiveness? Process their emotions in real time to address the issues and challenges they threw at them? The selection process was deliberately arduous. She knew that it was only when people were at their lowest, they showed their mettle, their capacity to dig deep and lean on the best versions of themselves. It was Gaia's version of the old US Navy SEALs Hell Week, minus the swearing and cajoling, plus different psychological pressures and complex problem-solving. The participants did not discover what the selection committee was really looking for until well into their own training, when the penny suddenly dropped. Gaia was about human development design, not just an engineering company's training ground.

"Maja?" She looked up as Claire called her name. Claire and Huw had been discussing the issues with one of the applicants' backgrounds.

"Maja, I'm not sure that Jonas is the right candidate. His psychometric profile shows a lot of unrestrained emotional outbursts. He hospitalised another kid on the *Sea Rover* with a karate kick. It appears anger management is somewhat lacking."

Maja paused a moment, pulling up Jonas's file on the table display. He was certainly an interesting candidate. Only son of the famous early world designers, Jenny and Don Seaborn, the pioneers of the travelling worlds. Huw was never that impressed with the engineering design and downplayed their fame. He always thought they got far too much kudos for what was essentially converting a cruise ship and adding an outrigger. Huw often said that fame made them arrogant. Maja secretly agreed. Reading the community

development reports of the *Sea Rover* showed a slippage of attention to the finer points of community design and management. She
wasn't sure they had grasped the subtleties of parental responsibility
in a community upbringing. Jonas's unfettered temper as a kid
might be a product of that *laissez-faire* environment. But for all
of his faults, Jonas might also be the perfect candidate for the
empathy-honing resources they had been developing.

Before responding to Claire, Maja addressed Huw. "What do
you think, Huw?"

"As much as I find the Seaborns to be overblown show ponies,
they have remarkable commercial acumen. Their innovations
onboard the *Sea Rover* for hydroponics, small-scale water recycling and waste management are impressive. They have been
self-sustaining for some time now. Plus, their reputation – however
over-inflated – would serve Gaia well to capitalise on. A second
generation of the Seaborn inventiveness, as it were. According to
his application, Jonas designed the terrawebbing and did a full
engine rebuild. He's the most qualified and well-rounded mechanic
we have among the applicants." Huw paused, steepled his fingers,
elbows on the table. His savant pose, thought Maja. "It would
bring a lot of interest to our work, raise expectations, and possibly
invite new funders. So, the young man is a bit volatile. That's
nothing we haven't dealt with before." Huw leant back and crossed
his arms. The usual signal he had made up his mind.

Claire wasn't giving up. "Violence is not usually something
that goes away easily. And those who are prone to it have a hard
time following the rules. Do we really want to introduce the potential for such drama in this intake? There is so much at stake."

"That's exactly why we need to take him." Huw and Claire
looked up at Maja who had been quiet, so far. She continued, "The
candidates need to be able to handle all sorts. And it's toughest
when they're peers. If they can manage the issues that come from
dealing with their peers under pressure, they will know what to

look out for and how to handle the challenges that are guaranteed to emerge in space travel and off-world communities. We shouldn't shy away from tough nuts. If anything, we should embrace them, show what's possible in human development by following our methodology." Maja saw that Claire wasn't shifting her position on this one, so she added, "Let's see how he goes through the selection process." That mollified the younger woman a bit. "He applied as a mechanic, right? Who else is in the final invitation pool?"

Claire shifted her focus back to the table display and answered, "Let me see. The final mechanic applicants include highly recommended Paul Johnston and Gina Casellatti. There's a number of other solid candidates too."

"Gina Casellatti – she was Xavier's recommendation, wasn't she?' asked Huw.

"That's right," Claire said. "She's currently working with Space Adventures. A real gun it seems."

"Well then, with Paul being well-vetted, and Gina being a strong candidate, plus the other candidates we can probably take a risk on Jonas. At least for the selection process. Especially if there are developmental benefits for the other applicants that might strengthen their experience overall. And, as I said, the Seaborn name wouldn't do us any harm." Huw was pleased with his own summary. He liked multiple win-wins. "How are we doing with the pilots?"

Claire's face lit up. "You worked your magic, Huw! Madison Floyd submitted her application. What an impressive woman! Top honours throughout her career in the U.S. Air Force. She trains all the space tourism pilots for suborbital flights. And – this is the best part – she's currently training Spaceward Bound pilots. But for some unknown reason they are *not* putting her forward on their bid. They just have her training their pilots. So, if she comes to selection, she will need to cancel her contract with them. And then they will be without trained pilots for their bid."

"You're not usually one to delight in the disappointments of others, Claire," Maja teased her gently.

"True. But I can't help it. Those cowboys! If we steal their prized trainer it will be a setback for them and put us one step ahead. Tell me you wouldn't be delighted too, Maja."

"It *would* be a happy accident in our favour," she said with just a hint of a smile. "Who else have we got applying for the pilot position?"

"It seems like the entire aeronautical and space tourism industry! We have all the first- and second-tier pilots from all the space tourism companies, and all of the fighter pilots with air force training. We also have a few earth-based pilots who work for world designed communities."

"Any stand-outs?" Huw asked.

"Madison is really the lead candidate. The others will have to pull out something special to beat her," Claire said.

"That's in the skills area," Maja reminded them. "Let's see how she does in the group dynamics."

"So, we have enough pilots for the selection process in James Bay?"

"We've got one from every continent, including a Helsinki designed world. The pilot is... " she touched the screen to pull up a profile. "... David Eriksson. And one from Singapore's offshore communities. Pabi Gupta. He has strong recommendations from all his senior commanders in the Singaporean Air Force."

"Good, good," Huw said. "That leaves life support technicians. I know we managed to get Max King to apply in time. I tracked him down from his latest Mount Everest expedition. His oxygen adaptation technology would be perfect. I can't wait to meet him!" He rubbed his hands gleefully.

"He is certainly an impressive candidate," Maja said. "He's been to all extreme zones on the planet as a private expeditioner. Mostly solo. So, we'll see if he can handle the confines of a team environment. There are also three candidates from the underwater worlds, if I remember correctly?"

"That's right," Claire said. "All very solid applications. There is one more for consideration that I'm not sure about."

"Who's that?' asked Maja.

"Serena Fox. A scavenger turned salvage diver turned engineer. She's been doing some cave design work. She worked on life support technology with her dive and caving experience. Her world designs are beautiful. She's the only applicant with design and life support experience."

"Oh, yes, I heard about that work," Maja said. "They're going underground for the cooling effect. Also fireproof. That's good. That's solid experience for the cave community focus on the Moon. But we already have enough life support engineers. What makes her stand out?"

Claire glanced at Huw who shrugged and nodded, indicating she should proceed. Claire pulled up Serena's profile on screen.

Maja stared at the displayed face. She was beautiful. Her skin was flawless. Blonde hair, soft and straight, framed high cheekbones and round blue eyes that drew you in under dark, moody eyebrows. But there was a hard edge to her. What was it? Defiance? Resentment? Resolve from a life of hardship as a scavenger? Maja found herself mesmerised by the young woman's beauty.

Aware suddenly of the silence as she studied the young woman's face, Maja sat back and said, "I see." They'd had good looking candidates before. They'd even argued about being prejudiced against the attractive ones – a kind of reverse discrimination. They wanted to check their own biases and be sure they weren't being swayed either way by someone's looks, good or ill.

"Aside from her distracting looks – and they are distracting, extremely so – why are you arguing for her? Huw?"

Huw shifted and uncrossed his arms. "Simple, really. She comes from the school of hard knocks. An orphan, a scavenger in one of the toughest districts hit doubly hard from sea rise and tsunami. Somehow, she's managed to survive and make good as a salvage diver. You need nerves of steel to do that work – diving in unstable wreckage to pull out possible goods for recycling or repurposing. The girl's got guts. Not only that, but she's managed to put herself through further study. The world might have passed her over, but she's not letting that keep her back. How much of her 'luck' is due to her looks?" Huw shrugged. "Don't know. But we can certainly get more of a sense of it at selection."

Maja looked over at Claire whose brows were drawn in concern. "And you, Claire? Why are you putting her forward?"

Claire pursed her lips as if trying to squeeze clarity into her thoughts. "I agree with Huw. I like the gumption, the self-starter. There's something in the edginess, though, that I'm not sure about. There's a hardness about her. Not sure if it's permanent, a protective layer, or something more…sinister. It's hard to tell. I'd like to see her in action at selection to learn more. Her kind of initiative is something that would be incredibly valuable to the cohort. And her looks? Well, that always creates interesting dynamics."

It certainly does, thought Maja. It was one of those fascinating aspects of human interactions she was still studying. The physicality of influence, no matter what cognitive filters and training they put people through. She'd love to see how this potential Moon cohort would deal with it. Jealousy and lust dragged people back to the primitive.

"Sounds like we've settled it, then. Serena's in. And we've got the medical candidates too," Huw said.

"Who's on that list?" Maja asked.

"The Sultan of Dubai's physician, Dr Mohammad Rasheed. Personally recommended by Aryanna Sharif. He specialises in longevity treatments. There's also Dr Pierre Martin, a Canadian surgeon who has been involved in various genetic modification research projects for human adaptation in low gravity. He's got quite a sassy holo cover message. Make sure you watch it – he's quite the character! And two more." Claire reached out to sort the applicants on screen. "There were so many for this position. Let's see, where are they…oh yes, Jade Mandez. Physician on both an underwater world and for one of the space tourism companies. And James Gregoire, sent by Harvard."

"We've been spoiled for choice. Well done, Claire, for narrowing it down. And Huw, for your special contacts and recommendations. How many applications did we start with?"

"Over three thousand," Claire said. Huw whistled in appreciation. "We have forty to invite for selection."

"It's going to be a busy time," Maja said.

"Any word on Xanthe, yet?" asked Claire.

Maja hesitated slightly. "Not yet. I've given her until this Friday."

"That's leaving it a little late, isn't it?" Claire said.

"It's getting close," Maja admitted. "If she refuses, we go to Plan B."

"And who's that?" asked Claire.

"Tony Boss."

"Tony! Have you told Xanthe that he's Plan B? That will drive her insane." Tony Boss was Xanthe's arch-rival. They had had many volatile disagreements during their training. Xanthe was a passionate student of community design for human development, Tony focused more on the commercial aspect of world design. Every one of his worlds had a commercial function. Xanthe argued that these often sacrificed community wellbeing and comfort. Their arguments were legendary. As far as Claire knew, they had not spoken since they graduated from the program – and had remained barely civil when Xanthe was employed with Gaia. Rumour had it that it was his growing influence on the commercial tenders that had pushed Xanthe to leave.

"I might have mentioned it," Maja said, and her eyes twinkled.

"Interesting bit of faci-pulation there, Maja," Huw said with a chuckle. That was his code-word for facilitation-cum-manipulation. Almost underhanded, but not quite. Maja liked to call it 'provocative motivation'.

"Well, hopefully it works. Xanthe would balance Xavier and Troy perfectly on this project. Much more so than Tony. Maja, if it's okay with you I will send out the invitations for selection."

Claire shut down the table display and stood, turning to leave.

Maja added, "Claire – Xavier Consus and Troy Bruin are attending selection. I would like to run them as observers in the expedition groups. Will you be okay with that?"

Claire hesitated. She turned her head back towards Maja, keeping her expression flat. "That will be fine." She paused, then nodded, "It will be good to see them."

She left the room, trying not to look like she was hurrying.

Maja knew Claire. She knew the news would rattle her a little. Claire had a thing for Troy. She made it out to be a professional crush, a respect for one of Gaia's most successful graduates, a world designer who kept stunning developers with his beautiful designs and sensitivities to human dynamics. His latest project, the New Baths of Caracalla, had intrigued them all. As a concept, it was fascinating: come and learn to harness your base impulses by indulging them in a controlled environment. That was the official marketing message. Maja wondered if it wasn't just an old-fashioned den of inequity dressed up as an educational centre. Maja smiled to herself. She was fond of Troy. He was charming, gorgeous and brilliant. But she knew well enough not to fall in love with him. Unlike poor Claire who had not managed to metabolise her attraction successfully. Oh well. This selection would be a good opportunity for her to make peace with her pheromones. Can we do that as humans, she wondered.

And Xavier, too! Poor Claire had been beset by jealousy and frustration when Xavier was a trainee. He was forever challenging the rules, pushing boundaries. And getting away with it. This had driven Claire to distraction. She loved an orderly school, felt the rules were there for a reason – to keep things in order and to ensure the best learning process for all. Xavier just refused to accept anything at face value. Maja admired this in him and encouraged it. This had likely added to Claire's frustration. Maja had held tight to her approach with Xavier though. And it had paid off. Xavier was a commercially successful world builder. His questioning mind had led to many innovations, including the remarkable Terra Verdi: a community that combined genetic research, seaweed harvesting and advanced hydroponics to be the largest producer of plant-based proteins and food on the planet. He had also licensed his technology out to many of the other world designers to include in their own designs. People and the planet were better off because of Xavier's work. If that meant putting up with a little boundary pushing, Maja was okay with that. Plus, they needed his expertise for the Moon pitch.

"Do you think she's the right one?" Huw's question startled Maja from her reverie.

"Who do you mean?"

"Claire. Do you think she's the right choice for your successor?"

"*What* do you mean?" Maja looked intently at Huw now.

"Maja, I know you're not well. I know you don't want others to know just yet. But you forget, I've got connections. They told me about the unusual requests for treatments coming out of Gaia. More than the usual experiments we order." Maja looked down at her hands in her lap.

"How bad is it?" Huw asked, quieter now.

"It's not *bad*, Huw. It's just as nature intended. Cells get worn out, don't function quite as well anymore is all."

He wasn't buying it.

"How long have you got Maja?" There was no getting around it, she could tell.

"Maybe a year." Huw sat back in his chair with a long, exhaled breath. "Jesus Christ, Maja."

"Don't worry. Gaia will be fine." He looked at her, the thin veil of pity leaking from his look.

"I know Gaia will be fine. Claire will be fine. We'll all be fine. But I'll miss you." He choked a little on the last words and cleared his throat. "What can I do?" All business again.

Maja looked at him softly, fondness and two decades of friendship weaving them together.

"Help me get ready. To answer your question, I'm not sure about Claire. She hasn't quite evolved as far as I'd like for someone to be at the helm. Developmentally she needs a broader perspective. The trouble is that she is expecting to be named successor, though I've made no promises nor any indications I was leaning one way or another – or indeed expecting to need a successor anytime soon."

"Well, we need to get a plan in place. I don't want you worried and harried towards your end. I want you to be comfortable, happy with where we've got to. Ready for what's next."

Maja could sense his inner turbulence below the surface of his brisk, pragmatic focus. She leant over and reached for his hand, holding his strong, thick fingers in her thin, slender ones.

"Thank you, Huw. I know you mean well. I *will* need your support and strength for the next little while."

He answered with a weak smile, holding back his pain. "Claire might rise to the occasion, she might not. There are others in the mix. Let's see how they do over the next little while."

They sat in silence for a while, comfortable in their own company, the warmth of their hands holding the warmth of their hearts.

Outside the door, Claire Edwards waited quietly, listening.

CHAPTER TWELVE

*An outsider always brings new eyes. This new vision often
gets far more credit than it sometimes deserves.*

CORONER'S REPORT, THE TERRA BLANCA TRAGEDY

Gaia Enterprises Headquarters: Claire

CLAIRE STOOD OUTSIDE the door of the Directors' meeting room until Huw and Maja finished speaking. She stepped quietly away, emotions rolling like white caps on a wind-blown sea.

Maja was dying! The thought collided with other snippets of information as her brain made new connections. She could see it now – Maja's extra test requirements, her thinner frame, the way she always seemed to be cold no matter the outside temperature. Maja had always been a slight woman. She thought it was just ageing.

Claire noticed with some consternation the competing emotions that swirled within her: grief at her mentor's impending death, hurt at being judged not yet worthy of succeeding her, hurt also that Maja had not let her into her confidence. And then the secret buried kernel of excitement that her time was coming.

Maja's passing would be terrible and tragic but that meant an opportunity for Claire to bring her vision for Gaia Enterprises to life. An ordered, structured institution, with graduates who were disciplined, focused and committed to everything Gaia stood for. A small stream of relief seeped through, too – Maja's 'experiments' in human development could be contained, dialled down. These were edgy and dangerous. After all, Maja, the guru, had been wrong – very wrong – about that early community, Terra Blanca. Maja believed the best of human nature would win the day. But without proper laws and boundaries, human beings turned to their more primal instincts. And people had died. Horribly. That could not be allowed to happen again. Ever.

But Claire's vision for Gaia and the future needed allies. The selection was now more important than ever.

She needed to make sure Maja saw her point of view and they only selected people who could see the integrity of what they had built, the solid rationale behind all of the teachings. Jonas Seaborn was a risk, Claire knew. He had all the telltale signs of someone with poor emotional intelligence. It would take him a lot of work if he was to rise to the standard of a Gaia crew member. This meant the selection challenges had to be harder than usual. The tests would push the applicants to reveal emotional trouble spots. No weaknesses could be allowed to come through the screening net. This cohort was critical. The future of humanity depended on it. Nothing but the most solid, most developed world designers could be allowed to build communities off world.

Claire turned her thoughts to the task at hand: designing the selection process. It had to be new every time. Word got out, no matter how much they told graduates to maintain confidentiality. Graduates wanted their friends to get a leg-up, so they shared insider secrets, just one or two, to give them an advantage. The first activity would have to set the tone. All in or get out. She would enjoy watching the candidates. And Troy. He was always so impressive.

Troy. The image of the tall, blond, sculpted man took hold of her. His smile spread in her mind's eye and blotted out every-thing else. Her heart thumped in response. All these years and she still hungered for his touch, to be near him. She cursed her own weakness. Unrequited love was an unresolved emotional state she needed to process and lay to rest. It would distract her from her mission during this selection. Besides, she would have to contend with Xavier, Maja's pet. Xavier had been a graduate, same as her and Troy, the three of them star pupils. Troy with his design genius and disarming good looks, Claire with her meticulous application of design principles, and then Xavier, the challenger. He ques-tioned everything, argued everything. It was so frustrating! He really rode the 'bad boy' image hard – always the rebel, always defying the status quo. And to Claire's amazement, Maja seemed to lap it up. Claire assumed Maja would clamp down on anyone who would defy the tenets of Gaia. These had been crafted after long and arduous research, forged in the crucible of brutal lived experiences. Maja had a right to assert them and claim them as the best way forward – she had lived through so much herself! Yet she indulged Xavier's arrogance. Why? What was it about him that led Maja to bend so easily?

It had confused Claire for a long time, these failings she saw in Maja. Maja was her mentor and a titan of intelligence, wisdom and compassion. She was everything Claire hoped to be as a leader and more. Then these cracks had appeared in the perfect picture, and Claire had felt the beginnings of doubt start creeping in. Maja was the Chief Executive Officer, but she was also human. Claire felt it her duty to make sure she stopped some of the big mistakes, prevented her icon from ruining her own creations.

If Maja only had a year at most to live, then Claire needed to make sure that this selection consolidated and set the standard for the future. There must be no ambiguity about the direction and regulations of Gaia Enterprises when she passed away. Claire pursed her lips and drew up her outline for the three-day selection. Now's the time, she thought. Now's *her* time.

CHAPTER THIRTEEN

Jealousy is as good a reason as any to do good in the world.

MAJA GARCIA, THE JOURNALS

Sydney: Xanthe

XANTHE ROLLED ONTO her back for what felt like the hundredth time and stared up at the ceiling. Sleep was impossible. The conversation with Maja over the holo had rattled her. After a week arguing with Simon, she had all but resolved to turn the project down.

She had gone back and forth with him about wasted space tourism dollars, the billions spent on Moon missions while millions struggled to live here on Earth, climate refugees dying of heat stress and disease in cramped temporary quarters. She agreed with him. Things on Earth were tough and needed immediate attention. It was why she'd given up her paramedic work to undertake world design. She wanted to make a difference to people, now. Especially since... the tsunami. She squeezed those memories back in to the small black box at the recesses of her mind.

Simon reiterated how space tourism was distracting the planet's best talent and redirecting it in service of the wealthy's thrills and spills, instead of focusing on climate rehabilitation. Not to mention the enormous carbon cost of endless rocket launches. Again, she agreed with him. Space tourism was a folly. There were some benefits though, but Simon didn't want to hear them, and time and again Xanthe found her voice getting shut down. It gnawed at her, like a mosquito bite that grows itchier even as you try and fail not to scratch it.

Xanthe believed that the future of humanity, the future of consciousness, was worth investing in. Her time horizon of concern stretched beyond this generation and the next. Humanity's fate was doomed if it stayed only on Earth. If an extinction-level event like a meteor didn't wipe us out, then the sun would, eventually. She felt the loss of humanity and life itself was a tragedy beyond all measure. She did not believe, as others like Simon did, that humans should hitch their fate to Earth. Earthists believed that we were born here, we die here, as Nature intended. From Earth's mud we emerged, with its dust we too should fade, they said.

But why? There is still so much goodness in humanity, in human civilisation, why let it dwindle to stardust?

Things with Simon grew tense and cold. Xanthe wondered if the future of humanity was worth the misery of a failed marriage. She had already suffered so much grief in the tsunami. She still loved Simon, even as she watched him harden and grow spurs. She could see that his anger against big tech, big pharma, and the Space Cowboys was a way to funnel his own grief. But the result was that the gentle man she had married now bristled with spikes. Maybe if she tried harder she could bring him back to tenderness. Maybe *that* mission was worth her effort: to save the man she once loved more than Earth itself. Whether it was a mission for one or a mission for many, love was a worthy cause.

She resolved to tell Maja she would pass on the Olympus Project. She buried her regret and resigned herself to focus on her community design work. Worthy work, she told herself. Simon wasn't so much delighted as relieved. "Good," he said. "You've come to your senses." She didn't let it show, but with this response, a dark termite burrowed in her soul.

Then Maja called. The conversation was brief. Maja was on a deadline with applications closing soon and selection on the horizon. They needed to confirm the third designer before selection invitations went out. If Xanthe was not on board, they would invite Tony Boss.

Tony Goddamn Boss. Good on him, she thought. He's been a successful designer with a multitude of high-profile projects. Sure, they had their differences, but she admired his work ethic and dedication. His arrogance? Not so much.

Xanthe turned on her side. She watched Simon's chest rise and fall as he slept. Calm. Peaceful. She rolled over again, stewing. At last, she slipped out of bed and padded out to the kitchen to make a cup of tea. Sleep was not coming to drown out her thoughts.

Steaming cup in hand, she went out on their balcony, the night air cool for once. She sat on one of the small chairs and stared up into the sky. There was the Moon, same as she ever was, pale face looking down on humanity.

Xanthe's eyes swelled with tears. What was she giving up? The chance of a lifetime. The chance to shape the future of human civilisation.

And Tony Boss. Was the regret professional jealousy? She pushed herself to confront this. Maybe a little. But she could get past that. Tony Boss would take the Olympus Project and make it a commercial success. The Moon Base would become a thriving economic hub for asteroid mining, for research and for space tourism.

But what about the people? What about community? If Tony designed it, the base would be functional, rather than inspiring. Troy might be able to temper the design a little, but his specialty was psych design and sensory stim, not community builds.

Not her problem. So be it. Gaia could make their own choices.

But could she let it go? Could she spend the rest of her life knowing she chose Simon over the Moon? The project was only two years. She didn't have to go forever. Design it, test the prototype, build it, come back. That's assuming we win the bid, she thought. *We.* Was she already back in Gaia's camp?

Two years and then back to working on the community designs here on Earth. That was a fair compromise, wasn't it? Make sure the Olympus Project was set on the right track, and then come back? Surely Simon would see the value in that.

She put her tea down and grabbed the holo. She sent the signal and moments later a groggy Maja popped into view.

"Xanthe," she said with a warm smile. "I've been expecting your call."

CHAPTER FOURTEEN

Any decision brings a loss as well as a gain. It's how we navigate the disappointment that determines how much we enjoy the upside.

ATHENA AI IN WISDOM OF THE AGES

Sydney: Xanthe

THREE DAYS AFTER she called Maja, Simon and Xanthe sat on their couch after dinner. She read her tablet; Simon read his. Simon hadn't said a word since she'd told him.

Finally, he broke the impasse.

"What happened to you?" The icy daggers were gone. His voice was sad.

"What do you mean?" Xanthe asked, on alert.

"World design was your calling after—"

"Don't." Her face hardened at the unspoken name.

Simon paused, then tried again. "All those communities you designed and helped. You built futures for refugees. You helped people reclaim dignity and hope. You helped *us* have hope. Even when you left Gaia you had a focus – to make this world better. This world, not the Moon."

Xanthe turned away from him to gaze out their window, left open to let a whisper of cool air in. She hugged the silence around her like a blanket.

"And what about us? If you do this, you'll be gone for two years. Maybe more." He put his hand on hers, his strong warm fingers covering her own thin, cold hand.

"I'll miss you," he said.

Still, she could not speak. The tears pushed up from deep within and spilled down her cheeks. In her choked and stubborn silence, Xanthe sensed his pleading shift from desperation to resignation. They both know she wouldn't change her mind.

PART TWO

SELECTION

CHAPTER FIFTEEN

"They say you're a playboy. How do you
respond to that description?"
"Well, I love play. And I'm a boy. So, I guess it's accurate."

TROY BRUIN, 'PERSON OF THE YEAR' INTERVIEW

*James Bay, Canada – Gaia Enterprises Recruitment and
Training Centre*

MAJA, HUW AND Claire celebrated Xanthe's acceptance only briefly.
With Xavier on board too, their lead design team was complete.
Huw initiated the press release and ran all the media interviews.
Claire issued the invitations to selection and started finalising
details for the exhaustive process. Maja helped her by liaising with
Troy, Xavier and the other graduates they'd recruited to help with
selection. At last, they were ready to receive the applicants.

Xavier spent a week with his wife and girls before his departure.
Despite his worries, his family were thrilled for him. They agreed
two years and a possible trip to the Moon were worth the sacrifices.

And the bragging rights, the girls told him. He called Troy as soon as his family approved his decision. His old friend was delighted.

Maja agreed to let Troy and Xavier arrive a day ahead of selection to 'get oriented', but really it was a chance for them to catch up in person before the arduous work of selection began. They spent a night on Gaia's training island laughing and swapping stories. The next day, Troy and Xavier drove the transfer boats from the training centre to collect the other graduates helping with selection. They ducked and weaved around islands, racing each other.

∾

Xanthe watched Troy and Xavier arrive with a flutter of nerves. They tied up the boats while the graduates waiting on the dock cheered, proud of their celebrity colleagues. The other graduates had been friendly but reserved around her. They all knew the history: the bitter split from Gaia over what Xanthe called mission creep. Still, they congratulated her on the appointment and welcomed her back to Gaia.

Xanthe noted the difference in reception for Troy and Xavier. It annoyed her, but she pushed that thought aside. As Xavier and Troy stepped on to the dock to back slaps and hugs, Xanthe turned away and busied herself with her luggage.

Troy strode down the dock when he caught sight of Xanthe. She shouldered her bag and then found herself staring up into the face of Achilles himself. Sweet Jesus the man was beautiful! The light in his eyes reached out and held her like a cradle of warm sunshine. *He is magnificent.* The thought caught her off guard. She knew him of course from all the media stories and Gaia news. Though colleagues when she worked previously with Gaia, Xanthe had not had a chance to meet him in person. He was not what she expected. More… vibrant. She summoned Simon's face to try and block her unruly response.

"Hello," he breathed and his smile widened to both sides. He held out his right hand and grasped hers, then folded his left around it. His skin was warm. She could *smell* him. A faint trace of musky soap. It sent tendrils of longing through her body.

"Hello. I'm Xanthe Waters. Pleasure to meet you." She stumbled a little on the last word. *Seven hells! What am I, twelve again?*

Xavier caught up to the two of them and the spell was broken. "*Bonjour!*" He exclaimed. He clapped Troy on the back and beamed at Xanthe, his black skin shiny in the morning sun. "Here we are – the three leads! Wonderful to meet you Madame Waters, I am a fan of your work." He thrust his hand out to take hers and shook it strongly.

"Thank you, Xavier. I am looking forward to working with you. Both of you," she said and covered her shyness well.

"I'm sure you'll fit right in, Xanthe," Troy said breezily. "Won't take you long to get caught up on the new Gaia protocols brought in since you, you know, *left*." He raised a knowing eyebrow, and a lopsided smile appeared on his face.

Xanthe felt his words as a jab. If he was trying to make her feel welcome, he had failed. She said nothing and followed them to the boats. Troy acknowledged his colleagues' comments and congratulations. Like a king and his subjects, she thought, with some disdain.

The rest of the day was a blur of briefings and logistics. Xanthe's apprehension about returning to Gaia was swallowed by the busy preparations. Troy and Xavier were to accompany an expedition group each, while Xanthe would work with Maja and Claire on the VR and other centre-based challenges. The buzz among the crew was electric. Tomorrow was the day – let the games begin!

CHAPTER SIXTEEN

Human development is much like the growth of an ash tree. It follows a familiar pattern, but then it sprouts branches in places you didn't expect. That's when you need to get out the pruning shears.

MAJA GARCIA, THE JOURNALS

James Bay, Canada – Gaia Enterprises Recruitment and Training Centre: Jonas

WITH AWKWARD HUGS from his parents, and the cheering waves of the *Sea Rover* community, Jonas left his floating home as it anchored near Montreal on the Fleuve St Laurent. From there, he took a plane with the other candidates to James Bay. They would be taken to the Gaia Enterprises training centre by boat. As they waited on the dock for the Gaia transfer vessel, he sized up the others, his rivals. A group of men chatted and laughed, standing together by the boat ramp. They looked fairly easy-going and fresh-faced. No stand-outs there.

Four of the women gathered on the end of the pier, gazing out to the far horizon of the lake. One of the women, short and stocky, lowered herself to the dock, flat on her stomach to point out something nearby in the water. A woman with brilliant white teeth and the blackest skin he'd ever seen laughed uproariously at something she said. Jonas smiled. That one had spunk! He made a note to get to know her better. The other two seemed average enough. Not that good looking. Unremarkable. He dismissed them as of low interest. Then he saw her, a fifth woman, all bronzed legs and long, soft blonde hair, which the breeze teased to float around her like waving fairy wands. She strode along the dock with a bright expression, opening her arms to the others as if welcoming long-lost friends. She made some remark that made them all burst out laughing. They stood around her as she told some animated story. Jonas was immediately drawn to her. He decided *she* was the one he'd get to know better. Now.

He jumped up and in his best saunter, approached the group and held out his hand.

"Hello there! I'm Jonas Seaborn. From the *Sea Rover*." He added the last bit to make sure they could place him correctly.

The blonde turned to look at him. Eyes blue, wide and fierce, so clear, as if made of crystals, they seemed to refract the light in all directions. Jonas felt electricity shoot through him from throat to tailbone.

"Serena Fox." She reached out and gripped his hand, looking at him directly.

"Mind if I join you?"

She gestured beside her. "Only if you bite. And then who knows! That might be fun."

"Where are you from?" he asked, chin jutting to punctuate his question.

"Sydney. Australia."

"Oh." Jonas failed to mask his pity.

Hearing his tone, Serena shot him a look. Sydney had suffered. The once glorious city was now an industrial mess. Residents had evacuated alongside other climate refugees. The ones remaining, refusing – or unable – to abandon their once glamorous properties eked out an existence through trade on the peripheries. The once gorgeous suburbs were little more than shanty towns now.

Wanting to move through the awkwardness, Jonas continued. "Where did you train, then?"

"On the docks mostly. Salvage operations, diving, then world design with caving quals."

Jonas nodded, acknowledging her experience.

"Which Worlds have you been on?"

"What is this? An interrogation! Lordy Mr Seaborn you are certainly not backwards in coming forwards."

"Just getting to know folks is all," he said, slightly abashed.

"Well, Jonas, there's plenty of time for pissing contests – we've got three weeks ahead of us. Don't get your knickers in a twist just yet."

The women stifled giggles.

Seeing his awkwardness, Serena continued. "Come on then, Jonas," she jibed, "Tell us about yourself. Training, quals, ribbons, trophies, gold stars – the works." She put her hands on her hips, slender, shapely shoulders catching the morning sunlight.

Jonas's face burned hot. For a moment he considered his response, then with an exaggerated flourish he bowed deeply, one leg poised in front, like an ancient courtier.

"Madame, ladies. I shall keep my knickers untwisted for the time being. I look forward to future said twisting, preferably at your most capable and welcoming hands." He winked and with as much dignity as he could muster, spun and marched off.

∽

The chatter continued as they boarded the shuttle boats to the training centre. Wind whipped their hair and reddened their cheeks. For a moment they forgot they were here for three arduous weeks of challenges that could mean the opportunity of a lifetime.

Once on the island, Gaia staff ushered the applicants to a large green lawn outside the main administration building. They dropped their bags and gathered in a circle. Maja, Claire and Huw waited and watched. To the side, the Gaia graduates lined up, including the Olympus Project lead designers, Xavier, Troy and Xanthe.

Xavier leant over to Troy and said, "Now *mon ami*, don't go making all the ladies fall in love with you again! They have work to do."

"I can't control the gifts of the gods," Troy replied with half a smirk.

Xanthe rolled her eyes while Xavier and Troy swapped barbs. Sensing her distance, Troy turned to her and said, "Xanthe, make sure you enjoy the luxuries of headquarters while we're out slumming it, half-starved."

"I'll be quite busy thank you very much," she snapped. "Plenty to do to set up the VR sims and challenges." She bristled at the suggestion that she had an easier workload. She glanced at him with all his self-assured cockiness and crazy good looks. She blurted, "Besides, I'm sure your ego could do with a little 'slumming'." She said it without mirth, just irritation.

"Oh la la!" Xavier laughed at the burn. Troy's face flushed red. He did not reply.

What am I doing here? Xanthe thought. Third wheel in a bro-mance on a project my husband loathes. She tried to breathe through her misgivings. Too late now. She gritted her teeth and resolved to relax and stay focused.

Then she saw her. Serena Fox. Dread stabbed her guts. She recognised the woman earlier when Claire briefed the staff on the candidates. Xanthe had first met Serena at her family's memorial after the tsunami. Xanthe had thought the other woman was a friend of her sister's. There had been a lot of people she did not know there. That's when she had discovered her father had had a lover: Serena. It's going to be a long few weeks, Xanthe thought.

❧

Claire scanned the crowd, putting names to the faces she had studied so rigorously in preparation for today. There was Serena, the tall, thin blonde. You could hardly miss her. Where was Jonas? She caught sight of him in saggy jeans, folded arms, nodding and jutting his chin at others who recognised him as the Seaborn heir. Madison, the pilot, in a bomber jacket and aviator shades. Each face was familiar. Having whittled the initial applications down to one hundred, she'd spent the past few months interrogating every aspect of these candidates' lives. She whittled the hundred down some more with psychometric testing, online questionnaires and holo interviews. Then referee checks, a second interview, and here they were, the last thirty. A few had dropped out after selection offers due to family commitments, injury or nerves. Thirty candidates for three spots on the build crew, and one spot for the medico. Tough competition.

"Welcome!" Maja's voice boomed out, loud for a woman who was so slight. Maja opened her arms wide. "Welcome to the selection for the Olympus Project tender. We are pleased to meet you all in person after such a long process. Consider yourselves privileged indeed to be here – it is no easy feat to make it this far in the process. Here at Gaia Enterprises, our work is to hone the thinking and world design skills for the future of humanity. This is serious work. The Moon Base is an enormous step for humanity and the future of planet Earth. We will need all the technical and interpersonal skills we can muster if we are to survive as a species on this changed world, and all the brave, new worlds.

"As such, this selection will not be easy. You will be tested in more ways than you can imagine. We can't afford to get our choices wrong. We need candidates who can endure the most difficult of pressures, the most serious of environments, the most extreme of conditions. We know you have the technical skills to design the physical spaces – the engineering, design and so forth. That's a core requirement. What we are looking for are leaders. Individuals who can shape communities, build safe and trusting environments; individuals who can guide human development. We need leaders who know themselves well, are aware of their shortcomings, and can lead on in spite of them." Maja paused and Claire saw how her words were landing: as intended, like the rumble of an earthquake. The applicants listened intently, nerves jangling.

"We want to see all of you in these next few weeks. You can't really hide. If you try and bluff your way through the activities, we will know. You must be raw and real. The staff are here to challenge you and to assess you. I'll hand you over now to Claire who will officially launch proceedings."

Claire stepped forward, serious and intense. "Hello, all. You will be issued with wrist comms. These will provide you with directions at critical points throughout the selection process. Your first task, so you can set your mind to it now, will be a team expedition. The wrist comms also provide you with biodata, as if you were wearing spacesuits. You have a set amount of oxygen programmed in for the duration of your trip. You need to manage your resources accordingly. There is no oxygen resupply until you reach the base in the next valley." She nodded to the support staff to distribute the electronic bracelets. "You have been divided into cohorts of five. Your wrist comms will tell you which cohort you belong to. Find your teammates. Your next task is to choose roles for each other. During the first phase of selection, you will need to choose leaders, navigators, supply managers and so forth. You have twenty minutes now to meet one another and find out about each other. In that time, you will also you need to nominate your team roles. Go."

❧

Madison slipped on her wrist comm. It activated on skin contact, animating with a message: *Delta cohort.*

"Delta! Delta cohort!" A stocky man called, waving his hand.

Following his lead, the other cohort members shouted their cohort names: Alpha, Bravo, Charlie, Delta, Echo, Foxtrot. Six cohorts in all.

Madison moved towards the Delta group, working her way around the calls and laughter. In a few moments, she gathered with four others who sized each other up. Troy joined them. He was their observing staff member. The stocky man who led the call signal spoke first.

"'Allo, there! Delta cohort, I presume. Shall we introduce ourselves? I am Dr Pierre Martin. Surgeon at *Humanité Plus*."

Madison took her measure of Pierre. This guy sure is up himself, she thought.

"Madison Floyd. Pilot." She nodded at him. He puffed his chest a little.

"I'm a pilot too! Hello – I'm David Eriksson. Of Archello in Helsinki. Good to be here!" David thrust his hand out to Madison, breaking the moment between her and Pierre. The tall gangly man beamed at each of them as he shook their hands in turn. "So, we ready to rock'n roll, crew of Delta?" He did a little dance.

"Steady on, Dave, my man! Got ants in your pants with those moves!" Madison laughed.

A short man eyed this exchange warily. "I am Dr Mohammad Rasheed, physician to His Excellency, the Sultan of Dubai." He spouted the announcement more stridently than he intended.

His sudden formal tone jolted them a little from the friendly exchange. Their smiles faded, not knowing what to make of this interjection. "Damn Mohammad, those are some kind of credentials!" Madison sung out.

"It is Dr Mohammad, if you please." he said curtly.

"Alright, alright," Madison replied. "Just trying to break the ice." She raised her hands in apology. Before she could say more, a tall, thin woman stepped into the space and put her hand out to Mohammad.

"Dr Rasheed, I am thrilled to meet you, I have read all your papers on longevity treatments. Your cellular rinsing technology is incredible! I am so excited to be in your group. It's an honour to meet you, sir." He shook her hand briefly and nodded an acknowledgement. She coloured and looked at the ground.

"And you are…" nudged Madison.

"Oh. Yes. Sorry. Dr Jade Mandez. I'm a life support medical technician."

"Holy guacamole, we got all the smart people right here!" Madison jibed. "Three doctors, I feel like we'll be right as rain no matter what happens trekkin' through the wilderness!"

"That leaves just one more introduction," David said, and they looked at Troy.

"Troy Bruin. Gaia graduate, of the New Baths of Caracalla."

"Oh, we all know who you are, Troy, my man! The most famous Gaia world designer around! Delta crew, we are blessed with design royalty! You'd better live up to your reputation, boyo, if we're going to take out the competition!" Madison waggled a finger at him.

Troy's smile drifted upwards on one side, devilish. His blond hair curled in a wistful flop.

"Great to be here," he said. "I'm looking forward to spending some time with you over these next few days." He looked at each of them with an encouraging smile. "Some of you may end up on the Olympus Project, in which case we'll be spending a lot more time together. Just so you know, my role on this expedition is purely as observer. Treat me as part of the team, a resource if you like, but I won't be helping you solve any of the challenges. We want to see how you tackle things. We want to see your leadership, as well as how you operate as a team."

"So, you'll be like a kind of – how you say – a freeloader?" asked Pierre with a grin.

"I say we just jump on him now and force him to give us all the answers. The big man couldn't resist all of us!" added David.

"Look at those muscles," Madison said. "I bet he could bench press all of us with one finger! What do you feed a brute like you, anyhow?" she asked.

"Cricket protein bars," he replied with a laugh.

"*Ah non! Merde! Dégueulasse!*" Pierre said with a grimace.

"Dega – what now?" asked Madison.

"Disgusting. I meant disgusting. Cricket protein – *c'est merde!*"

"Damn – I look forward to expanding my vocabulary with these great new French swear words on this little excursion!"

Mohammad tapped his foot in annoyance.

"Let's get to it, shall we?" he barked. "We need to pick a leader, navigators and what was it – supply managers. Who would like which role?"

They glanced awkwardly at one another.

"Why don't you take the leader role, Dr Mohammad, seeing how as you're so keen?" Madison suggested, with a challenge.

"Well, if no one else wants to…"

"Actually, I think Madison 'Mad Dog' Floyd would be good in the leader role to start, no? She has plenty of experience telling people what to do, as a pilot trainer. Smart to have someone used to giving orders to start with, no?" David proposed. Mohammad's face soured.

"Oh my, someone has done their homework," Madison remarked, one eyebrow shooting up.

"I agree," added Pierre. "Madison seems to have a good command style. I back that nomination. Jade, what do you think?"

Jade nodded. "Sure. Fine with me." She tried to keep her tone neutral. Her grey eyes flicked his way, then away again.

"Righto, settled then," Madison said. "Navigators – who's up for it?"

"I'll do it," Pierre said. "I've trekked all over and feel comfortable with map and compass in case there is no GPS tech. Jade, will you be my partner in crime?" He leant towards her and bumped her shoulder.

"Yes, that's fine. I can navigate," she said, not looking at him.

"That leaves Tweedle Dee and Tweedle Dum for supply. You two right with that?" Madison jabbed David in the arm and winked at Mohammad who just acknowledged her with an ill-concealed sneer.

"Nice work, Delta! First job done. We're going to cruise through selection at this rate. Now what?" Madison high-fived each of them, eyes glazing past Mohammad as she did so.

Claire called the nominated leaders over for the activity briefing. While the candidates made their way over, Xanthe studied the Gaia Enterprises training centre and its surrounds. The central gathering place had been carefully designed as a green oasis, bordered by a loose ring of maple trees and conifers. Nice and cooling in the summer. Buildings were set further back in the woods, mimicking the ring formation of the trees. The main gathering places formed an apex for the centre: the study and exercise hall and the dining room. Accommodation was in smaller units out further along the ring. There was a sense of community and belonging, of egalitarianism, a blend of work and play, of activity and rest. Clever, thought Xanthe. No one was left out, no one was elevated above the rest. Everything and everyone were equally accessible but had their own privacy. She had loved this place from the moment she first saw it, years ago.

Claire's voice cut short her admiration. "Candidates – make yourselves ready." Xanthe looked back at Claire and the expedition leaders. Serena Fox was among them. Xanthe took a deep breath and nodded at her. Serena smiled back and waved. She made a move to approach her when Claire started the briefing. It was a detailed explanation of the expedition and its objectives. All the group leaders listened intently. Xanthe enjoyed watching their growing consternation, not out of any malice, but in empathy. She remembered what it was like during her selection for designer training. It was a powerful experience. It was the hardest thing she'd ever done to date, and the most rewarding. She hoped the Olympus Project would recapture some of her original passion.

∾

Serena returned to the group after the briefing looking equal parts excited and overwhelmed. She gestured to the fledgling team, and they gathered around. Her super-fine blonde hair swished like water as she turned to each of them. Xavier, their supervising staff member, watched intently. Not intimidating at all, she mused.

"Listen up, Bravo group. The good news is that we know what we're doing. The bad news is that we're going over there." She pointed behind her to a hill towering some distance away. It looked steep and rocky. There was a murmur among the group.

Serena continued. "Here's the deal. Our task is to get our supplies, trek to Mount Precious, and design and set up a survival camp. There's a set of clues we need to decipher to get additional resources we might need." Serena eyed her team members. She cat-alogued them silently to cement their names. Two engineers: Gina, the tough-nut Italian loner, and Jonas Seaborn, the bumptious prat from the *Sea Rover*. Pabi the pilot smiled nervously and smoothed his immaculate dress pants. Military goon through and through, she thought. His shit's wired so tight he probably poops bullets. And then Max King. She'd read about him on the flight over from Sydney. Crazy mountaineer. Great inventions, though. Serena had used some of his oxygen-enriching tech in her first underground design projects. He's a bit of hot stuff too, she thought. Too bad he's going to miss out when I grab the life support spot for this gig.

86

I just need to make sure Xavier sees it the same way. She glanced at Xavier, their Gaia observer, who was checking his watch and eyeing her with a not-so-subtle hint.

"Shall we?" she suggested. They set off to the supply shed. Max chatted to Jonas, and they soon shared their favourite travel destinations. Jonas had been to every major port around the globe on the *Sea Rover* and was happy to let everyone know it. Max met him one for one, outdoing him every time. "You liked Puerto Vallarta? Wonderful! Have you watched the sunrise from the Mayan ruins in Guatemala? It's stunning. The raw power of the jungle and those ancient monuments gives spirituality a new meaning. It's not Everest by any means, but it's something special."

"I heard you climbed Everest," Serena baited him.

"A few times," Max replied with feigned humility.

"Oh. And which time did you do it blindfolded, with one hand tied behind your back? And wasn't there a time when you base jumped from the top and rescued five small children on the way down?" she teased.

"Not quite," he said laughing.

Good, Serena thought. He can take a joke. Not a complete knob after all.

They arrived at the expedition shed. Gina squatted down next to the pile of gear and swore in Italian.

"You're kidding," Jonas said. They stood around their supplies, stunned. There was one sleeping bag, a map and compass, a knife, one box of matches, one plastic sheet and one bag of oats.

"How are we going to stay warm with one sleeping bag between six of us? We'll starve with one bag of oats! How long are we out there? A couple of days? This is bullshit!" Jonas fumed. The rest stood uneasily, fearful of the unexpected hardship.

"That makes looking after supplies pretty easy!" laughed Pabi. He had volunteered to manage their resources. "I could do with losing a bit of weight, anyhow." They all looked at Pabi who was smiling sheepishly. His limbs were thin and wiry like a stretched rubber band. They all burst out laughing, and the tension from Jonas's outburst crumbled away.

"We got this, team!" Serena did her best version of cheer squad, trying to pump them up. "Jonas, Gina – here's the first set of clues." Jonas reach out and grabbed the envelope before Gina could. Gina grabbed the envelope back and said, "We do this together, Jon-ARSE," deliberately mis-pronouncing his name. "Two brains are better than one. Usually, anyhow," she added, with a sly grin.

"The rest of us can sort our personal stuff. We'll need warm clothes, wet weather gear, head torch and water bottles. Let's regroup in ten minutes," Serena said.

She sorted her belongings quickly and returned to find Jonas and Gina whooping happily. They had figured out the first clue – a jumble of letters and numbers. It was a name – Froggy Beach, and a six-digit grid reference. Max had the map out and brought it over to her.

"I think it's here," he said. He leant in towards her and Serena could feel the warmth of his skin against her arm. She peered at the map, checked the grid reference, conscious of where his arm touched hers.

"Yes – that's right. It says 'Froggy Beach'. About three kilometres along the shoreline." She smiled up at him and was rewarded with a giant grin. She noticed he had great teeth. Except for an eyetooth that spun the wrong direction with a tiny brown stain on the end. She tried not to stare at it.

"Let's go then!" Serena urged her crew to gather their goods and embark on their quest.

∽

"Jesus Christ Almighty." Jonas stood on the shore of Froggy Beach at a mailbox that was stuck in the water ten metres away, up a giant pole about three metres high, with a sign "Clue 2."

"We're going to have to get wet. Anyone bring swim gear?"

"No. But skin is waterproof!" Pabi was already stripping down, folding his clothes in a neat pile. Pabi felt free for the first time in years. Away from the suffocating pressure of his family and the oppressive discipline of the air force, this experience was liberating. He could be someone completely new. He could launch a whole new life.

⁓

Xavier sat down on the beach to watch them. This should be interesting, he thought. The tussles between Gina and Jonas were electric already. Xavier knew Gina was fantastic as an engineer from her brief stay at Terra Verdi, but could she survive a small team environment? Seaborn needed to show he could overcome bluster and ego. Max and Serena were contending for the life support technician spot. Max was technically better, but Serena had design skills. It came down to leadership, and who could be an able companion. Pabi? Xavier wanted to know if he could trust this pilot with his life.

"Okay, this is what we'll do," Serena commanded. "Max, you and Jonas can make a base at the bottom of the pole. Gina and Pabi, you two go next on their shoulders. I'm the thinnest, so I should be able to get to the top and grab the next clue." Xavier saw Gina bristle. He noticed she wasn't a waif like Serena, but she wasn't exactly huge either. Gina could have done this task easily as well. Was Serena stepping in to be the hero?

"Hang on a minute," Jonas said. "No reason for everyone to get wet. I think me and Max should be able to handle it. Max can just boost me up on his shoulders and I should be able to reach it."

"Nope. We do this as a team. All in."

"I think that's a waste of energy and puts others at risk." He crossed his arms, defiant.

Serena studied him for a moment.

"Any other suggestions?" she asked the group.

"Let them have a go first," Gina said, seeming to relish the challenge to Serena's leadership.

"Max, you up for that?" Serena asked.

He shrugged. "Sure."

Max and Jonas stripped down to their underwear and waded in, hooting a little with the cold water. Serena couldn't help but admire Max's muscular, fit form.

They watched as Max boosted Jonas to sit on his shoulders. Jonas wobbled a little, held on to the post and managed to stand on Max's shoulders. He stretched for the mailbox, but it was just out of reach.

"Maybe if I stand on your head?"

"Go for it!"

Jonas placed one foot on Max's head, then with a push upwards reached for the mailbox. He swung wide, lost his balance, and fell, arms windmilling. He hollered as he plunged into a bellyflop.

Pabi, Serena and Gina stifled their laughter while they watched from the shore.

"Are you alright, Jonas?" Serena called out once he surfaced.

"Yeah," he replied, dejected.

"Okay, that's enough. We're wasting time. We go with my original plan. We're coming in now." Serena commanded.

The three stripped down and joined the others. In a few minutes they had boosted Pabi and Gina to Jonas and Max's shoulders forming a standing ladder, then grabbed and heaved Serena upwards to the top. She retrieved a plastic container from the mailbox perch and jumped gracefully to the water below. The ladder collapsed and they clambered ashore to get dry and read the next clue.

"Bravo, Bravo group!" Xavier clapped their performance. The fledgling team soaked up the praise. Only Jonas was scowling.

CHAPTER SEVENTEEN

Language is a special tool of leadership. Our
words are weapons. Choose them wisely.

GAIA ENTERPRISES CODE OF CONDUCT

Delta cohort: Dr Mohammad, Jade, Pierre, David and
Madison with Troy

"THIS IS NOT acceptable," Madison growled. They were deep in the
forest, hot, hungry, and lost.

Pierre looked up from the map while Jade bit her lip and traced
the contour lines, trying to make sense of their location.

"Back off, Mad Dog," he bit back. "We're doing our best with
this piece-of-shit map. *Câlisse.*"

"What does that mean?" Madison asked in a menacing tone.

"What does *what* mean?" Pierre replied, exasperated.

"What you said. Just then."

"Piece-of-shit map? It's a piece-of-shit map. It's old and out of
date. We cannot use tech – no GPS, only compass,... ridiculous.
Many things not on the map."

"Not that – the other word!"

"What? *Câlisse?* It's French."

"Well, duh. What does it mean?" She demanded, alert to any insult.

"I guess the translation would be…" He thought for a moment. "Shit. It means shit."

Madison wasn't buying this. "What does it *really* mean?" Her voice was low and full of suppressed violence.

Pierre looked at her with raised eyebrows. "Seriously? Seriously, you want to know?" The tension was winding him up. They were lost, he was navigating. He felt the pressure to get them out of this, especially as the sun would be setting soon. She nodded. He said, "It means cup, a communion cup."

Madison's eyebrows shot up. "What the…?"

"It's how we swear in Québec. We use religious words. Like *tabarnak.* Say it like you've got something stuck in your throat." He swatted a fly, wiped his brow and leant back over the map.

"And what does *that* mean?" Dave asked, intrigued now.

"It means 'fuck'. Literal translation 'tabernacle'. Where you put the things for communion."

Dave burst out laughing. He sat on the ground, leaning on his pack. "You French Canadians know how to swing punches! Give it to me! What are you going to call me next, a pew? A prayer book? A stick of incense?"

Madison scoffed.

"How about *'petit con*?" Pierre said joining his laughter.

"And what does that mean?"

"'Stupid idiot'. Literal translation."

Dave laughed some more, slapping his pack and leaning over it to try and catch his breath between chortles.

"Okay, *putty con*," Madison said, stumbling on the new words. "Let's figure out where we are and get the *tabarnak* out of here."

"Not quite the right use of the word, but I understand the

sentiment," Pierre said. "Here – let me show where I think we are on this *putain* of a map."

Dave looked at him expectantly. "And that means, what? Nun?"

"No – that one means 'whore'."

"Oh my goodness, I'm dying!" Dave laughed some more, wiping tears from his face.

Mohammad sat apart on his backpack. He sipped a little water from a bottle, trying to conserve both his strength and fluid. He watched this exchange with disgust. These people were rude and crass. The profanity bothered him. He was a man of faith. He had worked all his life as a dedicated professional. And now he was here, in the middle of the Canadian wilderness with a bunch of imbeciles, at the personal behest of the Sultan. His left knee ached, and his privates chaffed from the sweaty cotton trousers. A poor choice for these conditions and activities, he lamented. Mohammad would never admit it, but he was struggling physically. For the Sultan's sake though, he would endure it. He glanced over at Troy who was sitting up against a tree, eyes closed, a smile on his face. He does not seem overly concerned, thought Mohammad. We cannot be too far from our objective.

Troy listened to the banter as he rested. He was enjoying the friction grinding away at the group. They'd manage to defuse a few tight moments, mostly through Dave and Pierre interjecting with jokes and Madison crumbling soon after. Mohammad remained aloof, and Jade was a mouse. Let's see if anyone will bring them together, he thought. Can I spend two years cooped up with any of these people? he wondered. Too soon to tell. We haven't got to the real tests yet.

Madison kicked his boots lightly.

"Look alive, Prince Troy, we're on the move."

CHAPTER EIGHTEEN

"It was like we forgot everything outside the gate. It was
like we became a universe unto ourselves, that we could
do whatever we saw fit to keep the community strong. We
made up our own rules, based on what we thought was right.
And for a while, it worked. People on the whole wanted
to get along and worked hard to look after each other."

TERRA BLANCA EYEWITNESS ACCOUNT

Bravo cohort: Jonas, Serena, Gina, Pabi and Max with Xavier

THEY WERE COLD, hungry and miserable. Jonas stared into his
mug of warm water, despondent. Selection was harder than he'd
thought. He'd done alright so far, sure. He'd aced all the clues with
a little help from Gina. Jonas was proud that it was because of his
problem-solving they'd got to Mount Precious first and claimed
the primo camping spot. Not that there was much of a campsite.
One small plastic sheet slung between trees with warm water and
a spoonful of oats for dinner. Christ he was hungry! And just
one sleeping bag to share between them! These selection planners
were brutes. Never letting us get comfortable. They'd have to slide

together like sardines. As long as he was in the middle, he'd be warm enough. And squeezed up against Serena couldn't be all bad. Damn what a hottie! A little too controlling for his taste, though.

Jonas stewed in his uncomfortable feelings. He was envious, sure. Serena had got first bite at the leadership cherry. Going first was always an advantage. Showed courage and determination. But what the group needed now was firm, strong leadership. Someone to take charge. Not be so damned consultative. Crisis needed clarity and a firm hand. That's what he'd learnt from his father: people respond to strength. Especially in hard times. And now, by jingo's balls these were hard times.

He glanced at his teammates. They were all as glum as wet terriers. Even the ladies' man Max had quit his flirting with Serena. Pabi had wandered off to 'water a tree' and Serena was studying the flames of their campfire. Even in the middle of the group she seemed apart. One moment she was a live wire, the next, sullen and removed. Couldn't figure that woman out.

Jonas's analysis was interrupted by a wrist comm alert.

"Here we go, folks! Look lively, incoming!" jostled Jonas. He sat up straighter and pasted on a happier look. If Serena wasn't going to bolster them, he sure as shit wouldn't let his opportunity to shine go to waste.

Claire's voice came through their devices. "Well done for making it to the summit. It's not one of our easiest jaunts." A few vented and mumbled agreement.

"We do have additional supplies for you. They are stashed in a small cave just around the corner from where you are now. There is enough for a hearty dinner with a few treats, and an additional sleeping kit to make your overnight stay a little more comfortable."

Whoops of delight and a wave of relief broke over the candidates.

"One more thing. There are only enough supplies for one group. You choose who gets it."

Shocked and frustrated, the teams turned back to one another.

Jonas turned quickly to Bravo group and gestured for them to huddle in. No way were they going to miss out on this bounty! The weary candidates pulled themselves to their feet and moved closer, groaning as they stretched out little aches and stiffness. The climb to the top of Mount Precious was notoriously challenging: steep, craggy and slippery with mossy rocks. A few people sported scraped knees and other injuries.

"Here's what I think we should do." He commanded their attention as Serena tried to speak. "We've got to get in there first. I'm happy to go around and claim it for the group. Pabi, you can come with me."

Serena's eyes narrowed and she interrupted Jonas's plan. "Hang on a minute. This is obviously a test. We can't go barging in there and take it all for ourselves!"

"Sure, we can!" Jonas said, fierce now. He wasn't going to let Little Miss Compromise show them up as weaklings. "It's like this. On the Moon we will be in survival mode. We've got to make sure our people survive – it's our responsibility. If some others – maybe the Chinese – want to move in and take stuff, we've got to put a ring around what we find. This is totally a test. We've got to show strength. Be bold. We don't come out on top in survival conditions by being diplomatic. We can't just roll over and let the others get in first! We'll be left out in the cold. What kind of world designers would we be if that happened? Dead ones, that's what." Jonas let his speech batter them into submission. He stared at each one, daring them to challenge his logic. Gina looked uncomfortable. Pabi was considering it. The big man Max was eyeing Serena, waiting. Serena was doing her nut, he could see. Too bad! This was their chance to make the right call, to lead. Jonas felt Xavier come fully to attention as this discussion heated up.

"Jonas – I'm pretty sure we should be collaborating with the others. Every man for himself is not the Gaia way. We've got to do this right, here, if we're going to do it right on the Moon," Serena said.

"You're right, it's not every man for himself – it's our tribe, our team, our people we need to look after." Jonas paused for dramatic effect. "These are just basic survival principles: if we share all the supplies out, we'll *all* be worse off. We've got to invest in the strongest. It's what anyone in a survival situation would do – you feed the warriors, the hunters, first, because at the end of the day they will ensure the survival of the rest of the tribe. No sense giving all the food to the babies and the weaklings. They just die anyway." It was so obvious. Why was she so blind to this?

"But we're not babies, we're adults. And as far as tribes go, we are all one tribe, even if we are in separate groups."

Jonas saw the other cohort leaders heading over to them.

"Listen, we've got to go and go now. We've got one shot at this. If someone beats us to the stash, we lose. Pabi, let's move."

He turned to go. Serena grabbed his wrist. He glanced at her grip as it tightened, then at her furious pinched face. No time for arguing now – he had to get this done. One chance to make an impression and make the right move. Leadership is all about timing and now was the moment.

He pulled away from her grasp and bolted. He could hear Pabi come scrambling after him, and Serena hissing for him to stop. Hiss away, serpent girl! He was going to make it all happen for them. He ignored the gasps and stares of the other groups as he made a beeline to where Claire had said the cave was. He found the opening just as Pabi caught up to him.

"Here it is Pabi! Let's get in there. Jonas got down on his belly and pushed himself under a low rock through a hidden opening.

"Jonas – wait!" Pabi called out.

Jonas ignored him and pulled out his head torch and shone it around. The entrance opened up with plenty of room to stand. He got to his feet and had a good look. A well-used fire pit with a vent above, some camp chairs, and then what looked like a stash of supplies. He ripped the tarp off. Score! Potatoes, mushrooms, carrots, rice, herbs, sauce and even chocolate. They would feast well tonight! And the promised sleeping bags – with sleeping mats no less! No head-to-toe snuggles required, now.

"Pabi – it's awesome! Grub, chocolate, a fire pit, chairs! We've got it made! Go tell the others!" Silence. Where was he? "Pabi?" He must have gone to get the others. Great – he'd make the fire and get everything ready. The perfect host.

The fire was crackling, the vegetables chopped and cooking, the beds all laid out. Where were they? They were taking their sweet time. Finally, he heard some movement at the cave entrance. Pabi wriggled through. His face was puckered like a cat's arse.

"Finally! I've got everything sorted. Where are the others?"

"They're coming."

"Good."

Why was Pabi all bent out of shape? The others shuffled through the entrance, and stood adjusting their eyes to the fire, looking at the awesome set-up they had for the night. Jonas was jazzed, pleased to be the one to offer comfort after their arduous day.

"You made it! Glad you came." They were quiet for people who had just left the bleak cold dreariness of hardship for the relative palace he had secured for them.

It was Serena who spoke. Cold and low, like a true Ice Queen.

"Of course we came. Where one goes, we all go." Her voice was full of reproach. Well, he'd get some hot soup into her and she'd soon be purring like a kitten. They'd see.

∽

They ate in silence. Except for Jonas. He continued to rattle on about the success of his initiative. That they had just shown they were the strongest group, the ones ready to make bold moves where others hesitated.

Serena was mortified. When Troy and Madison came over to the group, along with the other team leaders and observers, she had to confess that two of her team members had broken rank and rebelled. She'd lost control of that jackass Jonas. Now, they were all made to look like jerks. Madison and Troy were gobsmacked. They did not envy her predicament. This was a disaster. Her first opportunity as leader and her team disintegrated at the first major challenge.

Finally, she could take it no more.

"Jonas, what the hell were you thinking?"

He looked up from licking his plate, startled. "What do you mean?"

"This is selection for Gaia's most important project. It requires the best of the best. People who can work together in difficult circumstances. You went rogue. What happened to being a team player?"

His eyes narrowed. He put down his plate slowly and sat up straight. "I did this for the team!" He paused to get his emotions under control. "In leadership, there's a time to talk and there's a time for action. If we want our team to reach the valley floor in the best shape possible, we need food and a good night's sleep. Now we've got both, putting us way ahead of the others in the challenge. Exactly what is the problem with that?"

Serena opened her mouth to speak but Pabi interrupted. "Excuse me. I think Jonas meant well. But it made us look like arseholes."

"Does that matter?" demanded Jonas. "We're in competition for Chrissake! There are no rules about consulting the other cohorts!" He looked around at the others, seeking support. Gina met his gaze and glanced away. Xavier looked on, arms crossed. Jonas sensed a possible ally there. "Xavier? What do you think?"

Xavier squeezed his lips together, considering his response.

"You're both right. We are in competition."

"Thank you," Jonas exclaimed.

"And at the same time, there's no room for renegades on the Moon. The consequences there are extreme. No room for rushed judgements. It could mean life or death. Here, in this exercise, no big deal. If we didn't get the supplies we would have been a little cold and hungry. So what? We carry on." Xavier uncrossed his arms and leant forwards towards the others around the fire. "If you are going to win a place on the Olympus Project, you've got to be better than this. No more squabbling. You've got to unify, present as one team. It's the only way you get high performance. You can challenge ideas, sure. That's essential really. None of us is smarter than the rest. But you *don't* take unilateral decisions. That's how teams crack."

Silence settled in the cave, save for the pop and crackle of the fire.

"Thanks for that, Xavier!" Serena plugged the silence with forced enthusiasm. "That's what we needed – a right bollocking. Jonas – no more bolting like the house is on fire. Bravo crew, we've got this."

After a few minutes of quiet chatting, they readied for sleep. But the rift still hung between them, like the rank odour of something rotting.

The cave was warm, the food filling. The experience, for Serena, was bitter. Even though Xavier backed her and had brought the group back from the brink of conflict, she still felt deflated. It reflected badly on her as leader. She considered her group. Jonas was obviously a pig-headed brute who needed careful watching. Pabi was fairly compliant and even-keeled. Max was a godsend: measured and solid. Gina was tough as nails but not warming to anyone except Xavier.

Serena dragged her bedding and moved away, seeking solace in a cold, dark corner, bleak as her mood.

CHAPTER NINETEEN

*A fear conquered alone is a skirmish in the shadows. A fear
conquered with others is a battle in glorious sunshine.*

ATHENA AI IN WISDOM OF THE AGES

Bravo cohort: Jonas, Serena, Gina, Pabi and Max with Xavier

A MESSAGE BLEEPED on their wrist comms early that morning,
before dawn. They roused, groggy. Serena read the message aloud
to the group as they squinted at their displays. Xavier was already
up and packed, she noticed. He sat in one of the camp chairs,
watching them. Unnerving, she thought.

"Swap leadership roles. Your task is to navigate to the south
rock wall of the summit and descend to the valley below by way of
a multi-pitch descent. The rendezvous is at the base, three kilometres along the valley floor. All equipment is stashed by the largest
granite tor. You have until 5pm this evening to accomplish this
task. All team members must arrive together. Monitor your oxygen
supplies carefully, especially in the heat."

"Better move, yes?" Pabi said, throwing his sleeping bag open.

"Gina – it's your turn for the leadership role." Serena called out across the cave, hoping the smaller woman would embrace this as an olive branch.

"Okay." Gina sat up in her sleeping bag and pulled on her expedition clothes. She avoided Serena's glance.

"I thought we said no unilateral decisions?" called out Jonas, already stuffing his sleeping bag. A good night's sleep didn't seem to have improved his mood much.

"Anyone object to Gina being leader?" Serena asked.

A chorus of 'no's from Pabi and Max. They all stared at Jonas.

"Fine. As the lady wishes," he said. He did a cavalier flourish and bow. Serena mimicked the gesture in acknowledgement. Back on mocking terms.

∽

Gina took a deep breath as she ran through a mental checklist of what needed to happen next.

"Let's get packed up. Pabi, you're on breakfast since you're already up. No fire though – it will take too long. Serena and Max – can you sort out the route plan? It's still dark, so it will be night nav for about an hour once we get going. Jonas, you're on clean up." She enjoyed taking him down a notch.

"Yeah, sure," he said.

Serena glanced at him. The brashness was gone.

Breakfast was meagre. They finished the last of the supplies in the cave, except for a small reserve to make it through the day. They expected resupply at the base, but in this game, you never knew.

They emerged from the cave and saw that the other groups had already decamped.

"Where are the others?" Pabi said.

"Likely doing something similar," Gina said with a sparkle.

"You excited or something," Max asked, sidling up to her as they set out.

"A little. I enjoy rope work! I bet the view will be stunning! Jonas, how about you?"

"Yeah. Sure. Can't wait."

He was so sullen, Gina noticed. Where was his cave triumph bravado now?

They walked through the bush, headlamps like fireflies, until the dawn lit the sky bright with colours. They arrived at the granite tor just as the darkness eased enough for them to turn their torches off. The summit was a narrow ridge with granite boulders and a smattering of trees. There was a large rock platform that dropped suddenly, revealing a spectacular view of the green valley below.

Gina stepped up on the platform and eased her way to the edge. Serena joined her. It was a straight drop some thirty metres to another narrow, rocky ledge, about two metres wide, with another huge boulder.

"That must be the second pitch anchor," she said.

"Looks like it," Serena said. It was the only thing large enough to secure the ropes.

"What do you reckon – lower the packs, first?" Gina asked. For once, she was grateful Serena was there. Serena was a gun with ropes, having worked on salvage sites for years.

"I think that's our best bet. I'll go and find out what gear we've got and see if we can do it at the same time as the abseil."

Serena left the platform, grabbing Pabi to help her. Max crept to the edge, next to Gina.

"Long way down," he said.

"Indeed! How amazing is that view!" Gina was filled with awe.

"Beautiful," Max said, looking at her.

Uncomfortable now, Gina turned to join the others. Serena found the gear stash, and Pabi helped her to pull it free. They dumped the contents on the ground and started sorting through it.

Gina beckoned to Jonas who was sitting on his pack, well away from the edge. He walked over to her, hands in pockets.

"Jonas, can you and Max check the cliff face for suitable anchors, while Pabi and Serena get the gear sorted?" Max nodded. Jonas followed him, tripping on a tree root, stumbling towards the edge.

"Whoa, careful!" Gina called out. Don't want you going over the edge too soon!" Jonas looked back at her, his face white.

"Oh, shit." Gina said under her breath. Jonas was afraid of heights. She'd recognise that paralysed look anywhere. Working on building sites as long as she had, she knew when someone got the heebie-jeebies. They got quiet, then clumsy.

Gina watched Jonas follow Max along the edge, choosing his steps carefully. He wasn't saying much. At least he's moving, she thought.

She turned her attention to Serena and Pabi, who unfurled the ropes and placed the metal ware and helmets in piles.

"Hey, Serena," she said. Can you do the belaying? I think I will have my hands full looking after Mr Seaborn."

Serena looked up as she checked the harnesses. "What do you mean?"

"Methinks he is a little squeamish with heights."

Serena studied the webbing of the harness she was holding.

"Not sure I'm the best person for that job," she said and scowled. "That turkey is driving me crazy."

"I will do it." added Pabi. "Serena – she might have slippery fingers with Jonas. He is a pain in the you-know-what, right? I can belay. I will send him over first, okay? We will test the rope length on him." Pabi winked.

Max and Jonas returned.

"We've got the anchors picked. Ready for action stations?" Max clapped his hands and beamed at them.

"Just like on Everest!" Serena winked.

"Let's just check in first," Gina said. "How much experience do people have with abseiling?"

"Good call," Xavier said quietly beside her.

She nodded at his encouragement. "Pabi?"

"Okay. I have a bit. We did a lot in the air force. Even out of helicopters."

"Serena, I know you're professionally qualified for climb and abseil. Max, we know you're probably okay with ropes and heights, having been up Everest... what is it, four times?"

"Five," he said and flashed a full hand of fingers for emphasis. Serena flashed five back with mock admiration.

"Jonas?"

"I've done a bit. On the *Sea Rover*." He looked glum.

"How comfortable are you with this pitch?" Gina asked.

"I can do it." Jonas nodded, and took a deep breath.

"Sure?"

"Well, if there's another option, I'd do that."

Gina stared at him. The man was clearly freaking out.

"Max, can you check the map?" Gina asked. "See if there's an alternative route down to the valley."

"You can't be serious!" Serena said. "Are you thinking of walking around, instead? This is a major task for our assessment! We can't just opt out!"

"Let's just see what the options are, first," Gina replied, irritated with Serena's challenge.

"Looks like the cliff extends quite a long way. We can probably walk off the northern end of the ridge, but it will add another few hours. Plus, it will be a pretty rough trek to get there, by the looks of this," Max said, studying the map.

"Great. Then we'll miss the deadline *and* skip a major task." Serena fumed.

"I could walk alone and meet you in the valley," Jonas offered.

"No. We stick together," Gina said. "Wherever we go, we do it as a team."

They were all quiet.

"Jonas, how bad is it for you?" Gina asked.

"I get a little jittery. Honestly, it would be better if you just let me walk around."

"Not going to happen, Jonas. You're not walking through steep bush by yourself," Gina was tense now.

"We better decide soon. Either way, we are running out of time," Serena said.

"Max, what do you think?" Gina asked.

He considered the group for a moment. "I think we go over the edge. As a team. Jonas, you can make it. Just breathe your way through it."

Jonas looked dejected.

"Pabi? Your thoughts?"

"Let's do the edge. It will be faster. I will belay. I promise not to let you drop, Jonas. Maybe just a little!" He punched Jonas in the shoulder.

"Serena?"

"I want to go over the edge. Enough talking already. We've got to get this done. We are losing time here."

"Jonas… your call," Gina said.

Jonas shifted his feet. He didn't want to lose face, especially with his rival engineer, Gina. "Yeah. okay. Abseiling, it is."

"That's the spirit, man!" Max clapped him on the back.

"Okay. Let's get it done." Gina said. First crisis averted, she thought.

Gina sent Max and Jonas to organise lowering the packs while she helped Serena and Pabi set up the abseil. They worked quickly as the sun edged higher in the sky, waking the flies and bringing the heat.

Serena donned her helmet, harness and gloves and was soon ready to go over. Pabi checked her belay and prepared to lower her as she went backwards over the cliff.

"Okay, don't fall!" he said. Serena gave him the finger as she stepped smoothly over the edge and glided down the rock face.

"Safe!" she yelled back up once she hit the ground. Within moments she attached her abseil kit to the rope and tugged it twice to signal retrieval. Pabi hauled the equipment back up.

Serena started to receive the packs being lowered by Jonas and Max.

Gina tapped Max on the shoulder.

"You go next to help Serena. I'll finish this with Jonas."

"Sure thing!" He favoured her with one of his glorious smiles. Gina noticed how his blond curls stuck to his forehead with sweat. His shirt was soaked through. A little rivulet ran from his face down to the notch at his throat.

He strode over to the abseil and stepped into his harness. Gina snuck glances, watching his physique in action. He was always poised, relaxed power, sensuous... But he fancied Serena, didn't he?

Gina and Jonas lowered the remaining packs in quick succession. They untied the ropes and let them drop to the rock edge below where they could be used for the next abseil.

Gina checked Jonas. He was still moving, still focused. Not so pale.

"Ready to abseil?" she asked.

"Ready as I'm gonna be," he replied, with a feeble smile.

She helped him get geared up. Helmet, harness, abseil gloves, everything tucked in.

"Very good, Jonas!" Pabi said. "You look good! Let me drop you over." Pabi beckoned to Jonas to stand in front of him to rig up the abseil and belay. He clipped Jonas in and double-checked all the gear.

Jonas was pale again, Gina noticed. His hands trembled.

"Okay, Seaborn, time to get you 'airborne'. Ha! Funny, right? Okay, easy goes it. Step back, one foot then the next foot." Pabi was jovial as he talked Jonas through the steps.

"Breathe. Use your lungs. You have too much hot air – let it out!" Pabi grinned. "Your feet are like a pony. Stop prancing like that. Make a solid step back." Jonas was rocking from one foot to the other, barely moving, his gloved hands clenched around the belay rope.

"Relax the hands! Breathe! Move the feet! Stand tall! And, Jonas?" he waited for Jonas to respond. "Jonas? Jonas!" Jonas looked up. "Smile! You need to improve that face, okay? A smile is a good start! Go, now!" Jonas was at the edge where he had to step over and place the balls of his feet flat against the rock while lowering his body perpendicular to the cliff. It was the most precarious stage of the process.

"Lower the butt! Good. Very good. Champion!" Pabi continued to bleat encouragement.

Jonas's foot slipped and he banged his face on the cliff, knocking his lip. A trickle of blood ran down his chin.

"No problem, Jonas. That is an improvement, no? Do not worry, I have you!"

Jonas clung to the rope, breathing hard. Gina went to the edge so she could see the top of his head.

"You okay?" she asked.

"Just dandy, thanks."

"Good Jonas! Now feet flat on the rock and walk."

"Pabi?" Jonas called out.

"Yes Jonas?"

"Shut up."

"Okay, Seaborn. You just move."

Jonas pushed himself away from the cliff face and placed one foot and then another flat against the rock, so his body formed an L-shape. He started to lower himself again.

"Jonas, walk your feet down!" Gina called.

Too late – he let the abseil rope slide through his belay device while his feet stayed in place, his hips lowered, and then with a cry he was upside down, his feet above his head.

"Shit." Gina cried. "He's inverted!"

Pabi gripped the belay rope in a brake.

"I have you Jonas! You will not fall."

Jonas was white with terror, gripping the belay rope that wedged him hard against the rock face.

"Jonas – try and swing your legs to the side so you can go right side up," Gina yelled down to him. She watched him flail like a mouse with his tail in a trap.

Max and Serena came over and called up encouragement. Jonas struggled to get his head above his waist, his face beet red from the effort. He grunted and strained.

The voices below grew more concerned as the minutes dragged on, and Jonas became more fatigued.

There was nothing they could do from the top, either – all the ropes had been dropped below for the next abseil. If Jonas let go of the abseil rope, he ran the risk of falling out of his harness. His hips were so narrow.

"C'mon Jonas!" Gina pleaded.

Jonas tried flinging himself sideways. His toe caught on a crack in the rock. It was enough to give him some purchase. He grunted and heaved and managed to get himself upright again.

Cheers erupted.

"Well done! Good on you!" Gina yelled down to him. "Pabi can do the rest! Just keep your feet against the rock and Pabi can lower you the rest of the way."

Pabi lowered Jonas to the small ledge where Max and Serena grabbed him and unhooked him from the abseil system.

"Off belay!" Serena shouted to the top.

Jonas sat, heaving, his arms aching, hands trembling. His face was white, bar the trail of blood from his lip that stained his chin.

"Nice work!" Max said. Jonas said nothing. He was one metre away from the next edge and did not want to move.

Gina came down the abseil followed by Xavier then Pabi who self-belayed and pulled the ropes down after him.

The ledge was cramped with the six of them and their packs.

"Okay – round two. Let's go," Gina said, eyeing the sun, now high in the sky.

"I can't," Jonas said.

"Yes you can," Gina said.

"No, I can't. I'm wrecked. My arms are dead," Jonas said. "Look." He held out his hands to show her the tremors.

"Jonas – look around. You have no choice. We are on a tiny ledge. There is no way out but down. Get your shit together!" Gina's exasperation was icy.

"Take it easy! Give the man a moment, okay?" Pabi said. "He almost kissed his buttocks goodbye. You set up the next one, I will look after Mr Seaborn." Pabi sat next to Jonas and rubbed his back. "Breathe Jonas. Adrenaline will calm down soon."

"No dicking around – we're running late. It's going to be tight to get down and out in time."

"I promise – no 'dicking'," Pabi said. Gina glared at him.

Gina, Serena and Max worked carefully around Jonas and Pabi to set up the next pitch. When it was ready, Pabi got to his feet and set up to send them over again.

"Okay, princess, let's send you down," Pabi said to Serena.

"Don't call me princess." Her eyes sent him daggers. Then she grinned, finding her sense of humour once again. "I will accept 'Queen' only." She slipped over the edge. The rope whizzed through the descending device and she was down in moments.

The packs went over as before, followed by the ropes, then Max.

"Let's get you over quickly, Jonas. You know the drill. You've just got to keep moving. I'll be on belay at the edge and help you get over. It should be a bit easier – see, there's a little step that you can lower on to." Gina bustled around Jonas.

"Okay." Jonas seemed resigned.

"Focus on me, Jonas," Pabi said. "Listen to my voice."

Pabi gave clear instructions, no nonsense this time. Jonas approached the edge, Gina stood there with him, guided his footholds, and Jonas was over the difficult part without any incident. His descent was jerky, but he got there.

Gina let out a big sigh, not realising she'd been holding her breath watching Jonas.

"Your turn, Gina," Pabi said. "Be careful – there is a lot of loose rock. I do not like it." He spat suddenly. "Damn flies! I have eaten about ten! And one up my nose!"

"Thanks, Pabi." Gina clipped in and went over, pausing to admire the view. "This is stunning country. Nothing like this on the Moon!"

"Not yet, anyway." She smiled at him, and he nodded in return.

Once Gina was down, she asked Max to get the map out so they could plan their route. As they bent over the map there was a cry from above.

"ROCK!" bellowed Pabi. They jerked automatically towards the rock, standing tall, hoping their helmets would take any debris.

A chunk the size of a tennis ball thudded to their right and bounced down the slope. A few pebbles chipped at them, one hitting Gina in the cheek as it ricocheted off the rock face.

"Ouch!" she cried. That stung like a bitch, she thought.

Pabi thudded to the bottom of the abseil and unclipped.

"Everyone okay?" Xavier asked.

"Yeah. Though one of the rocks got me in the face." Gina said.

"Let me see," Max said. He moved in so Xavier had to step aside and leant down to examine her face. She could feel his breath on her cheek, smell his sweaty tang. He had his shirt off, hoping for it to dry while they packed up. His fingers probed the spot where the rock hit.

"Just bruised I think, no skin broken." He rubbed her shoulder. "You'll survive," he said warmly.

Damn this man, she thought. I can't think straight when he's around! Then she noticed Serena eyeing them carefully. That one's trouble, Gina thought.

"No rest for the wicked!" she cried. "Let's move out."

CHAPTER TWENTY

In world design, there are rules to be followed. Communities
need essentials like food, water, shelter, hygiene, a
place to gather. After that, rules do not apply.

WORLD DESIGNERS' MANIFESTO

"Whoa! Put those guns away, someone will get hurt!" Dave said, pointing at Troy's arms.

They were halfway down the valley after an arduous descent from the cliff face. Pierre was leading and they stopped for a break in the rising afternoon heat.

Troy flexed and posed for Dave.

"Just drying off after that sweaty work," Troy said.

"Dry somewhere else, no? My biceps wilt from inferiority complex."

Relieved they had made it through the tricky part of the task, they loaded the ropes and equipment into their packs. Mohammad moved slowly, exhausted.

"Any food left?" Dave asked. "I could eat my arm. Or Mohammad's arm. Maybe Troy's arm, it is the biggest."

"Sorry – no rations left until we hit the valley floor," Madison said. "We've got to hustle. That sun is showing late afternoon and we still have a tricky walk through this steep rubble."

"How are people's oxygen levels?" asked Jade. Her confidence was rising as she'd performed well on the abseil. All those afternoons she'd spent at the climbing gym close to the hospital research centre were paying off. She felt like she could contribute a little to the group now.

They checked their biometrics on the wrist comms.

"Whoa. I've got about two hours left on mine," said Pierre. "I think I used up quite a bit on that first pitch."

"Mine doesn't have much more than that," said Dave. The others were the same. Their readings were low. It was going to be a push to meet the deadline.

Sweaty, weary and hungry, they donned their packs and set off, picking their way carefully down the steep slope.

"At least there is shade in the trees," Dave said. "But damned flies! They are bastards, no?" He waved his hand in front of his face.

"Flies make good protein, Dave!" Troy said.

"Is that your secret weapon? All this time I thought steroids!"

"LOOK OUT!" Jade cried from behind them. Something massive crashed through the bush. Troy flung forward, grabbing Dave around the waist, and dragging him sideways as a boulder the size of an old TV smashed past them. Troy felt the wind of it and heard the crunch as it caught Dave on the leg.

Dave howled and then went quiet.

"Dave?" Troy asked. Jade came running down to them, flinging her pack aside when she reached them.

Dave was shaking. "My ankle."

"Let me look," Jade said. She lifted his pant leg. There was a purple egg-sized lump on his foot.

"Looks like a bad sprain. Maybe a fracture. Who's got the first aid kit?" Jade asked.

"I do." Madison said. She retrieved it from her pack and

brought it over. Jade was efficient as she strapped the ankle. Mohammad came over to inspect her work.

"Not too tight," he warned. "We don't want to cut his circulation."

Jade flinched at Mohammad's criticism and her lips drew to a tight line. "Of course, Dr Mohammad." She undid two wraps and re-wrapped them more carefully. Troy piled some packs behind Dave so he could lean back.

"Very good, Dr Jade," Dave said and winced as she cinched the bandage. "I have to work so hard to get attention around here!"

Pierre and Madison sat on their packs, watching. The shadows were growing long through the trees, and they hadn't yet reached the valley floor.

Pierre stood and faced the group. "Well, we have a bit of a situation here. Dave can't walk, so we are going to have to carry him." Silence. They all knew the terrain was steep, and their packs were already loaded with the extra abseil gear.

"We can call base and ask for a medivac. I think this qualifies for outside support. If we get him down to the valley, they may be able to drive in," Jade suggested.

"Good idea. Fire up the comms, Madison," Pierre said.

Madison pressed the call button on her wrist comm. "Base this is Delta group."

The line crackled then Claire's voice came through. "This is Base. Reading you loud and clear, Delta group. What is your message, over?"

"Base, we have a group member, David Eriksson, with a possible fractured ankle. We are requesting medivac support," Madison said. The others looked on, hopeful.

"Is he mobile? What is his condition?"

"He is in good spirits. Vitals good. He can be moved, but not on his own. We suggest carrying him down to the valley floor from our current position, then requesting vehicle evac from there." Madison chewed her lip.

"One moment, please."

The line was silent for what felt an age.

"Delta group, continue as planned. There is no vehicle support available, at this time. All parameters remain the same for the exercise."

"Base, I'm not sure we will make the deadline if we have to carry Dave out all the way." Madison looked startled. The others were wide-eyed in surprise.

"Understood. There is no vehicle support available, at this time. You will need to solve this on your own." Claire's voice was firm.

Madison took a breath before she replied. "Understood. Delta group out."

"Well, this is a real pile of *merde*!" spat Pierre. The others grumbled in agreement. "We'll never make it. Our biomarkers already show low oxygen – enough to get us to the valley base if we were walking normally, but not if we have to carry someone. If we were on the Moon, they'd be signing our death warrant."

"I think that's the point", Troy said. "We don't have the luxury of the cavalry rushing to our aid. We've got to be independent."

"It's a bit harsh, don't you think? If we stick together, we all run out of oxygen."

They went quiet. No one wanted to be the one to state the obvious.

Dave spoke. "If you leave me, you make it. You have enough oxygen to get there on time."

They all looked uncomfortable.

"We're not leaving you behind, Dave," Jade said.

"We might have to, if any of us are going to make it – to 'survive' in their Moon scenario," Madison said. Jade narrowed her eyes and stared down the other woman. Where was her compassion? Jade let it go as she pondered the bigger concern: what should they do next?

❧

"No one is being left behind on my watch," Pierre said with a clenched jaw. "We've got to sort this out. First, let's put up some shade over Dave while we come up with a plan. Mohammad, can you and Jade rig something up? Madison, can you look at those maps again."

Mohammad pulled the plastic sheet from his pack and he and Jade strung up a makeshift shelter. Mohammad was quiet.

"Is everything okay, Dr Mohammad?" Jade asked as she tied off the edge of the fly.

"Yes, of course," he snapped. He was disappointed his fatigue showed.

Pierre rifled through his pack and retrieved something.

"What's that?" Madison asked as she came over with the map. He put his finger to his lips, then pointed to his wrist comm. "I thought I had another energy bar in here. For Dave. Pierre gestured for Madison, Jade and Mohammad to join him under the shelter, alongside Dave, with a sign to stay quiet.

"Oh good. Cuddles," quipped the invalid. Troy came over as well to listen to the discussion.

"Very cosy!" Dave said. "I feel the love."

Pierre had them put their comms arms together and then pulled a circular device from his pocket. He pressed a button and a red light activated.

Mohammad recognised it immediately: a communications jamming device, the kind the Sultan and his officials used. He wondered how Pierre had got his hands on one. His eyes narrowed. This was underhanded, he thought.

"What the hell, Pierre?" Madison asked.

"It's a comms jammer. We can talk safely without them hearing us."

"Who? The Directors?" Jade asked.

"Of course, the Directors. Our wrist comms are not just for messages and bio monitoring. They've got cameras and mics. They're listening to all our conversations. Part of the eval and all that," he said.

"And you're carrying a jammer because – why?" Madison asked.

"For exactly this type of scenario. It's total bullshit about the vehicle. They want us to make a choice."

"What do you mean?" Jade asked.

"It's a Kobayashi Maru test. They want to see what we'll do."

"What's a 'Kobayashi Maru'? Another swear word, Pierre? What does it mean this time – 'Welcome to Church'?" Dave managed to wheeze as he moved his leg gently, seeking a more comfortable position.

"It's from *Star Trek*. It's an Academy test. All the pilots had to do it – you should know this! Anyway, it basically means a 'no-win' situation where there is no chance of survival. It's meant to be a character test." Pierre explained.

"I already said, you can leave me behind." Dave tried to ease the tension.

"Not happening, Dave," Jade said. "What do you mean about the vehicle?"

"The jammer is also a surveillance-quality listening device. I can hear all the comms in the valley. I've been listening as we walked down the hill. There is a four-wheel drive at the far end of the valley. They're not far from here."

"You're kidding!" Madison said.

"Wait – you've been listening in to the other groups all this time, but only tell us this now? What the hell, Pierre?" Madison's face was blotchy in frustration.

"*Bien, oui.* Didn't want to play all my cards, all at once."

"What do you know, then? About the other groups?" Troy asked.

"Alpha group is imploding – one of their group members is refusing to go on. They have quit selection and won't move. Sounds like a real shit fight over there. Claire sent Maja and Huw out to talk with the group. They're there now and settled in for a long discussion. That's where the vehicle is.

"Charlie group is completely lost. One of their crew dropped a map down a deep rock crevice when they did their descent."

"Sucks to be them!" Dave said.

"I think it sucks a little more to be us, right now," Pierre said. "Bravo group is doing okay – nearly back at the Base."

"So now what? We know there's a vehicle nearby, but they've given us directives that no help is coming…" Madison said.

Pierre smiled. "Time to change the game."

Hopefully their ruse would work. Breaking the rules felt like cheating. Or was it just being smart? Jade wondered which way the Directors would see it, at the end. And if Troy would dob them in. He'd agreed to be a resource for them and follow their lead. What was he really thinking, she wondered.

She nodded to Pierre, and he turned off the comms jammer. Time to play their hand.

"You want to build a stretcher?" Pierre asked.

"That's one solution," Madison said, playing along. "That will take hours. We don't have hours left of daylight," she said as she helped Mohammad pack up the shelter.

"I could carry him with a pack harness," Troy said. "If we empty most of the gear out of my pack, I can carry him piggyback style with the pack as a semi-support."

"Are you sure?" Jade asked.

"He weighs less than my usual squat load in the gym. I'll be fine."

"You do not help my ego, Big Man." Dave said.

They redistributed the contents of Troy's pack and eased Dave into the modified pack harness. He gripped Troy around the shoulders as Troy heaved himself upwards.

"How is that?" Troy asked.

"Never felt so alive!" quipped Dave.

They moved slowly, taking frequent breaks. At last, they reached the valley floor. They could see another group in the distance, a couple of kilometres ahead of them. The base was still at least an hour's walk away. Their oxygen levels were reading critical, with less than an hour left. They rested at the edge of the forest, where the land fell to a grassy open field.

Mohammad stayed on his feet and said carefully, "I'm nearly out of water. Anyone else?"

"Nearly out too," said Madison. "Troy, Jade, Pierre – do you have anything left?"

They shook their heads.

"How about Pierre and I go down to the river to fill up for the last leg out. What do you reckon?" suggested Madison. "We'll be quick."

"Okay," said Jade. "We'll meet you on the track." Madison and Pierre hurried off with the others watching warily. Jade was very uncomfortable with the whole situation. At least she and Dr Mohammad could monitor the casualty, Dave.

"Come on, then." Troy heaved to his feet with Dave in the harness. "We'll do our best. It's easier walking down the valley. We might just make it." Jade looked at him, grateful.

"My knight in shining armour!" Dave said. His head rested against Troy's back. "When I grow up, I want to be like you, Troy."

"No can do, brother. It's a patented design. One of a kind!"

"A man can dream, no?"

"When we get back, I can hook you up with some cricket protein. That will beef you up!"

"Oh, please no – not crickets. It is horrible. I ate a protein bar once and it had antennae." Dave said.

They walked slowly. Troy needed more frequent breaks. Dave's leg was agony as the piggyback jarred the ankle bone. He was becoming delirious with the pain, even with the heavy-duty pain-killer they'd administered. Soon they hit an old four-wheel drive track and the ground was firmer and more regular. The sun dipped past the edge of the hills and twilight breathed cool, damp air down on them across the valley.

Claire's voice crackled from the wrist comm, startling them. "Delta group, this is Base. We're not reading bio signatures for Madison and Pierre. Please report."

Jade spoke into her wrist comm. "We sent them ahead, Base. We've run out of water. They should be at the river."

"You've not heard anything from them?" Claire's voice with a trace of concern.

"Not for a while," Jade replied.

"Thank you. The four of you continue on. Your oxygen levels are running dangerously low."

"Thanks, Base. Moving now."

They could see the base in the distance through the evening gloom. They turned as headlights bobbed on the four-wheel track behind them and then shone full floodlights into their faces. They stepped off the track, shielding their eyes from the bright lights.

Madison and Pierre got out of the vehicle and hurried over to them.

"It's us! And aren't we righteous! It's the cavalry after all!" Madison cried.

"Bring Dave over here, Troy," Pierre said gesturing to the back of the four-wheel drive. Troy turned and eased Dave on to the ledge of the cab's door. He managed to pull himself inside.

Mohammad pushed passed Pierre and rummaged through the vehicle until he found the first aid medical kit. He opened it and found what he was looking for. "Here, drink this," Mohammad said handing Dave a solution in a small bottle. "It will kill the pain and calm you. Lie back once you drink it."

Dave swallowed it in one gulp. "Better than crickets, I hope," he said. He lay down with a grateful sigh.

"Better report in, Jade," Pierre said with a wink. "Our comms have been down. We were trying to hail base when we found this vehicle. Its comms are out too – looks like someone kicked the radio box by accident or something." He smirked.

"Will do." Jade walked away from the group to calm her nerves.

Their plan had worked. Pierre activated the comms jammer when they came close to the river. Instead of filling their water bags, they snuck up to the vehicle that was parked near the group being debriefed by Huw and Maja. Pierre disabled the vehicle comms and then hot-wired it to start. Their story would be that because they had no comms, they could not check who the vehicle belonged to, and so seized it to save their team.

"Base, this is Delta group. We have reunited with Pierre and Madison and are in-bound. On time."

Out of the frying pan, and into the fire, Jade thought.

CHAPTER TWENTY-ONE

*A leader, if they're lucky, will have an opportunity at
least once in their lifetime to answer the question, 'how
much is my life worth if it is in service to others'?*

GAIA ENTERPRISES CODE OF CONDUCT

Gaia Training Centre Headquarters: Xanthe

XANTHE SIPPED A cup of tea in the staff headquarters. The expedition groups were back on base, ragged and relieved. She watched them as they stepped out from the transport vehicles. They were gaunt after a week on survival rations and minimum gear. Some moved gingerly. For some it was too much, and they were scheduled to depart that afternoon after opting out of the selection process.

Xanthe felt for them. The expedition phase was tough socially as well as physically. They had to bond with strangers to meet crushing deadlines through difficult tasks. It was rough. What came next was rougher, she thought.

She watched the candidates stream in to the communal dining hall after they showered. A hot meal was waiting for them. She could hear relieved laughter as the hall filled.

"Hey!" It was Troy. He poured himself a cup of tea and joined her in one of the tub chairs at the observation window.

"Hey, Troy," she said. "How was it?" His hair was still damp from his own shower and his face glowed red from a week of wind and sun. In spite of the weariness he no doubt felt, he was the epitome of good health. Vigorous. His blue eyes electric. Too bad his vanity dulls his looks, she thought. In spite of herself, Xanthe felt a surge of attraction.

"It was an interesting week," he said. "Nearly killed one of our crew with a rogue loose rock. Had some questionable decisions from one or two leaders, and quite a bit of tension."

"So… the usual, then," she said with a smile.

"Indeed!"

The silence grew awkward.

Xanthe asked, "Um… find us some teammates yet?"

Troy tilted his head. "Too early to tell. Let's see what your round of challenges brings up. You all set?"

"Sure am," she said.

"What's up first?"

"VR crash scenarios."

"When?"

"Tonight."

He sucked in air with a grimace. "That's brutal."

"Yes," she agreed. "It is. Better to know now how they would handle the crisis than if they actually crash-landed on the Moon."

Troy smiled wearily. "You're right." After a few moments of quiet tea sipping, he asked, "Why did you say yes?"

"Pardon?" Her mind was immersed in selection and what was coming.

"Why did you say yes to the Olympus Project? I mean, it couldn't have been easy for you, coming back after all this time."

Xanthe was not in the mood to open up old wounds. "Why did *you*?" she countered.

"I want to build the best damn world on the Moon, obviously. It's the greatest design challenge there is. Aside from possibly Mars, but we're not likely to make it there in my lifetime. I believe I can add something special to the Project. That's why I'm here." When she did not respond, he continued. "I understand you've been a staunch Earth-ist. Something must have happened for you to change your mind?"

Annoyed now, she stood, picked up her mug, and said, "Something did happen. I realised I couldn't leave the fate of humanity's off-world civilisations in the hands of overrated, overblown brag-garts. Now if you don't mind, I have work to do."

∽

Bravo cohort: Jonas, Serena, Gina, Pabi and Max with Xavier

THE COCKPIT LIT up with flashing lights and screeching alarms. Pabi flicked the switches to no effect.

"I think it's an electrical system failure!" he said. I can't get anything to reboot! Jonas, what do you get?" Jonas studied a panel behind Pabi.

"Give me a second," he replied.

"Hurry! We are gaining speed and heading for collision with the surface!" Pabi cried out.

"I've got oxygen bleeding out into space, too – there's a leak somewhere!" Max yelled.

"Can you shut it down?" asked Serena. She was strapped in her launch chair next to his.

"The diagnostic is flashing red but not responding to com-mands," he replied.

"We have two minutes to impact, Jonas! I need something! I am flying blind, and the computer is offline!" Pabi's voice was filling with panic.

"Jonas, I can help!" Gina said. She craned her neck out of her launch seat to see what he was doing.

"I'm fine, thanks. I got this," he muttered. He didn't want to be upstaged by Gina. He stared at the flashing lights on the control board. One whole section was blacked out, dead. That didn't make sense. There were redundancy systems for everything. What was he missing?

"One minute!" Pabi yelled, flicking the switches uselessly.

"Fuck it!" Jonas said. Two heads, he thought. "Gina, get over here."

"Thought you'd never ask," she sniped and leapt from her chair. She followed his finger as they traced the line of systems failure over the panels.

"Okay, first principles. Think first principles," she said.

"THIRTY SECONDS! Brace for impact!" Pabi screeched. He pulled at the manual override controls hoping they'd start working and he'd be able to steer the craft off the collision course.

"First principles, first principles," Jonas repeated under his breath. "Of course!" He reached past Gina and ripped open a small panel. There it was. A shorted fuse. He ripped it out, grabbed another from the one labelled 'refuse processor'. They could worry about that later, he thought. The fuse floated out of his grasp in zero gravity, and he fumbled to retrieve it. Gina managed to swat it back to him. He grabbed it and jammed it into the shorted socket. "Reboot NOW!"

Pabi kept one hand on the steering control and leant forward to press the reboot button. Jonas held his breath.

Nothing happened.

"Fuck!" Yelled Jonas. He poked the fuse hard. "Again!"

Pabi hit his fist on it and there was a flash. The craft responded to the steering controls, and they were flung backwards as the nose of the craft soared away from the lunar surface. But not fast enough. The craft's rear slammed into the surface and bounced along before they ricocheted back into space. Gina and Jonas bumped into each other, both reaching for something to keep them from slamming into the walls or chairs.

"Damage report!" Pabi yelled.

"Oxygen still venting." Max checked all the indicators. "I can shut that one down now and initiate backup tanks."

"No other main systems affected as far as I can tell," added Serena.

"Gina, Jonas, get back in your seats," Pabi said. "We'll try that landing again, this time with less drama."

Xanthe's voice came over the comms system. "Delta crew, land your vehicle and exit the spacecraft for simulation debrief."

Jonas leant over to Gina as he climbed back into his seat. "*Grazie,*" he said.

"What for?" Gina said, surprised. "You solved it on your own."

"Maybe. But you inspired the solution. Teamwork, eh?" He put his fist up to bump hers.

"Okay Seaborn, teamwork," she smiled.

⚜

Delta cohort: Dr Mohammad, Jade, Pierre, David and Madison with Troy

"Now THIS is more like it!" Madison said as she strapped herself into the captain's chair of the spacecraft. She whistled in appreciation. "One sweet ride, my friends!" She ran her hands against the armrests and sighed. She loved being a pilot.

"Fly well, Mad Dog!" Dave said and gave her a high five. He strapped into the seat on the starboard side. He had had his turn at the simulation earlier that morning. It hadn't gone well. Jade and Mohammad had freaked out with the simulated launch and weightlessness and then the emergency landing had shattered their nerves. Doctors, he realised, were used to being in control. He glanced over at them now. Mohammad's face was glistening with sweat, and he looked pale. Jade smiled weakly at him but looked determined.

"Ready for some more fun?" He winked at her.

"Let's get this party started!" Madison rumbled. "Pierre, life support systems check, please."

"All good, Mad Dog. Ready for launch."

"Control, we are go for launch."

"Roger, we are go for launch." Xanthe's voice came through from Mission Control.

They ran through the checks, the countdown followed, and they were thrust upwards.

"Woohoo!" yelled Madison. They peered out the window and the small patch of blue eventually turned black. They were in orbit. So far so good.

"What do you think they will hit us with this time?" asked Dave. "I think broken life support, no? That would be a good one. Maybe Pierre will have to do some work for a change."

"*P'tit con, fous toi.*" Pierre replied with a rude gesture.

"Careful now, you'll upset Dr Mohammad," Madison said. They'd worked out Mohammad wasn't a fan of obscenities. "You okay, Doc?" she asked him.

"Fine. Thank you." He dabbed at his brow with his suit glove and tried to look more relaxed.

"Sure, Doc." She looked over the controls and everything seemed in order. The minutes ticked over. Surely, they'd launch a scenario soon, she thought.

Minutes turned into hours. Delta crew grew relaxed, then restless.

"Maybe they try to bore us on this one. See if we start to turn on each other, *joo.* See who we want to eject from the space capsule, no?"

"We only need one pilot, so I vote we eject you, Dave," Pierre joked.

"Well, I—"

"Delta crew, we have a situation." Mission Control crackled over the comms. This was it. They sat up and listened intently.

"Go ahead, Control," Madison said.

"The Chinese Space Station altered its orbital path recently. We project you are on an impact trajectory with them. They are warning us if you come too close, they will initiate hostile deflection manoeuvres."

"What does that mean, Control? Do they have weapons up here?" Madison was shocked.

"Affirmative. Evasive tactics recommended."

"Roger that, Control. What is the projected time to the hot zone with the Chinese?"

"Approximately ten minutes."

"Mad Dog – look at what else we've got around us!" Dave pointed to the display. They were travelling through the space junk belt. All Earth orbital flights had to be carefully timed to avoid the space debris from years of dilapidated satellites and rocket refuse. They had planned their launch and path meticulously to account for this. Now they had to veer off course to avoid the Chinese. All around them were objects that could cause minor damage if they were lucky, and catastrophic if they made one wrong move.

"Is that what I think it is?" Madison said.

"*Joo*. It is the Indian Space Station."

"I thought they decommissioned that thing years ago!" Pierre said as he leant over to get a look.

"They did. But they sent up a crew recently to salvage bits," Madison said. "Control – we have the Indian Space Station on screen. They are in our potential new flight zone. Please confirm number of people on board."

"We can confirm a crew of six."

"Shit," she said. "Athena, run possible new flight paths to avoid the Chinese red zone."

"Calculating…" The onboard AI's 'voice' was flat and toneless. "Deviation of any degree from current flight path will result in impact with the Indian Space Station, given current velocity, or impact with catastrophic scale debris."

"Athena, calculate damage to our craft and the Indian Space Station following collision."

"Calculating…" The wait seemed interminable. "The Indian Space Station will receive a one hundred percent hull integrity breach. Our space craft will receive a fifty percent risk of hull integrity damage."

"And if we stay on course we go through the Chinese red zone?" Madison asked.

"Affirmative."

"*Putain de merde*!" Pierre spat. "It is another Kobayashi Maru! We avoid the Chinese, we will likely die and kill the people on Indian Space Station. We avoid the Indians, and we die smashing into stupid satellite trash. We run the gauntlet with the Chinese, and they kill us, or they don't and we smash into them anyway."

The capsule was silent, warning lights blinking on screens.

"We still have fifty percent chance of survival if we hit the Indian Space Station." It was Pierre again.

"But then those people die, Pierre." Jade's voice was firm. She put a hand on his arm.

"Someone is definitely going to die today. Why does it have to be us?" he shouted.

"There must be some solution, no? Mad Dog you can fly like a demon. Do you think you can steer this through the hazard belt?" Dave was scrambling with the display, looking for a path through the debris.

She shook her head. "Not at this range, not at this speed. Even if we stop engines now, we would still jam into something, no matter which way we pointed." She steeled herself. "Delta crew, this is the way it is. I am going to deviate course to avoid the

Chinese and the Indian Space Station. This will put us in the direct path of this old satellite debris field." She pointed at the display. "I will go fast and hard so it will be quick. Prepare yourselves."

"*Câlisse!* What a stupid way to die!" Pierre slapped his forehead then braced himself. Jade grabbed his hand and smiled at him.

"Madison Floyd, it has been an honour to be with you. May Allah protect you and us all." Mohammad said. His prayers filled the capsule and a strange sense of serenity fell over them.

"Thanks, Doc," she said with surprise. It was the first compliment she'd had from the quiet, reserved doctor.

"A hell of a ride, Mad Dog! Let's leave in a blaze of glory!" Dave pumped a fist for her.

Their gaze went to the display window ahead of them. The silver flash of the debris was a dot, then they could make out its shape, then it filled the screen.

All went black.

CHAPTER TWENTY-TWO

As a World Designer, it's important to know when you've reached the limit of an idea. Wisdom is knowing your ideas are seeds, not fruit.

TROY BRUIN IN WORLD DESIGNERS:
PERSPECTIVE AND PRACTICE

Bravo cohort: Jonas, Serena, Gina, Pabi and Max with Xavier

GINA WATCHED DELTA crew file out of the simulation chamber. They were the fourth team to emerge over the course of the day. They looked particularly rattled. One of the crew – the Sultan's doctor, she thought it was – grabbed a vomit bag on the way out and made good use of it. She recognised Madison from the first day she met her on the dock. She looked haggard. Another woman, pale and trembling, helped Dave who was hobbling after his ankle injury, but even he did not have his usual smile. One of their crew just bolted without looking back. Who was that guy? She tried to remember. Oh yeah – the French-Canadian doctor.

"Geez – what happened to them?" Jonas said as he sidled up to Gina.

"Whatever it was, it doesn't look good," she replied.

"I'm glad we're done with that black box from hell."

"What makes you so sure we're done?" Gina asked.

"Just got word from Xavier. We're headed to Zone Four. I came to tell you. You're in the hot seat again." He patted her on the back. "Let's go."

❧

Serena, Pabi and Max waited for them outside the Zone Four challenge bay. Xavier opened the door and beckoned to them. "We're ready for you now," he said with an encouraging smile.

"Bravo crew – go time!" Serena put her fist in the middle of the group, and they joined her. They made the sound of a bomb dropping to an explosion and their hands shot upwards in unison. It was something they'd started after they hit the valley floor on expedition.

Xanthe was there, looking her usual serious self, thought Serena. Xanthe hadn't said two words to her since selection started. Serena had hoped to get a moment to talk, to clear the air. But so far, no luck.

Serena recalled their meeting at Patrick Waters's funeral. She didn't know he had a family. It had been a whirlwind romance. She only read about them in the obituary. Xanthe, Patrick's daughter, was the sole survivor. The shock of it – the deaths, the lies – spun her out for months.

Serena vaguely hoped she'd be able to make a bridge through grief. That if they shared their pain, it might somehow keep Patrick alive a little more, for both of them. She knew now that was naïve. She was Xanthe's father's lover. Some pains carve a canyon in the heart.

❧

Xanthe looked at each of them, her eyes neutral and unfocused as they passed over Serena. "Bravo crew, welcome to the Yellow

Submarine. This challenge is to see your problem-solving abilities within constraints, and under time pressure. Listen carefully as I will explain the briefing only once. Your task is simple. Retrieve the Yellow Submarine at the bottom of the tank." She waved at the enormous structure behind her, some four metres tall, with a small platform running along its edge. "You can use this box of resources to do so." She pointed at a large grey toolbox nearby. "There are two safety measures to abide by. To handle the equipment, you must wear this protective eyewear. She gestured to a table with oversized dark goggles. You may ONLY handle the equipment if you have this eyewear in place. The second safety measure is that you must not touch the fluid in the tank as it is extremely acidic. You have one hour to complete this task. Gina, you are the nominated leader for this task. Your team has three questions you may ask during the exercise. Your time starts now." A giant clock above the tank commenced a count down from sixty minutes of bright red numbers.

"Only three questions?" Jonas asked, incredulous.

"Correct. You have two questions remaining," Xanthe said, deadpan. Xavier stood beside her and smirked.

"Oh la la!" he said. "Got them!"

"What a ballbreaker," Jonas muttered as he turned to the group.

"Okay Delta, gather here. Just ignore Xanthe and Xavier for now until we figure this out," Gina said. "Let's start with the box." She walked over to the trunk.

"Wait!" Pabi said. "We need the eye protection!"

"Oh yes. Good call, Pabi." They donned the goggles.

"I can see sweet FA in these!" Max said.

"Same here. Totally black," Serena said. She pulled them off and squinted at them.

"What the hell use are goggles that make you blind?" Jonas said.

"Hmmm... maybe that's the point," Gina said. "Xanthe said if we are to handle the equipment, we need to wear the goggles. She did not say we needed to wear them if we were just looking."

"Are you sure?" Jonas asked. He still had the goggles on and looked like an enormous frog.

"We can use one of our TWO remaining questions to check," Max said with the jibe directed at Jonas.

"Good idea, Max. We all agreed?" Gina asked. She waited a heartbeat and then turned to Xanthe. "I'd like to use one of our questions to ask, 'do we need to wear eye protection to just look at the equipment, not touch it?'"

"You do not need eye protection to look at the equipment. You only need protection to *handle* it," she said. "You have one question remaining."

"Right. okay. Jonas, you still have your goggles on, can you please open the box and retrieve the items in there. Serena, you can walk him over there so he doesn't fall over."

Serena guided Jonas, who was effectively blind with the goggles on, to the trunk. She placed his hands on the trunk without touching it herself and stepped back. They gathered around as he opened it. He groped around and pulled out an assortment of items: rope, string, tongs, elastic bands, carabiners, party balloons, tape, a snorkel, purple underpants, pipe cleaners and a box of condoms.

"What the hell kind of submarine is this?" asked Max when the condoms came out.

Gina heard Xanthe whisper to Xavier, "Did you put those in there?"

"*Peut-être...*" he whispered back with a suppressed grin. She raised her eyebrows at him.

"I thought maybe we test their sense of humour, too."

Gina's face flamed red as her engineering mind kicked into overdrive. She watched Jonas sort the items into neat piles then step back, remove his goggles and look at the supplies.

"They want us to build a world on the Moon, and here we dick around with pipe cleaners and condoms? This is bullshit!" Max spat and skulked off.

"Come on, we can work this out," Pabi said. "We've just got to be inventive, that's all. Maybe we use the balloons to float it out of the tank."

"How would we get the balloons down to the sub? That won't work," Jonas said.

"I'll check to see if we can see the sub from the platform," Serena said and scurried up the tank's ladder.

Gina ignored the conversation as she stared at the objects. Her mind was spinning with possible solutions.

"What are you thinking, Gina?" Jonas asked.

"Maybe if we use the ropes and carabiners to create a z-drag pulley system over the tank, we could lower the tongs, and with the elastics rigged crossways, we could operate the tongs remotely. Yes, that could work." She put on her goggles and scrabbled at the equipment. Her hands worked deftly. Max returned to the group to see what Gina was doing.

"I can do a pulley system," he said. "I've rigged them many times for crevasse rescue. Let me help." He pulled on his goggles and started to rummage for the things he needed. Pabi stood behind them and directed their hands when they asked for different objects.

Serena climbed back down the ladder and came back to the group.

"I had a look in the tank. The water only comes up about halfway."

"Did you see the sub?" asked Jonas.

"Sort of – it's hard to make out. But it's about half a metre long. It kind of looks like a big yellow donut."

"You mean it's not solid?"

"Just what I said – a circular thing with a hole in the middle. Come and take a look for yourself."

Jonas followed Serena back up the ladder and they peered down into the tank. Jonas leant over the rail as far as he could. Serena grabbed his trousers just as he started to slip forwards.

"Whoa there, Seaborn! Not time for a splash just yet!"

"Thanks," he said, a little embarrassed. It looks like there might be rope around it. It reminds me of an old-fashioned lifesaving ring or something."

"Not much of a lifesaver if it sinks!"

"Let's go back to the others. I've got an idea."

Max argued with Gina. "That is not how you do a z-drag. We need to anchor one corner somewhere. We could probably do it with someone standing at one end of the tank to create the anchor."

"No, no. Give me back the carabiner. I need it for the pulley," she said.

"You're not listening, Gina. It won't work!" Max threw down his goggles in disgust.

"Just wait. Give me a moment," she said, and her fingers moved desperately over the gear.

The others stood back and watched her work the equipment. It looked incredibly complicated.

"We have fifteen minutes left," Pabi said.

They groaned. They hadn't even attempted to retrieve the object in the tank yet.

"Hey Gina," Jonas said. "I have an idea. I reckon we're making it too hard for ourselves. I think a grappling hook could be the go. Like an old fisherman's hook. We could do it with a rope and some pipe cleaners. I can have it rigged in five minutes. Less than." They all looked at the clock as Gina continued to fiddle with the gear, oblivious with her goggles.

"Gina?" Jonas asked.

"What? Okay, okay, you try it while I finish the pulley," she said and retraced the tongs, the elastics and the rope.

"Great!" He put on his goggles and knelt in front of the equipment. "Serena, can you be my eyes? I need pipe cleaners and a weight. Probably a carabiner. Max, Pabi, can you guys take a rope – one of the longest ones – and stretch it out across the tank? Make sure it's long enough to go across and lower down into the bottom."

With clear directions and a task to do now, they sprang into action. Pabi volunteered to go blind with the goggles and Max guided him up the ladder around the tank. Once they were both on the platform edge, Max put on his glasses and together they slowly edged their way into position on either side of the tank, each holding the rope taut over the tank.

Jonas twisted pipe cleaners together to create three little hooks.

"You think that's going to be strong enough?" Serena asked.

"Probably not. I'll add another pipe cleaner to each hook. That will have to do." He attached the makeshift hooks to the carabiner. "Okay, we're ready. Gina, we're going to test it now."

"Okay," she said, still fiddling with her pulleys.

Serena guided Jonas over to the tank and they climbed up to the ledge.

"How much time have we got left?" Jonas asked quietly.

"Five minutes," she replied.

"No worries. We got this."

They shuffled around to Pabi who was holding the rope taut at this end.

"Pabi, I am going to clip this carabiner onto the rope and then you can let it go slack so it can fall towards the water." Jonas found the rope and clipped on the device.

He pulled off his goggles and watched his contraption slide down the rope.

"Max – let some slack go through so we can lower the rope." Serena and Jonas held their breath as they watched the rope lower slowly to the water and then down to the yellow sub.

"Okay, now you two need to jiggle it. Like you're bobbing for something," Jonas said. They jiggled. They missed. Serena and Jonas let out a disappointed gasp.

"Try again," he commanded. Jonas and Serena stared at the carabiner and its hooks wobbling beneath the surface. Jonas could see the clock ticking over with one minute left to go.

ᴥ

Gina heard their cries and at last took off her goggles. She stared at the mess in her hands. Then she stood and climbed the ladder to see what her team had managed. Without her.

Xavier and Xanthe looked at each other as she passed them.

Xavier leant down to whisper to Xanthe, but Gina still heard. "Jonas just... took over!" There was a hint of disapproval in his voice.

"Gina let him," observed Xanthe.

"Hmmfff." He nodded towards the ladder. They climbed up to watch proceedings.

"Pabi, I think you've got it," Jonas said in a steady voice, drag it to your right and see if it will catch."

Pabi did as commanded and carefully dragged the rope to his right. He felt it catch.

"We got it!" He cried out.

"Okay, Max, Pabi, raise the rope slowly, slowly." Jonas spread his hands out over the water as if they could see him. Jonas and Serena cheered as the yellow object broke the surface, dangling precariously on the end of one pipe cleaner hook.

"Ten seconds, nine seconds, eight seconds…" The clock's mechanical voice announced over the tank, and they jerked at the interruption. The pipe cleaner hook wobbled, and the yellow object swung in a perilous loop.

"Six seconds, five seconds, four seconds…"

"Pabi, walk towards me taking in slack as you go. When it gets close enough, I'll grab it." Jonas anticipated where he might be able to grab the yellow donut and put his goggles on and outstretched his arms.

"Two seconds, one second…"

Jonas swung widely for the donut just as the pipe cleaner finally yielded under the weight of the object. It fell and the team groaned together.

They failed.

Gina felt the weight of disappointment sink with the yellow donut. She was gutted. The dark voice within crept up inside her like a wolf stalking its prey. *You failed*, it hissed.

"Close!" Xavier said with a whiff of encouragement.

"But no cigar," added Xanthe. "Bravo group, pack up the gear. You're on to the next challenge."

Troy waited with his team outside Zone Five. They lay on the grass, enjoying the tail end of the afternoon sun, now somewhat bearable. Troy marvelled at how Gaia managed to keep the grass green in the crushing heat.

He considered his group. They were emotionally spent. They had had a couple of hours to recover after the simulator, but it had not done much to revive their flagging spirits. He hoped they'd manage okay with this next one. Troy realised he was starting to favour his team. He'd have to watch that when it came to the vetting process. Not long now.

Troy noticed Xanthe walking up the path with Maja. He admired Xanthe's athletic frame. She had a pixie face that gave her a youthful look. But her deep green eyes showed an old soul, he thought. She was an interesting woman. Why she was so prickly and a bit spicy with him unnerved him. Unlike many others, she didn't bend to his charm. He could sense something walled up around her. It intrigued him. He was not used to friction of this sort. Still, he appreciated Xanthe's dedication to the job, now that she'd signed on. She'd been working her tail off through these scenarios.

He stood to greet them. Another chance to work his magic.

⚓

Troy's team stirred as Maja and Xanthe approached, summoning a vestige of enthusiasm.

"Hello Maja, Xanthe," Troy said.

"Troy," Maja smiled warmly and squeezed his hand.

"Is this the last one for today?' he asked Xanthe.

"Second last," she said with a sigh.

"Can I help?"

"Yeah sure. I could do with another pair of eyes in the tracking room."

He nodded.

"Is your crew ready?" Xanthe asked, eyebrows raised. Half of them were sitting down.

Dave noticed this exchange and jumped into action. He was team leader for this segment. "Team Delta, look alive. Chop chop. We don't keep Xanthe and Maja waiting, no?" He put out a hand and pulled Pierre to his feet. Mohammad and Jade were already standing, and Madison walked over wearily.

"Okay Team Delta, here's the deal,"Xanthe said. "The objective of this challenge is to see your performance under pressure."

"*Quelle surprise!*" muttered Pierre. Dave jabbed him in the ribs.

"Your mission is to enter the caverns and retrieve supplies. These are required for your next mission. There are oxygen tanks, medical kits and provisions. You may retrieve only one type of object per person. You must exit only by the same entrance. Other teams are already in the caverns. They have their own respective entrance and exit points. You may ask as many questions as you like before you enter but none afterwards."

Madison spoke up. "You said caverns, right? Do we get caving gear?"

"Thank you, Madison. Your protective equipment includes a safety helmet."

"And headlamps?"

"Negative. No outside light sources. To protect the environment."

"Night goggles?" Madison persisted.

"Now that would make it easier!" Xanthe said. "So, no. No night goggles."

"So we're just going to be stumbling around in the dark, looking for stuff?"

"I'm sure you'll work it out," Xanthe said.

"Is there a time limit?" Dave asked.

"Not this time. But it would be to your advantage to complete the task quickly."

Pierre piped up. "You said the other teams are already in there. Are we competing for resources?"

Xanthe smiled. "I'm sure you'll work that out." She looked around for more questions. None were forthcoming.

"When you're ready, let us know and we'll take you to the cavern entrance."

Dave assessed his team. Mohammad was stoic. Jade was nervous. Pierre looked as if he'd swallowed a turd. Madison was... was she nervous? Mad Dog?

"You okay, Mad Dog?" Dave asked.

"I've got a bit of the wobblies" she said.

"What's the problem?" he asked with concern.

"I'm not too good in caves. And definitely not good in total darkness. I get the heebie-jeebies."

"Are you going to be alright in there?"

"I sure as shit hope so! Don't want to let the team down, you know."

"Okay, well you stick with me. Pierre, you good?"

"*Tabarnak,* this challenge is total *câlisse de merde*! Pardon my French, Doc," he said to Mohammad.

"Still swearing like a trooper. So *you're* good then." Dave said. "Jade?"

"I'm okay. A little nervous. As long as we stick together, I'll be fine."

"Doc?"

"I have never been in caves. Darkness? I will be okay with that. I agree with Dr Jade, stick together." He nodded to Jade who smiled gratefully at him.

"Alright, then. Well, this won't get the baby bathed, let's get to it, yes?" They grabbed their helmets and headed over to Xanthe.

The cavern mouth was a small opening they'd have to crawl through. Madison started taking deep breaths and shaking out her arms.

"Remember to keep a hand on the person in front of you. Madison, you follow me. Then Jade. Then Mohammad. Then—"

"I prefer to go last, if you please," Mohammad said.

"Okay, then," Dave said. "Pierre, you go after Jade, then Mohammad last, after Pierre."

Dave saluted Troy, Xanthe and Maja as they readied themselves to enter the darkness. Dave crawled in first and called back what he discovered as he went.

"It's only narrow for a little bit. You have to crawl for ten metres then it opens up. I can stand up here."

"Dave. Dave, come back – you're too far away!" Madison cried out. She took some more deep breaths, trying to stay calm.

"I'm here!" He popped his head out and smiled with a goofy grin. "No problem. Let's go." His head disappeared again.

Madison took another deep breath and dropped to the ground.

"Dr Mohammad," she said, "If you're doin' any prayin' right now, do some for me, if you wouldn't mind?"

"Of course, Madison. I will pray for you. But you can pray for yourself, too."

"Me and God got a lot of reconcilin' to do before I go askin' any favours," she said. "How about I start with a good word from you." She gave him one last look before entering the darkness.

"Of course. Consider it done."

Xanthe, Troy and Maja watched them enter the caves and then retreated to the observation room, a small nearby hut. Xavier was in there, along with the four other team leaders. The fifth leader was stood down when his team was dismantled after the expedition with the exodus of a few candidates. The team leaders sat in a row, glued to monitor screens.

Troy bumped fists with Xavier.

"How's your crew doing?" Troy asked him.

"*Mon Dieu! Quelle bordelle!* It is a disaster!"

"Really? Let me see." Xanthe came over to watch the monitor. They had infrared cameras installed throughout the caves and were tracking each team through the maze of tunnels. In reality, it was a small contained system with easy access and egress points. When experienced in total darkness, however, it was disorienting and seemed much larger than the few hundred metres the web of tunnels really was.

"Look," Xavier pointed. "Pabi is in charge. He led his group to the middle of the caves, and then insists every time they find an object, that he personally goes back to the entrance to remember the way they came. He has been backwards and forwards five times already. I think Max is going to punch him in the head."

"I've never seen any leader do that," Maja said.

"There's a good reason for that," Xavier said. "It's completely stupid!"

The three of them watched Pabi make it back to the entrance, then turn around and make his way back to the group. It was painful to watch.

"Can you turn up the audio?" Xanthe asked.

Xavier moved the dial and the candidates' voices drifted to them.

Gina: He's only trying his best.

Max: Well, his best is shit. This is a stupid strategy. We are burning time with this backwards and forwards.

Serena: Got any better ideas, Max?

Max: Yeah. We do a scatter and regroup here. We'd cover way more ground.

Jonas: That's actually a pretty good idea, as long as we're each confident of staying oriented.

Serena: Hell no. I'm not bumbling around in the dark on my own! Gina, I'll go with you.

Gina: We should wait for Pabi to get back first.

Max: Chrissake.

Pabi: I'm back.

Max: At last! Listen, Pabi. Your strategy is bullshit. This is what we're going to do. We are going to bombshell it. We'll go and each do a recce down a finger of the caves and come back to here when we find something.

Pabi: No! You cannot do that.

Max: Why the hell not?

Pabi: Because I am the leader. We follow my plan.

Max: But your plan is ridiculous. I'm sorry Pabi. I'm not doing it.

Pabi: You must do it! I am the leader! I am in charge.

Max: Whatever dude. I'm going down this tunnel to my left. I've found an oxygen canister and a first aid kit. I just need provisions and I'm done. I'll shout out if I find anything that someone else needs.

Xavier turned the volume back down again. "*Merde!* I cannot listen to this. Troy, you watch my team. I will watch yours."

"Sure thing, brother!" Troy sat down to watch the disaster that was overtaking Team Bravo.

Xavier moved to the neighbouring monitor and found the camera where Delta team was making their way through the caves.

"Now this is more like it!" Xavier said. Xanthe peered over his shoulder. The team seemed intact. Dave was at the front, and they were making good progress through the cave. Xanthe moved away to check in with the other teams. The leaders were mesmerised by the action on screen, watching their teams progress.

"Hey Xanthe! I think Alpha group will exit shortly."

"Thanks, Denis. Maja, can you meet them and send them to the next challenge?"

"It would be my pleasure, Xanthe," Maja said warmly. "You are doing a fine job here. Well done."

"Thanks, Maja. Not over yet!"

"*Ah non! Les cons!*" Xavier smacked the desk in front of him. Alarmed, Xanthe returned to Xavier's monitor.

"What is it now?"

"Troy's group has run into two of mine. I think Troy's man is stealing from mine."

"Really?" Troy came over to watch this development next to Xanthe.

The three of them peered at the screen. Xanthe felt the shared focus of her colleagues. She was conscious of a creeping sense of camaraderie between them. Of being equals.

"Watch him – this man." Xavier pointed at Pierre. Pierre bent down and felt the pile of supplies beside Serena and Gina who seemed oblivious to this inspection.

Xanthe dialled up the volume.

Pierre: Serena? Is that you? Where's the rest of your group?

Serena: Who the hell knows? It's a shit fight. We were following Pabi's directions then it all went to hell in a handbasket. Max and Jonas have gone rogue. Gina and I have been left to guard the kit.

Pierre: What did you find?

Serena: Amazingly, most of what we need. You?

Pierre: Bits and pieces. Just started.

Serena: Best be off then. Off you tot!

Pierre: Will do.

Xavier, Xanthe and Troy watched Pierre shoulder one of the medkits and an oxygen tank.

"The cheeky little bugger!" Troy exclaimed.

In another screen they watched Dave move forward and his crew follow.

"What are they doing now?" Xavier asked.

They watched as Dave's crew went around a bend in the caves.

"Turn it up Xanthe!" Troy urged.

They caught the last bit of what Pierre was saying to Mohammad.

Pierre: You stay with the team, Mohammad. I'll be right back.

Mohammad went to put his hand on Jade's shoulder then recoiled.

Jade: You okay, Dr Mohammad?

Mohammad: Yes. If you don't mind, I prefer not to touch your shoulder. It's not... proper.

Jade: Stay close then.

Mohammad: That's fine. I am fine. I'll be just here, right behind you.

The team moved ahead. Mohammad waited a moment and then followed. He stumbled and fell.

Jade: Dr Mohammad?

Mohammad: Fine. I'm fine. Just tying my shoelace.

෪

Mohammad was mortified. He stood up and brushed his hands together. They stung. He must have cut the skin as he fell. Stupid. Then he listened for the team. He heard them faintly. He waved his arms around looking for a wall, something. He found one. The right side, that was the right one. He followed the sound of his companions' voices. But they seemed to grow more faint. He hurried. Still, they grew fainter. Then he heard nothing. He stopped and strained to hear something. He called out: "Hello! Hello! Jade? Madison? Dave? Pierre?" No reply. It struck him then that he was completely alone. In the dark. And lost.

෪

Xavier, Xanthe, and Troy watched it unfold: Pierre leaving to stash his hoard and steal some more; Mohammad trailing behind the team, falling and shuffling forward. The moment where he moved two steps away from them and picked up the wrong tunnel, separating finally from the group.

"Oh, boy," Troy said. "The good doctor is not going to like this much."

"Who would?" Xanthe asked. "Has the group worked out he's missing yet?"

"I don't think so," Xavier said, horrified.

They dialled in on Dave's mini group.

Dave: Where's Pierre?

Pierre: I'm coming. Had to go back for the medkit I dropped. I stashed it back at the last tunnel entrance. We'll pick it up on the way back out.

Madison: What if we go back through a different tunnel, numb nuts?

147

Pierre: *Putain!* Don't worry! It's the only tunnel entrance back to the start.

Madison: Don't 'poot-ayn' me, you dipshit. How do you know it's the only tunnel back?

Pierre: I have really good mental maps.

Madison: If you say so, noodle brain. As long as we don't have to stay in this infernal cave any longer than we have to because of your over-cocky 'mental maps'.

Dave: Quiet. Where's Mohammad?

Jade: He's right here. Dr Mohammad?

They waited for his reply.

Jade: Dr Mohammad?

All: Mohammad!

Dave: Quiet! We can't hear him if he replies.

The silence seeped.

Madison: Well, shit sticks. We lost the Doc.

Xanthe and others watched Delta group hash out a plan. They turned about and followed Pierre back to the tunnel entrance, walking past the tunnel Mohammad had taken. Xanthe checked the camera on Mohammad. He'd had the good sense to stop. He was at the far end of a tunnel, at a dead end.

"They'll take hours to find them unless they double back now," Troy said.

"I will leave them to you, *mon ami*. I will return to my dysfunctional halfwits, thank you very much." He stood and surveilled his team's monitor. "It seems that in spite of themselves they have managed to regroup with most of the necessary equipment."

"Minus what Pierre stole," Troy added.

"Oh la la!" Xavier slapped his forehead. "Yes, minus that."

❦

Mohammad felt around the end of the tunnel. He discovered a pile of equipment: an oxygen tank and medkit. He would have preferred food supplies, but this was good. One of the teams would have to come this way to get the supplies. He was bound to be discovered. But then again, he realised, he was making an enormous amount of assumptions. What if these were extra supplies? What if teams left the caves without taking all the required kit?

Surely his group would have worked out he wasn't with them by now. Jade would notice. Wouldn't she? Pierre would know that he was no longer there to hold his shoulder. Wouldn't he? It can't be much longer, he thought.

Mohammad shuffled around until he found a flattish rock to sit on. He peered into the darkness, looking for any hint of light. He waved his hand in front of him. Nothing. They'd been in the caves long enough not to get any residual impressions on the retinas. They had removed all electronics too so there was truly nothing to illuminate the space. So, this is what it's like to be completely blind, he thought.

He shivered. He grew cold sitting, waiting. He strained at every noise. Occasionally he heard voices in the distance, and he yelled out, hoping they'd hear him. But they passed by. A sudden choking sense of loneliness rushed up his throat. He'd been abandoned. Forgotten. Left out. No one cared. They just left him here. Did he matter so little they wouldn't notice him missing? They were a group of five, surely someone would realise? Why didn't they come for him?

These feelings were familiar he realised. He'd shut the door on them decades ago. But here, alone in an unknown cave, exhausted physically and emotionally from the trials of selection, the door that had been safely shut for so long suddenly flung open. The memories came now. His father stern and angry, yelling at him and pointing him to his room. His brother laughing and sticking his tongue out as he was banished from the family gathering. At school, being teased and then ignored as others played marbles. They never invited him to a game, not once. He remembered too how he started to build his personal armour. He drew his intelligence and ambition around him like a shield and forged forward, alone.

And here in the cave, he was alone again. He wept.

Hours must have passed, he thought. He was hungry, cold, shivering and desperate to urinate. He dared not. He did not want to be discovered having soiled the cave and himself. The shame!

Mohammad heard a clatter, louder than anything he'd heard previously. At last!

"Hello! Hello! Down here!" he yelled.

"Geez! You gave me a fright!" A male voice said.

"Who's that?" Mohammad asked.

"Jonas Seaborn. Who are you?"

"Dr Mohammad Rasheed, personal physician to the Sultan of Dubai." He said his full title in an effort to re-establish his dignity.

"Ah! The Doc! Your group has been looking all over for you!"

Mohammad felt a surge of mixed feelings: relief, gratitude and vengeful anger.

"Good. They should never have left me!" he blurted.

"No kidding! Well, don't worry, I can take you out to them. Did you find any kit down here Doc?"

"Yes. Here." He waved at the pile, remembering just then that Jonas could not see what he was doing.

"Great. I'll help you carry it out." Jonas shuffled closer to Mohammad's voice and together they gathered the gear.

Mohammad put his hand on Jonas's shoulder to follow him out of the tunnel, the warmth of the younger man's body a balm to his bruised and shivering soul.

"Thank you, Jonas," he said.

They made their way back to a hub, a small slightly open space in the cave system where several of the tunnels branched off and where Mohammad had gone missing.

"Hey Delta Team!" called out Jonas when he could hear their voices. "Guess who I found!"

"Mohammad!" The relief in the voices washed over Mohammad as he approached them. He wanted to weep but he dared not. He would not give them the satisfaction of revealing his weakness. He squashed his emotions with a hammer of bitter contempt.

"The Lone Ranger rides again! Good to have you back on board, Doc! We missed you!" Dave's attempt at lifting the tension, thought Mohammad. Well, not yet. All is not forgiven.

"Whoa, Doc, you gave us a fright. You alright?" Madison's voice was warm.

"I am fine. Can we exit now?" he replied curtly.

The group's friendly banter fell silent with Mohammad's icy tone.

"Yes, of course, right away. We're not far. Let's go," Dave said.

"Here, Mohammad, put your hand on my shoulder," Pierre said. Mohammad did so reluctantly. But he desperately did not want a repeat of his recent experience. He stumbled a little and gripped Pierre hard as they moved forward. Pierre patted his hand.

"It's alright," Pierre said.

But it wasn't.

᠅

Bravo cohort: Jonas, Serena, Gina, Pabi and Max with Xavier

THIS WAS IT, thought Serena. One last challenge. Team Bravo waited outside what looked like a shipping storage container. She was bone-tired. Only the thought of a shift in activities tomorrow helped her stay focused. Whatever this was, no doubt it would be hard. And after the failure with the tank activity and the weirdness in the caves, she doubted this challenge would be easy. Not by any means. Plus, Max was leading this one.

She couldn't believe she'd found this bozo attractive at one point. He was a complete narcissist. Let's see what he makes of whatever this next challenge throws at us.

Xanthe and Xavier arrived, and they steadied themselves. Serena didn't even try to be friendly with Xanthe this time. She was too tired to care about building bridges right now.

"Bravo crew," Xanthe began. "Last team challenge. This one is about decision-making under pressure. Here's the situation: this is an outpost on the Moon. You've been sent here to do research work. You are waiting for a replacement crew, but the buggy has broken down. A replacement may not arrive for another seven hours. Your main concern is oxygen supply. You will have whatever is left in your spacesuits and the tanks you've got with you that you collected from the caves, along with the medkits and food supplies. The shelter is just that: a shell but with no atmospheric support. When you enter the shelter, don your spacesuits and check your oxygen gauges. Good luck. And I forgot – your comms with the main base are down too."

"Sounds like a real shit-stinker, Xanthe!" Max said. "Thanks for that!"

She smiled and nodded her head. Contrary to what they likely thought of her as the architect of these challenges, she died a little inside when she sent the teams through these ordeals.

"*Bonne chance*, Team Bravo!" Xavier gave them a thumbs up.

"Bravo Group, gather in!" Serena found a vestige of spirit and put her fist in the middle of the group. They joined in and did a lacklustre cheer of bomb fizzle and explosion. They filed into the shed and donned the cumbersome spacesuits.

"These stink like sour cheese left to rot in a jock strap!" Jonas complained. "Oof!"

"We're the last ones to use them," Gina said. "There must have been at least five bodies through these suits before us."

"Ahhh, this takes me back!" Max said. "Eight weeks on Everest in the same thermals. It's the smell of success, team!"

They ignored him. They'd heard enough about Everest.

Pabi grimaced. He was a fastidiously clean person and wearing someone else's steamy training suit sparked images of creeping bacteria colonies.

Max opened the inner door to the shelter.

"Well, we won't die of excessive luxury, that's for sure," he said. It was an empty steel room, with a narrow window running the length of one side. It had a projection of the lunar surface beyond. They traipsed in and Max closed the door, waving to Xanthe and Xavier as he did so.

"First things first," Max directed. "Suit lights on so we can see in this tin hut. Next check your oxygen readings. It should be on your arm panel."

"Oh wow!" Gina said. "My suit reads four hours left. Is that right?" She showed it to Serena. She tapped at it.

"Yeah, mate, I think so," she replied. "Mine's at three and half hours. Pabi, what's yours?"

"Five hours."

"I'm at four hours," Jonas said.

"I've got six hours," said Max. "Okay, this is a concern. Not enough before the rescue buggy arrives. Xanthe said seven hours, right? Let's check the tanks, see how much we have there."

It was more bad news. The tanks were less than half full. If they topped up the suits with what was in the tanks, they'd each have between five and a half and six hours of oxygen.

"What's in the medkits?" Max asked, suddenly inspired. They unpacked the kits: sleeping pills, aspirin, mild pain relief medication, eyewash and bandages. Damn, he thought, nothing heavy enough to go into partial hibernation.

"I think we should sit down," Serena said. She'd worked out the situation alongside Max. They were fucked.

"This is what we're facing," Max began. We've got base seven hours away by Moon buggy. So walking, assuming we know which way to go, is at least fourteen hours. We have no comms with base. Presumably they know what supplies we have and would be hustling to get us some help. Given the buggy is down, that means a foot expedition. If we start walking now, we might meet them on the way, assuming they leave right now. That's a big assumption."

"But our oxygen will run out well before that…" Gina said, with dawning awareness.

"Correct," Max continued. "So walking is only an option if we combine all oxygen into one or two suits, and they go."

"And the others?" asked Gina.

"We're cactus," said Jonas flatly.

"In the walking scenario, two people live, the other three die."

"Our other options?" Gina pressed.

"Another option is that we all stay and hope for the best. Likely outcome is that we all run out of oxygen and die. One after another."

"Terrific!" Jonas said.

"Our last option is that one person donates their oxygen to the others," said Max.

"And then what happens to them?" Gina said.

"They die," Pabi said quietly.

"In summary, the choices are: we all die, three people die, or one person dies. Obviously, I think we should go for the least amount of people dying," Max said.

"So. We draw straws," Serena said flatly.

"Hang on, not so fast," Max said. "This is an expedition, with expedition rules. Like on Everest. We make decisions that are rational, not emotional. We choose who goes based on who is likely to survive and who is likely to help us survive, not only now, but in whatever scenario happens next."

"You can't be serious?" Serena said gobsmacked. "We're all human beings here. We're all equal contributors."

"We're all humans, but not all of us are essential for survival, Serena," he said with a low threat in his voice.

"And who would you see as 'less essential'?" she countered.

Max looked slowly around the room, all faces staring at him through their ghostly helmet lights.

"Jonas, engineer, strong and good at fixing stuff. Gina, good too, even if you flubbed the submarine test. Engineers are always useful. You stay." He turned to Pabi and stared hard at him. Pabi stared right back, drawing himself up taller. "Pabi, you're a shit leader. But an awesome pilot. We'll need a pilot to get us off this rock. You stay." They all turned to look at Serena. "Serena. We don't need two life support specialists," he said flatly.

"Oh what? And that's it? I'm redundant? Let me guess – you stay, I go?"

"I have more experience in extreme conditions," he said carefully.

"Like hell you do! You know fuck all about me, you son of a bitch! You don't know what I've been through! I've survived alone as a teenager, I lived on the streets, fending off criminals, gangs, rapists. I made it through all that, became a salvage diver and fought my way to an education with the odds stacked against me to end up here. That's worth something. It's not... not NOTHING!"

The silence boomed.

"It's not enough. I'm sorry," Max said quietly.

"Like hell you are! This isn't fucking *Survivor*! You don't just vote people off!" Jonas joined in. He was going to fight for Serena.

"We're NOT voting," Max said. "I'm the leader. I'm making the call."

"Just like you let Pabi make the call in the caves?" Jonas said.

"That's different. Pabi's plan was stupid, and it was costing the group. I'm trying to save the group." Max's voice stayed even.

"You son of a bitch!" Serena said. "How many bodies did you walk over on your hundred freakin' trips up Everest?"

"As many as I needed to," he said, voice like ice.

Emotions skidded across the room. Eyes turned on Max. They were suddenly aware of the extreme nature of the mission, and the cold and clinical mind of the man amongst them.

"I'll go." It was Gina.

"Wait. No – Gina, no!" Serena cried.

"It's okay. I thought about it. I may be an engineer and I am great at fixing bikes and machines, despite the tank incident, but Serena – I can't let you go. You bring heart to this team. And despite what Max says, that is worth something." She stood up.

Serena jumped up too. "Gina – NO! You are not leaving. Max is right, we need people who can problem solve and fix things. You stay. Here, take my O2." She started dismantling the oxygen feed to plug into Gina's suit. "See, I know how to do stuff too," she swiped.

Gina and Serena watched the suit indicator levels drain and then top up Gina's. Jonas and Pabi stood too. It was like watching an oncoming train in the dark and they were cemented to the tracks.

Serena's mouth went dry. She felt paralysed. Was this really happening? Somewhere in the back of her brain she knew this was just a training scenario, that they would all be fine, but right now, this was *real*. They were about to let her go to her death.

"I'm leaving myself ten minutes," Serena said. "Enough time to get out of here and get the fuck away from *you*!" She jabbed a spacesuit finger at Max. "Pabi, Gina, Jonas, it's been a pleasure being on Team Bravo with you." Gina hugged her awkwardly, bumping helmet visors.

Max opened the door for her. She strode through and was gone.

"My God," said Jonas. "What have we done?"

CHAPTER TWENTY-THREE

*Self-knowledge is the leader's best weapon. No one can take
you down if you already know how low you can go.*

GAIA ENTERPRISES CODE OF CONDUCT

Gaia Training Centre: Interviews Round 1, Jonas

SELECTION CONTINUED APACE. Expedition and team challenges
were now over, replaced by a sequence of psychometric testing,
physical test reviews, biophysical assessments, mental agility tests,
character interviews and peer assessments. Camaraderie grew
among the candidates, along with nervous expectation. The days
started early and finished late. The candidates were mentally, emotionally and physically worn out. Next up were the final series
of interviews. This process was intended to put them off balance
– again – and poke all their vulnerabilities.

Huw, Claire and Maja sat behind the enormous mahogany
desk, ready for the candidates. It formed a massive barrier between
them and the interviewees. It was an old-fashioned technique,
designed to intimidate.

To date, the candidates had interacted with the Gaia Directors in various contexts: the formal welcome address, rugged outdoor campsites, casual interactions over meals. They were sometimes formal, sometimes familiar. It kept the candidates off balance.

Maja nodded to the staff member at the door who acknowledged and beckoned to the first candidate, Jonas Seaborn.

Jonas sauntered in and gave the panel a breezy smile. Just show confidence, he thought. That's what they're after.

"Welcome Jonas." Maja allowed a smile.

"How do you think you've performed so far in the selection process?"

Okay, they're going straight for the jugular! No worries. Play it cool. "Pretty good. I think I handled the expedition phase really well. I'm pretty tough physically, so that was okay. Problem-solving was pretty straightforward. I didn't get too stumped." Too right. He was one of the strongest and smartest ones there, that's for sure. He tried not to think of the abseiling incident.

"How did you get along with the others?"

Jonas shrugged. "It's like anywhere. You like some. Others, not so much."

"Who did you get along with most?"

Jonas twitched his left foot, shifted in his chair. "Hmmmm. I'd say Troy. That guy is cool." Let's warm them up with a casual approach. The panel remained implacable.

"What do you think about the other candidates?" Maja's face was a block of wood. He was getting nothing from her. Jonas felt a tinge of something drift through his gut. He sat up a little.

"Ahh – which ones?"

"Any ones. Pick three. Give us your assessment of them."

Jonas felt prickles of anxiety on the back of his neck. He licked his lips to steady his thoughts.

"Okay. Yeah. So, in my group, there's Pabi. The pilot. He was pretty solid in the flight scenarios. But he really stuffed up the cave task. Wasn't too good outside of his area of expertise."

The panel nodded, almost in unison. Jonas had the distinct impression of wooden puppets bobbing to an unseen hand. He pushed that thought to one side and concentrated.

"And then there's Max. A bit of a loner. And a dictator rather than a leader in my opinion. Didn't really stand out in a good kind of way." Yeah – that's good. Give them some critiques too.

"And for the third?"

"Hmmm. Well, Gina. She's confident. Capable. She's got a bit of attitude. People like her."

"And Serena?" Claire interjected.

Jonas glanced at her. He felt an invisible chasm open under him. Any moment he might plummet.

"Oh. Ahh. I think Serena's pretty good. She's a good designer and all that. But she's a tough nut to crack. Can't seem to put my finger on her." Literally, he thought to himself. She was a wildcat – all skittish. Jonas noticed Claire make a note on her electronic writer.

"Changing tack a little now, Jonas. Why should *you* join the Olympus Project?" Maja reclaimed lead interviewer role.

He sat up. This was easier territory. He felt the chasm close a little beneath him.

"Thanks for asking, Maja." He gave her his best, sincere smile. "Simply, it's this. I've had a lifetime on the *Sea Rover*. I've literally been born to world design. I know all the theory and the engineering. But I also know the social dynamics. What it takes to run a contained community."

"And what is that? What does it take?"

"Strength. Focus. You've got to be clear on the standards. Let people know there is a steady hand at the helm."

The interview panel all bent over their writers and scribbled something. Good. He was scoring a few points, he thought.

"And fair. You've got to be fair. Firm. And fair." Touché! That sounded good, he thought.

He waited while they captured his comments. They seemed to

be writing A LOT. The tinge that had crept through his belly earlier made a reappearance. He clamped down on it.

"Last question for you at this time, Jonas." Maja paused and leant forward. "What rules do you think we should have for choosing which people get to settle on the Moon? Or Mars, for that matter?"

The tinge circled and squeezed his gut, causing his heart to thump erratically. "Wow. Big question. Well, yeah. I've thought about this a lot, actually. The Moon, and then Mars, well, they're kind of like Noah's ark, right? There's not enough room for all of humanity, at least not at first while we build the settlements. So, we've got to take the best representation of us. The strongest, the fittest, the smartest. The most reliable. The most stable." Jonas took a breath and leant to the edge of his seat, focused. He felt his passion burn through him. "We'll need people to go the distance, to put in the hard yards, year after year. We need people who won't give up. People who can work things out. People who've got guts. I mean, this is the future of the human species! So, we've got to send our best to to do our best." Jonas felt the electricity in his words spark in the room. He knew he landed his message. He felt a new twinge – what was it – pride? Yeah, that was it.

"Thank you, Jonas." He was dismissed. Jonas sagged a little in his chair. The effort of attention and the emotional surges left him drained. He was spent. This was tougher than he thought it would be, he admitted.

Jonas rose as steadily as he could from his chair, trying to hide his residual nerves. He walked up to the big desk, shook hands with the panel members, looking at each of them earnestly. He realised he didn't need to fake it. He genuinely wanted this. He wanted to be a world designer on the Moon. Maybe even Mars. He wanted it more than anything he'd ever wanted before. He hoped he'd done enough.

～

Interviews Round 2, Serena

"SERENA FOX. YOU'RE next."

Serena rose from the bench with the grace of a tigress. She was ready. Tired, but ready. She had recovered from the eviction scenario, but only just. It was harrowing. But then the first round of interviews had gone fairly smoothly. She'd responded with ease to the tough questions, giving her honest and fair appraisal of her colleagues, as requested. This round would be tackling the grittier issues.

The panel of Directors observed her as she entered the room and slipped into the chair before the giant solid desk. She held their gaze with bright grey eyes and waited calmly for their questions.

Huw began this time. "Serena, thank you for your patience and contribution so far. We appreciate this is an arduous process. Second round interviews are more detailed and specific than the previous round so we can get a better look at candidates' perspectives." Serena waited, silent and attentive.

"In your opinion, what do you think is the biggest threat to a Moon community?"

She thought for a moment. "Aside from the obvious physical threats of system breakdowns and environmental disasters?" she asked.

"Yes. Aside from those."

Serena paused, looking inward to her own thoughts rather than trying to decipher what they were after.

"Success on the Moon depends on social harmony. Because of its remoteness, and because there are no escape valves so to speak, Moon community members need to be able to work through issues together, without ostracising anyone. Exclusion in such a community could be the single most personal threat to any individual. And

161

that kind of social distress could cause a lot of dysfunction. The ripple effects would undermine social progress."

The panel was quiet, unmoving. Then Maja leant forward slowly. Her voice was slow and low.

"Tell me, Serena, have you ever felt like an outsider?"

The words sliced across the table and pierced Serena's bubble of confidence. Like icy fingertips, they reached through and plucked at the hidden wounded strings of her soul. The strum of pain reverberated and pushed tears into her eyes.

"All the time." Her voice was half whisper, half croak.

Interviews Round 2, Madison

"MADISON FLOYD. SECOND round interview – your turn."

Madison sprang to her feet. *Let's get this show over with.* She strode through the doorway, glanced at the implacable panel of Directors, and took her seat, posture erect.

"Madison, thanks for your patience. We are always appreciative of the effort the candidates bring to this process." Huw repeated his well-worn spiel.

Sure you are. Madison noticed her cynical internal voice and tried to quash it.

"These second-round interviews give us a chance to dive a little deeper with each candidate." Huw raised his eyebrows and tilted his forehead forward to emphasise 'deeper'.

Got it. Deeper. Let's do it.

"What would you do if someone broke the rules of the community?"

This caught her off guard. Oh shit. They know. That damned comms jammer Pierre brought out on expedition. "What do you mean? Rules like, 'Pick up after yourself' or something like that?"

"Sure. Let's start with that."

"Okay. You'd hope that if people were on the Moon, they wouldn't be slobs. But I get that sometimes people fall into bad patterns. But in that kind of situation, you just gotta speak up. Can't let it fester. That kind of stuff sends people crazy in small communities." Madison smiled coolly and shifted in her seat as she waited for the blank-faced Directors to finish writing their notes.

Claire spoke this time, in a nonchalant manner. "Tell me Madison, if you were expedition leader, what would you do if someone committed a violent act?"

What the hell? Where did that come from? Were they expecting violence on the Moon?

"Again, I'd hope that people selected for a Moon expedition would be screened for violent tendencies! No room for that kind of nonsense." She felt the heat building in her as she imagined a violent scenario.

"But if it did happen, then I'd follow what Gaia says: atonement, not punishment. Try and make good. Give them a second chance. A chance at redemption. After all, there's no walking the plank on the Moon! There's nowhere to go. And prison? I've seen what prison does to people." Madison thought of her mother holed up in the backwater penitentiary for years on end while she floundered alone outside. "Prison serves no one and is a huge waste of money. So, atonement is the thing. Give someone the chance to make right. Of course, as long as the person is no longer a threat. And the victim is okay with it too. I mean it would be weird to go on living and working beside someone who had hurt you, done you wrong. What a thing!" Madison stopped herself. Better stop riding that high horse, she thought. The panel had their heads down and were scribbling madly.

Am I getting this right? Could I really do that? If someone hurt me, would I be okay getting up the next day and saying 'good morning' and carrying on as if it had never happened? She felt the palms of her hand grow a little damp.

Once the scribbling stopped it was Maja this time, all casual: "What would you do if someone was incapacitated on the Moon? So much so they couldn't do their job?"

Holy crap! Man, this is rough! I mean these are all my worst nightmares being tabled. She pursed her lips and rubbed her trousers, trying to find the best way forward.

"Well, of course, we would need to look after them. They would be part of the group."

"Let's revisit the incident with David on expedition." Maja's face pinched and sharpened, like a hawk, her voice quick.

Here we go, thought Madison. She took deep breath. "Yeah?"

"Imagine his injury was a little more severe. He's badly hurt and difficult to move." Madison nodded, waiting. "What if there was no vehicle nearby. Base is hours away. You're running out of oxygen. If you stay, you both die. If you go, David dies. What do you do?"

"That would be awful. I'd do my best to save him of course."

"And if trying to help him meant the community would lose you, their pilot, endangering the rest of the community, what would you do *then*?" Maja's words swooped around Madison and landed with claws on her heart.

The image of a colleague, a friend, in pain, lying there looking at her, not able to move, loomed in Madison's mind. What would she do? If saving him meant endangering herself, and therefore risking the mission, risking the lives of others… could she leave him there to die alone in the cold and dark? Would that be the right thing to do? Sacrifice one for the many?

The room felt heavy around her. She thought of the last scenario in the shed. Her team had fought viciously about who should be sacrificed. They agreed to keep the doctors: Mohammad and Jade stayed. They only had one life support technician – Pierre – so he would stay. That left her and Dave. They didn't need two pilots. In the end, she and Dave had flipped a coin. Dave lost. She watched him walk out the door, letting him die for the greater good. She felt disgusted with herself. But when it came down to it, she wanted to live, and if there was a chance to survive, she'd take it.

She steeled herself. "If I had to, I'd walk away."

ॐ

Interviews Round 3, Jonas

"JONAS SEABORN. THIRD round." The staff member ushered him forward from the waiting room.

Jonas struggled to his feet. He was physically and mentally exhausted. The first round of interviews had gone well. The second round, not so much. He'd stumbled on the ethical questions, making it up as he went, losing confidence with each answer. And all that mad scribbling! Feeling this uncertain was a new experience for him. It was like he'd left the *Sea Rover* and was standing on land again. That weird feeling like you were still at sea, rocking.

He sank into the interview chair, trying not to slump, and looked wearily at the panel. Claire, Huw, Maja, faces blank as ever.

"Jonas. Welcome back." Claire, this time, brisk efficiency in her tone. She really had it in for him, he thought. Nothing he did or said seemed to loosen her up. He'd tried all his tricks.

Jonas acknowledged her and waited for the questions to slam.

"Have we seen enough of you in the selection process? Is there something else we should know about you?" Claire's eyes searched his face. He felt himself recoil a little. Geez, she was a tough nut.

But here it was. At last, a chance to win them over! He would take his time, slow right down. Be careful. Outwit them.

"Thanks Claire. I'm grateful for this opportunity." All modesty now. "I've worked hard for this. I mean, I know I have some advantages, being a Seaborn and all that. But I like to think that I've earned my right to be here, and to be selected." Yeah, that's it, that's the right tone. He felt a little rush of strength travel the length of his spine and lift him straighter in his chair. "I've put 100 percent into every task. I didn't always agree with the others, but hey, you win some, you lose some. And then you get on with it. Plus, I'm a good designer." Damn straight he was too. They all said so.

"Tell me, Jonas, what would others say was your greatest strength?" Claire was prodding here. Jonas had the distinct impression of being a fish circling a hook.

"Others?" He stalled. He never thought about what others might think of him. He just expected them to fall into line. "Ahhh... I guess they'd say I was... determined? Strong-willed? And capable. Yeah, they'd say I was capable." Good. Not too up yourself, and certainly a fair assessment.

"And what would they say were your weaknesses?" The fishhook seemed to dangle and flash in front of him.

"My weaknesses?" Jonas adjusted his posture, rolled his shoulders, seeking relief from the tension. "My weaknesses... okay. Yeah. I'd guess they'd say I was stubborn. I don't tend to let go when I want something. I just hang on and hang on." Jonas met Claire's eyes as she stared at him a little longer than he thought necessary before bending over her writing tablet to scribble some more. He imagined the fishhook scraping the inside of his cheek. He desperately wanted to spit it out, end this.

Huw spoke next. "I'm curious about your family, Jonas." Huw allowed a gentle smile as he propped his elbows on the table and made a tent with his fingers. Jonas met his gaze and felt his heart rattle. Huw had been kind to him through the whole selection process. He had an ally here, he thought. Or did he? With some surprise Jonas noticed he felt damp in the armpits.

Huw continued, a slow, easy pace to his words. "Tell me, what's your relationship like with your parents?"

Jonas tried to stop himself from stiffening and going rigid. "What do you mean?" His heart thumped hard.

"Your parents. Do you get along with them?"

"Oh. Yeah. Sure. We get along just fine." He wanted to end this topic, but Huw raised his eyebrows, waiting for more. "They're good, I guess. I mean, they're busy and all. It's quite a lot of work to be designers, builders and leaders on the *Sea Rover*. Always something to do, you know." Still the eyebrows! What else does he want? "Being a Seaborn has certain expectations with it, you know. Everybody thinks you've got some sort of gift. You've got to be a leader all the time. Always on show. You never really know what people want from you. Why they're talking to you. Do they like you for you, you know? Or just because you're a Seaborn..." What was happening? His mouth was running away with itself. Why was he talking about this stuff? The thought was a leaf in the current of his emotions. He felt the wash of them rise and flush old thoughts free from their rotten moorings. He babbled on. "It was tough, really tough being an only kid. I mean good, too, because I got a lot of attention. From others. The other adults looked after me mostly while my parents ran the *Sea Rover*. Sometimes I got into trouble just so I could see my parents." Jonas really wished he hadn't let that one slip. Too late. And more flowed through him. "I wasn't the best kid." His lip trembled. This was crazy! He was about to lose it in front of the three stooges. He steeled himself and tried to stem the flow of his emotions, like putting a plug back in a draining bath. "I wasn't poster-child perfect. But they weren't the best parents either." He wiped his sweaty lip with the back of his hand.

"Tell me, Jonas." Huw continued, slowly, carefully. Gently tapping his fingertips together as he considered his next question. Claire and Maja stole glances at him as the pause dragged on. Jonas noticed, but all he could do was wait, grim, spent.

"Jonas, are your parents *proud* of you?" Emphasis with eyebrows on 'proud.'

Jonas felt the silvery sharp hook bite inside his cheek. The emotions unleashed like a tsunami. The tears spilled from his eyes. He stared at Huw and let them roll, one after another, down his burning face.

❦

Interviews Round 3, Mohammad

"DR MOHAMMAD RASHEED, please proceed."

Mohammad nodded to the staff member at the door and took his seat in front of the Directors.

"Dr Rasheed," Maja began. "This has been a most arduous process. I'd like to congratulate you on your performance thus far."

Mohammad nodded at the compliment. He felt a surge of pride and relief. He had not let the Sultan down. He ran dangerously close a few times to losing his composure and letting his disgraceful emotions take over. He thought with some shame of how he had made his teammates repent and grovel for a full day after the caving incident. They had each pleaded for his forgiveness. They tried at first to laugh it off, make light of it. But the desolation and fear of being alone in the darkness still clung to him and he had snapped back at them bitterly to hide his terror. He rode the spite all afternoon, gaining a grim sense of satisfaction with their genuine remorse. He felt ashamed of his behaviour. He knew they did not leave him deliberately. And it was partly his fault – his unwillingness to hold on to Jade's shoulder had led to the unfortunate stumble and disorientation. Decorum had superseded safety and he had worn the bitter consequences of that. His shame and fear and hurt all rolled into one and he kept his teammates, his friends, at arm's length, twisting a nasty knife of guilt in their sides.

He knew they wouldn't put up with this kind of pettiness for long. Thankfully, he managed to placate his inner turmoil and let go of his punishing resentment. He softened and reached out with an olive branch. It was a long lecture on the biochemicals of fear and the anxiety of ostracism and its impact on the human endocrine system. They listened and heard his forgiveness, as well as his own thinly veiled apology. All was well again.

And then they went into the shed and sacrificed Dave.

"Dr Rasheed?" Maja repeated. Mohammad had not heard the question.

"I beg your pardon," he said. "Can you repeat the question, please?"

"Having gone through all of these ordeals, how would you assess your own suitability for the Olympus Project?"

Mohammad breathed slowly as he recalled all the activities and events to date. Finally, he said, "Well. I have walked and scrambled up steep cliffs in stinging heat with mouthfuls of flies. I watched a colleague almost get killed by a flying boulder. My pilot ran our ship into an asteroid on a suicide run. I was left alone in complete darkness for five hours in a cave. Then we had to sacrifice a colleague for the greater good. I can assure you, I am most certainly *not* suited to a life in space." He paused. They waited. "I do know however, that what I have seen in the character and resolve of my colleagues, the determination to cope with the most onerous of situations, that it would be the honour and privilege of a lifetime to support such a crew, such a mission, to the Moon, to Mars, or anywhere else. For that I'd willingly sacrifice a life of comfort for a life of purpose."

૰

Interviews Round 3, David

"DAVID ERIKSSON, YOU'RE next."

Dave hobbled through the doorway and eased himself into a seat in front of the Directors. His ankle was improving quickly thanks to the rapid healing injections and the protective casing they'd applied after the incident on expedition, but it was still a bit tender.

Claire smiled at him and began.

"David, thanks for your patience. This is the last round of interviews, so we will make this succinct."

Dave took each of them in: Maja with her smooth brown face and dark, dancing eyes, Huw with his pensive look, and Claire with her earnest energy. They're working hard, he thought. Still focused after all these interviews. He felt admiration for their commitment.

"David," Claire continued, "You've had some setbacks throughout this selection process. How would you summarise these experiences?"

Dave laughed. "Setbacks is one word for it, no? I smashed an ankle on expedition, crash-landed my aircraft in simulation and nearly gave my accompanying doctors a heart attack, then I lost one of them for hours in the cave. Then my team sacrificed me in the Moon shed. So yes, some setbacks. But really, how would I summarise it?" He considered the events, and his feelings through them. "It was really good fun. I mean, it was terrifying and hard and gut-wrenching, but good fun. I learnt something about myself."

"And what was that?" Huw asked, learning forward.

"I like being part of a team. It's like… family." He thought of his husband Sven and daughter Sophia and the family bond he felt for his teammates, which was so absent from his home.

Maja spoke now. "What did you think when your 'family' chose you to leave the Moon shed?"

A trace of emotion fluttered across his face. "Well, it had to be someone, no? One person dies or we all die. I was glad it was me. What a thing – to die so others may live. What a way to go, too, no? Walk out onto the giant wasteland of the Moon's surface and watch the Earth hang like a big beautiful blue dot until you just fade away." He looked wistful then. "But I would have wanted one thing to be better."

"What is that?" asked Claire.

"A great soundtrack. I would have liked amazing music to send me off into the wild, dark yonder. Make sure you add THAT to the design specs."

CHAPTER TWENTY-FOUR

Selecting candidates for Gaia Enterprises is a thorough process.
But in spite of it all, sometimes we make mistakes. No matter
how hard we try, we don't always see clearly into someone's soul.

MAJA GARCIA, THE JOURNALS

Gaia Training Centre: Maja

THE DIRECTORS MET to make their choices for the next phase of
the Olympus Project: the year-long training. This was it. From
three thousand to thirty, they were choosing just seven people to
join Xavier, Troy and Xanthe through the next phase. Two pilots,
two life support technicians, two engineers and the physician. The
final crew for the Simulation Hub would be decided later, with the
training phase providing further assessment, as well as creating a
back-up crew.

Maja studied the display table with the candidates' images.
This was their chance to get it right. The future of humanity
depended on them finding the best way forward. Only the best
leaders should be allowed to continue, to become candidates for
the Moon mission. She had her favourites – they all did. Then there

was always a tough deliberation about the final few spots. She was curious about how Claire would respond to her choices. Huw was obvious – he was pragmatic and would back the candidates who were stable and solid in reputation.

"Let's start with the pilots, shall we?" Maja gestured to her colleagues to gather around the display. "Madison Floyd. Outstanding in all aspects: problem-solving, supportive leadership, challenging the status quo, maintaining an even keel."

"I agree. Totally solid. Claire? Your thoughts?" Huw turned to study the woman's face. It was drawn and frowning.

"She is clearly a cut above the others. It goes to show how experience can create steadiness. She does have a ruthless streak that worries me a little, but she's clearly the number one pick. Let's look at the next tier. I think you'll agree that Pabi and David were the next best."

Huw jiggled his leg as his face scrunched considering this next list. "Pabi's okay. His technical skills are strong, but his leadership is weak. He doesn't have much charisma, but we could work with that – perhaps a program at the New Baths of Caracalla would do the trick. But David was a standout for me. He showed tenacity and humility and, importantly, a sense of humour. David's a good sort. He lacks finesse, but somehow, he manages to make his deficits a source of strength. He gets the others laughing when tensions escalate, and he does seem to have a good moral compass. He's the kind of man you want when the ship is sinking: someone to keep the spirits up. While he didn't hog the spotlight, he worked hard in the background. Good support, a solid adviser. He's worth the next project stage. He had excellent peer reviews as well. He gets my vote. Maja – your thoughts?"

Maja was listening intently to their considerations. She already knew these were the top candidates and was pleased they agreed. She listened instead for the tension in Claire, wondering how much resistance she might get for the next recommendations. "Your observations concur with mine. Those three are strong." She drew up the remaining candidate profiles.

Claire jumped in, relieved their conversation had been easy so far and progress was being made quickly. "Let's talk about the life support technicians. We've got Serena, Max, Pierre. The other candidates withdrew."

Huw's leg jiggled again, and his face did more contortions. He blew out some air, trying to find some ease in his body as he stared at the screen. The three candidates' faces lit up, smiling and eager in their photos. Maja, Claire and Huw all focused intently on these next candidates.

Huw broke the silence. "Technically, Pierre and Max are the strongest. Their expertise is impressive, although Pierre is a little volatile and reactive."

Claire nodded in agreement. Maja added, "There's something not quite right about Pierre though. He strikes me as a little perverse."

"Oh?" Asked Huw, "How so?"

"In one of his interviews he mentioned that he was an avid researcher and experimenter. And that included doing plastic surgery on his pet dog, to test his enhancement technology."

"Animal testing is nothing new in science, Maja," Huw said.

"True. And yet when someone takes their own pet and experiments on it, it seems a breach of..." She reached for the right word. "A breach of morality... or trust."

"Hmmm. I think you're exaggerating a bit, Maja!" Huw said. "As I understand it, no harm came to the dog. It's still perfectly healthy. And proved the enhancement technology worked just fine."

"Still, it makes me uneasy."

"I'll make a note of it," said Claire. If we select him for the training, we will need to explore this further at Caracalla."

"Serena and Max then?" Huw asked.

"They both bring something different to the table than Pierre.

Their showdown at the Moon stranding scenario was interesting," Maja said.

"What did you make of that, Maja?" asked Claire.

Maja thought for a moment. "Max made a hard call for the sake of the group's survival. That shows nerves of steel." She paused. They waited. "And the unilateral nature of it shows a heart of steel. Serena on the other hand, is far more compassionate and volatile. She is group oriented in a way that is beyond mere survival principles. Belonging is a strong value for her, not having had much of it. She is well respected and liked by the others."

"Which do we need more for the Olympus Project? Hard calls or a soft touch?" asked Huw.

"That's a little reductive, Huw." Claire admonished.

"Across the balance of the group we might have both," added Maja.

"There's something else we need to consider when it comes to Serena," Claire said. She pressed full screen and the stunning face of Serena seemed to fill the room.

"Serena Fox." Huw's leg stopped jittering. He leant back and clasped his hands behind his head, stretching backwards, getting a better perspective on the woman's image.

Maja watched Claire. The younger woman's face rippled with confused thoughts.

"What is it, Claire?" She asked.

"Well, there's nothing actually wrong with Serena. She handled her leadership role skilfully with a strong hand, even with all that conflict at the cave with Jonas. She shows dedication to team in spite of the self-sacrifice. She shows good self-knowledge, her psychometrics are strong, and she got good peer reviews."

"But?" Huw asked.

"Well… she *disturbs* people."

"What do you mean?" Huw asked.

Claire seemed reluctant to continue as her peers waited in anticipation.

"The woman is..." she searched for the right word, "too... attractive."

Huw burst out laughing.

"Since when are good looks a crime? I mean, it certainly hasn't harmed the career – or contribution – of our superstar, Troy Bruin! Good God, woman! We've moved beyond such primitive biases, surely? Come now, Claire, your objections wouldn't be based on jealousy, would they?"

Claire looked flustered.

Maja asked gently, "Tell us more about how she disturbs others, Claire. Does she manipulate them?"

"No, it's not that." She thought again how she might describe her observations. "The women bristle around her, and the men go quiet."

"Surely that's *their* problem, not hers?" Huw asked, still incredulous they were actually having this conversation. "I can't believe we'd consider dismissing a candidate simply because others thought she was too attractive. That's ridiculous. Frankly I'm disappointed in you, Claire."

Claire looked grim.

"Seriously, now. I back Serena's candidacy because she's a fighter. Look at her background. She's had a tough go of it as an orphan, fought her way through everything. She earned her stripes as a diver and salvage operator and did well with her engineering degree. The only thing I'd be concerned about is how aloof she is. No clear friendships despite the intense experiences they've shared. It seems people respect her enough, but can she build real bonds? The Moon is a long way with nowhere to run."

"That's my point exactly, Huw." Claire's tone was low and biting.

Claire and Huw stared at one another, at an impasse.

Maja intervened. "Serena's looks are not her fault, nor her

responsibility. How others respond to an attractive human is their issue. Jealousy and lust are things we can work on at Caracalla. Serena seems a solid candidate, as Huw said. I'm a little concerned about her lack of rapport building. She will need social networks to manage the pressures." Maja looked again at the screen with Serena's beautiful face. "That's something we can develop over a year. Or not. That's why we have the training phase to really see if they are up to it. Huw's right. We can't dismiss someone for their looks, especially when she has such crucial other qualities. I've noted your concerns about the impact on others, and that we need to be mindful of how the dynamics unfold. Can you live with that, Claire?"

Claire looked concerned but nodded. "So who do we take? Serena, Max, or Pierre?"

"Let's leave them for the moment. We have the engineers to discuss. Who do you each nominate?" Maja asked.

Huw jumped in, bolstered by his win over Claire. "If this is the second-chance place, I'd pick Gina. She's got guts. Love her attitude." Huw smiled remembering the tall woman's belligerent attitude, defiant. Gina was a self-reliant, independent engineering genius.

"I was thinking the same," admitted Claire. "She is opinionated, and this does blind her a bit, but being outspoken can be a good thing. Challenges default thinking. I wonder—" She stopped short as Maja interrupted the conversation.

"I'd like you to consider Jonas."

They stared at her, stunned. At last Claire spoke.

"You can't be serious? Maja, he led a selfish rebellion at the cave, he undermined and challenged Serena's leadership at every point during the expedition phase. He tested low on the psychometrics. His leadership maturity is well behind the others. We can't take him!" Claire was flabbergasted.

Huw stayed quiet, waiting for Maja's response. When Maja

held a contrarian position she always had an interesting rationale for it.

"What you say is correct, Claire. He is behind developmentally compared with the others. That's exactly why he should be included in the group. They'll need to contend with people who are not as mature as them. World designers on the Moon, and then Mars, will need to plan for and respond to all stages of development. If they can't handle someone like him here, in training, they certainly won't be able to handle them on the Moon."

Claire remained unconvinced. Her frustration was evident. Huw waited, foot bouncing as his thoughts processed.

"Jonas is also a great candidate for the emotional intelligence training program we've developed using the full Virtual Emotions Stimulator. It should accelerate his maturity and get him up to speed with the others." Unofficially known as the 'Empathy Suit', the VES was one of Maja's latest investments. Designed originally for military and surgical virtual reality training, she had commissioned programming to help its wearers experience the full reality of another human's experience, complete with simulated physical sensations delivered through the body suit. It had been very successful in curbing violence in delinquent teenagers.

"So, Jonas is a project for you?" Claire was incredulous. "We are selecting these people to design long-term communities in the most remote and isolated of environments, where there is no backup and no second chances. These world designers will set the course of human development as a species, not just as a temporary space colony. Jonas has been an arrogant prat since he arrived on the island. Cocksure and brash. He mentions his Seaborn heritage at every opportunity. He lacks self-awareness and empathy. And Maja – you want to include him? For what? Another developmental experiment?" Claire covered her mouth to rein in her outburst. "Huw? You don't support this, do you? Jonas could jeopardise the whole project – his insensitivity sets entirely the wrong tone."

Huw let out a long breath. "Jonas is an interesting character. A total show pony. But maybe Maja is right. The Olympus Project is a legacy project for every billionaire out there, keen to make their mark on off-planet human migration. If our world designers can't handle an upstart like Jonas, they'll never be able to negotiate and work with the egos of that lot. Besides, there is the commercial advantage of the Seaborn name. It *does* come with kudos. That would bolster investor confidence in our program. They don't need to see the details as we progress. Besides, we've got a year to shape him up, and he *is* an excellent engineer. I say we take him."

Claire felt the weight of anxiety drop into her guts. In every fibre of her being she felt this decision was wrong. Maja, and now Huw, were gambling on too many unknowns, too many risks, when what they really needed was a rock-solid set of candidates from the outset. So much was riding on this decision! Why couldn't Maja see that? She could run her development experiences elsewhere, not on the Olympus Project. Claire felt the shiny glow of her mentor, so long respected, start to dull. In its place, she felt the beginnings of that particular sense of grief that comes with the end of innocence.

"Claire, I know you have your doubts. Trust in the process. Jonas will serve us well."

Huw and Claire watched as Maja ticked 'successful' over Jonas's profile. It was done.

"And now – the doctor," Huw said gleefully.

"Was there ever any real doubt as to who would take the spot?" asked Claire. "Aryanna Sharif is very persuasive. No one else really had a shot, did they?" Bitterness filled her mouth.

"Aryanna Sharif may be funding this project, but she does not call the shots," Maja said with a hard look at Claire. "We had many fine candidates for the role of project physician. Nothing is guaranteed."

Claire held back her retort, sensing its futility. She was getting ground down by the failure to persuade.

The discussions continued long into the night. At last, they had their final list. The new recruits would start in the morning. Maja clicked 'publish'. The list would be posted on the common room announcement board. She bade her colleagues good night and retired to her personal quarters, satisfied.

Claire watched her go, followed quickly by Huw. Claire breathed out slowly. Selection was done.

Now, she thought, it begins.

CHAPTER TWENTY-FIVE

One always has choices, even if it feels like there are none.

ATHENA AI IN WISDOM OF THE AGES

Gaia Training Centre: Pabi

PABI STARED AT the announcement list in the common room, his expression unreadable. He left the room quickly, seeking fresh air and quiet. He made his way to the waterfront and sat on the grass under the shade of a maple tree. A rivulet of sweat ran down the back of his neck and soaked into his shirt. It was barely dawn and the heat clung to him like a needy child.

Pabi smelled the earthy tones of the fading summer on the breeze as it drifted across the water. It was the smell of endings, of closure, of death and decay. Of change. He closed his eyes, savouring the moment.

He pulled his holo comm from his pocket and hit connect without the visual feed.

"*Beta?*" His mother's voice pierced the quiet.

"Mummy-ji, hello," Pabi said.

"Oh, thank goodness! I thought you might be dead, or starving, or injured somewhere, Pabi! Tell me, tell me! What is the news?"

The moment stretched like a lazy cat. Pabi noticed the deep blue sky of late summer, the chirp of a wren and the muted patter as it tapped a merry dance around the base of a nearby shrub. He saw his future etched before him: returning to Singapore, a wedding to the suitable girl of his parents' choosing in a ceremony both lavish enough to show the false narrative of appropriate wealth, and simple enough to pretend humility. He saw the years unfolding in the sameness of domestic chores and a comfortable, passionless existence.

He gave himself this moment, just a little longer, poised between destinies. And for the first time in his life, lied to his mother.

"They haven't told us yet, Mummy-ji. A few more days."

His mother replied with rapid fire questions interspersed with a litany of chastisements and general complaints about his father's inability to put socks in the laundry hamper, the neighbours' cat pissing on the balcony and Auntie Shilpa's chronic gout.

Pabi listened respectfully until she had vented all her news. When she was done, he said goodbye, promising he'd call with an update in a few days.

A few days. A small buffer before he stepped into a life he did not want.

A pair of swans swam up the bank and eyed him warily. He met their gaze. One of them honked and they swam on.

CHAPTER TWENTY-SIX

*I fear that I misjudged the leader's ability to operate beyond
early stages of development. Fear and power and pride remain
primal forces that are, as yet, untamed. And still I hope we can
overcome our darker nature to let our better selves prevail.*

MAJA GARCIA, TERRA BLANCA JOURNALS

Gaia Training Centre: Xanthe

XANTHE SAT ON the narrow bed in her private room. Everything
was in its place now, as cosy as she could make it. Xanthe stretched
back on the bed, feet up. She and the new recruits had a rare few
moments of peace and quiet before the training kicked off. After
the onslaught that was selection, she was grateful for the chance
to be on her own.

The announcement that morning of successful candidates was
as strange as it was wonderful. There was no surprise about the
standout candidates: But Serena? Xanthe pressed her lips together
in irritation. Serena did a fair to middling job of her leadership
tasks, Xanthe admitted. She handled Jonas well enough.

Jonas! She was surprised he made it through. Xanthe frowned.

What were the Directors thinking? The Olympus Project was so important. Surely Gaia Enterprises needed to be on top of their game? The best of the best. Jonas was far from that. Was it the Sea-born name? Were they making exceptions to leverage his heritage? Surely not...

Maybe there's something they see that I haven't yet, she thought. The Directors wouldn't make such a strange choice without a good reason – a really good reason. Xanthe thought back to all the inter-actions she'd had with Jonas. There were glimmers of insight. He was bloody determined, she gave him that. Xanthe parked her apprehension. She resolved to find out more about Jonas.

Mr Jonas Seaborn, let's see what you've got.

CHAPTER TWENTY-SEVEN

One of the delights of human experience is the deep sense of
connection we can have with others. If we allow ourselves to be seen.

ATHENA AI IN WISDOM OF THE AGES

Gaia Training Centre: Serena

IN HER ROOM, Serena stood and assessed her surroundings. Clean, bright, functional. A bed, chair, desk, fitness mat, meditation cushion, and wardrobe for training gear and recreation clothes. Nothing decorative. Each of the trainees had a room of their own for the duration of their training program. A large window drew the eyes outwards to a green lawn. The swaying trees set in a carefully crafted garden were designed to give the impression of no design at all, mimicking a grove one might come across on a stroll through the forest. Though the room was spartan, the view to the natural world gave the viewer a sense of abundance. Serena felt it expand her spirit as she took a deep breath, watching the wind and sunlight play with the willow leaves. Home. Or something like it. For now. She was used to impermanence. Living in tsunami refugee camps for so long she knew not to get too attached, to anything. Or anyone.

Serena grabbed her electronic writer, Gaia issue to all trainees, and sat at the desk. She wanted to capture her thoughts about the selection process before the training began. She knew that if she was going to be one of the final candidates chosen after training for the Olympus Project, she had to be at the top of her game. She needed to figure out the success code, track her achievements and progress. And those of her rivals.

Serena jotted her observations of the process: "kept us off guard, threw us in the deep end, challenges pushed group dynamics rather than built them. Interviews were heat-seeking missiles, looking for those soft vulnerable parts."

They'd found hers, too. She never felt quite safe anywhere. She'd never really had friends. She had tried. But then the men would go all creepy, or worse, domineering and bullish. And the women, they puffed up like frightened cats around her. Like Xanthe. Xanthe was always a little rough with her. She tried to cover it up, Serena knew. But you can't hide the bitter poison of resentment: it sours the face.

Serena had been delighted that Xanthe had joined the Olympus Project selection. She thought it a chance to make amends. Not so. Not yet. Xanthe kept her at arm's length, cold.

Serena thought about Xanthe's leadership role. Very directive. Almost too much so – a bit curt even. Was it just when she was around though?

They had months of training to smooth things out. Then the final choice for building the Simulation Hub for the tender. A good amount of time to get to know each other.

She was glad of one relationship: Xavier. Her connection with the tall Frenchman was a surprise. Serena was focused on the one goal only: get through selection. Her rapport with Xavier sprang up over a meal after the expedition phase. He saw her sitting alone in the dining hall, gazing out to the welcome lawn through a rain-flecked window, the remnants of a salad wilting on her plate. He sat down in a chair across from her and handed her a mug of steaming liquid.

She glanced at the mug and then up at him with a questioning expression.

"*Chocolat chaud.* Hot chocolate. It's good for endorphins and nervous system therapy. No sugar." Xavier smiled broadly at her. "Thought you needed a little lift, judging by the look of you."

Serena noticed that he did not seem to get edgy around her like other men. He held his own, comfortable and relaxed.

"You make a lot of assumptions," she said, a bit shirty.

"I call it how I see it. And to me, you look like a person who needs a little boost. Anyhow, expedition phase is over, so we can relax. Thought it would be good to get to know the future world designers for the Olympus Project."

"We haven't made it through yet," Serena said in hushed tones. She did not like to get ahead of herself. Jeopardise her performance by letting her guard down. She needed to stay vigilant, focused.

"*Mais vraiment!* Really, you're a natural, Serena," Xavier countered. "You have passion, you take on anyone – even that jackass Jonas – with fairness and an even keel." He picked up a spoon, stirred it slowly through his chocolate. "You have spunk." He tapped the spoon on the rim of the mug before popping it in his mouth to suck it clean. He pulled it out again and pointed it at her. "But that's not your real talent."

"No?" She asked, perturbed by the pointing spoon.

"No. Your real talent is what you keep hidden, deep under that tough, brash exterior of yours that you wear like a samurai." He put the spoon down, leant forward and said in a conspiratorial whisper. "Underneath all that tough girl act is a soft, warm heart, desperate to love." Serena felt herself holding her breath. Then frightened anger bubbled up inside her. She sat back, arms crossed.

"Horseshit. You don't know me from a bar of soap."

He was still leaning forward, staring into her face.

"Is that right?" He said it slowly, holding her gaze.

"What do you want, Xavier?"

He said nothing for a moment, scanning her face. "I'm not sure exactly." He sat back and crossed his arms to mirror hers. "But I'm pretty sure it involves you." The tension hung between them like a strand of a spider's web reaching between two distant points.

Then Xavier smiled and so did she. They burst into laughter.

Serena smiled at the memory, bringing her attention back to the room and her writing tablet that had shut down as her mind wandered. She started her notes again.

Impressions of fellow trainees and world designers:

Troy Bruin – very confident. Talented, proven world designer. Party boy. Who has the hots for Xanthe, that silly little fish.

Xavier Consus – Serena paused, enjoying the pleasant thoughts that swirled. *Capable. Valuable asset in his horticulture innovations. Ambitious.* How ambitious? she wondered.

Xanthe Waters – The Dictator. Likes to be in control. And also – the Diplomat. Wants everyone to feel heard. Except for me.

Jonas Seaborn, engineer–bulldozer. As subtle as a sledgehammer. With about as much self-awareness.

Gina Casellatti, engineer – tough nut. Rogue operator. Hell of a chick! A bird of a feather.

David Eriksson – pilot. Flies under the radar. Very 'punny', she thought.

Madison Floyd – pilot. Goddess? Gladiator? The woman was fierce.

Dr Mohammad Rasheed – physician. Kind of creepy and reserved.

Dr Pierre Martin – life support technician. Opinionated technical expert. And the man she needed to beat. Serena couldn't believe it was her and Pierre as the last candidates for life support tech. They'd beaten out Max, hardcore international explorer. Such an arrogant prick, she thought. He was so ungracious when they'd met up in the common room and the trainee list was published. Serena comforted Jade, who was quietly weeping her disappointment in a corner. Max strode in and stood feet spread, hands on hips, glaring at the noticeboard.

"This is complete bullshit!" he exclaimed. He looked around the room seeking a target for his frustration and his eyes set on her. "Fox – who'd you sleep with to make it onto that list?"

Serena refused to dignify his outburst with a response, but it had cut deep. Max stormed out of the room and spent the rest of the morning packing up his things, ignoring anyone who tried to speak with him.

Good riddance, arsehole, she thought.

She resumed her writing to complete the list.

Serena Fox – life support technician. Serena paused as she thought of how to describe herself. *The Contender.*

There were three spots on offer to join Xanthe, Xavier and Troy for the Simulation Hub. Come hell or high water she would be one of them.

CHAPTER TWENTY-EIGHT

*In any venture, there is no guarantee of success. There is only
hard labour. Sometimes it works, sometimes it doesn't.*

*DON AND JENNY SEABORN IN WORLD
DESIGNERS: PERSPECTIVE AND PRACTICE*

Gaia Training Centre: Jonas

JONAS LET HIS kick whack hard into the training bag hanging in
the gym. He was alone. The others must be catching up on sleep
or some shit. He had been way too fired up to sit for long in his
poxy little room. When he saw his name on the trainee list he'd let
out a big hoot. Fuck yeah!

It had been a tense few hours, waiting to find out. Especially
after that last interview where he'd blubbered like a baby. He
thought he was a goner for sure, showing such weakness.

But nope! Here he was. One of the freakin' trainees for the
Olympus Project. What a rush!

Those old windbag Directors had to rain on his parade,
though. They'd called him in for a 'debrief' and read him the riot
act. Develop more self-awareness, listen more, seek feedback, yadda
yadda yadda. He'd nodded diligently like a good boy, making notes

on his shiny new electronic scribbler. Inside he was fist pumping all the way. He'd made it. His parents could go suck it. He'd shown them.

Jonas punched the bag with a hook, a cross and then a flurry of jabs. He'd made it! He stopped, heaving and dripping sweat.

He'd made it. He stepped over to the bench against the wall and sank on to it. He grabbed his workout towel, covered his face with it, breathed deeply into the clean cotton fibres. He curled over, head in his hands. He took a deep breath. Then another. Then a deep shuddering sob racked his body.

He'd made it.

CHAPTER TWENTY-NINE

World designers create best when they are at home
in their own bodies, their own emotions. You can't
build cathedrals with rickety foundations.

WORLD DESIGNERS' MANIFESTO

Gaia Training Centre: Xanthe

XANTHE STOOD IN the morning sunlight outside the Conversation Hub, waiting for the others to arrive and Maja's first session to begin. She breathed deeply, savouring the smell of pine trees and damp earth. *We'll definitely need a bit of this on the Moon.* She wondered if they would be able to replicate the subtle nuances of the ground: the mulching leaf matter, the grass, the movement of insects. How much could they build there to make it feel more like home?

Her reverie was interrupted as she caught a glimpse of Troy sauntering across the green lawn towards her. *He moves like a panther.* Not for the first time, Xanthe drank in the sight of him. Every movement fluid. Every cell seemed to vibrate with a quiet self-assurance that was neither arrogant nor unnatural. The kind of confidence of someone who knows themselves well and likes what they find. Xanthe focused on dialling down her attraction. She thought of Simon instead.

Troy stepped slowly up to her, his beautiful full mouth holding a smile for her, his blue eyes bright. He came to a stop in front of her, looking her over as a dog eyes a steak.

"Xanthe, hello."

"Hi." She held his gaze then looked away quickly as she felt the nearness of him trigger a flush of warmth to her cheeks.

"Hey – congratulations on a great selection. You did a terrific job." She glanced at him. He meant his words, she could tell. "It was never in doubt. You've got heart and vision the size of the Eiffel Tower."

"Thanks, Troy."

He moved closer. He put his hand on her shoulder and looked into her face. "I mean it. You've got something special and valuable for the Olympus Project."

Xanthe was holding her breath, swirling in the rush of happiness that flooded her body with his touch, his big warm hand on her shoulder. "Thanks," she said, annoyed with the shyness that crept up on her.

"Come here." He pulled her to him and hugged her gently. Her face pressed against his firm broad chest, breathing in the delicious smell of him. His arms around her, the firmness of his body against hers. Xanthe's mind flew ahead to scenarios with Troy that did not serve her. She shut them down.

"Okay, thanks." She pulled away, steeling herself. Troy felt her stiffen and let her go, disappointment dragging the corners of his mouth down a little.

"Apart from the whole Moon thing, we'll get to know each other better too. I am looking forward to that." He smiled encouragingly at her.

"Yup. That will be good." She shuffled her weight from one foot to the next. The door opened behind her. Maja ushered them in, just as the other trainees arrived. Xanthe stepped quickly inside.

CHAPTER THIRTY

Human development takes so damned long. Most of the time I
have patience for it. Then mortality fingers my joints, suckles at my
energy and I wonder if I will run out of time to see it all through.

MAJA GARCIA, THE JOURNALS

Gaia Training Centre: Maja

MAJA SAT IN silence, waiting for the trainees to settle. The soft tub
chairs were arranged in a circle, the warm intimate space of the
Conversation Hub lit with floor to ceiling windows, letting the
natural light dance in patterns. They used to call it the lecture hall,
but Claire insisted they change it. Too hierarchical. Maja smiled
at that. She was right, of course. Claire was so egalitarian. About
most things. She still liked the privileges of authority: the better
accommodation, private workspace – and better remuneration.
Maja admired Claire's obsession with the messaging of minutia.
"It's the little things that make or break a plan. Think pebble in
your shoe. Or the kindness of a handwritten note. We've got to pay
attention, Maja, to the details." And so they did.

   Maja felt rather than heard the shift in the room as quiet

settled over the group, like dust particles drifting in an afternoon sunbeam. She looked at each of them, soaking in their anticipation. Her mind flashed forward to the Moon. These were the true pioneers. They would develop a new home, a new habitat, for humanity. Maja's heart swelled in satisfaction. At last, her vision was edging closer to fulfilment.

She began.

"World design is human development design." The words were like musical cords, strummed from a place deep within her. "For a long time now we've been aware that environments cause evolution. The polar bear developed clear, hollow fur to match the ice sheets, to hide herself from prey, and to keep her warm. Every species on this planet has found ways to adapt its biology to its surroundings. Humans too. But we did something different, unprecedented. We started changing our environment, the first species to do so on a massive scale. As we changed our environment, we adapted to what we created. The internet was one environmental change that catapulted human evolution: all of a sudden, we needed to communicate faster, better. Mobile technology was another exponential change. And robotics, artificial intelligence and human biotech. All of these changes in our environment have had an impact on human development." Maja saw a few of them nod. One or two were already starting to lose interest: Jonas and Pierre. Time to shift gears.

"Our opportunity with the Olympus Project is to craft an environment where we fast-track human development for its future residents. We want to accelerate ego development so that we avoid the tragic missteps of our forebears. No more world wars. No more slavery. No more oppression. We want something better for the human race. It's your turn to guide it. And you can do this with your designs. How you develop the Moon habitat will guide the future of the species." Emotion slithered around the room. The scope of their work was becoming more real to them.

"Here is the first world building principle you must hold

central to all your work: 'As within, so without'. How you see yourself, how you experience yourself, the stories you make up about who you are determine what you create in the world. How you see the world is how you build the world. Our objective in the next twelve months is to make *damned* sure that your view of the world is one that elevates humanity rather than destroys it." She noticed a few of them flinch at her tone. She'd added just a hint of venom. That got their attention! They hadn't seen her passion yet. Throughout selection she was a stoic and benign figure. Now they would experience the full repertoire of her influence skills. Time to break out the magician, she thought.

"Perspective is power. We start your 'training' by unpacking what you think you know. Our first step is to map out your worldview. We want to know what you value. Not what you say you value, but what you feel in your bones. Now, beware. This is confronting work. Where there is light, there are shadows. Know where they fall and what they hide." Her gaze narrowed as she looked at each face in turn. Some open: Xanthe, Dave, Troy. Some blank: Jonas. Pierre. Madison. Some darkening: Xavier, Serena, Mohammad. Gina. Interesting.

"Our values shape our choices. We can, however, choose our values, and thereby make new choices. You have completed your values profiles. Now I want you to spend some time mapping your value system to past choices. What worked, what didn't, what you learnt. Then you will debrief with a partner." They started to shift in their seats, glad of the change of pace.

"Hear this!" Her words sliced the air and stopped them cold, as if the edge of a sword had flashed beside them trailing a subtle rush of wind across their cheeks. "You cannot bluff your way through this exercise. It's time for you to confront your own truths: good and ill. It's how we lurch forwards in our own personal development. As within, so without."

They bent their heads to work.

CHAPTER THIRTY-ONE

Your best source of knowledge is other
people. Be humble. Get curious.

GAIA ENTERPRISES CODE OF CONDUCT

Gaia Training Centre: Jonas

"Hey, Jonas." Xanthe leant over to his tub chair. She'd deliberately sought him out, grabbing the chair beside him as they entered for the first session with Maja. "Can I debrief with you?"

Jonas looked up, startled. He'd been staring at his values profile, trying to make sense of what it all meant.

"Yeah. Sure." He sat more upright, trying to find a strength he did not feel.

"Great!" Xanthe sparkled. She was determined to figure Jonas out. "How did you go? What do you think about your profile?"

He glanced down at he tablet. The graph of his results stared back at him, an embarrassment, like dirty underpants left offending side up on the floor. A flag of secret shame.

"Dunno. Still thinking about it. How about you go first?" Buying himself some time.

"No surprises. It says that I am socially conscious and sensitive. That totally makes sense given the work I've done in community building back in Sydney. I always wanted to make sure everyone had a home, somewhere to belong. Fairness has always been really important to me." Her big green eyes looked down at her lap, hiding the flicker of pain.

"That's interesting. Growing up on the *Sea Rover*, everyone had a place. I mean how could you not? You were stuck on a giant floating island! I always knew my place. I was son of the famous founders, Don and Jenny Seaborn. I was destined to be a world designer, right from the start. Family expectations and all that." He tried to keep the resentment from seeping out.

"Hmmm. How do you account for such a low score on the 'belonging' values? Is it because you scored so high on the 'power' ones?" Xanthe knew she was leaning into a sensitive spot as Jonas's face muscles pinched. She backed off a bit.

"Power. I guess... well, I DO like to be in charge."

"I noticed!" Xanthe smiled at him, a bit teasing, a bit of gentle encouragement.

"I've got strong ideas and I back myself. I like to make my own rules. That's probably why the 'rules and law' values aren't so big."

"A rebel then?" She smiled at him again.

"Something like that." He felt himself relaxing in Xanthe's easy conversation. She leant over to take a look at his tablet.

"Do you mind?" she asked. He shrugged and handed it to her. "Is it okay if I do a bit of horoscoping for you? I tell you what I think is going on in your profile, and you let me know if I've got it right."

"Sure." He relaxed. It was much easier to let Xanthe do the interpretation than work through it himself.

"By the looks of this, and from what I've seen of you through selection, I'd say you're a pretty energetic kind of person. Passionate, lots of energy. Maybe a little impulsive – that's the lack of 'rules' values failing to temper your 'power' values. You've got a strong achiever streak – want to make your mark, highly competitive. How am I doing so far?"

"Yep. Go on." He was enjoying this.

"And then there's your shadow side. All this focus and drive can burn people around you. They don't always sign up to your ideas because you're too busy haranguing them, not listening to them." Blood flooded Jonas's cheeks crimson. "True?"

"Not sure. I guess I never really thought about it."

Xanthe leant back in her tub chair, watching Jonas process her insights. It was clear he was having trouble with this new awareness.

"Can I give you some advice?" He nodded, sitting back in his chair, bracing himself.

"If you want to make it to the final cut for the Olympus Project, you're going to have to pay a lot more attention to other people. Figure them out. Listen more. There's more to leadership than power."

It was like the Directors' lecture all over again. Jonas felt himself switch off.

"Yeah. Okay. Thanks." The words came out chilled. Xanthe felt it. "Hey – can I do yours now?" he asked, reaching for her tablet with intent. She handed it over.

"Okay, let me see here." He looked at her profile results. "I'd say you're big into team bonding and stuff – lots of belonging, lots of community. But you got a low power score." He paused as his thoughts bound together. He prepared to unleash them like a whip, just enough to smart a little. "I bet you desperately want to fit in, but you're scared. Scared to show yourself. You hide. You don't speak up in groups. I bet you want everyone to belong, to be equal because you're actually terrified of being a leader. A little scaredy cat. Yeah. That's it, isn't it?" He watched her eyes grow wide as he spoke. He'd nailed it. "That's what I'll call you. Scaredy cat. Little kitty cat." He gave back her tablet and exchanged it for his own. He felt the sting of the nickname do its job.

"Just joking!" He tried to ease the awkwardness that stuck to them. She smiled feebly. "Hey if I call you Kit Cat, you can call me—"

"Jackass!" she spat.

He stared at her, feeling the moment hang like a wave reaching its peak. He laughed. "Nice one! We can be Jackass and Kit Cat."

Xanthe laughed too, uncertain.

The moment and its awkwardness receded, the wave broken, washing the exchange behind them.

CHAPTER THIRTY-TWO

*Designing a legacy is like launching a ship without a
captain: we'll never know where the currents take it.*

MAJA GARCIA, TERRA BLANCA JOURNALS

Gaia Training Centre: Maja

THE FIRST TWO weeks of the training program flew by in a haze of
conversations and Gaia Enterprises World Design theory. Claire
and Maja repeated many of the crucial principles through their lec-
tures and debriefs. Slowly, they were growing into the Gaia ideals.
Each trainee wore their special Gaia pin, its compass emblem
sitting proudly on their lapels.

Maja had enjoyed watching the trainees soak up the teachings.
She was pleased with how they were interacting and developing
as a cohort. Any one of them would be an asset to the Olympus
Project – which would make the final decision a whole lot harder,
she knew.

Following the overview session at the Gaia centre, they would
be sent to the New Baths of Caracalla where Troy would host
them. First mission: self-mastery. Meditation, physical training and

emotional expression were Troy's preferred training methodology. Then to Terra Verdi for study of Xavier's space-ready hydroponic experiments and space-travel food cultivation. Three trainees would be nominated at this point for the Simulation Hub. After space engineering study, they would build the Olympus Project prototype in the desert, just as if they were landing on the Moon.

The last portion of the program was the Simulation Hub, at Gaia Enterprises' desert base, its remoteness intended to simulate the harsh reality of the lunar and Martian landscapes. For twelve months the trainees and world designers would live and work exclusively in the Simulation Hub, in a small team of six. During their long seclusion they would be tasked with the fundamentals of setting up the Hub to support human life, and then design and implement together the extension of the Hub, making it ready for the next set of Moon tourists and the expansion of the Lunar Commission community.

Maja walked the length of the Gaia training base. Her limbs ached and she stopped often to catch her breath. Still, she was determined to remain limber and fit. This Project needed her. Without her, she felt the direction of Gaia Enterprises might be stymied. She knew Claire was more conservative than her for its future. But if the company was to survive and make its contribution to the planet, to humanity, it needed to push the boundaries. If only she could outlast her body, they might have a chance.

CHAPTER THIRTY-THREE

Gaia Training Centre: Xanthe

XANTHE LAY HER few belongings out on the bed in her room. They were heading out to the New Baths of Caracalla the next day for the month-long regime at Troy's famous power training palace. *The Den of Iniquity.* That was its unofficial moniker for the traditionalists. There was a retro regression movement going back to purist practices. 'How humans were meant to be', went the slogan. And that meant anything that used drugs or artificial intelligence or bioengineering was anti-human. They were a small but radical group, causing problems for all the lab-grown meat producers and micro-dosing communities. Not that Troy's place did any of that. Officially, anyhow.

Damn! She'd left her training gear in the gym. Xanthe pulled on her shoes, left her accommodation and made her way across the common lawn, damp now with the cool night air. In a month or so, the frost would arrive. No more big, heavy snowfalls, though. Those days were long gone, she thought.

The other accommodation huts were shut, the trainees snug and sleeping after the long arduous day. Xanthe envied them. Sleep did not often come easy to her.

Just as she reached the edge of the accommodation huts near the common facilities, a door opened across from her, flooding the dark with a sword of light. Xanthe stopped to adjust her eyes.

Troy was in the doorway of the cabin. His large, broad shoulders unmistakable framed against the internal light. Her heart leapt to her throat as it always did when he was nearby. Who was he talking to, Xanthe wondered.

She moved a little closer in the shadows, careful not to reveal her presence. She was not sure why she felt the need to hide. Something about this scene pricked her senses.

Troy shifted in the doorway. Xanthe had a clear view into the interior. *Claire!* Xanthe watched as Troy gave Claire a small box. She put it in her pocket. Troy reached a hand and placed it gently on her cheek. Claire pressed her lips to it. Then Troy leant forward and kissed her deeply. Claire's arms slid around his back. They stayed in their embrace, savouring each other. Troy pulled away gently, kissed her once more, then turned to leave.

Xanthe pressed against the neighbouring cabin, out of sight, holding her breath.

A jealousy she knew she had no right to feel battered her heart. Then a huge sense of betrayal threatened to swallow her whole.

I'm an idiot. All this time getting sucked in by his charm, his outrageous good looks. It didn't matter that Xanthe had no intention of reciprocating his interest, she still felt betrayed. Turns out he was a pants man after all. He seemed so genuine! But he was just screwing around. With Claire. One of the Directors.

Claire! What a hypocrite! Always banging on about the rules, and here she was breaking the biggest one – sleeping with a staff member. Xanthe knew Troy and Claire had trained together, years ago. But still. She was a Director now. Troy was a designer for the Olympus Project. There were principles.

Xanthe blinked back tears. Her disappointment in Troy paled against the despair she felt at discovering the moral vagaries of a Director. She had always seen Gaia as her inner compass: a beacon of hope for the future of humanity. But what was it really if its lessons were just empty words?

Once she was sure Claire was locked up in her cabin and Troy had gone, Xanthe continued to the gym. She gathered her training suit and paused, looking at the equipment in the small space. This was supposed to be a whetstone for the best of the best. A place where dreamers and designers could come and carve out the best version of themselves. Now it seemed just another room full of junk and empty promises. All the vibrant colour of excitement faded to grey. She left, as cold and empty as the now-vacant gym.

CHAPTER THIRTY-FOUR

"Sensuous indulgence is a spiritual experience. To
be so immersed in one's physical pleasure is not to
be transported, but to merge with the divine."
"Is that why you smoke pot?"
"That's why I do anything."

TROY BRUIN, 'SEXIEST HUMAN ALIVE', INTERVIEW

New Baths of Caracalla: Xanthe

TROY WELCOMED THEM at the enormous entrance to the New
Baths of Caracalla. The doors were dark and gargantuan – meant
as a throwback to an ancient fortress, with giant gold doorknock-
ers. Troy stood on the sweeping steps and bid them up into the
famous venue.

Caracalla remained something of a mystery. The people who
explored its programs certainly seemed transformed: more relaxed,
more focused, more energised, or more thoughtful – whatever their
intention was going in. His programs received nothing but rave
reviews, without divulging any of the secret experiences.

Xanthe was at once thrilled and anxious at the prospect of
undergoing a program there. Standing out was not her forte.

Standing out with all one's vulnerabilities dangling free made fear rise, its cold fingers squeezing tight around her throat.

Troy led them through the facility. It was glorious with its high marble ceilings, intricate mosaics and gorgeous fountains. Ever since he had visited the ruins of the original baths in Rome, Troy had wanted to bring the ancient centre of health and leisure to life once more. He'd designed this venue on similar principles of grandiose scale. The spectacular hallways led through to light-filled chambers with sparkling fountains. There were rooms for all sorts of exercise, both solitary and group oriented. There were halls for racket sports. There were steam rooms, saunas and a sun-drenched swimming pool with sea-themed mosaics. Lush plants framed the whole thing so that swimmers felt they were floating in a jungle oasis. Cold plunge pools flanked several other hot baths. Domed ceilings invited the gaze upwards while bathers felt their aches wash away.

On the outer circle of the property, he built accommodation and the tech-training rooms: virtual reality simulators and all manner of sensory chambers, both for stimulation and decompression. A whole room of flotation tanks glowed like watery cocoons.

The grounds were gorgeous. Gravel paths led across green lawns dappled with light filtered by enormous trees. There were secret nooks for quiet contemplation and higher points for looking out across expanded vistas.

"The original Baths had spaces to worship the gods," Troy told them as they wandered back to the main building from the outdoor meditation pace. "They favoured Mithra, a Persian god popular with soldiers. Guardian of Truth."

"Wasn't Caracalla himself a bit of a tyrant? I thought he had his brother murdered so he could be undisputed Roman emperor," Serena said.

Troy paused in the atrium so their eyes could adjust to the softer light and their bodies could cool a little. The heat was steamy in the garden.

"Yes, it's true," Troy said. "Caracalla was formally known as Marcus Aurelius Antoninus. He was co-ruler with his father for a time, then with his brother, who was murdered by the Praetorian Guard, allegedly at Caracalla's behest. He didn't like to share power," Troy said with a smile.

"I'll say! He was a blood-thirsty mass murderer! As I recall, he ordered many massacres during his military campaigns. Why did you name the baths after such a barbarian?" asked Serena.

Troy considered his response. "The Romans didn't whitewash their gods. Many were violent and impetuous. I think they painted the gods to mirror our own human nature: at once glorious and terrible." Troy led them to a marvellous statue in one corner of the atrium. It was a bearded man with tight curly hair and a grim, angry expression. "This is Caracalla. He had the gumption to create something spectacular, the original baths, in ancient times, open to the public. They were impressive and uplifting. He was also a power-hungry, murdering tyrant." Troy looked up at the statue's face for a moment, then to his colleagues. "The good deeds of men are often marred by their bad ones. None of us are all good, nor all bad. Many a wondrous creation was born of a flawed and awful human. The story of Caracalla inspired me not because of the deeds of the man, but as a reminder that each of us can shine light or cast shadows. These Baths are here to help us put a candle to those shadows so that we each might walk more in sunlight than in darkness."

Serena opened her mouth for a retort but thought better of it and stayed silent.

"Our task here is to dig into those shadows. Unearth the dark corners. It's not easy. But on the other side of it is deep personal strength and an inner calm."

The trainees were at once unsettled and awed.

"Well, I am not sure about anyone else, but with all these fountains trickling I need to make water, myself. Troy, where is the nearest facility?" Dave broke the spell and the trainees murmured once again to one another, admiring the mosaics and statues throughout the atrium.

Troy showed them to their accommodation. Single rooms with beautiful, luxurious finishings. Xanthe sighed and marvelled at the sense of relaxation the room instantly evoked as she entered. She welcomed the brief reprieve from group activity and took her time settling in.

An hour later, they gathered for their first training session with Troy. Here they were, the Gaia trainees and world designers, the future architects of day-to-day life on the Moon, sitting in a circle on a padded mat, cross-legged on colourful cushions. This was Troy's private training room. He'd decorated it himself: deep rich colours, lights soft, incense snaking from a burner in the corner, quiet acoustic music feeding the room from surround-sound speakers. A real sanctuary, thought Xanthe.

The others looked fairly relaxed, she observed. Jonas studied every detail, bouncing a crossed knee, leaning back with his arms keeping him upright in a slouch. Xavier whispered to Serena who smiled broadly. Dave cracked jokes and played the clown. Pierre looked bored, Gina was in a corner on her own. Mohammad looked uncomfortable, as he usually did. Madison lay back, relaxed and grinning.

Troy emerged from behind a panel, bare chested under a long, purple silk robe, which flowed around him. He wore thin, wool mid-calf trousers that lingered over the tight muscles of his legs. Xanthe tried not to stare and felt the heat rise in her face.

He floated to a kneeling position on the empty cushion waiting for him.

"Welcome! Today we learn the power of Voice." His words were rich and warm like custard. "Today we access the inner force of You and unleash it."

"Inner Force! This is dangerous, no? My Inner Force is the

Love Beast! Look out! He's coming out today!" Dave thudded his scrawny chest. The others smiled nervously and glanced at Troy, waiting to see how he would handle the interruption.

"I hope so, Dave." Troy seemed to elevate to a standing position. "Love Beast, Hate Beast, Fight Beast, Tender Beast…" He sauntered over to behind Dave. "We want to see and hear all of them." Troy squatted and said in Dave's ear, loud enough so everyone could hear, "We want those Beasts tamed, controlled." He paused looking at each of them in turn as he hovered by Dave's ear. "They will submit to our will." Troy put his hands on Dave's shoulders and pressed his knees into his lower back, forcing the smaller man to sit up straight. "But first we choose who we become. We believe that we are our own Masters. We command ourselves first." Troy patted Dave on the shoulder. "Sit up straight, feel the power and stability of your spine. See yourself as a tower. A giant. Feel the power of the Earth surge from beneath you, up through your spine and out the top of your head." Troy stood and walked around correcting each of them as they adjusted their position.

Xanthe felt herself pulse with heat when Troy's big warm hands pressed on her shoulders, his fingers adjusting her neck, lingering just a little.

They sat that way for what seemed hours while Troy lectured on self-mastery, tuning into the body's sensation, developing a heightened awareness of their tissues, tendons and the energy swirling within them.

"I want you to imagine your voice starting in your belly, growing a deep red then orange then yellow, pulling up the energy from the root of your spine through your sacrum to your solar plexus, feeling the power and force of your energy building there. Tend this fire, fan its flames, feel the heat build and build. When you feel you're ready, raise your hand to let me know. I'll tap you on the shoulder. Then let your voice be expressed in a way that feels meaningful to you."

Xanthe tried to imagine a burning fire, but all she felt was a lump of coal, stubbornly refusing to glow red.

Then she saw Serena raise her hand slowly. Serena sat tall and majestic, a sheen on her smooth pale skin. Her face was intent and relaxed. Troy walked over to her and gently touched her shoulder. Serena leapt to her feet in a deep fighter's stance, opened her eyes wide, raised her head and let out an almighty bellowing stream of non-sensical syllables.

"Oom-bella-bella-bum-ba-lah – AHHHH!"

They all jumped in response. She stared at each of them in turn with a warrior's ferocious gaze, and then threw her head back and repeated the bellow.

"Oom-bella-bella-bum-ba-lay – AYYYYY!"

Like Neptune commanding the ocean she raised her arms and cried, "Oom-bella-bella-bum-ba-loh – OHHH!

Oom-bella-bella-bum-ba-LAH, bum-ba-LAY, bum-ba-LOH – AHHH-AYYY-OHH!"

They sat stunned while Troy clapped his hands in glee.

"Fantastic, Serena! That was terrific."

Holy crap. Xanthe's heart pounded in terror. Serena was magnificent: every cell was dialled in to the full expression of her power. Xanthe felt herself wither in face of Serena's force.

"Wowee! Serena – most impressive." Madison beamed in appreciation. "Not bad for a skinny little thing! I'll go next. Serena's chant has awakened the tigress!"

Madison jumped up and also took a fighting stance. She let out a roar and raked the air with imaginary talons. The others hooted and clapped, except for Mohammad, who watched nervously.

Dave went next. He got to his feet with a little less grace, a little uncertain. But he gathered himself and screamed, fists balled at his side, neck muscles straining. He burst out laughing afterwards, delighted with himself.

"Dave – yes! Well done!"

Each followed in rapid succession, with different iterations on the theme. Gina bellowed. Pierre screeched. Xavier growled. Even Mohammad tried to bellow a resonant "Allah". Xanthe felt more and more panicked with each one. At last, it was her turn. She raised her hand cautiously. Troy touched her shoulder gently. With all the grace she could muster, Xanthe stood, planted her feet, stretched her arms high in a victory stance, took a deep breath, and let out a long raspy 'ahhhhhhh' that cracked in the middle. Her face burned with embarrassment.

Troy considered her carefully and said, "Good. Good." He turned away to take them all in. "Voice is something to cultivate. The more we access it, the cleaner and stronger it becomes. That's enough for now. Let's take a break. This afternoon we move on to fear mastery in the virtual reality chamber."

He bowed to them, and they returned the gesture. Xanthe scurried from the room, seeking fresh air, space, anywhere but this cloying, stuffy place.

CHAPTER THIRTY-FIVE

"An important aspect of the training here is to have participants
face down their darkest fantasies, the part of them so repressed
and buried that any association to themselves seems an
aberration. They need to see their shadow or be doomed to live
it out. Most people don't like this part of the training much."

TROY BRUIN, 'PERSON OF THE YEAR' INTERVIEW

New Baths of Caracalla, VR Chamber: Jonas

JONAS STARED RELUCTANTLY at the virtual reality garment. This was
what Maja had called the 'empathy suit'. It was skin-tight with a
special flexible glass visor. It was equipped with sensors everywhere
to simulate physical senses.

They were being put through multiple scenarios to learn fear
management underwater, in confined spaces and at height. Jonas
hated heights, always had. He dodged a fair amount of rigging
training on the *Sea Rover*, but his father insisted he do the minimum. He clambered up the ladders, arms shaking, brain jittery
with terror. All he remembered from those experiences was the
desperate urge to flee and the warped sensation of the ground

flying away from him. The memories hovered around him now, drumming his heart into a frenzy.

They were paired, alternating being the subject and the support. Jonas was disappointed he was paired with Xanthe. He'd lost an opportunity to build rapport with Serena, the scrumptious minx. So far she'd evaded his charms at selection, but here he could play hero and all that. Though it was probably a good thing she wouldn't see him at his weakest. Be cool, he thought, it's virtual, not real. Just don't piss your pants.

The Virtual Reality chamber was an empty space with padded walls and floor, big enough to hold five pairs. There were sensor harnesses strung up in different parts of the room. These were to help simulate resistance when required. Under the weblike harness was a multi-directional moving floor that would allow walking or running.

They entered the chamber, in nervous excitement. Troy directed them to their respective areas of the room where a staff member would look after one small group each. The staff member had comms to the pair who could only hear each other.

Troy started the briefing.

"Welcome fellow trainees! A few reminders before we begin: our team will monitor safety. Remember your fear management techniques: breathing, focus, anchoring. The brain doesn't know the difference between reality and virtual reality, so this will feel like physical reality. You need to manage your fear the same way you would do so in the physical world. Any actions you take here have consequences, biochemically. You won't *actually* fall from a skyscraper, but your brain will think you do, so it's up to you to remain calm throughout. This is what we'll need for the Moon: absolute modulation of our fear response. We need to THINK our way through a crisis, not react through it. Your fellow trainee is there to assist you, just as they will be on the Moon expedition. This is just as much an exercise of support. Okay, let's go."

Xanthe helped Jonas get into the webbing. Jonas moved his arms and lifted his knees alternatively, testing the stretchiness of it. Like a fly caught in a web, he thought. Xanthe gave him a thumbs up before she switched her face visor to virtual mode. Jonas did the same. Gradually the room view faded out, and the scenario came into focus. He was on the deck of large sailboat, at the foot of the main pole, where the ladder was. The ground started to sway under him, just as if he were on a ship. He could feel the warmth of the sun and the breeze of the ocean on his face. The smell of salty air was vivid.

"This is amazing!" Xanthe said. "I've never been on a tall ship before!" She looked around, taking in the details of the scenario, stumbling a little, getting used to the rocking sensation. "Geez that rigging is high."

"Yeah." Jonas said flatly, his pulse hammering.

"You ready?" Xanthe clapped him on the back. "Let's do it."

Jonas's adrenaline surged and needles of panic jabbed at him. Breathe, you bastard, breathe! He took deep breaths and paced back and forth at the bottom of the ladder. He stood still, drove his feet into the ground, hands on hips, and breathed slowly and smoothly. Gradually his heart rate slowed.

"Good job, Jonas!"

He glanced at Xanthe. Great, just what I need, Miss Congeniality. He took hold of the ladder. It felt so damn real! He knew it was the sensors creating resistance in the shape of a ladder rung, but damned if he could tell the difference.

"Just one step at a time."

One foot went on, then another. He focused on the ladder. Each rung became his whole world. One foot, then another. One hand up, then the next. His peripheral vision caught sight of the deck below when he was ten metres up and his head swam. He grabbed the rungs and hugged them. Stuck. "Fuck." He breathed, chest tight. "Fuck, fuck, fuck." He trembled.

"Hey Jonas!" Xanthe's voice seemed to come from a long, long way away. "How are you doing?"

"Fabulous."

"What?" she shouted.

"Freakin' fabulous!" he yelled back.

"Good job. Keep going. You're a third of the way there."

Jonas focused on the rung that was at eye level. He noticed all of its details: worn steel, a bit of paint chipped. Ten centimetres from the main pole. He noticed the sway of the ship as a wave pulsed below. He knew it would only get more exaggerated the longer he waited and the higher he went. He just had to keep moving.

He felt a dribble of sweat sneak down his back, soaking into the suit. The observers would notice this. He had to get control – this was a make-or-break activity. If he couldn't control his fear here in simulation, he was a liability on a Moon mission. No room for fear to take over. And there would be a lot of height work there, setting up antennas, working on the habitat roofs, any number of things. Maja and Claire had badgered him with these requirements.

Claire in particular had emphasised the working-at-height rule. "There's no getting round this one, Jonas. You either pass the heights test or you don't move forward in the training." She'd tapped the damn desk with her stumpy square finger to highlight the message. Claire had it in for him.

"Fuck it." He wasn't going to let that bitch get in the way of his career breakthrough. Breathing forcefully, he unwrapped his arms from the ladder and started moving again, trying hard not to grip too tight. He couldn't burn his muscles out now or he'd just peel off from lack of strength at the top.

One rung after another. He sensed the deck growing smaller below him, Xanthe but a speck below. Jonas was highly aware that there was no belay holding him either. He really had to manage this ladder climb without relying on any physical security. The sea air whipped around him. The sway of the pole grew more exaggerated.

Jonas felt his muscles strain to keep his balance on the steps. This giant pendulum action heaved him to and fro.

"Don't fight it, Jonas!" Xanthe's voice was a distant wisp. Good reminder, he thought. Thanks Xanthe. He focused on the rhythm of the sway and timed his steps so that he stepped up at the zenith of the swing, sank with the fall of it, stepped up again at the top, and moved with the sway to the other side.

The sky darkened around him as the program fed a storm into the scenario. The wind blew hard in his face. How did they do that? The thought skittered like a cockroach in the corners of his brain. He kept to his step, swing, step. The ship began to pitch and roll, no more steady swing. Jonas focused on bracing his legs as he adjusted to the new rhythm. From down on the decks he heard the urgent shouts of the crew members. This is amazing programming. "Shut up." He said aloud to his inner voice. He was another thirty rungs from the top. He glanced up and saw the small platform he was aiming for. It was tiny. Just big enough for two feet. He dared not glance down.

The wind tore at him, little pellets of rain hit his body. He even felt them on his face! The sensors were so vivid. Up he climbed. His legs started to tremble. The boat lurched with a large gust. He grabbed at the rungs, losing his grip as his body was flung sideways. He hung on with one hand as his feet slipped from the rungs. He scrambled for the ladder, flailing mid-air, dangling from his right hand. His feet banged against the rungs of the ladder, and he managed to hook his right toe under the rung. He had just enough strength to reach his left hand out to the rungs, fingers slipping against the wet metal. The boat pitched again, and he grabbed the mast with his thighs, straddling it. His right foot found a rung, and he wrapped himself to the ladder, like a cat climbing a tree. His fingers like claws, white from the strain. He felt the blood drain from his face. He leant his forehead against the rungs as the boat rolled and swayed, thunder sounded, and the wind brushed

216

him first from one angle and then another. Jonas felt a sob lurch from his chest.

He heard Xanthe's muffled voice, straining to reach him against the wind. "Fuck this." Jonas felt the anger and terror wash through him in rapid succession. He thought again of Claire's judgemental pinched face and channelled some of his resentment. No way are you winning, you sour-faced witch.

"You got this. You got this." That will show them. He knew they would record everything he said, so he might as well give them a good show.

His hands were cold and aching, but he looked up, reached for another rung, pulled himself up, then again. At last, he was just below the platform. He did the final few steps in quick succession and stood on the last rung, gasping. He stepped on to the platform, slick with virtual rain, and lost his footing. His feet dangled either side of it as the ship pitched again. His legs were battered by the platform. Feeling his grip losing strength, Jonas emitted an almighty guttural growl and heaved his legs skyward and jammed them on to the platform, his lips pressed against the metal rung.

He just had to ring the bell. It hung above him, behind his head. He had to turn around and face the world below to ring it. Having come so far, his strength waning, Jonas jammed his body against the ladder. He looped his right arm between the ladder rung and the ship's mast, and slowly pivoted his feet in a small circle. The ocean stretched all around him, the sky dark with clouds moving with the fierce wind. He swayed with the ship, the horizon dipping and rising. Jonas felt his stomach lurch and he swallowed hard, forcing the sensation back. The bell dangled in a taunt in front of him. Somewhere below Xanthe was shouting. He took a deep breath, made sure his right arm was firmly jammed, and imagined his feet were giant magnets. He stretched, felt the bell's rope twitch between his fingers. He scrambled at it, got his third finger hooked around it, and rang the bastard!

"Fuck yeah!" he shouted.

He spun and grabbed the ladder in both arms once more. He stared at the rung in front of him and breathed forcefully, the grey, rain-spattered ladder his whole universe. He savoured the victory, felt tears well. Not now, he told himself, not now. Get down.

Jonas stepped off the platform, jamming his feet on the rungs. He moved downwards, one painstaking step at a time, firmly facing the pole. He turned into the wind, to the roll and pitch of the ship, and kept moving. He felt his shoulders cramping, his fingers gnarled, but forced himself to keep going. He hooked his arms around the ladder to give his fingers a break. Going down felt a little easier, and gradually the pitching of the ship lessened, and he could distinguish voices again.

He tuned into Xanthe's voice. She was ecstatic.

"Jonas, that was amazing! You absolute legend! Keep going!" He glanced down and saw her jumping up and down on the deck. At last, he reached the last rung, and stepped on to the deck. Xanthe leapt to him and hugged him. His knees buckled.

"Easy now." Xanthe helped lower him to the deck.

"Meant to do that," he mumbled.

"I'm sure you did!" She laughed and slapped him on the back. "Good on you! You did it."

He panted and his arms shook. He looked at her, her eyes dancing, her smile wide.

"Your turn next," he said.

"Yeah. I know." Her smile faded.

"We've got the dunk tank, right?"

"Yeah." She scowled.

"What is it?"

"I'm afraid of water."

He stared at her, chest heaving.

"Serious?"

"Yeah."

"Your last name is Waters and you're afraid of *water*?"

"Yeah," she said, despondent.

He snorted.

"Shut up, you – *jackass*! Ever since the tsunami, I freak out at the shore."

He lay down on the deck, adrenaline and relief scrambling his nervous system. He knew it wasn't right, was probably hurtful, but he just laughed and laughed.

CHAPTER THIRTY-SIX

Fear is a reminder that one very much wants to stay alive.
The trick is to lean towards life, not away from death.

ATHENA AI IN WISDOM OF THE AGES

The New Baths of Caracalla, VR Chamber: Madison

MADISON STARED AT the coffin. They'd picked her challenge well. Confinement and darkness. The dread seeped through every cell in her body. It pulled her heart up to her throat. She looked around for Gina, her partner on the challenge.

"Listen up Gina, you gotta talk me through this. I am no good in the dark. And tight spaces? Really not so good. I need you in there with me. Just keep talking to me."

Gina nodded. She brushed her black curls off her neck. Madison thought she looked a little bored.

"Damn, Gina! You're one cool customer!" Madison said.

Gina shrugged. "Small spaces don't worry me. And I like the dark. It relaxes me."

"Well, send me some of those chilled vibes when I'm in the box, if you wouldn't mind." Gina nodded again.

Madison focused on her breathing as Troy had taught them. She felt the anxiety in her chest and turned her attention there. She imagined it as a black band around her lungs. A few more deep breaths, and then she climbed the steps and lay down in the coffin.

Damn this is morbid, she thought.

Gina's face appeared above her.

"You ready, Mad Dog?"

"As ready as I'm ever gonna be."

Gina's face disappeared and then the lid of the coffin closed. She heard a clunk as Gina slid the bolt shut.

"Gina! Gina!" she cried out as the darkness took hold.

Gina's voice came to life in her headphones.

"I'm here, Mad Dog. How is it in there?"

"Dandy. Just dandy."

Madison sighed with relief. She had company. She could hear Gina. Madison squeezed her eyes shut. Just pretend you're sleeping at home. This is just like your bed. Why do they put cushions in coffins, Madison wondered. The dead don't feel discomfort.

Coffin. The word reminded her she was in a very small space with very solid walls to it. She reached out her arms to the side and knocked against the panels. She tried to reach her arms above her head, but the coffin didn't allow her to move much. She put her hands up in front of her and discovered she had a mere handspan of space between her face and the lid of the coffin. All of a sudden, she just wanted to sit up and take a deep breath. She felt a surge of energy and she contracted her abdominals and pressed her arms above her against the lid, trying to sit up and raise the lid. It did not budge.

Panic was a white fever shooting across her consciousness.

"Get me out get me out get me out!" she shouted. She pounded on the coffin lid.

"Mad Dog – you okay?" Gina's voice was distant.

Madison breathed deeply, fighting the panic as her mind raced with thoughts of oxygen running out, of them forgetting about her, about being trapped in here forever, of the image of the mummified woman she saw once in Mexico. The leathery figure of a woman who died in terror, scratching at her own coffin, having been buried alive by mistake.

Tears started to stream down her face. "Gina, Gina, talk to me, talk to me."

"I'm here Mad Dog. Stay calm. Chill out. You'll be fine."

"Yeah. Yeah." Madison gulped and breathed, felt the panic roll up her chest again, and her hands seemed to attack the lid of their own volition. She cried and hammered. She panted like a woman giving birth, and worked hard to slow her breathing.

"Gina. Talk to me."

"Okay, Mad Dog. What do you want me to talk about?"

"Anything. Say anything. Just talk to me."

There was a long pause.

"Gina? Gina? Are you there?"

"Yeah, Mad Dog. I don't know what to talk about."

"Chrissake, Gina. I'm in a freakin' coffin! Talk about anything that's not a coffin! Tell me about the room you're in."

"Okay, okay, calm down. Well, the room. I am sitting in a chair. It's red. Made of tough fabric. The room is painted deep purple, like Troy's other room. The floor is…"

Madison strained to listen. Gina's voice was fading, getting hard to hear.

"Gina? Gina? Can you adjust your audio, I can't hear that well." No response. "Gina?"

There was nothing. No sound.

Panic ripped through her like a lightning bolt. She screamed in abject terror and pounded on the walls. She was alone, stuck, and they were going to let die in here, asphyxiate. Alone. Alone. Alone.

Outside the room, Troy's team waited for a change but saw none. Her panic did not abate. Her biometrics surged to acute distress. After twenty minutes – that, for Madison, felt like a life-time – they reinstated comms and released her from the coffin. Madison sprung out of it as if electrified, wetting her pants and jumping into Gina's arms, wailing with relief.

Gina held her awkwardly. Mad Dog Madison was undone.

CHAPTER THIRTY-SEVEN

Water is a magnificent thing: it gives life and it can take it away. World designers can harness this extraordinary power, but must never take it for granted.

XAVIER CONSUS IN WORLD DESIGNERS:
PERSPECTIVE AND PRACTICE

The New Baths of Caracalla, VR Chamber: Xanthe

XANTHE SLIPPED INTO the water tank. She noticed simultaneously the coldness of the water and the warmth of her breath as it filtered in through her nostrils and out again. She clenched her jaw and then consciously relaxed it.

Jonas was there in the tank with her. They both wore SCUBA gear and could move around a little. Floating in the water was pleasant, Xanthe realised. She relaxed a tiny bit. Easy does it, she repeated to herself.

She felt her feet touch the ground and her shoulders grow heavy. They were draining the tank. She felt her body grow heavier as the water disappeared and she had to support her own weight again. The water disappeared. Her memories rushed in.

This was just like the tsunami. That sense of wonder and

curiosity as the water receded. The few moments when she thought it was just a big dumping wave pulling back from the shore. Then it kept retreating. The next terrifying moment when she realised this could only mean a tsunami. Even though this never happened in Sydney. Her brain observed the usual pattern of water movements, accessed the databank in her brain and spat out: *tsunami*. The next moment of terror when she realised how far they were from shore, how far they'd have to run. And running, tripping on the wet sand, up the beach, seeking higher ground, and then the roar behind them…

Xanthe felt the rush of water come back into the tank and knock her and Jonas to the ground. She scrambled to regain her footing but was pinned down by the force of the water. She reached out and grabbed Jonas. She had two hands clutched around his arm as the water pummelled them. This time she did not let go.

CHAPTER THIRTY-EIGHT

"I do not use drugs in my work. I use sensory enhancers.
Nothing happens for participants that wasn't there
already. The tea simply allows them to experience their
shadow self. Bringing the shadow to light in a controlled
environment is a powerful way to transform limitations."

TROY BRUIN, SCIENCE MAGAZINE INTERVIEW

The New Baths of Caracalla: Serena

THE MONTH AT Caracalla passed in a daily regime of meditation, yoga, physical conditioning and emotional management workshops. These were interspersed with the fear management scenarios. They each went through the fear management training multiple times. Madison's trips to the coffin simulator did not get any easier. Each time, the panic found its way in, no matter how much breathing and meditation she did beforehand. Serena felt a deep pity for her.

Jonas tackled height scenarios on tall buildings, tight ropes and space walks. His fear mastery improved with each one – albeit with a fair amount of cursing.

Serena peered through the crack to Troy's private training room. Intrigued, she watched him prepare for one of the last training sessions he called 'the Journey'. They dragged mattresses and blankets into the cosy warm space and loaded them with soft bright cushions. Troy lit multiple candles and dimmed the lights. The incense was a thick and heavy smog. Jugs of water, cloudy with lemon slices, sat on side tables placed near the mattresses.

The trainees entered, apprehensive. They didn't know much about the Journey, only that Troy had told them it would be 'mind-blowing'.

Troy welcomed them one at a time, hugging each of them. He was back in his purple flow robe, Serena noticed. She kneeled down on one of the cushions and waited while the others chose spots on the mattresses and cushions around the room.

"Welcome to the Journey," Troy began. He sat in full lotus position on a purple cushion. "This Journey is an exploration of your inner world. It's a chance to examine old stories of your life and make sense of them, letting them go, rewriting them or celebrating them. We want you to leave this room – this womb – feeling reborn and complete."

"Don't slip on the way out! Wombs can be messy things, I'm told." Dave said. The others smiled at his feeble attempt at humour.

"You'll each be on your own trip. But you can still help each other. Sometimes the comforting touch of a friend can help stabilise you."

"I'll need plenty of touching. Just letting you know up-front," Dave said.

Serena threw a cushion at him. He whacked it away with a grin.

Troy ignored Dave's interruptions. "The Journey is different for every person. There is no right or wrong. Just an opportunity to clear and focus."

"What can we expect?" Serena asked. She hated not knowing what was coming. She did not like to feel out of control.

"It will be a gentle easing at first. A relaxation. Just go with it and notice all your senses increase in receptivity. You may see wonderful things. You may see troubling things. Your job is to witness and experience it fully, letting the stories rise and pass. The whole journey will take four hours or so. There is water nearby – make sure you stay hydrated throughout. I'll get the tea now and we will begin the ceremony."

He stood with lithesome ease and retreated to a small kitchen at the back of the room. He returned with a small Japanese tea pot with matching cups. He placed it in the middle of the room.

"Zeus, play the Journey." Zeus was the AI programmed for the training room. The sound of haunting flute music filled the room. "Zeus, a little softer please."

Troy poured tea into each cup. His movements were slow and precise, mesmerising. Serena noticed how exquisite his gestures were. Troy was a big muscular man, yet each gesture was controlled and graceful. Not dainty. She had the sense of watching an artist paint with one bristle.

Troy lifted the tray and offered it, one by one, to each of them.

"Please drink all of it."

"Bottom's up!" Dave said and thew the liquid down his throat with a nervous smile.

Serena stared at the dark murky liquid with its feather of steam. She brought it to her lips and smelled the earthiness of it. She took a sip and winced at the bitterness. She swallowed and then sipped some more. The warmth of it slid through her belly. She drained the remainder and placed the empty cup on the side table nearby. She sat on her cushion, waiting. She felt nothing.

The others settled back on the mattresses, or lay on the floor, heads propped on pillows. Dave was whispering to Jonas, lying on the floor, propped on an elbow. Jonas lay on his back, laughing, with Pierre next to him. Xanthe took up space on another mattress, eyes closed, in corpse pose. Gina was on her own as usual.

Madison lay near Mohammad who looked relaxed for a change. Serena caught Xavier's glance, and he crawled over to her, across the mess of cushions.

"Mind if I hang with you?" he asked.

"Sure." The music piped and lilted.

After a moment she asked, "Notice anything?"

"*Un peu.* I feel woozy. Like my arms and legs are turning to melted cheese." He lay back and grabbed a cushion to put under his head. "You?"

"Not yet." She chewed her lip.

"Why don't you lay down on the mattress? It might help you relax." He patted the mattress next to him.

She shuffled over to the mattress and lay down. She noticed the incense seemed to grow thicker. It was cloying and sickly sweet. She sat up again and poured herself a glass of water.

"Want some, Xavier?"

Xavier's eyes were closed, his face relaxed and blissful.

"*Non, merci.* I'm good."

Serena drank the cool lemony water and felt the liquid streak through her. Her arms felt heavy. She settled back on the mattress, eyeing the others. Dave was lying down giggling with Jonas and Pierre. Everyone else seemed out of it. Troy sat on his cushion in lotus position, back upright, observing them.

Serena closed her eyes. She felt the weight of her arms sink into the mattress. She could hardly move them. Her legs too – they felt like cement blocks. Everything felt dark and heavy. She took a deep breath, trying to find space in her body. Her chest felt like it had a weight on it.

Colours erupted in her vision, she tried to open her eyes, but they stayed leaden and shut. Like an Egyptian mummy, she thought. I'm being prepared for the journey to the underworld. She had the feeling of being sucked through a tunnel. Jackals snarled and lunged at her as she flew along the tunnel. She saw screaming children, the rush of water, the roar as buildings collapsed. She was back on the docks when the water rushed in and took her friend, snatching her in its watery jaws, and there was her neighbour reaching out to her, beckoning, and the building collapsing on top of him, snuffing him out in a cloud of dust, and then there were faces, taunting and cruel, the big kid with his dirty jeans stealing her muffin at the refugee camp and pushing her aside. Devon's face loomed too. He smiled with a golden tooth and held out his hand, but his fingers were snakes hissing and striking at her, and she was running, hiding, finding a corner in the rubble where no one could hurt her, no one could leave her, no one could find her. She cowered in the darkness, alone, so alone. There was no one for her. No one with her. Alone in the darkness. And the jackals came again, hunting her, snapping at her. They came with the heads of women who spat at her and clawed at her, trying to rake her eyes, her hair, her clothes. She stumbled away from them, but they kept coming. She fell and curled into a ball, hearing their taunts and growls, waiting for the attack.

"Serena! Serena!" The voices slithered around her, hissing.

"Serena! Serena! You're okay!" Another voice, a man's voice, muffled like she had cotton wool in her ears.

"Serena – listen to my voice. I've got you. You're okay."

Who was that? Was it Patrick? She listened for his voice again, hoping for the man's big hand to reach down and pull her into the light like he had so many years ago.

It wasn't Patrick. He wasn't there. She buried her head and covered her ears, trying to block out the hissing jackal heads.

"Serena, it's Xavier. Can you hear me? I've got you! You hear me? You're fine." His voice poked through the cotton wool that seemed to block her ears. Serena noticed a hand on her back. She tensed, waiting for a blow, waiting for an assault.

"No no no!" she cried.

"It's okay, Serena. You're safe. I won't hurt you."

The hand stroked her, warm, gentle.

She focused on the hand as it moved in a circle on her back, soothing. The voice came again.

"Serena, it's Xavier. You're okay. You're in the training room. Come back."

She felt the gentleness of his hand flow through her, like cream stirred in a soup. She relaxed a little. She noticed her hands clenched in a ball around something. A cushion? She felt her awareness come back to her body. She unclenched her hands and realised she was huddled on the mattress, head buried in cushions. The back of her neck was drenched in sweat.

She heard the flute music, mournful. She heard Xavier's voice again, clear now, close.

"That's it, Serena, come back. You're safe. I've got you."

She felt him kneeling beside her. His arm came around her. His face near hers, his breath on her cheek.

"I've got you. You're okay. Trust me."

The word was like a mallet. It smashed down on her awareness, scattering the jackals back into the shadows. She fell to the side, but Xavier was there, holding her.

"Easy now, I've got you." She opened her eyes, and his face was fuzzy. She closed them again and breathed deeply. The incense filled her senses, but this time it was cleansing. It swept the rubble and wash of the tsunami from the room. She opened her eyes again and rolled to face Xavier. He was lying down next to her now, face to face.

"Welcome back," he said, his eyes concerned. "You had quite the trip! Where did you go?"

She took a breath and looked at him. "To hell. Where I've been for quite some time." The tears spilled from her. Xavier held her close and let her weep, nestled against his neck.

"It's okay. We've got this. We've got this."

❦

Gina let the tea take her quickly. She closed her eyes, and the room quickly became the canopy of the open road as she sped along on a motorbike. She felt the rush of air, the thrum of the bike, the surge of adrenaline as she went faster, faster, faster. The bike was magic, hurtling around hairpin bends, climbing mountain passes, shooting to valleys below. The exhilaration saturated her consciousness.

Then the voice whispered somewhere at the back of her brain.

"What are you doing? Where are you going?"

Shut up, she told it.

"Who are you?"

Shut up. Leave me alone.

"You can't run forever," it said.

Yes, I can.

"You can't outrun who you really are, Gina."

The bike hit something and suddenly she was soaring into the sky. Then plunging back to Earth. The ground was fast coming into focus. She had a strange lurching sensation and she smashed headfirst into the ground. She lay there conscious of her hammering heart, the heaviness of her body as it lay on what felt like hard asphalt. She thought she smelled the acrid burn of rubber and petrol. She pushed herself to her feet and looked down at what had brought the bike to a sudden stop.

It was a body. A woman. Long curly hair matted with blood. Gina knew who it was even before she bent to roll it over. The body flopped over, and she stared into her own bruised and battered face.

"You did this," the voice said.

I know.

"How long are you going to deny it?"

As long as I can.

"Admit it. Your sister is dead because of you."

The words grabbed Gina and flung her back to a different time. Two little girls, dressed in the same white frilly dresses, blue satin ribbons holding their black curly hair back from their round faces.

"Bellissima! Angela!" Their mother and father preening over the little girls. But one was smiling, and the other was scowling. One little girl twirled and paraded for the parents. The other pulled the ribbon from her hair and flung it to the ground and stamped on it.

The scowling one yelled at her parents. "But I don't want to go to the party! I want to play with Eduardo and Riccardo. They are riding bikes to the beach and—"

The father reached over and slapped her across the face.

"Good girls don't ride with boys. Good girls wear dresses and go to parties."

Gina felt the sting on her face and down to her gut all over again.

The smiling girl pulled a face at her sister and Gina felt herself again in that seven-year-old body, lurching at her sister, hitting her, biting her, trying to ruin her perfect beauty, trying to punish her for the trap her parents held her in. And there she was at the top of the stairs again, pinching and shoving her sister, and then the long wail, the arms flailing, and the beautiful, shocked little face tumbling backwards, so slowly, and the horrible crack and silence that followed, forever.

Gina ran from the house, jumped on her bike and kept riding. She was still riding from the shadows.

"When are you going to face it?"

Maybe never.

Gina felt herself pulled into a dark room, alone with the voice. The pit of her stomach was a lead balloon that shortened her breath.

"Gina. It's time."

Not yet.

"Gina. Gina." It was someone else's voice reaching through the darkness.

There was a hand in hers. For a moment she felt a connection, a warmth. Something she had not felt since… well, since *before*.

She opened her eyes, and it was Pierre.

"*Salut!*" he said. "*Bon voyage?*"

She pressed her palms to her face and sat up. "No. You?"

"*Formidable!* I was an artist and a surgeon making great sculptures out of different animal parts." Gina looked horrified. He laughed. "It was *magnifique!* Trust me, Gina, there is sometimes great beauty in the grotesque."

CHAPTER THIRTY-NINE

Troy Bruin loves to dance. He sees it as a fundamental
human experience. Plus, he's a show off.

XAVIER CONSUS, WORLD DESIGNERS MAGAZINE

The New Baths of Caracalla: Xanthe

THEIR MONTH OF training was finally over. Xanthe felt relieved. It had taken every ounce of her courage to show up each day and face down her fears and her tumultuous emotions. She had also worked hard to build relationships with her colleagues.

She felt a grudging respect from Jonas, especially with her support of him through the various challenges. He'd done a decent job of supporting her, too. The water tanks had tested all of her emotional fortitude. The grief from the tsunami remained sunk in her deepest depths. Somehow, she managed to push it down every time it threatened to bob to the surface.

Xanthe enjoyed the easy friendliness of Dave. He was upbeat and fun. He seemed to know himself well – foibles and weaknesses accepted, he exuded a quiet confidence in most things. He enjoyed all the activities with good-natured jibing. He was easy to be around, Xanthe thought.

Xavier was a different kettle of fish. Arrogant and hard. All task focused. Except when it came to Serena. Xanthe wondered at their friendship. Xavier was a dedicated family man with a longstanding relationship and two daughters back home. His relationship with Serena was not sexual, as far as Xanthe could tell. It was more like brother and sister. It was interesting to see a man engage with Serena without being affected by her beauty. It was interesting too, Xanthe thought, to see Serena disarmed by the platonic friendship. She seemed almost vulnerable around Xavier.

Serena. Xanthe thought she had her simmering resentment of her father's lover under control, but she realised, with a sense of bitterness, that there was also a tinge of jealousy. Serena's looks, her brash confidence, her biting directness. It was hard to hold her own next to this electric ball of female power. So, Xanthe avoided her where she could.

Then there was Troy. Xanthe fought her attraction around him. Her body failed to comply with her directives, and she felt heat run through her anytime he was near. It was frustrating. She had a life – a good life – with Simon. This man, this strutting, hard-bodied hulk hijacked her senses anytime she was near him. Xanthe tried hard to keep a professional distance between them. Was he genuinely interested in her? she wondered. He was smooth and flirtatious with all of them – men and women alike. He seemed to enjoy seduction in all its forms. She thought again of the kiss she had witnessed between Troy and Claire. So many boundaries had been crossed in that incident. Why had she not spoken up?

Overall, Xanthe felt ready for the next stage of training. They were off to Xavier's Terra Verdi the next day. They had a few weeks there to learn the advanced food production techniques his team were pioneering, and that they would use in the Simulation Hub, or SimHub as they'd been calling it. Xanthe was looking forward to a change of pace. Less deep, personal reflection and more tangible, practical skills.

In the meantime they had the dance party. Troy had billed it as the final challenge. A true liberation of the senses, a chance to be fully self-expressed and free. Xanthe felt only quiet discomfort at the pending ceremony.

They gathered for the event outside Troy's private training room, dressed in loose clothing as instructed. The doors flew open of their own accord, revealing the room transformed again, this time into a sultry lounge. Music pulsed in the background.

Troy reclined on a high-backed fuchsia empire chair elevated on a small makeshift stage, leaning an elbow on the plush armrest. He wore a loose, white linen shirt over his taut, firm chest. His clothes allowed his animal-hard physique to shift in smooth, relaxed movements. His pale blue eyes were made more mesmerising by the kohl he had fashioned around them, Egyptian style.

He stood, or rather seemed to rise, from his chair and stepped down from the pedestal to greet them. Each movement had a slow, relaxed gait, like a tiger assured of its power and strength.

"Hello, dear friends," he said, smiling with his slow, lopsided grin. "It's time to party. It's your opportunity to feel free and enjoy yourselves. Let your bodies move in whichever way feels good to you. Let yourself be transported, transformed. To assist you, we have my personal freedom tea blend." He gestured to the stand-up table where he had his Japanese tea service laid out, waiting for them.

"Again with the tea!" exclaimed Dave. "What's in this one?"

"You know I never reveal my secrets," Troy said slyly. "Don't worry, this tea is perfectly harmless. It simply lowers personal barriers, if you let them. All you have to do is go with it."

"Oh, I always go with it," Dave said. "And after it. Your tea makes me pee. A lot."

"I think you will sweat it out dancing, this time," assured Troy.

"Then, let's do it, no? I love a good dance!" Dave grabbed his cup and tossed back the fluid. He grimaced. "Couldn't you make it taste nice? My God, it is like arse of a dog."

"You had much experience with that?" said Jonas, as he swigged his own tea.

"Not lately! And I hope never again!" Dave was already moving to the music and beaming ear to ear. "By God I love to dance!" he said.

"Then it's time we let the Love Beast out and dance up a storm!" Troy said. "Zeus, play the Odyssey." The AI responded and switched music tracks.

Doof doof doof doof. The music was a staccato jabbing. It thrashed through the air, dominating all other sound and movement. It stretched and latched onto bodies in a sticky frenzy.

Xanthe felt the music pierce her tissues and wrap around her spinal cord. It throbbed. It squeezed the length of her spine, birthing a snake of fear from the base of her back, along her vertebrae. It moved with the beat, slithering anxiety into her chest cavity. She trembled. Her arms and legs seemed to move of their own volition, and she hoped the movement would disperse the panic that seemed to strangle her nerve endings.

The tea-imbued trainees swung their bodies against the rhythm, being wrung from the inside out by the frenzied beat. Their hearts raced, trying to metabolise the tea's stimulants as sound thrashed their nervous systems. Serena and Xavier linked hands and twirled each other like kids in a playground. Jonas was in a corner on his own, mixing dance moves with martial arts. Dave laughed and spun, hopping and flailing like a puppet with elastic tethers. Pierre tried to drag Gina to dance but she stood sullen against the walls. Mohammad was doing a bit of a shimmy with Madison's loud encouragement. Xanthe fought the beat as it thudded through her, straining her senses. She caught sight of Troy.

He smiled and arched his back in a stretch as the music pounded the room. "Zeus, turn it up." The drumbeat grew louder.

Xanthe felt strange as she watched him. It was as if she could feel what was happening inside his body, not just hers. She felt the music reach down into Troy's chest, filling his lung space with vibration. "Louder," he said. The beat throbbed downwards into his groin. He moved his head in time to the beat, felt his feet thud in response. He sang along to the lyrics, allowing the words to thunder in his chest and out into the room. He swung his arms around his hips, allowing the music to move his body in a grind to the beat. His body felt electric. He whirled and stomped, a physical expression of the song, giving it life, bringing it into being. He became Odysseus. The legend took form, a giant in the room, an integrated pulse of sexual energy, electrifying and torrid. Troy was slick with sweat, his muscles taut and straining, as if a nest of serpents were wrestling to bust free from the membrane of his skin.

Xanthe was moving too, transfixed by the experience of being inside Troy's body, of feeling his energy pure and free-flowing. Suddenly, she was aware of her own body. She felt herself being sucked back into her own form. It was moving, straining to be released from the clamps her mind had put on it. The darkness that was sunk deep inside threatened to burst from its moorings, to bubble up and explode to the light.

Xanthe keeled over, holding tight to the dark stone in her stomach, forcing it back down into the cold blackness. Her body racked with shivers and drenched with sweat. She felt sick. Her dance was over.

CHAPTER FORTY

*I have often marvelled at the power of language. One
word spoken can change the course of everything.*

MAJA GARCIA, THE JOURNALS

The New Baths of Caracalla: Xanthe

TROY FOUND XANTHE the next day in one of the grounds' meditation corners, under an enormous oak tree. He sat down beside her.

"How are you? I noticed you had some trouble with the tea
last night," he said delicately.

Xanthe kept her gaze on a swirl of starlings just visible beyond
the Baths' towering arches. "I'm alright," she said quietly.

He waited for more. When she said nothing, he continued. "It
seems you have a lot on your mind. Your body is trying to speak
it out. Won't you share with me? It helps to release when we say
what we carry within."

She shook her head. She felt the nearness of him, the heat of
his body, in the space between them.

"Xanthe, I care about you, deeply. I admire your commitment
to the project. I love your vision for humanity." He moved so he

could look her more fully in the face. She could feel something different about his attentions. It was lust, yes, but something more. Something dangerous. He reached to take her hand in his.

"Don't." Xanthe pulled away. The sexual energy clung to them in the torpid afternoon. Xanthe saw the future that would unfold before her if they dared utter the words, giving their feelings form and substance. She wasn't prepared for that shift in direction, the radical falling away of trust with Simon, the irreparable chasm this enlivening would bring to her existing relationship. She could see and anticipate the pain that such a birthing would bring – with no guarantee of happiness – hanging a word away from being spoken into existence.

No, that world would have to lay dormant, alive elsewhere in an alternate universe, and not this one, not now. She let the unsaid drift on the emotions' currents, grieving what might have been, grieving the unmade.

CHAPTER FORTY-ONE

The history of humanity is the history of food. Once we got past
survival, into hunting and gathering, and then into mechanism
farming, only then did we free up resources for other pursuits.
Technology gave us mass food production, and food gave us freedom.

XAVIER CONSUS IN WORLD DESIGNERS:
PERSPECTIVE AND PRACTICE

Terra Verdi: Jonas

JONAS WAS EAGER to get to Terra Verdi following the intense training at Caracalla. Xavier's man-made island enterprise was not far
from Naples. Their mission was to taste-test the food supplies on
offer for the SimHub. They would be selecting from tried-and-true
space food, as well as Terra Verdi's pioneering new products. They
would also learn how to set up and maintain the food production
system, essential for the future Moon development.

Xavier led his colleagues to Terra Verdi's showcase hall. It was a
high-ceilinged glass rotunda with trays of green plants stacked to the
top in carefully monitored micro-ecosystems, specifically tailored
to the individual plant's requirements. Each plant received just
the right amount and wavelength of artificial light. Temperatures

were regulated carefully by highly sensitive equipment reporting all performance and environmental feedback to a central monitoring system. Each food tray had recycled water dripped to exact specifications. With their analysis and decades-long studies, Terra Verdi had managed to increase yields by a whopping fifty percent for some food varieties. Raspberries were Xavier's favourite. He had them stacked for easy access here in the rotunda as he passed through. Jonas snuck a few when he wasn't looking. Delicious!

The real game changer, though, was the seaweed protein products. In their high-security secret laboratory, Xavier's scientists produced the most astounding, delicious plant-based meat replacements that no one could distinguish from real meat. Never mind that few people remained who had actually tasted real meat, these days. Land was in such high demand from climate refugees and other industries, that animal production on a mass scale had all but folded in recent years. Real meat, produced from live animals, remained an exorbitant, hard-to-find product, only for the wealthy. The remaining producers clung to their farms, fiercely defending their last land rights after having much of it annexed by governments wishing to eliminate refugee shanty towns and settle people permanently. Xavier's Green Meat had arrived just at the right time, giving various governments the leverage to reclaim land that was no longer needed for meat protein production. It could all be grown at sea on the various Green Meat algae sea farms, or on the floating worlds. Real meat was now a high-end luxury item, out of reach for the general consumer. Xavier did well in this market, too. His family had been land farmers for generations, and he inherited the property, greatly reduced after the land repossessions, but still managing a productive and sustainable piggery. His father had the foresight twenty years before the rise in sea levels and global temperatures to invest in a small plant-based startup enterprise. This eventually became Terra Verdi, with a research and production base on one of Gaia Enterprises' first archipelago projects, designed by none other than Troy Bruin. Troy and Xavier continued as friendly rivals, both being stellar graduates.

Here in the rotunda, Jonas stared up at the impossibly high vertical stacks and the vibrant greenery clinging to every visible space. The air was humid and earthy in a way that Jonas had never experienced. They had a small Terra Verdi farm on the *Sea Rover* but nothing on the sheer scale of this! And this was just the showcase room.

Jonas's reverie was broken as Xavier called out to him. Jonas always felt an instinctive self-consciousness about his own poor looks around men like Xavier. Xavier was a giant of a man, broad and muscular, handsome with smooth black skin and startling brown eyes under heavy black brows. As always, Jonas tried to stand a little taller. He channelled his martial arts sensei and anchored his feet. He felt a trickle of confidence come back to him.

"Jonas! You and Gina will spend special care with the waste management system since you are the engineer specialists for our project. Serena and Pierre will also look to this as part of the life support specs." Xavier emphasised their respective roles ahead of their intensive immersion at Terra Verdi. "Madison, Gina, Mohammad, Xanthe and Troy – you will need to know the ins and outs of food production set-up and maintenance. Can't have me being the only person who knows what to do."

The tour seemed to go on forever and Jonas was fascinated the whole time. Endless corridors packed with plants of all varieties, drippers, lights, sprays. Automated harvesters came through for product collection. Staff in green uniforms hurried past, nodding at Xavier, and he greeted each of them by name, with a friendly cheer. Xavier picked produce as he went, offering samples to Jonas and the others. Jonas was amazed at the taste and vibrant green colour of all the plants. These were just the in-house staff supplies. The export products were in another tier out in the archipelago, in enormous warehouses, strictly monitored for biosecurity protocols. Jonas asked to see the Green Meat algae farms.

"Sorry, Jonas. Those areas are strictly off-limits. They are high-security research facilities with sensitive equipment and product. We need to be careful of corporate espionage. You'd be surprised what people will do for a well-guarded secret."

They circled back through the main rotunda. Xavier grabbed some raspberries for them off a nearby plant. The fruit was enormous, almost the size of a plum.

"These are my pride and joy! Genetically modified for additional sweetness and triple the size of an old-fashioned raspberry." Xavier gobbled three in quick succession. Following his lead, Jonas followed suit. He marvelled at the flavour, like distilled syrup. His mouth erupted in pleasure. He wondered at the manipulation of plants to produce such deliciousness.

"Let's go to the staff quarters. There is someone I want you to meet."

Staff quarters were designed around central hubs where employees could gather after hours. It seemed like a vibrant community. Xavier's accommodation was at the far end of the archipelago's peninsula so he could walk past and greet his employees on a daily basis, checking on community morale and any surreptitious shirking, while also maintaining a modicum of privacy. His accommodation pod was beautifully appointed with plenty of natural light and soft furnishings. A sophisticated bachelor pad. His family lived in the family home on the mainland so they could access schooling more easily.

"Ahh – there she is! Jonas, meet Sophie." Xavier reached behind a plush sofa and retrieved a little grey kitten, a blue-pointed Siamese. Sophie mewed and hung awkwardly in Xavier's big paw of a hand. "We keep cats to help with vermin. Even with all of our controls, rats and mice seem to find their way here for an easy lunch."

Jonas had never held a cat before. Pets were forbidden on the *Sea Rover* as an extra hindrance no one needed, especially in high seas. His father had been ruthless about enforcing the rules. Jonas shuddered at the memory of his father's treatment of the poor disallowed animals.

Jonas reached out to pat the little furball cradled in Xavier's hand. Sophie hissed and raked at him, a claw catching the skin on the back of his hand. He snatched it back again, smarting at the pain and rejection.

"Sorry about that. She takes a while to warm to strangers. Don't worry though, she'll come around."

Jonas sucked at his own wound, offended. He nursed his hand, still raw and irritated from the scratch, all the way back to his own room. Stupid cat! He only wanted to pat it. Nasty little beast. He added 'kitten' to his list of things he wouldn't miss if he made it to the Moon.

"May I give her a cuddle?" asked Pierre. He stretched out his hands. Xavier shrugged and held out the kitten. She hissed at Pierre and raked at him, too.

"*Putain!*" Pierre waved his hand in pain. "*Maudit tabarnak!*"

"*Mon Dieu!* That is some kind of swearing!" Xavier said. "What is it about religion that you French Canadians get so wound up about? Eh, *mon cousin?*"

Pierre bristled at that. "I am not your '*cousin*'. You French bastards are such snobs about language. Us French Canadians just have more imagination, *câlisse.*"

"If you say so, *mon petit ami Canadien.*" Xavier nuzzled the kitten and then lowered it into a big pocket on his green jacket, cooing to her.

"Careful Xavier. Pierre could make a sailor blush with his expletives!" Madison laughed.

"Battle of the frogs!" added Dave.

"Not sure the Doc would approve," Madison said, looking at Mohammad.

"*Au contraire*," Mohammad said. "I've been finding it all rather educational." And he favoured them with a small smile.

Dave and Madison stared at him, looked at each other, and burst out laughing.

"Doc! You are full of surprises!" Madison said, clapping him on the back.

The first weeks of their secondment passed in a blur. There were endless plant varieties to learn, alongside hydroponic principles, pollination, genetic modification processes – those permitted and those not – fertilisers, pests, blights, irrigation systems, equipment electronics, harvesting equipment and processes, packaging and export systems, data analysis. Jonas was intrigued by it all.

Still, he was not allowed anywhere near the top secret Green Meat section, though they were fed regularly on the results of the laboratory's experiments. Most of these were delicious, except for the Chicken Lickin, a dodgy looking meat substitute created from lichen. It was rubbery and had an aftertaste of chemicals – was it phosphorus?

Jonas grew bored. The days were rinse-and-repeat. No excursions to the mainland, no offer to check out the Green Meat project, not even a diving expedition for the oysters he knew were growing on the eastern wing of the archipelago. What a waste.

Jonas pressured Serena to join him in a sneaky after-hours dive to see if they could get some oysters. Serena was reluctant.

"That's not really allowed. Diving gear is supposed to be for equipment and facility checks only."

"That's what we're doing – checking on the east side warehouse pylons. If we happen to come across some oysters, then that's a bonus. What are you, a wimpy-ass pussy?" He punctuated his goad with a chin jut. "C'mon. We can share them with the others if you're that worried about it."

"No one calls me a wimp-ass pussy, Mr Seaborn big shot!" Jonas noticed her hesitation, but she agreed.

That night, her heart pounding, they snuck out of the dive gear room for an unapproved expedition. Down at the shoreline, they hid in the shadows.

"I'm not sure about this," she whispered.

"Too late now, chicken shit! Besides, this will only take ten minutes. No one will miss us. If anyone catches us, we can say we noticed something odd about the drippers in the spinach shed and thought it might be a problem with the waste outlet. We can say we used our initiative. They're always banging on about that." He gave her a big grin, knowing it was his most winning attribute.

"Okay let's do it."

Sure enough, there were oysters. They bundled three dozen into a net and snuck back in with no further incident, exhilarated.

"I think we should tell Xavier," Serena said as they put the dive gear away.

"Are you crazy? Why would we dob ourselves in?"

"Think about it. Oysters could be an additional product for Terra Verdi. They're growing all over the pylons, so we know they're viable. He could set up an oyster farm easy-peasy through the archipelago. He'd make a ton of money." Jonas considered this.

"Okay. Let's tell him tomorrow."

❧

The next morning Jonas sought out Xavier to tell him about the oysters. Serena found them talking excitedly in the common room of their accommodation hub.

"Serena, come and see. Jonas – The Man – Seaborn, has discovered oysters on the eastern pylons. He suggested Terra Verdi could grow these easily alongside our docks."

"Did he, now." Serena gave Jonas a death stare.

"And the quality is amazing. Here – try one." Xavier offered Serena an oyster, glistening, taunting.

"I'll pass. Thanks." She left without a word to Jonas.

"She doesn't know what she's missing," Jonas beamed.

He noticed Sophie the kitten popping her head out of Xavier's pocket. Thrilled by his recent win over Serena and now elevated as a favourite in Xavier's eyes, Jonas reached out to pat the cat. She growled and spat at him.

"You gotta work a little harder to make friends, I think Jonas." Xavier gave the kitten a reassuring stroke around the ears.

As Xavier left, Jonas whispered, "Screw you, cat."

§

Serena gave Jonas the cold shoulder for a week. He tried jokes, teases and taunts. She ignored him.

And now he had sanitation maintenance duty. With the plant-based diet, the waste was voluminous and awful. The bulky waste matter was scooped, dried and repurposed for the crops. Most of these processes were automated, but sometimes the equipment got clogged and a human had to go in and clean it out. He was now said human. For two long weeks. Crap. Jonas smiled at his own joke.

On day eleven, he was called out to the main tank. One of the filters had a split and needed to be replaced. David and Xanthe were his support crew. Xanthe lowered Jonas on a bosun's chair over the churning pond of liquid shit. Jonas tightened his gas mask but the smell still seeped in. All day, every day he breathed in shit. You'd think he'd get used to it. He double-checked his safety harness, and leant over the greeny-brown soup. He reached through the muck with his industrial gloved hand and felt the lumpy mess press against the rubber. He tried not to gag. He felt around and found the broken filter with its gaping crack widening against the pressure of the shit soup pushing past it. He worked at the clips, but they refused to budge.

"Son of a bitch!" He stretched awkwardly to get a better reach and felt himself falling forward. His safety harness strained but held as he swung free of the bosun's chair. He stabilised, calming the panic until he stopped swinging. He was now planing like Superman over the pond. He reached in again, pulling himself further into the tank to see if he could get behind the filter to loosen it. He was eye to eye with the seething shit soup, dangling in a rigid plank form to keep from dipping into the pond, eyes watering from the fumes, even with his full hazmat suit and gas mask sealing him tight. He jiggled the clips and with one mighty yank pulled the filter loose. He cheered, triumphant. He hooked it to the bosun's chair and grabbed the replacement. His abdominals burned from the strain of holding him parallel. Carefully he plunged the filter down into the mess. It slotted in nicely. Relieved the job was done, Jonas pushed away from the filter and reached out for the bosun's chair that dangled nearby.

He heard it first. A creaking tear. Then he felt the webbing in his harness give way. It burned against his hazmat suit as it slipped through the buckles, leaving a gaping tear in the rubber. He flapped in a panic for two long seconds, trying to grab the chair, the safety rope, anything – and then flopped in a full-frontal splash into the green-brown shit slurpee below. Cold, brown, lumpy fluid seeped into his suit.

Xanthe and Dave dragged him out quickly with a rescue hook, and hosed him down on the deck, keeping him a good six metres away. The stench was unbelievable!

"Jonas, you do like to make a splash, but this does seem a little bit over the top, no?" laughed Dave.

Jonas glared at him. He had to strip down naked since his suit had been breached. Xanthe hosed him down again, a crowd gathering, adding to his humiliation. Dave tossed him disposal bags and made him bundle his clothes, suit and harness into the bags. Dave hosed Jonas again before throwing him a towel and ushering him from a distance to the decontamination chamber.

Jonas spent an hour in the decontamination chamber scrubbing his hair and body with soap over and over again. When his skin was rubbed raw, he dressed in the green uniform Xanthe had left for him and exited the chamber. A cheer went up as he came through to the main sanitation entrance.

"Hey, Shitstick!" Serena laughed.

"Nice work, Poopy Pants!" Dave added.

Xanthe gave him a friendly hug. "Talk about a baptism of fire! You sure made a stir Mr Big Shot! Or should I say... Mr Big Shit?" Jonas shrugged her off and stomped off back to his room. Good-natured ribbing from others who had heard the story continued all the way back to his accommodation. Jonas felt every catchphrase as a small burning dagger. Little nicks whittling away at his self-esteem.

Jonas burned with shame and embarrassment. He was a Seaborn! Son of the two most famous world designers in history! He'd risked his life going into that pond and they had laughed at him!

Jonas arrived at his accommodation common room hub. He glared around the room, looking for some way to burn through his mortification. Seeing nothing useful, he flopped on the couch. He stared up at the skylight above, the fading light of the evening captured in the plexiglass frame. He slumped forward, head in hands, feeling the misery ooze through him. Under the lounge chair he caught a glimpse of grey fur. Cat. Loathsome pest.

Pierre arrived to interrupt his misery.

"*Salut*, Jonas."

"Hello, Pierre." Jonas said curtly.

"What's the matter with you?"

"I fell in the sewage tank."

"What – right in it?"

Jonas nodded.

Pierre guffawed. "*Ah merde! C'est dégueulasse!*"

Jonas glowered.

"Ah, come on. It's funny, *oui?*" Jonas said nothing.

"*Vraiment, mon vieux.* It's hilarious." Jonas rolled his eyes and plonked back down on the couch.

Jonas's embarrassment swamped both head heart. He had a long way to go.

CHAPTER FORTY-TWO

*There is kindness in truth, but you must be careful
how you deliver it. There is a difference between
speaking the truth and slamming it on the table.*

GAIA ENTERPRISES CODE OF CONDUCT

Terra Verdi: Xanthe

DAVID, TROY AND Xanthe were in the equipment maintenance
room, scrubbing hoses and trays. They heard voices arguing down
the hall. Serena and Xavier.

"Serena, thank you for your suggestions but you don't know
merde about food engineering. Stick to toilets and air filters."

Xanthe looked up and saw Xavier stalk past the doorway.
He'd been in a foul mood lately. Serena appeared at the doorway
looking grim and then found a spot and picked up a scrub brush
and a hose. She shrugged it off and looked around at the others,
nonplussed.

Xanthe watched her colleagues out of the corner of her eye as
she bent over a particularly mouldy piece of filtration gear. She was
also in a sour mood. Since her repudiation of Troy at Caracalla,

she felt her emotions swirling mercilessly. She knew she'd done the right thing. She did not want to start something with Troy, she was faithful to Simon. At least in deed. But it didn't help her resolve that every conversation with Simon ended with some snide remark from him about Gaia Enterprises, or a criticism of the Olympus Project, or some other admonishment. The truth was, she was sick of it. She believed in this project, she believed in the future of Earth through humanity's expansion into space. She could hold love of the planet at the same time as love for space exploration. Why couldn't he see that? Why didn't he respect her decisions? And why the hell did she just take it? She never said anything. She just let it all slide past her as if it didn't affect her. She scrubbed at the dirty filter a little harder.

Then there was Troy. Flirting outrageously with Serena and Dave. And Gina. And Madison. She berated herself for feeling jealous. She wondered about Troy. He seemed to be no substance, all sensuality. Did he have any depth to him at all?

"Xanthe! What do you think?" Serena called out to her. Xanthe glanced up. She had not been following their conversation at all.

"What do I think about what?" she said, irritated.

"About having a space fashion parade while we're in the SimHub. We can add it to the list of SimHub activities for Moon visitors."

"Yes! I have fabulous outfits that will liven up the place!" Dave exclaimed.

"I bet you do, gorgeous!" Troy added, gracing him with a glorious, suggestive smile.

Xanthe watched them and bitterness filled her gorge.

"So, what do you think, Xanthe?" Serena was trying hard to engage her.

"What do I think? I think that is a ridiculous idea that reinforces stereotypes and the lamentable social obsession with physical appearance. It is vacuous and superficial. Much like those who propose it." She said the last, not quite under her breath.

The words ripped through the room and stunned them to silence. Xanthe studied the filtration device, scrubbed it a little more, then chucked it in the clean bucket.

Serena walked over and squatted next to her.

"What the hell is up with you?" Serena demanded in a low voice.

"Nothing is up with me," Xanthe said. She worked hard to keep venom from her voice but failed.

"That was a nasty remark and uncalled for. We're trying to create a fun environment. That doesn't mean it's superficial."

Xanthe said nothing. She picked up another pipe to clean and inspected it. Shame and resentment swirled through her. She did not trust what would come out of her mouth next.

Serena stared at her a little more, then stood and resumed her cleaning station with a huff. She rolled her eyes at Dave who shrugged his shoulders and carried on cleaning.

Troy watched it all with a considered look. After a few minutes of silent scrubbing, he approached Xanthe and sat down on the bench next to her.

"Hey," he said.

Xanthe glanced at him and said nothing.

"Are you okay?" he asked.

"Just fine, thanks."

"It's just that you don't seem yourself today," he said and put his hand on her back.

Xanthe flinched and moved away.

"I told you, I'm fine."

"You sure don't seem like it."

"What is it to you, anyway?" Xanthe said in exasperation. "You swan around, oozing and flirting with everyone, like a moth going from one warm flame to another. Is that all you're after? A bit of slap and tickle? Anyone will do?" Xanthe regretted her words instantly, but too late. They were boiling up from deep within her.

Troy looked at her and considered his response. "I care about all of us on the Olympus Project. I care about all people. I have plenty of love for all," he said.

"Is that what you tell yourself?" Xanthe said. "Because from where I stand it looks a lot like hedonism. Radical self-obsession. All physicality, no intimacy. No real emotion beyond basic primal urges. You have no, no…" she searched for the word, "depth." The emotion spilled over, and she covered it with anger, telling herself she was right, but feeling guilty for it anyway.

She glanced at Troy. She saw something in his eyes she had not seen before. He was about to say something when Jonas and Madison burst into the room. They stopped in their tracks as they sensed the tension.

"Whoa. Who died?" asked Madison.

"Xanthe's self-restraint," said Dave. "Look out, she is speaking truths with a sledgehammer today."

Xavier appeared in the doorway again. He considered the group, which seemed off-colour and awkward, then decided to push on. "Listen up. We have a problem. Spaceward Bound has announced today they are producing Eco Meat for their Olympus Project bid."

"And so?" Serena asked.

"It looks and sounds a lot like Green Meat. Either some *trou du cul* has shared our proprietary process, or those imbeciles have somehow managed to move ahead of us in food production. I am ordering a complete lock down of Terra Verdi while we investigate. This will take some time to consider. In the meantime, we will need to move quickly and get onto the next stage of our project. We have enough experience and training to start building the SimHub. I say we call the Directors and ask them to make the final cut. We need to get going. We can take some of the research with us and continue the project during the SimHub build." The others nodded, grateful that something had come up to distract from the tension with Xanthe.

"No way are those pieces of *merde* at Spaceward Bound going to beat us on this tender!"

"Hear, hear!" said Dave.

Xanthe kept her head down, her face burning. Shame filled her. She knew lashing out at Serena and Troy had nothing to do with them. Not really. She was failing to process her emotions as they had been taught at the Baths of Caracalla. This kind of petty outburst, even laced with truth, did not serve. She would have to do better.

CHAPTER FORTY-THREE

*They were drunk. Not on power, but on the fear that drives
us to do the unspeakable in the name of self-protection.*

CORONER'S REPORT, THE TERRA BLANCA TRAGEDY

Gaia Enterprises Desert Base: Maja

MAJA SHUFFLED DOWN the corridor of the desert base headquarters. She paused, leaning against the wall. The pain was getting worse, making walking a constant challenge. She just needed to hang on a little longer. They had the space engineering training and then the simulation exercise to get through. This was the essence of the pitch for the Lunar Moon mission. They needed to get this right, or they lost out. And with that, the future of Gaia was on the line.

The pain eased and she made her way to the headquarters room. Claire and Huw were waiting for her.

Maja sank into one of the big leather chairs and poured herself a glass of water. It was so damn hot. The cooling mechanisms were at capacity, but they had been built to tolerate an Earth that was much cooler and less volatile.

"Where are we up to?" Maja asked.

"We're working out the final group for the simulation." Claire brought up the hologram images of the trainees.

"What are you thinking?' Maja asked.

"I'm in two minds. Either we combine for dynamics, or we combine for skill."

"And commercial success overall," Huw added. "The Commission is going to consider value for money too. We might have the best design but if it blows the budget, forget it." Claire nodded.

"That's where it gets a little tough. The most skilled candidates aren't the best mix of people, there's fireworks there. It's a long time to be in a pressure situation – twelve months in close quarters. And then the trip to the Moon if our bid wins. They've got to get along." Claire chewed a fingernail as she stared at the candidates.

"What's your first choice look like – the skills-based mix?" Maja asked.

Huw jumped in. "My skills mix are the three designers of course. Xavier, Xanthe and Troy plus Pierre on life support tech. Madison as pilot. We disagree about the engineer."

"Not *just* the engineer," Claire interjected.

"Explain your rationale, Huw," Maja said.

"Pierre is the best life support technician. And Madison is the best pilot. Simple."

"So far so good. Claire, what are your concerns?" Maja asked.

"Xavier complained about Pierre. Said he mistreated his kitten. I don't like that."

"What happened?" Maja asked.

"It's hard to tell. Xavier has been very distracted with the possible corporate espionage issue. He's been critical of everybody. But still, there's no smoke without fire. Pierre's animal experiments are concerning."

"Who's the alternative again? Serena?"

"Yes. And that's the next problem. It's Serena and Xanthe. They are long-time rivals. I think this could be a real pressure cooker.

Selection really highlighted their differences, and they haven't built any bridges since."

"This could be their chance to mend things. They're both mature young women. Often rivals end up being allies." Claire considered this. "That leaves one spot. We've got up to six places for the pitch. Who is the last person?"

"This is another issue where we can't agree," Claire said.

"Oh?" Maja asked.

"I want Jonas," Huw declared.

"And I want Gina," Claire countered.

"Why Jonas?" Maja asked, inwardly delighted. Her hypothesis about Jonas was proving right. They had pushed the trainee's buttons, and he had responded and evolved. Their processes were causing human development, just as she intended. But she wanted to hear it from one of the others rather than having to point it out herself.

Huw jumped in. "Primarily, it's the Seaborn name. It carries heft and I think it will add the commercial edge we need. But it's also a practical choice: Jonas is actually quite good at design and a very good engineer," Huw tapped his finger on the table to emphasise the point.

"Maja, you know I've had reservations about Jonas right from the start. He's the biggest risk we have. He has nowhere near the emotional maturity of the others. He drags things backwards!" Claire said, exasperated.

"Has he shown progress through the training?" Maja asked.

"Yes. I suppose he has," Claire grudgingly admitted.

"The reports say he nailed the VR simulations at Caracalla. Xavier says he shows an aptitude for the hydroponics. He's even made a friend in Xanthe." Huw was animated. Maja glanced at him. Her friend was digging in on his point.

"What exactly do you see is the risk here, Claire?" Maja asked.

Claire searched for the right words to express her concern.

"I think it's his opportunist side. It's very active, always close to the surface. I just don't think that twelve months in a contained environment, trying to deliver as a team, is going to be the best environment for him."

"How do his engineering skills compare with Gina's?" Maja asked, still hoping Claire would make the decision.

"His are better," she admitted.

"Is it possible he might rise to the occasion?" Maja prodded.

Claire held Maja's gaze. "I know where you're going with this Maja. You want Jonas. You've been hell-bent on proving we can cause development by design since we first looked at selection candidates, but—"

"You *don't* believe we can cause development by design?" Maja interrupted, quick as a whip. This principle was at the heart of the Gaia philosophy. She knew she had caught Claire in a bind.

"Yes. Of course, I do. You know that." Claire was flustered now, realising she'd contradicted her own beliefs.

"And so?" Maja was giving her one last chance to make the call.

"There's just something not quite right. Call it an instinct. Intuition."

"Is that enough to scrub him from the SimHub crew? Where he might in fact rise to the occasion?" Maja knew she'd nailed it now.

"No. No, I suppose it's not." Claire looked dejected. "But if we are going with Jonas in the SimHub, I'm stating my concerns for the record." She met Maja's gaze with a new determination. Maja was surprised at the steel in her eyes. She hadn't seen that in Claire before. Not just disagreement and disappointment, but defiance. Interesting.

"Concerns noted. Jonas will either live up to expectations, or not. I am betting on his better nature," Maja said.

"I hope you're right, Maja. I really do."

"Good. It's settled then," Huw said. He clapped his hands in satisfaction.

"Not quite," Claire said. "I've got my own concerns. About Madison."

"Oh? And what are they?" Maja asked.

"She did not respond at all to the fear management training. No progress whatsoever."

Maja frowned. "Has she shown any progress in other areas?"

"She didn't need to, she was strong in every other dimension – though I did find some of her comments about the challenges to be revealing."

"How so?" asked Huw.

"She has a self-preservation streak that might be seen as a little heartless."

"Any more than the others?" Maja asked.

"Less so than Max. But more so than Dave. If we're choosing between Madison and Dave, my judgement is that Madison has more experience and skill as a pilot, but Dave has sensitivity as a human." Claire said.

The three of them sat quietly, thinking. Maja studied the holo-grams of the last candidates. On one side they had Xavier, Xanthe, Troy and Dr Mohammad. On the other they had Madison, Pierre, Serena, Dave, Gina and Jonas.

"What shall it be then?" Maja asked. "Skill or potential?"

PART THREE

THE SIMHUB

CHAPTER FORTY-FOUR

Water, air, sunlight, earth. It's all so damned elemental.
That's why I love plants so much: they give
and take in equal measure.

XAVIER CONSUS IN WORLD DESIGNERS:
PERSPECTIVE AND PRACTICE

SimHub: Serena

SERENA SAT WAITING in the transport hangar, sweat trickling down her neck. They were moving out that morning to the SimHub. It had been several long months of training with the Space Centre. They learnt about design and engineering constraints with building materials and the Moon environment. Then there was the design phase. This was planning and haggling with the others about design concepts, each with their own particular pet project.

It all seemed a bit more real now they were focused on the actual construction phase. The final cut for the SimHub crew seemed a long time ago now. She remembered Xanthe, Xavier and Troy waiting for them in the accommodation common room. The three lead designers had just been in conference with the Directors, and all looked bewildered. It was Troy who announced it. Serena was glad it was him. Xanthe and Xavier weren't so great at masking their feelings.

Serena wondered at the final choice. Jonas over Gina? Gina was a gun. Jonas was a bit of a buffoon. Dave over Madison? Dave was nice enough, but they were saying goodbye to Mad Dog? That seemed crazy! And she of course won out over Pierre. That one she was glad of. Pierre was a better and more experienced life support tech, but Serena would back herself every day for initiative and self-reliance. Every. Single. Time.

Pierre had been nonchalant over the announcement. He brushed it off and made some comment about getting back to his enhancement research.

Gina was surprisingly calm about the whole thing. She said something about getting back in touch with family. Some unresolved issue. Serena wondered if the trip she had at Caracalla had something to do with that.

The worst part was watching Dr Mohammad say goodbye to Madison. For such a stiff, he was genuinely choked up. He shook her hand vigorously, covering his grip with his second hand.

"Goodbye Madison," Mohammad croaked. "May Allah protect you and yours." He gave her a little bow as he let go of her hand.

"Thanks Doc," Madison smiled bravely. "It's been a pleasure. Good luck on the project. I'm still backup, in case Dave crashes the ship." She punched Dave on the shoulder. Dave was at a loss for words. He truly did not expect to be selected. Not when Mad Dog was in the running.

And now they were getting ready to start building, small groups working on different aspects of the SimHub. Just Serena's luck she'd been lumped with Xavier, that son of a bitch. They hadn't spoken much since the Terra Verdi incident, and when they did it was usually an argument of some kind. A kind of hostile tension bristled between them ever since.

"Hey."

Serena looked up as Xanthe sat down next to her. Serena gave her a half smile and said nothing.

"All set?" Xanthe asked.

"Yep." Serena looked away, watching the logistics team load the gear into the transport vehicles. Silence slid between them.

Xanthe tried again to break the awkwardness. "What personal item did you pack?"

"Nothing. I'm not sentimental," she snapped.

Xanthe flinched at the tone and said nothing. Serena regretted the outburst.

"Look, Xanthe, I'm just having a moment to myself. We're about to spend twelve months in each other's pockets."

Xanthe said nothing and did not move away. Serena felt Xanthe studying her face.

"What?" Serena said, flustered.

"Serena, something's up. What is it?"

"Nothing." Serena rested her elbows on her knees, moving away from Xanthe.

"Serena, I know we've not been that close. But I can tell something is bothering you. And as you said, we've got many long months together."

Serena hung her head, considering her options. She'd tried to be friendly with Xanthe because of her history with Patrick. But Xanthe had remained hard towards her. Selection and the training process hadn't closed the gap that much. But she was right, twelve months with five other people in close quarters was a long time. She desperately needed a friend, especially since she'd lost the one connection she'd made in Xavier.

Serena sat up and looked again at Xanthe. Her huge green eyes were concerned. Genuine, Serena thought. She took a deep breath and let it out slowly.

"It's Xavier," Serena said, her voice a whisper.

"Oh. What happened?"

"We had a full-on scrap over product development."

"Really? That doesn't sound like Xavier."

"I told him the Chicken Lickin sucked. Which it does. I suggested he add cricket protein to boost the profile and change the texture. Maybe some yeast flavouring."

"Sounds sensible. Why did he argue?"

"He called me a 'meddling, know-it-all blow-in' and then swore a lot in French."

"That *does* sound like Xavier."

"But it isn't like him to lose his temper. Very uncool."

"Maybe it's the breach of security he's worried about. Someone sharing his corporate knowledge with Spaceward Bound. That would eat away at anyone. The betrayal. Plus, it jeopardises our project."

"Yeah, I guess. Doesn't excuse his atrocious conduct towards me, though."

"No, it doesn't. But if we're going to be successful, we've got to sort our issues out."

Serena glanced at Xanthe with that comment. Was she ready to talk about Patrick?

"We've got twelve months together, as you said. More if we win," Xanthe said.

"When we win, you mean," Serena smiled.

"Yes. *When* we win." Xanthe reached out and patted Serena's hand. It was the first time she'd ever touched her, Serena thought. Strange.

"Thanks, Xanthe," she said, and meant it.

CHAPTER FORTY-FIVE

We can't underestimate how good for morale it will be to have living, growing things in off-world communities. To remind us of the miracle of life, its fragility, and how lucky we are.

XAVIER CONSUS IN WORLD DESIGNERS: PERSPECTIVE AND PRACTICE

SimHub: Jonas

JONAS STEPPED OUT of the transport vehicle into the searing heat, wearing a full spacesuit. Even though dawn was just breaking, his skin was slick with sweat, the suit recycler struggling to process it. Dr Mohammad had fussed over the suit readings, concerned about skin irritation and dehydration. He's a good sort, thought Jonas. It will be good to have him monitoring them from headquarters. Mohammad was tasked with documenting the physical, emotional and mental impacts of confined living on the SimHub crew. Xanthe, with her paramedic background, would look after the day-to-day immediate medical issues. Mohammad would also work with them to trial various longevity and performance boosters.

Jonas felt like an animal in a cage already after the Space Centre training. They had been probed and poked endlessly to ensure they would be suitable for space travel. Now at the SimHub, in the oppressive heat, he wished he was back in the relative luxury of the Space Centre clinic. The need to escape the environment would simulate the experience well. Damn it was hot, he thought. He missed the sea already. Jonas stomped slowly in the heavy suit over to the habitation pod. The tiny fledgling base, Artemis, was already set up as it would be on the Moon expedition. Their job during the simulation would be to build out the first community accommodation, ready to receive the cave-exploration and build-ing crew, first, and later the climate migrants and space tourists sent by the Lunar Commission. The SimHub was a proof of concept for the pitch – for the design, build and human experience during the process and afterwards. Gaia Enterprises would include the research findings along with the design, and their designers, as part of the pitch.

Xavier gestured to his colleagues with his suited arm, heavy and slow. Jonas clomped towards him. Xavier was nominated as the first commander for the SimHub Build. The three lead design-ers, Xanthe, Troy and Xavier, had pulled straws for the leadership rotation. Four months each. After Xavier was Troy, then Xanthe to lead it to completion and inspection by the Lunar Commission. Xavier's voice came into Jonas's headset.

"*Merde! C'est l'enfer* in these damn suits. Let's get moving. Troy, you take Dave and the girls and start unloading the habitat materials. Put them close to the far end of the pod so we can access them easily for the construction phase."

"We're *women*, actually," Xanthe's voice snipped. Jonas smiled to himself. Xanthe would sock it to him every time.

"Yes, quite right. *Absolument.* Jonas, give me a hand with the plants," Xavier said. Jonas walked over, moving slowly so as not to increase his body temperature too much in the already sweltering suit. They loaded the plants in their sealed containers from the base of the imitation Moon lander onto the rover. It was hot work. Not as hot as those poor bastards, though, thought Jonas, watching the others use the second rover to lift one panel at a time. They'd be out in the sun for twice as long as he and Xavier. The two of them would have those plants inside the pod and set up by the time the others had returned. With the plants piled on the rover, Xavier and Jonas slid into the driving capsule. Jonas gave the others a royal salute as they trundled past.

"We'll put the drinks on ice on for you. In a few hours. So long suckers!" He sniggered into his headset mic.

"Seaborn! Always the gentleman!" Dave quipped and somehow managed to give him the middle finger in his thick suit.

Jonas and Xavier unloaded the plants through the pod decontamination entrance and ran the cleansing and atmosphere-adjustment cycles before they peeled off their suits. Now in their moisture-wicking undergarments, they unsealed the main entrance and stepped into the pod itself. It was narrow and cramped, three sets of bunks lined up on the right-hand side, facing a wall of storage units and a nutrition dispenser. There was a small table at the entrance with three boxes serving as stools.

"Are you sure the Directors got the dimensions right?" asked Jonas.

"Yes, I'm sure," Xavier answered. "I double-checked the measurements myself. This is an exact replica of the Artemis Moon habitat pod."

"Clearly, they did not have a world designer working for them, poor buggers," he said. "Imagine days in a compressed tin can together only to land and move into this."

"And then we show up!" There will have been just the three of them for a year in this space. Six more bodies suddenly squeeze in, with a load of plant experiments."

"A real fart tank!" Jonas said, a little grim.

"Hopefully not, with our plants changing up the diet. Let's get it set up."

They worked quickly, knowing the others would need space to operate in. The plants were gently removed from their containers and stacked vertically against the northern wall, framing the entrance. Xavier attached the hydration drip system and checked the monitors were online. Within three months they'd have fresh produce to supplement the freeze-dried rations. Once the extensions had been built, they could start to establish the community hydroponics farm so they could cultivate enough food for the first fifty arrivals to last a year. The food system was essential for future Moon and Mars communities. Once the cave extension had been accessed and sealed, they could get the protein printer set up for the lab-grown meat. They needed to make this supply system work, or they would all die of starvation when the supplies ran out. Jonas worried about the food. He didn't like the meat products and he was constantly hungry on his plant-based diet, especially since he had started doing more martial arts training. It helped calm his nerves. Being confined with this crew was going to stretch his patience. He longed for the big, blue horizons of the *Sea Rover*.

But here they were, in the desert. He'd had have to adapt fast if he was going to stay part of the crew. And they needed him, thought Jonas. His mechanical and engineering skills were central to the life support functions. It surprised him how good it felt to feel needed. How different it was to always trying to prove yourself.

He'd better not cock it up, he thought.

CHAPTER FORTY-SIX

*Some designers say that the focus should be on the shape of the
built space. Others say it should be about the self-sustaining
elements. For me, it's always been about the people: how we come
together and stay together while building a future together.*

XANTHE WATERS IN WORLD DESIGNERS:
PERSPECTIVE AND PRACTICE

SimHub: Xanthe

XANTHE SAT ON the floor of the newly sealed central plaza of the
SimHub. Four months into the build and they finally had this
section up and running. Xavier was relieved he could finish his
leadership rotation on a high. He made a show of handing over
the commander's data tablet to Troy. Their bromance was thriving,
Xanthe thought. Sometimes Xanthe felt like the third wheel in
their company. She managed to push that thought aside. Too much
to do to worry about those two.

She stared up at the atrium. She was pleased with the SimHub
design, and this aspect, in particular. It would house various plants
to provide a lush garden experience. The skylight would be an
aquarium to help manage the cooling and heating system, with

exotic robotic fish doubling as water filters. Though a small space, she felt it was integral to keep the human inhabitants connected to their planet of origin, all the while with a view to the stars. She was proud of it.

She sipped water from her hydration bag and then stood to finish rearranging the baby plants. They needed to test the lighting and air flow on the plants' resilience.

Xanthe thought about how hard the team had worked the past few months. It hadn't been easy at first, all crammed together in that tiny Artemis replica. But the hard work was forging friendships. She was even getting along better with Serena. Things with Troy remained the same: awkward. She sighed. Xanthe's feelings for Troy were complex. She was glad the work was all-consuming.

If they won the bid, the real trip would unfold in a similar way. Once they arrived at Artemis, the NASA station, they would be tasked with extending the community underground, the best protection from radiation and meteors. The first Artemis habitat had suffered badly when a meteor hit it and ripped through the outer layer of the structure. Luckily the one remaining astronaut had managed to seal off the breach while the others returned from a science expedition. Repairs were swift, but it brought home how vulnerable an above-ground community was on the Moon.

The team had an elegant and simple design for the Olympus Project. From a central plaza with an aquarium skylight, activity areas spun out from it in spokes underground. Everything was built on redundancy to allow for system failures. They divided the community into bio-function areas: food production, bedrooms, exercises, toileting including a shower. Jonas worked out the engineering to make it possible. Though in low gravity the shower would be more of a wipe-down cupboard.

The habitat pod housed the air scrubber dome, waste management and water recycling. Then the human side of things came into play with areas for 'head' and 'heart'. 'Head' was the research and work aspect of the community, with its computer interfaces and flexible desk spaces. 'Heart' areas included the kitchen and dining area for social connection, along with a comms room for speaking with Mission Control and family 'back on Earth'. They also allowed for various AI avatar resources for their own counselling and intellectual support. They had several programs including Gandhi, the Dalai Lama, Jesus Christ, Tony Robbins and Ken Wilber among others. And Troy's favourite, his masterpiece as he said, was the Stim Room. It was a private space, richly appointed with soft cushions and vibrant colours, with a suite of VR experiences and sensory stimulation they knew they would miss from Earth: rain, wind, grass, scents. The room could change ambience to be a beach scene, forest, or even the manic hum of a cityscape. The Stim Room could also be used for immersive learning experiences and training.

Xanthe focused on the central plaza. Once they arrived on the Moon, they would cram into Artemis with the existing astronauts until the excavator bore had cleared the space for Olympus. They would assemble the 3D printer specially calibrated to operate in Moon atmosphere and gravity and let it fill in the space. Before they sealed it, they would assemble the life support functions: air scrubbers, water recycling, waste management. Then the aquarium roof would be installed, and they would move in to test it all.

The SimHub build was a Lunar Commission requirement for the bid. They wanted to know not only how the future community might be built, but how the designers and builders would cope in confined spaces, working in lunar conditions. All aspects of the build were simulated. It was a tough ask in the desert.

So far so good, she thought.

CHAPTER FORTY-SEVEN

Money? I Don't care about money. I am motivated by life,
pure and simple. I intend to get as much of it as I can.

ARYANNA SHARIF, THE UNAUTHORISED BIOGRAPHY

SimHub: Jonas

JONAS PULLED ON his soft tracksuit pants. Time to test the water recycling system again. They'd spent their first days in the SimHub firing up the systems and getting them established. After the air filtration system, water recycling was the next priority. Both systems needed constant monitoring. Jonas worried most about waste management. Can't have all that piss and shit piling up for too long. That would make for a most uncomfortable experience. It's the fundamentals that make the difference.

Geared up, he knocked on Dave's sleep pod door.

"Dave, you ready? Let's go sort out the piss machine."

"One moment," Dave replied. He appeared in a bright yellow tracksuit.

"What the hell is that?" Jonas asked, stunned.

"It is my plumbing outfit," Dave said.

"Hell's bells, it's ugly! You want to *scare* the piss machine into working?"

"Beauty is in the eye of the beholder, my friend!" Dave did a little strut and pose.

"Okay, then. Let's get on with it, Mr Banana."

They made their way to the water recycling unit in the bio-function area of the SimHub. The others hooted with delight as they trundled past.

"You like to make a splash, don't you Dave?"

"We're here for a long time. Might as well have some fun, no?"

Jonas shook his head. He pulled out the toolkit, wrapped as per space protocol with velcro tabs. He peered at the gauges and tested a few valves for pressure.

"I see where the problem is," he said. "Banana Brain, can you hand me tools as I ask for them?" Jonas got down on his back and slid around the side of the unit.

"You're the Boss."

"You're the idiot!"

Jonas wrestled with various parts of the machine, interspersing curse words with requests for different tools. Dave waited patiently.

"Say Jonas, what do you think of Aryanna Sharif being the sponsor for this bid?"

"Is that confirmed now, is it?"

"Came out in the broadcast, last night. Gaia finally announced it."

"Well, that's certainly interesting. Sharif has always been very anti-space tourism, and now she's in the game with the others. I guess the lure of more profits tempts the best of them."

"Don't you think it's a bit strange to shift focus like that? This must be costing her an arm and a leg."

Jonas grunted as he tightened a bolt on the unit. "She's got plenty of cash. I doubt she'd feel the hit."

"But why do it? I think about it. There's something they're not telling us."

Jonas sat up and put his wrench back in the toolkit.

"You got a theory, Banana Boy?"

Dave frowned, thinking. "What if the project is just a ruse? What if she has no intention of going to the Moon? What if she wants us to build this unit for her to live in here?"

"What? That makes no sense! Why would anyone willingly seal themselves into a self-contained space if they didn't have too? And why bother going through the scam of pretending to be a tender applicant? That seems like wasted effort to me," Jonas said.

"What if there is something else going on. Something bigger," Dave continued.

"Are you some sort of conspiracy theorist now?"

"Think about it, though. Sharif founds the Earth Alliance. Then she invests in terraforming technology – which is not designed for the Earth. It's designed for other planets, moons, asteroids. And what do we know about terraforming?"

Jonas stopped wiping his hands as he followed Dave's logic. "It destroys before it settles the new weather patterns," Jonas said quietly.

"Exactly." Dave slapped his leg for emphasis.

"You think Aryanna is building this project for her own little Noah's ark while she floods the planet to reset its ecosystems?"

Dave nodded, wide eyed.

Jonas stared at him for a moment, then laughed.

"Good one! You crazy bastard! You almost had me!"

"I'm not joking. I think she could be that ambitious. Maybe she sets up a project on the Moon while she floods Earth, then when things settle, goes backs to Earth where she has some special units just in case it doesn't work properly."

"No one has that kind of money. Or that much time! How old is Aryanna, now? Maybe 80? Terraforming takes decades."

"She's also invested in longevity technology."

Jonas stared some more. "You're very well informed on Sharif's business matters. A little obsessed, maybe?"

"I just want to know who I am working for. And why. That's reasonable, isn't it?"

"I guess so. And right now, you're working for me. Do you understand this recycler now? I need you to be fully up to speed in case I get conked on the head or something."

"Yes. I know it inside out."

"Well let's hope you don't have to go inside the shit tank! I don't want to have pull you out."

"I hope not too. It would ruin my banana suit."

CHAPTER FORTY-EIGHT

We found no evidence of sabotage. Goading
to violence? Yes. Sabotage? No.

CORONER'S REPORT, THE TERRA BLANCA TRAGEDY

SimHub: Xanthe

XANTHE SLIPPED INTO the comms room. Troy, as commander, had just finished the evening debrief with the team and it was her time to connect with Simon. It was getting harder and harder to have these conversations as the weeks went by. She felt the distance between them as if they were already on the Moon. Still she sensed his constant judgement, his disappointment in her for pursuing this project. For leaving him.

She breathed deeply as she clicked the connection link on the holodisplay. Simon's face appeared with a weary smile.

"Hello darling," she said.

"Hello," he replied.

"How are things?" she asked.

"Hot as hell. It seems to have gone up a notch in the last few weeks. It's putting everyone on edge."

"Who is 'everyone'?"

"Colleagues. The public. Politicians. Workers. You know – everyone stuck in Sydney."

And there it was, the first little barb. She ignored it.

"How is the project?" she asked. Simon was working on his own building design. A strip mall to be converted to food production. A green cooling corridor in a dense inner-city living precinct.

"Moving along well. Except for the nightly raids of the plant stock. We've had to employ armed roboguards to deter the thieves."

"That doesn't sound good."

"Well, things you've gotta do when you're stuck in the city."

Xanthe refused to take the bait and stayed quiet.

Simon let the silence fill the space between them for a minute.

"How are things, there?" he asked, trying to lower the tension.

"Good. We've done a number of experiments and scenarios. The hub design seems to be holding well. Except for this weird green growth we keep finding in the air scrubber dome. We have to wipe down neon green slime twice a day on the water recycler. It's pretty gross actually. Yesterday I—"

Simon interrupted her. "Xanthe, there's something you should know. The Earth First protesters are reacting badly to the news of Aryanna Sharif's involvement in the project. They are making noises about protesting on site."

"Really? They'll have a hard time finding us. We are in the middle of nowhere out here. The location is top secret. And all roads are blockaded. Plus, we have aerial surveillance."

"I know all that. But some of these crazies have advanced tech. They can hack satellites and find your location pretty quickly."

"They still have to get in. It's not an easy place to access. They would need insider info to get anywhere near us."

"Hey, I'm just letting you know what I'm hearing on the ground." He pushed away from the monitor and waved his hands in surrender. "This project was always going to be a problem, I told you that from the outset. It's a billionaire's ego trip. And now Sharif has bought into the immoral and outrageous waste of resources too, along with the rest of them."

Xanthe looked away and said nothing. It was the same old story with Simon. His judgement and derision were just getting worse.

"How do you do it, Xanthe? Waste your time and talent like that? You could be doing so much more for people. Here. For people who need help. Climate refugees. We're bursting at the seams. We can't keep up with the work. And you're out there, God knows where, tinkering with some biosphere bubble. And why? So more rich people can have a jaunt to the Moon?"

"Simon, that's enough!" They were both shocked by her outburst. Xanthe let her anger roll through her. "This is not just a pleasure jaunt! We are doing real work here, setting up projects and prototypes for the future of humanity."

"Assuming there will be any humanity left," he said.

Xanthe felt the heat rise in her face. "We're in a race against time, Simon. We need to do both: shelter people *now*, and build something for us to live in, *in the future*. Maybe on the Earth, maybe off it. If we need to run a few tourist trips alongside to fund it, so be it. But my work is just as important as yours." She even slapped the table to make her point.

For once, Simon was quiet. He had never seen her so animated. She never raised her voice with him. Ever.

Hurt crept between them like a fat, wet slug. Simon started to speak when Xavier came busting in.

"Xanthe! We need you! We've got trouble with the water recycler! All hands on deck!"

CHAPTER FORTY-NINE

*The leader of the rebellion had a peculiar kind
of charisma. He divided to conquer.*

CORONER'S REPORT, THE TERRA BLANCA TRAGEDY

SimHub: Jonas

"Shit," said Jonas. He lay on his back, inspecting the far end of
the waste management system.

"You said it!" laughed Dave. He applied sponges to stem the
leak from the faeces processor as foul fluid seeped onto the floor.
"You seem to have a knack for getting into shit!"

"Ha ha, Banana Boy. It seems I'm not the only one. Apollo,
what is the diagnostic report?" Troy named the AI system Apollo,
indulging his penchant for Roman mythology, and to fit with the
Olympus theme.

"All systems operating as per specifications. Overflow breached
container seals at 19:32."

"What caused the overflow?" asked Jonas.

"Overflow caused by excessive fluid input."

"What? That must have been a massive shit!" quipped Dave.

"No one's turd is that big. This system has the capacity for fifty people," said Troy as he checked the gauges on the processor.

"Apollo, what kind of fluid?" asked Jonas, ignoring the others.

"One moment please… fluid type undetermined."

"What the hell," muttered Jonas. "Apollo, what are the possible sources of excess fluid?"

"Fluid source options are the input pipe, flush mechanism or manual input." Jonas sat up, confused.

"Apollo, is the masticator functioning properly?"

"All masticator functions are within range."

"What do you think, Jonas?" asked Troy.

"Well, could be that Apollo's sensors aren't doing a correct diagnostic. We'll have to do a manual check. Troy, shut down the tank. We need to see if it's a gauge or input pipe causing the problem."

Serena crowded into the small space, bringing a biohazard bag over for Dave's sponges. "Here you go, Dave. Don't get the banana suit dirty, for goodness sake!"

Xavier and Xanthe appeared in the doorway.

"Jonas – sitrep please," she said.

"The waste management system is malfunctioning, and we've got an unexplained overflow leak. So far, the water recycler seems to be isolated from it and functioning okay."

"That's good news, right?" Serena asked, as she adjusted one of the system levers.

"So far, yes. No poo detected in our drinking water. But we'll have Apollo run full diagnostics," said Jonas. "Xanthe, can you and Xavier prepare for a full scrub down? We can't have any leaks out of this room into the main system. Otherwise, it will smell like shit for months until we process it all out of the atmosphere."

"I'll close the air circulator down on this room until we can clean it out," said Xavier.

"Troy, can you shine a spotlight in here for me?" asked Jonas.

Troy moved over with the emergency lamp. His face wrinkled in disgust. "That really does stink," he said.

"It will get worse unless we figure this one out," Jonas said. "Okay, I'm going in." He donned the splashguard, gas mask and rubber gloves. He plunged his left arm into the muck. He grunted, as he felt around the tank. "Masticator seems okay," he said. "Could be a problem with the input pipe."

"Apollo, run the input pipe cleaning cycle, please."

"Input pipe cleaning initiated."

Jonas stared into the unit while it whirred, sending a blast of air and biochemical rinse down through the system.

"Apollo, report please."

"Input pipe clear."

"No problems there," he said thoughtfully. The others stood around as Dave sponged at the remnants of turd water. "Let me check the gauge." He fished around and pulled out a plastic sphere.

"What is that?" asked Troy.

"An old-school toilet gauge. It bobs on the surface of the system. When it sinks below a certain level, like when the waste is pushed through to the next processing tank, it lifts a flap that initiates a flush of tank fluid. It looks intact." He reached back into the tank. "Ahh!" His face lit up. "Here's the problem. The flap is jammed up. Looks like there's something stuck in there." He grunted and wrestled with the offending object until he wrenched it free. He held up a bottle cap.

"Which one of you buggers swallowed a cap and didn't notice?" Serena exclaimed.

"Is that even possible?" Xanthe asked.

"Not likely! Maybe it fell in when we were setting up and it just got jammed, now," said Dave.

Jonas extracted his arm carefully and gestured to Dave to bring over the biohazard bag. He stripped his outer gloves into the bag.

"That doesn't explain the leak. Those seals should hold, even with extra flush. I'll check them again," Jonas said.

Still wearing the inner liners, he inspected the rim of the tank. "They look okay. But to be on the safe side, I'll use the 3D printer to print a new set." He closed the lid and snapped it shut, double-checking the safeties.

"Dave, if you could process all the gear as per biohazard protocol, including these," he removed the glove liners and placed them in the bag, "that would be terrific. Xanthe and Xavier, you're on scrub down, if that's okay with you, boss?" Xanthe had taken over the role of commander from Troy the week before, as part of their shared leadership roster.

"Sure," she replied.

"Serena and Troy, we can do an inspection of the toilets and shower to make sure we haven't missed anything."

"In the meantime, team, no excessive fluid consumption!" teased Serena. "And that's especially you, Banana Boy! Lay off the smoothie machine! You'll turn green if you drink anymore of that stuff."

"I thought you had a thing for little green men," he said.

"If we were on Mars, maybe."

"So, there's still a chance..."

She punched him lightly on the shoulder. "Only if you wear that outfit. Green bananas are good for cholesterol management."

CHAPTER FIFTY

We've come full circle. We've decentralised food production so people can access food from their buildings, their homes, public spaces. Food is no longer an afterthought, but a central life force to all human functions. Which it should have been all along.

XAVIER CONSUS IN WORLD DESIGNERS:
PERSPECTIVE AND PRACTICE

SimHub: Xavier

XAVIER INSPECTED THE seedlings under the grow lamps. They looked healthy enough. All the readings were positive. He moved down the length of the shelves, checking for trouble spots.

Mon Dieu, he loved plants. Such a simple relationship. Set them up with good conditions, and they respond to your directions. Why weren't people like that? he wondered for the umpteenth time. No simple directions allowed without endless bloody consulting. It was infuriating!

Xavier squatted behind the shelves to check the irrigation feeds. All seemed in order. Wait – what was that? Down in one corner, tucked out of view, was some sort of tape wrapped around the tubing. How did that get there? He turned off the water gauge for that tray and removed the tube.

What the hell? The tube was slit open. Was this a poor attempt at a repair job? How did that slit happen? The tubing was very durable material. Why would someone cover this up?

Xavier moved the shelf carefully, sliding behind it to access the rest of the tube system. Nothing seemed out of order. He replaced the misfit tubing with a new piece and pushed the shelf back into place. He took the tape over to the workbench and slid it into a plant tissue slide.

"Apollo, run a diagnostic on the compounds in this sample." For once, he did not wince at the AI's name. When Troy had declared it be named after yet another Roman god, Xavier had laughed. "I think you fancy yourself a god too, eh *mon ami*?"

"Why can't we aspire to walk among the gods?" Troy replied, full of mischief. "After all, some of us are clearly closer to them than others." He stood tall and put his hands on hips, and raised his chin. "What do you reckon? Mars, God of War? "

"You are too much, Troy!" laughed Xavier. "Just remember – things did not go so well for the city of 'Troy'. Best not to live too much in the shadow of a name. "

"Analysis complete," said the AI.

"Apollo, read out summary, please," said Xavier.

"Sample includes compounds typical of adhesive tape."

That's a relief, he thought.

"Sample includes traces of limestone."

Limestone? Where was that coming from? There were no soil components – this was a strictly hydroponic setup. The only place limestone should be going is through the plant food tubing.

"Apollo, double check the pH levels of the tanks."

"There are rising pH levels in tank 6. The pH level is currently at 7.5."

Way too alkaline for tomatoes. They liked slightly acidic

conditions. Xavier checked the plants again. Yes, there it was, a slight yellowing.

"Apollo, check the plant food drippers. Are there any irregularities?"

"Plant food solution corresponds to the set chemical composition appropriate for each tank."

Damn. How did the limestone get in there? Through that dodgy repair? Someone adding it to the tank? Stupidity? Sloppiness? Or sabotage?

Xavier twirled the slit tubing, deep in thought.

If it was sabotage, why? Why would anyone wreck the food crops? *Merde!* Didn't make any sense. No, couldn't be that. Stupidity seemed more likely. He made a note to talk with Xanthe about it.

CHAPTER FIFTY-ONE

Food in space has to be more than just fuel. It's comfort, it's joy, it's morale. It's an opportunity to come together, to pause and be thankful.

XAVIER CONSUS IN WORLD DESIGNERS:
PERSPECTIVE AND PRACTICE

SimHub: Xanthe

SERENA STRODE INTO the kitchen, blonde hair floating behind her.

"I'm absolutely buggered!" she announced as she reached to refill her plastic water bag. No one answered. Jonas scanned his datapad, while Troy shuffled a deck of cards. Even Dave was quiet, doing the thousand-yard stare, his yellow jumpsuit crumpled and worn thin. Serena flounced into a chair and sucked her water bag noisily, tossing hair over her shoulder.

Xanthe braced herself for the annoyance she always felt in Serena's presence. *How does she always manage to look like a glamazon? Even at such a late hour?* Xanthe mused with a twinge of bitterness. Serena still made her feel small and podgy, even after all this time confined together. Xanthe stood up taller and pulled her shoulders back. I can't change my height, but I can manage my posture, she thought. She maintained the straight back as she filled her bag of tea.

It was their Thursday SimHub Crew Night. They had established the ritual early on. One night a week to check in and clear the air, if needed. So far, they'd managed to be fairly civil. No outright conflict. Yet. Damn, she was tired. They had been running hull breach scenarios for two days, taking turns getting into and out of the heavy simulated spacesuits, working in the full glare of the desert sun and then well into the night. Mission Control said it was necessary to test their resilience and ability to perform in difficult circumstances. They were all beginning to think that Claire took a fiendish sense of enjoyment in their suffering. Ten months into the build now and she wouldn't let up.

Xavier was late. That was so like him, Xanthe thought. His work was always more important than anyone else's. She felt the irritation crawl over her and poke at her thoughts. She took a deep breath, tried to settle her mind. The fatigue sparked and crackled along her nerves. She reached into the cupboard for the allotted SimHub Crew Night treat: one small block of highly coveted chocolate. They had to ration it carefully. It was one of the things they couldn't manufacture in the Food Hub. Jonas grabbed his, ripped open the package and gobbled it instantly with a look of relieved satisfaction.

"We're supposed to wait," Troy reprimanded.

"Stuff that," Jonas said. "He's late anyway."

Xavier appeared as if on cue.

"Nice of you to join us," Serena quipped.

"Apologies," he breathed as he slid in beside her.

"Anyone need a hot beverage before we start?" asked Xanthe.

"No thanks," said Dave. "Coffee is just not that appealing drunk from a bag."

"Well, it's all we've got," snapped Xanthe. Five pairs of eyes latched on to her face. Shit, she thought. I am more tired than

I realised. "Shall we get started, then?" she continued, trying to smooth it over with a more even tone.

"Who'd like to go first? Check in and share something you're grateful for." Eyes flicked away. Silence.

"I'll go then, you miserable buggers," Serena said. "I'm absolutely exhaust-ipated. This has been a week from Hell. Nothing is going right in the excavation. The drilling robot keeps breaking down, the excavated dirt keeps getting trapped in the clearing mechanism and the shower is on the fritz again. And I can't get the bloody dirt off my spacesuit. Which stinks to high heaven by the way. They could have designed that with better odour control."

"Anything else?" Xanthe asked wearily.

"Yes. Jonas is driving me nuts." She waved a finger at him. "You keep leaving the repair tools lying around. And you don't finish the job. I've had to come in twice and finish the drill repair."

"That's because I keep being called away to fix the damn shower!" He replied. "Don't want Your Majesty to go without a shower, do we?"

"Maybe if you did it right the first time, you wouldn't have to keep going back. You're supposed to be a qualified mechanic and engineer for Chrissake." She sat back, folding her arms in a huff.

"I am an engineer. Not a plumber. Besides, I don't see you signing up for checking the toilet and waste clearance system."

"Alright enough!" called out Xanthe. "Serena we'll come back to you in a few minutes after you've calmed down to hear what you're grateful for."

Serena's face grew dark against her golden hair. "Grateful? I'll tell you what I'm grateful for! Nothing! I'm being treated like a child! I've raised some serious issues here and you're just blowing them off, *Commander.*"

Gauntlet thrown. Xanthe felt the years of hostility surge from deep within. "Well maybe if you stopped acting like a child, you wouldn't be treated like one," she said bitterly.

"What the hell is that supposed to mean?"

"It means you expect the whole world to do what you want. You take what you want, you do what you want, regardless of other people's feelings."

Serena stared at Xanthe. Then she said quietly through gritted teeth, "People are free to make their own choices. I don't make anyone do anything they don't want to do."

"And damn the consequences," Xanthe shot back.

"Ummm – what are we talking about, here?" Dave asked.

Xanthe threw her hot bag of tea on the table. "Serena fucked my Dad." And there it was. Shit.

"Okay, then. We might be needing a timeout, right about now," suggested Troy.

"No. No, we don't," said Serena. "I've got nothing to hide. And you might as well know, since we'll be living together for at least another two months. More, if by some miracle we manage to get this project back on track and win the bid." She sat back in her chair. "Yes, it's true. I had an affair with Patrick Waters. Except I didn't know he was married, or had kids, until his goddamn funeral. That's where I met Xanthe. I thought Xanthe was a niece or something and went to share my condolences and introduce myself. Imagine my surprise. The man I loved was a bold, two-faced liar living a double life. So, then I had the lovely experience of grieving both the man I loved and the lie I bought, all while being viewed as the enemy by total strangers. Not my best day."

"I think *I* need a timeout," said Xavier.

"If I may suggest something," said Troy. "Xanthe, you and Serena need to work out how you are going to, ah, navigate this past experience. And Serena, you and Jonas need to work out a better way of working together."

"Why am *I* the bad guy all of a sudden?" Serena demanded.

"You're *not* the bad guy," said Troy. "You're just the first person to open Pandora's Box."

"Thanks for that!" Jonas gave her a sarcastic thumbs up.

"Fuck you, Jonas."

"Wow. This is getting out of hand," Xavier said.

"Xavier's right. We need to calm down. We are all tired. We can do better than this," Troy said.

They sat simmering for a few moments.

"I think time out may be a good idea, no?" said Dave carefully. He was watching the others retreat into their own thoughts. "I'll make some shit-arse coffee for everyone and then maybe we try again."

Xanthe smiled weakly at that. "Thanks, Dave. Okay. Let's take five and reconvene." She stood and left the room, heading for the sanctum. Though the plants were still tiny, it was still her favourite spot, with the view to the stars that made her soul ache and stretch each time. She sat on the narrow bench, staring up into the night.

She sensed someone behind her and turned. Serena. She looked away again, her emotions tumbling like desert-blown weeds. Serena perched on the edge of the bench.

"Xanthe, I'm sorry," Serena said. "But I didn't know—I would never have—"

Xanthe felt the hot sting of tears and her throat growing tight. She glanced at Serena and saw the pain in her face.

"I'm sorry, too. For what I said. I didn't know you didn't know. It's just that my Dad—" She choked on the words.

"He was a good man, Xanthe. I loved him. But he lied. He was a liar. He lied to me, to you, to your mother, to everyone. If I'd known… God, if I'd known! I would have killed him, myself!"

Xanthe found herself half-sobbing, half-laughing at that. "He was a son of a bitch," she said. "But I just miss him. All of them. My Mum, my sisters. I lost so much in the tsunami." The grief poured out of her in body-racking sobs. Her head filled with the blinding white pain of loss. Serena moved closer and Xanthe found herself leaning into her embrace, hugging the one woman she'd hated all these years. The one woman who shared a connection with her lost loved ones. She clung to that distant connection as if it were the tail end of a kite in a windstorm.

"It's okay. It's okay," Serena said, rocking Xanthe back and forth. Her own tears fell on Xanthe's head. Then her nose started to run. She sniffed and wiped the snot with her sleeve. Xanthe was sniffing too, her sobs easing.

"I think we need to blow our noses. This ratty old top will only soak up so much snot," Serena said.

Xanthe laughed at that and pulled away slowly. "Serena. I'm sorry."

"It's okay. The past is done. We get to make it mean whatever we want. And now, we have now. Let's make that good."

"Agreed."

They rose and walked slowly back towards the kitchen.

"You'd better make things right with Jonas," Xanthe said.

"Oh, that little turd bottom. We'll get him sorted, no worries!"

Serena gave Xanthe another hug, and they rejoined the others, renewed.

CHAPTER FIFTY-TWO

If we're not careful, we can justify anything
with our own moral code.

ATHENA AI IN WISDOM OF THE AGES

Gaia Desert Base Mission Control Headquarters: Maja

CLAIRE STORMED INTO the Mission Control boardroom. Maja looked up from her tablet as the younger woman stood over her.

"Is it true?" Claire demanded.

"Excuse me. Is what true?"

"Is it true Aryanna Sharif is really looking to terraform Earth with a flooding event?"

Maja put her tablet aside and placed her hands in her lap. "I'm not across all of Madame Sharif's business projects," she said.

"Flooding the Earth is not a business project, Maja!"

Maja stood and walked over to the observation window, glancing at the other woman. The heat of the day weighed down the branches of the few scrappy trees peppering the desert landscape.

"Sounds a little improbable, don't you think?" Maja said after a moment, turning to look at Claire.

"It sounds crazy!" Claire said, distressed.

"What gave you this idea, Claire?"

"Dave was talking about it with Jonas." Claire said flatly.

"You were listening in again?"

Claire looked flummoxed. "I was passing by the monitors. They were working on the water recycling unit. I wanted to see how they were progressing."

"Did you let them know you were observing? As per the privacy protocols?"

"I didn't get a chance to." Claire's mouth hardened.

"And what else have you heard? By accident." Maja held Claire's gaze, until Claire broke away.

"Nothing. It was a slip. I should have let them know I was observing." Claire pulled out a chair and sat.

Maja returned to her chair to join her.

"Anything else on your mind?" she asked.

Claire paused, pursing her lips. "Why is she supporting this project? It's a massive expense."

Maja shrugged. "That's not for me to say. I'm just grateful for her support. Madame Sharif is, after all, bankrolling the entire project. Our job is to make sure we deliver. And on that note, how are the scenario experiments coming along?"

Claire reluctantly acknowledged the change of subject.

"So far so good. The team has handled all incidents and crises remarkably well. In fact, they seem to be enjoying it."

"And morale? Group dynamics?"

"They seem to be working just fine together. Serena and Xanthe avoid one another but are civil. Serena does seem a little short on patience with Jonas. She snaps at him often."

"Anything we should be concerned about?"

"When it comes to Jonas, I'm always concerned. But no, nothing out of the ordinary to worry about."

"Good. I know Huw is looking forward to the report at the

end of this week. Is that all, then?" Maja moved to indicate the conversation was over.

"Just one thing. How are succession plans going?"

Maja breathed a little deeper. Only the most astute observer would notice the change in her breath, her pulse.

"No plans, as yet. Just talking through the process with Huw. Why?"

"Maja, you know why. I would love to be considered the prime candidate to take the reins. I've been dedicated to Gaia for ten years. I love the enterprise, I'm committed to its vision. I want to see it succeed in the long term. I want to honour your legacy."

Maja smiled. "Legacy! Not sure about that. We all blow to dust in the end. If we have the chance to live well, to love well, then that is a life worth living. The constructs of business are the ego's foolish deception if we are to turn to that for meaning." Claire looked deflated by Maja's response. Maja leant over and patted the other woman's hands, which were fidgeting. "Yet I do appreciate your intent. And your commitment. You have been a most loyal partner in this enterprise." She stilled Claire's fidgeting, then smiled.

"Now, let me get on with the work of this business. There is much to address."

CHAPTER FIFTY-THREE

Green Meat is less about animal rights and more about practicalities. With climate pressures there is less arable and liveable land. Green Meat is a two-for-one solution: food production that decarbonises and cools habitats. Don't get me wrong, I still love meat. I'll take a bacon sandwich any day over a green smoothie.

XAVIER CONSUS IN WORLD DESIGNERS: PERSPECTIVE AND PRACTICE

SimHub: Xavier

XAVIER COUNTED AGAIN. He checked all the ration packs for the third time. There were definitely packages missing. None of the big meals. Just the snack packs and a few flat breads.

He put all the supplies back in their storage units. He sat down at the supply workbench, deep in thought. Someone was sneaking supplies. But who? All they needed to do was ask for more food and he'd give it out. They did not have an endless supply but if people were struggling, adjustments could be made.

The Food Hub was behind schedule in its production, so this breach in supplies would mean they would have to ration carefully. It was doable, but unpleasant.

But who was sneaking food? It was such an enormous betrayal! So selfish! The faces of his crew mates swam in front of him. None of them seemed the type. Xavier felt his anger growing as he ruminated on the thievery.

They still hadn't found who had leaked the Green Meat intelligence to Spaceward Bound, or even if they had. Someone must have. It was just too implausible for the Bounder buffoons to have suddenly developed such advanced food tech. Not their expertise.

And now someone here might be sneaking food? *Merde!* It was infuriating.

Well, there was one way to sort this out. Time to call a crew meeting.

He marched down the corridor to the dining hub, looking for Xanthe. He found her in the comms room, talking with Claire on the holo.

"Yes, Control, we are up-to-date with construction. The second corridor is excavated, and we will start the robodrill on the third one tomorrow. We're about two weeks behind, at the moment."

"You'll need to step up the pace, Commander. Two weeks behind with just six weeks until the inspection, that's getting pretty tight."

"I understand. But we've had the drill break down several times and soil clearance hasn't been running all that smoothly. It needs human surveillance so it doesn't get jammed. And that takes someone off other duties in the meantime."

"Figure it out, Commander. You need to get back on schedule."

"Xanthe – we need to talk. Now." Xavier interrupted. She glanced at him and gave him a 'wait a minute' sign.

"Control, I need to go. I have Xavier here. He has an issue I need to attend to."

"Oh? What is it?" Claire's image on alert.

"Nothing of significance, Control," Xavier said, moving into her view. "Just had a plan I need to run past Xanthe for improving crop output is all," he lied.

"Alright then. I look forward to hearing about it. I'll leave you two to it. Mission Control out."

"Xavier – how many times have I asked you not to interrupt when I'm talking to Claire? She gives us such a hard time as it is! Now, what is so important that it warrants barging in like this?"

"There's no easy way to say this, so I'll just say it. Someone is stealing food."

"What? Are you sure? How do you know?"

"I redid the stocktake three times. There is stuff missing. Snacks and flatbreads."

"Did you check anywhere else? Maybe the supplies got stored somewhere out of the ordinary?"

"Xanthe, it's a small operation here! Not too many places to misplace food supplies!"

"Well… maybe someone took it to their room and forgot to bring it back…"

He looked at her, eyebrows raised. "I know you don't want to believe it. I don't want to, either. It is *merde*. But someone is doing the wrong thing, and we need to sort it out. Now, maybe there is an innocent explanation for this. I hope so. But in the meantime, we need to address it and stop it. We will run out of supplies and be rationing hard, especially towards the end of the sim. And that is a bad look for the bid."

"Okay, okay. We'll raise it after dinner tonight. But let me take the lead on this. You can be a little…"

"What?" he asked.

"Direct," she answered.

"Oh. I thought you were going to say 'clever'."

"And arrogant!"

"Okay. *Merci*. You take the lead. But don't let people get off the hook! We need to get this addressed. Pronto."

⤚⟋⤙

They chatted amiably around the table after dinner. The Clean Meat cooker had finally grown enough cells to produce a pork cutlet each. They'd all salivated and exclaimed over the meat. All except Jonas.

"I don't do pork," he said.

"Why not?" asked Troy.

"I know what pigs eat," he said.

"But this didn't come from a live pig, Jonas. It's grown in serum. No animal died here," said Troy.

"That's true, but I had a bad experience once. My parents sent me to an old-school boutique farm that used to produce real meat, back in the day."

"Why did they send you there?" asked Dave.

"Punishment. I was a bit of an arse growing up on the *Sea Rover* and they thought a dose of real work would smarten me up. So, they shipped me out to this piggery where a friend of theirs was trying to make a living hanging on to old-school farming techniques. Not much demand for real meat these days with the prices sky high and all the effort that goes into producing it and all."

"The hard work put you off eating pork?" asked Serena.

"Nah. I liked working with the pigs. They're clever animals. Social, too. Really curious. And that's the problem."

"What do you mean?" asked Dave.

Jonas was enjoying being the centre of attention, now. "Pigs have a great sense of smell. And they love to chew on things. That's why they used to dock their tails, way back when."

"Pigs had tails?" asked Xanthe.

"Yup. Before they engineered that out of them. Turns out tails were these curly little things and for a curious pig, right fun to chew on. And if one started chewing and biting tails, they all got the habit and taste for it. Nothing like a pen full of butt-chewing pigs to ruin a herd!"

"So, wait – you don't eat pork because the animals used to chew each other's tails?" Xavier was getting sucked into the story now, too.

"Nah, that's not it. It's what happened to Jorge."

"Who the hell is Jorge?" Serena asked.

They were all drawn into his story.

"Jorge was the farm manager. And he really liked the pigs. He'd go out there all times of the day and night and just chat with them. He liked pigs way more than he liked people. One day he was up in the big open pen where there were some six hundred pigs. He got up real early so he could get some alone time with the piggies."

"That's kinda weird," said Troy.

"Each to his own," continued Jonas. "Anyhow, Jorge was out in the pen, way up the back end of it and he stumbled and fell over. So we think, anyway."

"What happened? Xanthe asked, her big green eyes even wider.

"We're not exactly sure. But we think he fell, as I said, and knocked himself out on something. Maybe one of the drinking taps out there. Anyway, the pigs being curious creatures, came upon an unconscious Jorge and started sniffing away at him. Then had a little chew of him, and then maybe a little bite. Once there's the smell of blood, pigs being omnivores and all, they have a go at poor old Jorge. When someone finally came out to see what the pigs were making a racket about, there were bits of Jorge all over the place. I came out too and I saw three big sows squealing over his leg, tearing bits and pieces one way and another."

"Oh, my goodness! That's horrible!" exclaimed Xanthe.

"Yep. Pretty nasty. Haven't been able to eat a bite of pork since. It's a shame, too. Because I tell ya, there's nothing more delicious than fresh bacon fried up and dripping in a sandwich. Yum! But I can't do it. Even if it *is* clean meat in a Petri dish."

"Wow. That must be bullshit," said Xavier.

"No it's true, actually," said Dave. "There used to be huge piggeries in the Netherlands. My friend Harold worked in one. He told me stories about pigs. They eat anything! Very strong jaws. They could eat a human, bones and all. And they shit out the teeth!"

"What?!" Serena said.

"Yeah. Teeth are protected by enamel, so they don't get digested much." Jonas said, smiling and showing off his own great teeth.

"Okay, then," said Xanthe. "On that note, we actually need to talk about something different. Not a great segue from human-eating pigs, but there you go. It turns out, according to Xavier, that some of our food stock supplies have been... misplaced."

"What do you mean 'misplaced'?" asked Troy. "Like... they didn't arrive with us? They were left in storage somewhere offsite?"

"No. Rather that, when doing the stocktake, we came up short on some items," Xanthe continued.

"Well, count again," offered Serena.

"I did. Three times." Xavier said.

"What are we missing?" asked Dave.

"Snacks and flatbread," answered Xavier.

"That's strange. Did someone take extra by accident while out on expedition and forget to pack it back in?" suggested Troy.

"Maybe it got mistaken for other packages in the storage area. I can go and have a look." Dave stood to go and check.

"What I am suggesting is that maybe someone forgot or miscalculated their ration..." Xanthe suggested.

"Someone is stealing food!" exclaimed Xavier. They looked at him in shock.

"No... no one would do that here!" said Serena, looking at each of them. "Maybe it was Dave, sleepwalking again. Maybe he is a sleep eater."

"Not likely. My sleepwalking is usually to the bathroom and

back. Nothing so complex as rifling through storage containers and opening ration packs," Dave responded.

"I'm sure no one did it on purpose," Troy said, hoping it was true.

"Well, I didn't do it," said Serena, folding her arms in defiance.

"Obviously, I didn't do it," said Xavier.

"I don't even like flatbread," murmured Troy, thinking.

"Me, neither!" said Dave.

"Well, it wasn't rats, since there are no other animals in this bubble apart from us," said Xanthe. "Any other explanations?"

"I want to know what Mr Seaborn has to say over there. You've been awfully quiet, Jonas," Serena said, staring him down.

Jonas jiggled his knee and toyed with his drink bag. "Yeah, okay. It was me."

"*Putain* Jonas! That's just shit!" cried Xavier. "This is crew food. It's for all of us."

"I know. I know. It's just – well – I've been starving. Doing a few extra workouts – trying to burn off some nervous energy. Then with all these late-night scenarios we've been running, I've been feeling subpar. It's not just the pork I don't eat. I really can't stomach any of the meat – the clean meat, the printed stuff, it all weirds me out. Plus, half of you don't even like the flatbreads, so I thought no one would notice or mind that much."

"Typical bloody Seaborn – always putting themselves ahead of everyone else. Disgusting." Serena said.

"You're not eating the meat? When were you going to tell us?' Xanthe asked. "We can't afford anyone to be getting sick and run down. Especially not now when the project is so far behind!"

"I know. I know. Stupid. I know." Jonas rubbed his head, running his hands through his matted hair.

"What's this about nervous energy?" asked Troy, his face concerned.

"I'm worried about the waste management system. When I

replaced the seals, they looked liked they'd been damaged some-how. We don't have an endless supply of materials for printing seals. We can't afford another breach. Anyway, it's been keeping me awake at night."

"Who cares about a bit of damaged rubber! You've been steal-ing food!" Xavier glared at Jonas. "Now we are all going to have to ration. We're all going to pay the price for his selfish choices."

Jonas stared at the floor.

"Okay, hang on a minute," Xanthe said. "Jonas, why didn't you tell us you were hungry? Why sneak around?"

Jonas wriggled a little in his chair. "Dunno," he said, face burning hot.

Xanthe raised her eyebrows at him. "Mate, you've starved on expedition, leapt down cliffs, hiked through scrub and survived some tough VR sims. And you can't speak up about food rations? What gives?"

He avoided their eyes, knee bouncing, hands twisting his water bag. "It's just that…" he struggled to find the words.

"What?" she prodded.

"I don't like appearing weak, okay?"

"How does being hungry make you look weak?" asked Troy gently.

"I know it sounds… immature. I just don't like to be singled out. I should be able to handle it."

"This is nuts," said Xavier. "So, you steal food, putting us all at risk, so you can feel a little better about yourself? Pfffff." Xavier made a dismissive gesture. "Sounds like Daddy issues to me."

"Or Mummy ones," added Serena.

"Not far from the truth," Jonas said. It was their turn to stare at him. "My Dad was a right bastard about being strong and stuff," confessed Jonas. "He believed that leaders needed to be strong, show no weaknesses. I learnt martial arts just so I could show I could kick some arse. He sent me to that piggery to toughen me up. 'Learn some real work' as he said. I could never tell him that it put me off meat for good. Can't even eat fish now. He'd have been disgusted by me for having such a weak stomach. So to speak. Anyway, I guess all that kinda hung around in my head. It wasn't a great choice, I know," Jonas said, truly dejected now.

"Anything else you've been hiding from us, Seaborn?" challenged Serena.

He looked at her miserably then shook his head.

"Anybody else have some childhood trauma that needs revisiting before you start binging the rations?" asked Xavier.

"Okay look," interrupted Xanthe. "This is obviously not a great situation. There are a couple of issues. Jonas, thanks for fessing up. I'm sorry you didn't feel comfortable enough to raise this with the group. And as a group, we need to get better at making it easier to talk about this stuff. Sarcasm doesn't help." She eyeballed Xavier and Serena in turn.

"Xavier, you'll need to recalculate rations with the depleted stores. We'll have to double down on boosting food production in the fledgling crops. We might be able to get some more productivity out of them, especially if we use the recycled waste."

"Is that safe?" asked Serena. "It hasn't had the required processing time yet. We can't afford microbes along with a food shortage to take us down."

They paused, considering the risks. It all became more real now with the crops not producing enough yet.

Jonas spoke up. "We can accelerate the decomposition and processing life cycle with more air circulation. I can divert some more power into the processing containers."

"Alright. Jonas, you will be on the accelerated waste management project as of tomorrow. Dave, you will go out with Serena to handle the excavation site." They nodded. "And now we have to deal with something else. The breach of trust." The words fell heavily on the table.

"I am truly sorry. I know it was stupid. And selfish."

"Apologies aren't quite enough, Jonas," said Serena.

"What do you want me to do? Penance?"

"No, not penance," said Xanthe. "Gaia Enterprises doesn't believe in penance. And neither do I. It's a waste of emotional energy. But we do need to rectify this situation. You've breached our trust and it's going to be very hard to earn it back. Especially over an issue like food. Atonement is what we do instead. You'll need to find a way to make it right." Xanthe let the message float for a moment. "Getting the crops growing better with the waste recycler would be a step in the right direction."

Dave raised his hand. "Suggestion?" he asked, Xanthe nodded. "I would be happy if Jonas cleaned out the toilets for the rest of this month. He seems to be good with getting in shit!"

"That sounds like penance," Xanthe warned.

"Nah. I'll do it," said Jonas. "It will help with the waste decomposition if I accelerate it with the bio cleaners anyway."

"Then maybe you can clean my underpants and socks," said Dave. "I'd trust you a lot if you tackled that and survived!" He said with a mischievous grin.

"This is not a joke," Xavier said. "I've got my eye on you, Jonas. No more clipping our ticket. You'd better get those crops humming." Jonas nodded back at him wearily. "And from now on, the food cupboards will be locked."

"Is that really necessary?" asked Xanthe.

"Is anyone else hungry?" challenged Xavier. "I know I sure am. So, we'll protect ourselves from our lesser nature. At least until we get those crops back on track and we know we've got enough to last."

"From now on," Xanthe added, "if you feel unwell, hungry or otherwise, you need to tell me or Troy. We're the medico team and we can work with you to sort it out. I'll also discuss it with Dr Mohammad at Mission Control to see if there is anything we can adjust with our given supplements for you. Our individual health is a communal concern. What affects one, affects us all. And on that note, I'm off to bed. I'm sure Mission Control has something cooked up for us tomorrow."

CHAPTER FIFTY-FOUR

*Trust is a by-product of good systems. Set things
up right, and fewer things go wrong.*

ATHENA AI IN WISDOM OF THE AGES

Excavation site: Serena

SERENA AND DAVE trudged out to the excavation site. The sun
was squatting on the horizon like a fat lady at the markets. The
flies were already out and humming. One good thing about the
spacesuits, thought Serena: no flies running up your nose.

Dave was unusually quiet. Serena glanced over to him. He
stared down at his feet as they did their slow spacesuit waddle.

"Hey," she said. "What's up with you, today?"

He looked up and curled his lips in a half-hearted smile.

"Oh, not much. Just thinking about last night."

"Hmmm. Certainly not our most pleasant crew meeting."

"Do you think we can trust Jonas? After what he did?"

Serena snorted. "I wouldn't trust that guy as far as I could
throw him! He's nothing but a sneak."

"Really? You don't think we can trust him at all?"

Serena thought about the question as they stopped at the excavation site's access pit, a deep shaft that dropped to the tunnels dug out for the SimHub's next extension.

"I believe that how we do one thing is how we do everything. Jonas cuts corners – he has since the start of the whole selection process."

"You don't think he could earn our trust back? You don't think atonement can work?"

She considered the question as she punched in the access code to review the excavation data.

"Well… maybe. I also believe that if you can change one thing, you can change everything." The machine whirred to life, and she turned to face Dave, peering at him through the helmet lens. "If he can get those crops working, if he does toilet duty, if he cleans up after himself, then maybe he has a chance at being trusted. But really, what I need to see from him is for him to speak the truth. Every time. No matter how hard it is to say. As humans we're pretty resilient. We can handle any truth, no matter how harsh, as long as it's shared. I bet on that with Xanthe." She scanned the data feed, checking for glitches, then looked back at Dave. "It's been worth it." Dave held her gaze then looked away.

"What do you think, Dave? You think he can redeem himself?"

"I hope so. I like to think people are worth a second chance. Especially if we are to live together so closely on the Moon."

"We won't get to the Moon if we don't get this project back on track. We're losing the competition at the moment with all these stupid setbacks. Let's hope we can get the excavation finished today. Then the print-bot can get in there tomorrow and start building those walls."

CHAPTER FIFTY-FIVE

*I've always believed that creating conditions to cause
human development is not manipulation, it's optimisation.
When you give people a chance to rise to the occasion,
they often do. But after Terra Blanca, I'm not sure that's
always the case. Humans are complex creatures.*

MAJA GARCIA, TERRA BLANCA JOURNALS

Gaia Desert Base Mission Control Headquarters: Claire

CLAIRE STUDIED THE recording of the SimHub crew team meeting. It wasn't usual practice, but she'd been alarmed when she'd overheard Xavier's report about missing supplies. She kept her finger hovering over the off switch and listened to his report. Food stealing was a serious threat to the project. Team dynamics could disintegrate quickly with such a breach of trust. And of course, it was Jonas. That man was trouble from the start.

Claire turned from the recording as Maja entered the Control comms room. She wanted Maja to see this for herself.

"Hello, Claire. What is so important that you are summoning me so late?" Maja asked, wrapping her cardigan more tightly around her thin, bony shoulders.

"We've got a serious issue in the SimHub," Claire said.

"Oh?" Maja asked, as she sat next to Claire in front of the comms panel.

"Jonas has been stealing food." Claire let the weight of the news settle on Maja with the heaviness it was due.

"Oh. I see." She thought for a moment. "Does the crew know?"

"Yes. Xavier discovered missing food packs and told Xanthe. They've just had a crew meeting to address it."

"And they invited you to observe?" asked Maja with surprise.

Claire was caught out, but she persevered – the issue was too important. "The seriousness of the issue overrode permission protocols, in my view." Maja's eyes narrowed just a little. "I'm concerned that this will wreck the progress we've made to date. A team without trust loses enormous productivity."

"Yes, it does," Maja responded quietly. "Tell me, what has the crew decided to do about the situation?"

"Xavier has locked the supply cupboards."

"And what are they doing about Jonas?"

Claire bristled a little. "That's the problem. Nothing. Apart from putting him on toilet duty."

"Is there an atonement plan?"

"Jonas has suggested he could focus on the waste processing to accelerate decomposition."

"And the group was satisfied with that?"

Claire looked uncomfortable. "They've agreed to it."

"Let me review the footage." They watched the meeting recording together in silence.

Maja pursed her lips and studied the ceiling as she considered the ramifications of the situation.

"It seems to me that they've addressed it correctly, as per Gaia Enterprises protocol: group discussion, an atonement plan they agree to. What else would you have them do?"

"Something to address the actual issue: Jonas. Jonas is a serious problem. If he's stealing food, what other rules is he playing fast and loose with? Where is his commitment to the team? To the project?" Claire felt her pent-up frustration erupt. "He needs to be removed from the project before anything else is compromised."

"I don't think that is necessary, Claire. The crew addressed the issue head on. They are all hungry with the food production not meeting targets. It could easily have been one of the others."

"But it wasn't!" Claire leapt on the gap in Maja's argument. "It was Jonas. And he's becoming a serious liability."

"I think we need to wait and see. The crew needs to manage this, just as they would on the Moon. We can't go imposing our imperatives on them. They need to feel autonomous and self-sufficient, otherwise they will never be confident or able to handle the issues off-planet."

"They may never *get* off-planet if they have someone like Jonas screwing things up!" Claire blurted.

Maja eyed Claire for a moment. "Why don't we do this then: since we were not invited to attend the meeting and we did not ask permission to record or review the meeting, why don't we see if Xanthe raises it as part of her report? If she does, we can lean into it a little with her and press her on the points you raise – of group dynamics, productivity and so forth. If she finds the situation with Jonas untenable then we can step in and assist. Otherwise, we let this run its course."

"Maja, this is not an experiment! Our whole project is on the line here!" Claire jabbed her finger into the comms table to emphasise the point.

"Yes, it is," said Maja with an infuriating, quiet calm. "If they can't handle this little issue, how will they handle something even more challenging? I say let's wait and see." Her tone indicated the conversation was over. She stood and nodded to Claire as she hugged her cardigan closer against the late evening chill. "See you in the morning."

Claire watched her leave. Damn her! Maja was hell-bent on treating this whole project as a science experiment, to prove her human development theories. But Jonas should never have been chosen from the outset. He was far too volatile. Too underhanded. It spoke volumes about his character and trustworthiness. And now this! Who could trust anything he did when he was prepared to steal food!

Maja was becoming more stubborn as she became more frail. She used to listen more. They used to see everything eye to eye. But this thing with Jonas… she was so obstinate about it! She seemed blind to the ramifications. Claire felt the frustration squeeze her chest tight. She wondered if she might be able to convince Huw to take a stand about this. In the meantime, she'd have to step up her scrutiny of the SimHub. Put them under some more pressure – that would flush out the weakness and scourge that was Jonas. No way she was going to let that spoilt, reckless punk ruin their chances at the Olympus Project. There was too much riding on it.

CHAPTER FIFTY-SIX

*Nature has been taking a life to feed a life since
the dawn of time. Life is violent and tragic.*

XAVIER CONSUS IN WORLD DESIGNERS:
PERSPECTIVE AND PRACTICE

SimHub: Xanthe

THEY GATHERED FOR their nightly evening meal and ate in weary silence, each person chewing away at the rations. Rubbery synthetic meat in dry tortilla wraps. To add to the food woes following the stealing incident, the food printer was on the fritz again and the lab-grown meat was taking much longer than expected to incubate the chicken breasts. They had all been looking forward to fresh and not freeze-dried food for a change, and they were all thoroughly disappointed.

Xanthe struggled to her feet and headed to the comms room. Time for her check-in with Dr Mohammad. They were nearly eleven months into the simulation. It felt like six years, thought Xanthe. Their bodies were withering under the tight rations and constant work.

It had been a particularly trying week. Nothing seemed to

go right. Xavier had found more problems with the food crops. First the bad repair that no one remembered doing, then another tomato crop failed. Apollo had run several checks but found the input solution was correct. That meant running diagnostic checks on Apollo. Was the AI malfunctioning? Were its sensors incorrectly wired? All this was delaying the rest of the Hub setup. At this rate they'd have to default in the bid.

To make matters worse, Mission Control was riding them hard. Insisting they keep up their expedition experiments and emergency response scenarios alongside repair and construction work. Xanthe was bone tired. All her strategies for team motivation had run their course. She did not have the energy to rouse enthusiasm in anyone else.

This sucks, she thought. Simon's face loomed in her mind. Crossed arms with a bitter 'I told you so' on his lips. She sighed and sucked on the protein slurry from its plastic bag. I long for grass and wind on my face, she thought. Living in a self-contained bubble was an exercise in mental persistence. And she was running thin on that.

"SimHub, this is Mission Control." Dr Mohammad's voice boomed in the quiet space.

"Go ahead Mission Control. Dr Mohammad – how are you?" Xanthe asked.

Mohammad appeared on the holo. He looked prim and well groomed as ever, thought Xanthe. No struggling with rations on that end.

"I am well, thank you for asking, Commander Xanthe." She had graduated from Commander Waters to Commander Xanthe in this last week. When it was Troy's command shift in the first half of the build, he was never referred to as anything other than 'Commander Bruin'. Xanthe took it as a sign of approval and found herself amused by her own vain response.

"Where are we up to, Doc?" she asked.

"Well, I am quite concerned. Everyone's bio readings are poor. You have all lost a lot of weight. The fatigue we can put down to slight dehydration and lack of variety in the diet. I am sending over new supplement directives to try and address the deficiencies. Please, Commander Xanthe, make sure everyone drinks more water."

"Will do, Doc. Thanks for being in our corner."

He smiled, slightly embarrassed and nodded in acknowledgement. His image dissolved.

The fatigue has more to do with the cracking pace and relentless tasks, thought Xanthe.

Claire's voice came through the comms. Groans all round. Xanthe moved back to the comms interface.

"Go ahead, Control," she said.

"We need an inspection of the perimeter. There are incoming protesters flagged by the surveillance drones."

"We secured that yesterday!" said Jonas, exasperated.

"Control, are there any security breach readings in the system?" asked Xanthe.

"None so far. We want an analogue check."

"This is such bullshit," mumbled Serena. "Make-work projects so that Mission Control – Claire – can push their weight around."

"We also need a full assessment of the power and water system." Claire's voice was clinical. Xavier and Jonas rolled their eyes. Troy screwed up his face.

"Why is that, Control?" asked Xanthe, shooting them a warning look.

"If we have a breach, we need to know what the resources are."

"We did a full check three days ago. Will that do?"

"We would like it confirmed and double-checked."

"Affirmative. We'll get on it." Xanthe said. She kept her voice even then shut down the comms.

"I'll go, Xanthe," Dave said. "I don't mind. I've been having trouble sleeping again. The exercise might do me good."

"Are you sleepwalking again, Dave?" asked Troy.

"Is he sleepwalking! Lordy, the man walks as much at night as he does during the day! I caught him wandering through the food hub, lost and gibbering last night. You do talk rubbish, you know!" Serena gave him a friendly punch on the shoulder.

"Right, then. Dave and Troy, you're on perimeter check. Xavier, Serena – water. Jonas – that leaves you on power check. I'll manage the comms. I'll have something warm and delicious ready for you all when you get back."

Jonas saluted and pushed himself to his feet. "As long as it's not that heinous cricket cake again."

"Crickets are a—"

"'Great source of protein'. We know, Troy!" They responded in unison. It was a small moment of levity in face of the drudgery ahead.

⋘

SimHub Perimeter: Troy

It took an hour to suit up into the heavy spacesuits. Troy and Dave lumbered through the airlock into the desert night air. They felt the coolness through the thick insulated layers.

Dave's voice came through on the private comm link in Troy's helmet. "Troy, what say we divide and conquer? I'll go left, you go right?"

Troy looked at him through the bleary light of the helmet. "That's against protocol. Analogue requires two sets of eyes for redundancy."

"Come on. You're going to pull procedure on me right now? It's 1:30am. We've been on the go for three straight days. Besides, we know this is just Claire power tripping on us. Plus, we did this check yesterday, no?"

"Xanthe will know."

"Oh, I see… still trying to romance Ms Waters. You know she's married, right?"

"I know. And it's not that. I just don't want to…"

"What?"

"Let her down." Troy confessed.

"Well, I'll be damned. Mr Hedonist himself is showing signs of – what is it called – affection?"

"Shut up."

"I thought it was unprofessional for a psychologist to form attachments with their subjects."

"She's not my 'subject'. None of you are. We're colleagues. And caring is not the same as 'attachment'."

"Sure. You tell yourself that all day long. But in the meantime, we are freezing our balls off here. I think making a judgement call in the face of a stupid decision is the right thing, no? Besides, we just play along if Xanthe reaches out to us. Say we had to split up when we found an anomaly and wanted to check it upstream."

Troy hesitated. They *were* tired. If Dave was sleepwalking, that was a sure sign of fatigue and overwork. And fatigue was a real risk on these missions, especially in space. The lure of finishing earlier and getting into bed tipped his decision. "Okay. But don't cut any corners! Do this right."

"Of course! I am a highly trained world-designing professional. In a fake spacesuit."

Troy smiled. They fist-bumped in their bulky gloves and set off in opposite directions to check the security perimeter around the excavation site. The boring machine had nearly completed its tunnelling, ready for the 3D printer robot to go in and start layering the framework for the Hub extension. This was a major milestone in the project and the centrepiece of their design. SimHub crew was enormously proud of it.

Incoming protesters were a concern, Troy thought. Their site was top secret, but somehow, they'd discovered their location in the remote reaches of the desert. The security system should keep them out. Activated by infrared, heat sensors and motion control, nothing got through the repellent energy field. Its only weakness was the sensor wiring. Occasionally a curious bird would come in on top of it, avoiding all the sensors, and tug away at the casing. It had happened previously, but the backup sensors kicked in right away. It would be unlucky to have two go out at once. But that's what the analogue checks were for – see if there were any signs of decay or tampering and fix it up to ensure the redundancy was okay.

Christ he was tired. These spacesuits were cumbersome and sweaty, even in the cool of the desert. He just wanted to peel it off and slide into bed. With Xanthe. He admitted it. He liked her. Found her attractive. But it was more than that. He hadn't lied to Dave. He cared for her. There was a thread of sadness to her he hadn't been able to reach yet. She carried that pain, tightly wound somewhere deep. It made her seem more ethereal somehow. Intangible. Was that why he liked her so much? She was... inaccessible? Few women resisted his charms. He couldn't think of a single one before Xanthe. Nor many men. Troy was used to easy engagements. An attraction, a consummation, a letting go. It was a pure and simple interaction. No attachments, just human connection.

But Xanthe made him rethink all that. There was nothing easy about connecting with her. She was a mystery to him. What was inside that box of secrets?

Something moved in his peripheral vision. He shone his torch across the bushes beyond the perimeter. An animal? Nothing. He took a few steps closer, not wanting to activate the sensors. He traced the edge of the perimeter, looking for tracks. There was something, he felt sure of it...

"Hey, Big Fella!" Dave called over the helmet comms.

"Dave – where are you?" he said, peering into the edge of the shadows.

"Right behind you!"

Troy whirled and there was Dave, plodding in his enormous suit towards him.

"Dave! You scared me. You done?"

"Sure am."

"Hey, you see anything move beyond the perimeter? I swear something is out there."

"No. It's quiet as a graveyard. A little creepy. Maybe it's your imagination getting the better of you. It has been a long day."

"Maybe so." Troy swept the perimeter once more for good measure. Nothing.

"Troy, Dave, how are you travelling?" Xanthe's voice nudged them back to task awareness. They were at the eleventh post, all sensors and backups intact so far.

"Nearly done. We'll be back inside within the next twenty minutes," he replied.

"Good. I'll have something ready for you."

"Cricket cake?" Troy asked hopefully.

"Better than that – algae soup."

"If my face turns green, it's on you, Xanthe!" Dave cackled. "I've already been given a bow shot from Serena about too much green stuff!"

"You'll be fine. I'm more worried about the waste recycler going down again. Can you imagine mopping up neon green turds?" Troy added.

"That's enough you two! Hurry up and finish the job so we can all wrap up for the day."

"Yes, Commander. On our way."

CHAPTER FIFTY-SEVEN

*Allegiances formed for the most tenuous of reasons. Simply naming
a group was enough to create a sense of tribe, an 'us against them'.*

CORONER'S REPORT, THE TERRA BLANCA TRAGEDY

SimHub: Xanthe

XANTHE WAITED FOR Claire to appear in the holo comms. The other
team members were already on their assignments for the day. Jonas
was determined to get the waste recycling ramped up while Serena and
Dave marched off to the excavation site. Troy would help Xavier with
the crops, testing the system, looking for leaks. She hoped the atonement agreement would hold and they could build connection again.

Claire's image appeared on the holo.

"Good morning, Control," said Xanthe.

"Commander, hello. What is the food situation there?"

The question caught her off guard. Claire was always straight
down to business, but food was not at the top of the agenda. This
was usually Mohammad's purview, while Claire focused on the
excavation since it was so far behind schedule.

"What do you mean 'food situation'?"

"Rations. How are the rations?"

Does she know about the food stealing, wondered Xanthe. But how? No one would have sent her a message. Holy shit! She was listening! Xanthe thought she'd turned off Mission Control comms during their team meetings. No, she *knew* she did! Claire must have watched the security cameras, and somehow activated the audio she'd turned off.

"Good, under control," said Xanthe. Her mind raced on how to best address this, since lying was not an option. Claire obviously knew Jonas had been sneaking food. "We had one crew member needing to adjust their rations, but we have it sorted now."

"Is there anything else about that, Commander?" Claire challenged.

Damn her. Well, she wasn't going to throw Jonas to the wolves. "Yes. Jonas thinks we can ramp up waste processing to give the crops a boost. We might be able to get food production back on track if he rejigs some of the power to increase the airflow in the processing tanks."

"I see." Claire let the unspoken hang between them. The discomfort was heavy, but Xanthe held her ground.

Claire broke the silence. "And how is the excavation going?"

Xanthe notched that up as a win and cheered silently to herself. She gave the report. They should be on track for printing the walls tomorrow.

"Good news, at last," said Claire.

Xanthe let the barb flow past her. Claire was always critical, obsessed with detail.

"I look forward to the day's report at 16:00."

"I'll be ready. As usual," Xanthe said. She threw her own little barb back over the fence.

"See that you are. Mission Control out." Her image shut down before Xanthe could retort. She was such a bitch! At least there were no extra assignments today. They really didn't need that after the food issue. They were all just hanging on by a thread, at the moment. And she wasn't sure how the team would react to finding out they were being spied on, too. That was a bigger concern. Privacy was a big deal for them as they were living in such a self-contained space. They didn't need Claire meddling in their team issues. Xanthe had it under control. This was her crew! So, they had a rough spot. But she felt they had made progress with the atonement plan. And Jonas had turned a corner with that sharing about his family. Vulnerability and truth always build bridges. She wasn't going to let Claire tear them down!

How would she tell the team about the comms breach without alerting Claire? She thought for a moment, then an idea formed. Time to go analogue.

⊰

Three days passed and the team was exhausted. Claire had them run scenarios and do perimeter checks every night. The protesters had managed to sneak around the road barricades. The security team had not yet managed to locate them in the desert scrub. They must be using some kind of comms jammer. It was making Mission Control nervous. Xanthe wasn't worried. She knew the perimeter security was solid. They'd checked it enough times.

As she expected, the crew reacted with outrage to the news of Claire's spying. She left a message on an old-school paper-and-pen notepad, in the main toilet cubicle. The one place she knew there were no cameras or microphones. The team had vented disgust. Then they started drafting code words to drop into casual conversation in the dining room so Claire would not be alert to their own internal team matters.

⊰

They grabbed their respective meals from the food cupboard after Xavier unlocked it and settled into companionable, silent munching.

325

They jumped as the room comms activated: incoming call from Mission Control.

Xanthe pushed her chair back and said pointedly, "I have some discomfort in the posterior," *Claire is really riding my arse.*

"Perhaps you need a suppository?" said Dave. *Claire can shove it up her arse.*

"Or a long ride on a short pony," said Serena. *Claire can go and get fucked.*

"Go ahead Mission Control," she said, activating the comms, trying not to laugh.

"SimHub crew, you will need to prepare for night ops. Perimeter check and siege rescue scenario." There was a collective groan.

"That's an interesting opportunity," said Xavier. *That's fucked.*

"Prepare for the briefing in one hour." said Claire.

"I'll put my hand up for that," said Jonas. *I've got an issue to raise.*

"Well, I've got a big one to unload," said Troy, getting up. *Important message in the toilet.* "Jonas, perhaps you'll join me?"

"Thanks Mission Control, we'll be ready." Xanthe signed off. She nodded at Troy who gave her the thumbs up. Claire must be wondering how they all became so comfortable sharing their bodily functions, all of a sudden.

When Troy and Jonas returned, Xanthe ducked out to the toilet. The message read: "I've got a comms jammer I confiscated from Pierre at selection. Thought it might come in handy at some stage. If Jonas can get the comms jammer to work in the SimHub, I've got an idea. Jonas?"

Xanthe tagged Jonas back at the dining room table, "Jonas, can you check the toilet – I think the bio flush is on the fritz again."

Jonas returned after his trip to the toilet with a big thumbs up to Troy and Xanthe. "All good now! Systems are go in the SimHub!"

❧

They gathered in the Comms room, kitted out for night ops. They'd agreed via the Throne Room Comms, as they'd dubbed it, to dress as if ready for action. Jonas would hide the jammer in his pocket and activate it as they were about to get the briefing. They bubbled with nervous excitement, enjoying the subterfuge.

Xanthe waited at the holo for Claire to come online. Soon her image appeared. "SimHub, this is Mission Control." As if they didn't know.

"Go ahead Mission Control," said Xanthe, appearing stoic.

"Your mission is—" the message crackled and came through unclear. They all leant in, pretending to try and decipher the message.

"Sorry Control, you're breaking up. Do you read, over?"

"Night—ops—" the message crackled and Claire's image flickered in and out.

"Sorry Control – say again, over."

"Perimeter—" the image went blank.

"Comms are breaking up, Control. Do you read, over?"

Static popped and nothing re-emerged.

"Control, I'll try message bank, over."

Xanthe made a show of going to the data pad and pressing 'connect' multiple times.

"Control, comms are down. Repeat, comms are down, over. Try the emergency channel." She went over to the emergency unit and dialled the connect number. It went through, as they expected.

"This is Mission Control. Is that you SimHub?"

"Affirmative, Control. There seem to be problems with the comms. The holo and data pad aren't connecting. And this line is very sketchy too."

"What do—" the line continued to hiss.

"Control, this is SimHub," Xanthe repeated. "I believe you

can hear our signal but yours is very weak. Permission to suspend night ops and repair comms?"

"—night ops—"

"Say again Control."

"—night ops"

"Negative Control, we do not read, over."

"—mission granted."

"Affirmative, Control. Understood permission to suspend night ops granted. We will work on restoring comms."

"—tive."

"Understand, permission granted. We will call once comms are restored. SimHub out."

Then all the comms went silent. They looked at each other.

"And done!" said Jonas, beaming. "Comms are down, security cameras are offline."

"Even the backup power on the cameras?" asked Serena.

"Please! I'm not an amateur. They can't see us, hear us or hail us. We are free, my friends!" Jonas threw his arms into a victory stance.

"You're sure? Absolutely sure?" Troy asked.

"One hundred percent. Troy, my main man. The show is all yours!"

"Fan-bloody-tastic!" Troy said, "Listen up SimHub crew, meet in the Stim Room in twenty minutes. Dress Code 5."

"What's that one again?" asked Dave.

"Party clothes!" Serena said clapping her hands.

"SimHub crew!" Xanthe called out, stopping them. They turned, excitement turning to anxiety at her tone. "You've worked hard. It's been a long few days…" She let them hang on her words. "Now, it's time to party!" They hooted and high-fived. "See you in twenty! Best dressed wins a prize!"

CHAPTER FIFTY-EIGHT

"Sometimes you just need to dance."

TROY BRUIN, 'PERSON OF THE YEAR' INTERVIEW

Stim Room: Xanthe

XANTHE RUSHED INTO the room, straightening her dress. Troy was waiting for them in the Stim Room. He had his favourite white linen shirt on, open at the top as if beach ready. He'd managed a shower in the brief twenty minutes and looked electric.

"Oh!" She said as she caught sight of Troy. He looked amazing! She'd managed to numb her feelings for Troy to neutral over the past few months. They'd been so busy with operations, always dressed in overalls or spacesuits, casual wear was mostly tracksuit pants in their rare free time. Nothing provocative about work clothes, she thought. Tonight he'd showered and looked... what was it? Happy, she thought. Or maybe it was *her* feeling happy? She realised she hadn't felt happy in a long, long time. The thrill of fooling Claire and getting a break from the constant scrutiny made her giddy.

Troy caught her looking at him and favoured her with one of his slow, lopsided grins. His lips were so lush, she thought.

Jonas appeared in tight jeans and a clean white t-shirt. *Damn!* thought Xanthe. Jonas had been working out! He looked good, too! Serena strutted in and posed, mini-skirt and silver top flashing with sequins.

"You brought a silver sequinned top? To the SimHub?" Xanthe was incredulous.

"Darling, one should never go anywhere without a little spangle!"

"Holy shit!" said Troy. Xanthe, Serena and Jonas spun to see what he was staring at.

It was Dave. He wore a tight bright pink top and even tighter and brighter pink pants. Enormous sunglasses covered half his face.

"My word!" said Serena. "Do you dress in anything but neon?"

"My dear, dull in dress, dull in heart. If you're going to a party, dress like a party!" He blew her a kiss.

"We're all here now?" asked Troy.

"Nope! Guess who's missing?" asked Serena.

They smirked, and called out together, "XAVIER!"

He lumbered into the room, tucking his collared shirt into his jeans. "Sorry I'm late," he said.

"Wouldn't want to let us down by exceeding expectations, would you?" said Serena. Xanthe noted they were back on friendly terms after months of tension. Serena had worked hard to rebuild the friendship after his belligerent antagonism regarding all things food. Serena had changed her approach. Instead of trying so hard to impress him with suggestions, she got curious about his work. She asked more questions. She listened intently. In turn, Xavier became more open to her ideas. They started to collaborate more on food projects. This was new for her, Serena told Xanthe. A friendship built on mutual respect.

"Okay, SimHub crew, listen up," said Troy. "I've prepared a nice little experience for us. We're going to Paris – warming up at a nightclub there. Then to Rome and the Colosseum! And if you're good, to New York. The New York that was before the floods," he added. Now to help you get in the dance mood, I've prepared a little tea."

"Not that shite from the baths?" Serena asked, concerned.

"Nope. A different one. This will help you get into the beat of the music. It will loosen your limbic system." He turned and grabbed something from the corner of the room. A teapot and six small ceramic cups.

"You brought your teapot?" asked Xanthe.

"It was my personal sentimental item," he replied. That smile again, she thought. She let it wash over her instead of pushing it aside like usual.

Xanthe took a teacup and sipped. She appreciated the feel of the ceramic edge. She hadn't anticipated missing things like cups and glasses and dishwater in the SimHub. Their commitment to space-like living highlighted all the familiar comforts that they – and future moon visitors – would miss.

The tea was sweet and flowery. She inhaled deeply and felt the warmth of the beverage seep through her. It was like a gentle undertow, dragging her softly out to sea. She felt the warmth flood her limbs as she drained the last bit. She gave the teacup back to Troy and he took it gently from her. His whole head was a giant smile, she thought. How did one human have such enormous warmth, she wondered.

Troy handed out the VR glasses, wraparounds they wore like sunglasses. "Let's get this party started! Apollo, bring up Paris." The walls lit up with a pristine street scene of cobblestones in a narrow street of apartment housing rising above them. On one wall was a silver doorway pulsing with light, beckoning.

Xanthe slipped on the glasses and dialled into the experience Troy had programmed for them. The scene faded in. They stepped through the doorway and arrived in a dance club, lights started to twinkle and then flash. They could see each other, while immersed in a VR world with a heaving group of dancers all around them. The music grew louder. It thrummed and pulsed.

Xanthe felt herself moving to its rhythm. She discovered she was enjoying the feel of the beat riding her body. She moved with it, ecstatic. She laughed and danced, enjoying watching her friends dance alongside her. Dave was outrageous of course – doing high kicks, spins and even the splits, his pink pants surprisingly stretchy. They hooted and egged him on. Jonas followed with some martial arts manoeuvres and a backflip. Serena floated and sizzled, flashing silver and gold as she spun. Xanthe stomped and shimmied and sang to the chorus. Troy grabbed her and swayed with her side by side, then twirled her and lifted her up to the sky. She laughed and laughed. Even Xavier sauntered across the dance floor, doing a casual strut and nod, all angles and edges, but suave and sophisticated.

They danced and danced, heaving and sweating, and singing to the songs they knew. There was the old classic *Earth Monsters* from the Glitterati, *Vapid Vibes* from Julius Cesare, and song after song from Titanium Ricochet. Anthems from a familiar past. The VR program shifted from the Paris nightclub to Rome, where they walked through the gates of the restored Colosseum and joined fifty thousand spectators in a spectacular concert of Pink Reimagined. The roars of the crowd, the dazzling pyrotechnics and aerial acrobatics – including boot-powered flyovers of the band – were stunning. The music hooked and moved them. They felt free and alive and… together.

Gradually they grew tired. The music seemed to take its cue from their shifting energy and ebbed. Troy said, "Apollo, bring up the New York lounge scene." The lights dimmed and the scene projected on the walls was a comfortable and cosy room with flickering candlelight and mellow music, softening the room and their spirits. They dragged the bean bags from the corners of the room. This was one of Troy's design preferences for the Stim Room: soft and flexible for all sorts of VR journeys, as well as for regular use.

"I haven't danced like that in bloody years!" said Serena as she flopped into her bag.

"I don't think I've *ever* danced like that!" said Xavier.

"I've certainly never seen anyone dance like Dave!" Jonas said.

Dave did a tired bow, with a cavalier flourish of his hand.

They sat quietly, listening to the music, enjoying the post-exertion elation.

"Of all the people on the planet, and off it, I am glad I am here with you lot," said Troy. They turned and looked at him. It was not like Troy to get sentimental.

"Well, well, big boy! What's got into you! Is it the tea making you all soppy?" said Serena.

He smirked. "No, not the tea – that has well and truly worn off. Or been danced off. I just feel grateful for your company. I mean, this has been a tough gig. Much harder than I expected. And I'm a damned psychologist! I never realised how much I'd miss the freedoms we had on Earth."

"Like what?" asked Xanthe.

"Like… the freedom to breathe fresh air. Or walk in the rain. Or go for a swim. Or simply go outside! This sealed SimHub is a real challenge. Not just for human development, but for human sanity." He paused, looking at each of them. "I've learnt a lot from each of you."

"Is there some*one* you miss? On the outside?" asked Xanthe. She sat leaning up against the wall, next to him, and turned her head so she could see him better. His shirt was damp with sweat.

He thought about it for a moment.

"No, not really. I'm not that close to my family. My parents passed away a few years back and my brother is busy doing his own thing. I haven't been one for… attachments. I've lived my life pretty freely. This is the most time I've spent with anyone! Excluding my executive assistant. Odette has organised my world for years."

"Do you miss her?" asked Dave.

"Maybe a little. But no, not really." Troy looked at Dave, who was sitting cross-legged, pulling at his shirt to try and air it dry. "How about you, Dave? Do you miss your daughter? How is Sophia anyway?"

"She's doing okay. She's disappointed she can't start university this year."

"Why's that?"

Dave sighed and said, "Sven." They noted the flat tone as he said the name.

"Sven? Your husband? What happened?"

Dave hesitated. "Sven is… a gambler. He recently got a hold of Sophia's savings and blew them in one of those underground private gambling rooms. She stupidly believed he was going to use the cash to pay down the mortgage on our apartment."

"Oh my god! That's horrendous!" Xanthe said. "You can't lend her the money? Surely you have enough from this job to pay her fees?"

Dave shook his head sadly. "I'm still paying off his debts from years ago. Everything I have is paying the bare minimum on our loans and the rest goes to his gambling debts."

"Are you still together?" Serena asked.

"It's complicated. A lot of water under the bridge, I think is the expression." Dave looked uncomfortable. "What about you, Serena? You missing anyone?"

"Nah. I cut all ties when I applied to this gig. My best mate at work stabbed me in the back right before I headed to selection. And my last relationship, well…" she glanced at Xanthe, "that ended badly. Hard to find a bloke who can be honest, it seems."

"Xavier, do you miss your family?" asked Troy. The big man was playing with a locket on his necklace. Troy knew it had tiny images of his wife and two teenage kids.

"Of course!" he said. "My kids are terrors. Luckily, my wife is a hard taskmaster. She keeps them well in line."

"Tougher than you?" asked Jonas.

"She makes me look like Santa Claus." They laughed at that, trying to imagine anyone more regimented than Xavier.

"Jonas, who's in your world? Got anyone you're missing?" asked Troy.

"No one special. I had a girlfriend, last year. But it got too hard. I was working on building my career. Then I went back to the *Sea Rover* for a while. Had to get out of there though. The *Sea Rover* is a big place, but with parents like mine it can feel very small."

"What are they like – the famous Don and Jenny Seaborn?" asked Xanthe.

Jonas shrugged. "They're a little... distant. I guess that's the best way to describe them. And harsh, too. Everything was always about the *Rover* – getting it right, making it better, experimenting, staying ahead of the world-building profession. They weren't the most caring of parents. Everything was always a lesson to be learnt. There were always rules to follow." Jonas found himself disclosing more than he usually did, but he felt comfortable here, and the words just wanted to come out. "My Dad is a real ballbreaker! Can't take a joke. When I was about ten, me and this other kid had a great idea. He had a dog – a little dachshund called Samson – and we scooped its poo from the kennel run, put it in a bag and set in on fire outside the captain's lounge when my Dad was in there. He ran out and stomped on it to put out the flames, and well, you can imagine. He was not happy. But then – " Jonas looked bleak. "Instead of ranting and chewing us out, he ordered my friend Jinn to hand over the dog. Jinn brought up little Samson and then—" Jonas swallowed hard to keep his emotions in check. "Don Fucking Seaborn grabbed the dog and threw it overboard, just like that. Didn't say a word. Just threw the dog over the side, like it was nothing. He didn't say anything. Not one word! Just gave us a long hard look. Jinn never really got over it."

"*Putain! Quel con!*" swore Xavier.

"What a dick!" said Serena.

"Yeah. Well. So, you can see why I'm not all that keen to hang out with them. I haven't talked to them in months, in fact. All they want to know is if we're winning the competition or not. And since we're behind on all the milestones, there's nothing parent-worthy to report."

The reminder of their struggles in the SimHub was a nagging prickle.

"How about you, Xanthe? Do you miss Simon?" Serena asked gently, hoping to change the subject.

Xanthe flinched a little at the question. "Some days," she said. "We've been together for a long time, been through a lot. But he doesn't really support my work, here."

"Is he anti-space?" asked Jonas.

"He would call it 'pro-Earth'. But yes, he is part of the protest movement. We end up fighting about it every time we speak." The team knew things weren't good between them. Raised voices and arguments were hard to miss, even in the confines of the comms room.

"Did you ever want kids?" asked Xavier. They knew she didn't have any.

Maybe it was the exhaustion settling in. Maybe it was the tea and its after-effects. Or maybe it was the strange letting go she was feeling as they shared with one another, but Xanthe felt the floor shift beneath her. The question hit her hard. She was used it to by now, of course, the topic of kids, and bracing for the question that inevitably came in new social settings: "Do you have any children?" She usually responded with a simple and solid 'No' and let others use their imagination to work out why. The awkwardness of the unspoken questions – 'Why not? Did you want them? If not, why not? And if you did want them, but couldn't have them, what was the problem?'. Most people gauged by her tone that she didn't want to explore it further and so left the itchy, unasked questions alone. How do you answer any of those questions without making everyone feel uncomfortable? Without dredging up the dark and violent past? The secret place in her heart where she felt equal parts terrible dark grief and wistful relief?

But here in this space, in this small bubble of humanity, she felt safe. She felt held. She felt cared for.

"I did want kids," she whispered, staring at her fingers twisting the edge of her dress. "We had one. A son," she breathed. She looked up at their surprised faces. This was a secret they hadn't guessed. "But then being a mother... well, it was hard. It was not what I expected. I felt so trapped! I just wanted to build my paramedic career. I was exhausted all the time. Felt guilty all the time. Don't get me wrong – I loved him. I love my son. But I missed the freedom of not being a parent." Xanthe rubbed her face and took a deep breath.

"Then he died. In the tsunami. He was... he was only four." There were gasps and sounds of sadness from them. Her words came faster now, rolling out like waves, breaking on the shore of her consciousness. "I held him. We ran. God, it was loud! All that water! Then it hit me, swept me off my feet like I was a feather. I held him tight as I could. So tight. But the water tumbled and spun and he was wrenched from me. I grabbed for his hand. I held his fingers for just a moment. I can still feel the touch of them as he tried to hang on. Then he was gone. Just... gone. And we never found him." The tears washed over her, and she let them fall, quiet and silent. A river of grief with no end. "And I just can't help how much I miss him. And how much relief I felt at the same time – no more parenting. No more divided focus. I hate myself for feeling that. God! I am a terrible human!"

They were quiet as Xanthe's grief swept through the room.

Troy moved closer and put his arm around her shoulders. Her lip trembled. Xavier moved to her other side and put his arm around her too. Jonas, Serena and Dave all shuffled in, making a tight circle, and put arms around each other. Serena reached out across the circle and placed a hand on Xanthe's foot.

"What was his name?" asked Troy.

Deep from the depths, the silent word, forbidden all these years, the name unsaid, drifted upwards and she whispered, "Jack." And then a little more loudly, with a bit more certainty, "His name was Jack." His name filled the room, bright as sunlight.

"Jack." Troy said. "It's a good name." He squeezed her shoulder and she leant in to the warm, gentle strength of him. "Tonight, we honour Jack. We dedicate our work and play to him, for all the days he didn't get to live on this sweet planet, or on any other. May this little band of misfits design a world worth living in, in honour of those like Jack who didn't get the chance."

"For a world worth living in," said Serena.

And then together, "For a world worth living in."

CHAPTER FIFTY-NINE

Once broken, trust is an ugly and discarded thing.

ATHENA AI IN WISDOM OF THE AGES

Air Scrubber Dome: Jonas

"SEVEN HELLS!" EXCLAIMED Jonas. It was his turn to check the air scrubber and wipe down the slime that accumulated in the processing chamber. The walls were thick with mucus and mould. Way more than usual. So odd, he thought.

He checked the readings on the output vents – they all seemed normal, no extra moisture or pathogens detected. What would cause this build-up? He was going to have to do a full service of the machine. He hailed Xanthe on the wrist comm to let her know.

"Xanthe, the air scrubber looks like it's malfunctioning. I'm going to give it a full service."

"Damn!" came her response. They both knew a full service would take him out of action for most of the day and delay the excavation project yet again. They were meant to start the last wing today and that needed an engineer on site. Serena needed him as engineer support, and Dave who was nominated to assist, on site to run the excavator safely while she checked the tunnels. But the air scrubber took priority. Excess carbon dioxide or unwanted microbes would cause an imbalance in their crops. They didn't need that – just as the crops were starting to come good again, with the waste processor turbocharging their growth. They were so close to the end of the project now! Any delay spelt disaster for their pitch in the comp.

"I'll be as quick as I can," Jonas said, trying to sound positive.

Jonas shut down the primary scrubber. He opened its interface and peered inside. The honeycomb filters needed cleaning for one. He grabbed the suction vacuum and passed it over the fragile layers of the filtration system. Something clunked into the vacuum. What the hell? He opened up the vacuum to see what made the noise. A plastic cap. Another one of those damn things?

Jonas unscrewed the entire unit. Was the intake hose compromised? As he lifted the unit out of the wall, he saw it. Was that an empty water bag? He pulled the item out of the wall space and stared at it. How the hell did that get there? There's no way into the intake mechanisms for anything of that size. It had to have been left there. Who did the last damn service? Some idiot must have placed it there while they were working on it and forgotten about it. He checked the log. It was Dave. And Serena? This was normally a one-person job. Oh that's right, Dave suggested that Serena help him that day so they could get out to the excavation site sooner.

He unscrewed the panels of the scrubber. This was going to need major surgery to make sure the delicate honeycombs weren't wrecked.

What the—?! Jonas stared at the honeycombs. They were slashed. Could the water bag have caused that? No. It couldn't have. If the bag had been left there by accident, the lid could have been loose and got sucked into the scrubber, in theory. It would have jammed in the system but that's about it. These honeycombs were damaged by something more forceful. Did those idiots drop something on it and not check? Unlikely.

Shit, thought Jonas. The unthinkable dawned on him. This was deliberate damage. Somebody had taken something sharp – maybe a screwdriver? and then driven it through the honeycomb. But why? Who? Why would anyone want to wreck the air scrubber for Chrissake? If you were going to sabotage a project, there were other ways of doing it that were more effective. Hull breach for one. That could wreck their crops pretty quickly. Poison their water for another. They'd all be sick for days. Wreck the comms. This was sneaky. Hard to find. Only a trained mechanic would be able to spot the damage to the honeycombs.

Jonas sat down on the floor with the scrubber in front of him. He thought about each of his crew mates. Which one of them could do such a thing? Xavier? Nah – he was too busy and obsessed with the plants. He avoided slime duty like the plague, saying he didn't want to risk contaminating the crops. Serena? She didn't go much for subtlety. Troy? What possible reason could he have for sabotage? There *was* something odd about him, though. The way he was so noncommittal. Or Xanthe? Or Dave? There must a be another explanation for the damage. But Jonas came up blank.

And what should he do about it? Tell Xanthe? But what if she was the saboteur? What if she was secretly in league with her anti-space husband? Possible. His heart sank. This would break the SimHub crew. The food stealing had been bad enough. It had taken him ages to earn back trust from the others and even now the stores were still locked. But this? It was horrible.

Jonas put the unit back in place. He wiped down the slime carefully and rebooted the machine. He was going to have to print some new filters, taking even more time. He hadn't had to print anything since the waste management seals. The seals! Shit! He knew there was something off about that whole thing. He hurried to his room and rifled through his container of belongings. Ahh! There it was. He'd kept the piece of the seal that didn't look quite right. He scrutinised it again. Yes. There it was. The rubber was sliced, not worn. It was possible to do that damage if something sharp had pressed against it during installation. Possible. Not likely. The seals had been sliced. And that freakin' cap – put in the water processing gauge – on purpose?

Crap. Was he just being paranoid? All these setbacks in the SimHub. It felt like the universe or something was against them. Jonas sat on the edge of the bed and stared again at the seal.

It wasn't some*thing*. It was some*one*. And he was going to find out who.

CHAPTER SIXTY

We can't always foresee the consequences of our actions. But our actions always have consequences. That's why it's so important to ask, 'Can I live with this decision, no matter the outcome?'

MAJA GARCIA, TERRA BLANCA JOURNALS

SimHub Comms Room: Xanthe

XANTHE STARED AT the comms screens and holos without seeing them. She was lost in thought, replaying the conversation she had with Simon the previous night. He told her that the anti-space protests were ramping up. Reports were saying the Olympus Project was really about creating an off-world sanctuary for the extremely rich. Another rumour suggested that increasing ocean temperatures with even more severe storms were to come, with the likelihood of global food crop failures causing mass starvation. Simon insisted they could still reverse the effects, if only they dedicated the resources to saving Earth's atmosphere instead of planning to escape it. Simon called the Olympus Project a folly and a waste. She threw it back at him this time, refusing to be cowered by his criticism. The Olympus Project was essential to humanity's future, not an obstacle to it.

What they were learning on the project could be applied to life on Earth as well as life on the Moon – or anywhere else. If they could grow crops safely, live in a self-contained environment, then there was hope on Earth and off-planet. Humans had a future here and now, and well into the future.

And the long-term future of humanity, of consciousness, was off-planet. They both knew that. The purists insisted that humans were meant only for planet Earth, and when the Earth boiled dry as it got closer to the sun, that was its fate – along with all other living creatures. Who were we to mess with the design of the Universe? Back and forth the arguments went. Save Earth, save Humanity, or let it be.

Xanthe hated that Simon refused to consider her point of view. He was full of venom. Was it the loss of their son? Had this turned him into the angry man he'd become? One who blamed the lack of action on climate change for the tsunami that had killed their little boy? Climate change was possible, but the more likely explanation was that the tsunami was man-made – a massive explosion out to sea that caused the surge. Many thought it was the Russians. For Simon, the fault of their current predicament was squarely on the shoulders of the big corporate giants and their relentless appetite for more.

Xanthe sighed. The distance between them was more than the breadth of a desert and the length of the project. In the depth of her grief, she had chosen hope. Simon had chosen blame and fury. And now she had become the object and symbol of everything he despised. She felt the last of their relationship fraying like a rope rubbed thin under tension. One by one, the strands of their connection were splitting, leaving the weight of the future hanging by the tenuous and fragile thread of their shared past. Was it enough?

Xanthe was startled from her reverie by Troy who handed her a bag of tea. She thanked him. Though she was grateful for the gesture, drinking from a bag was never that satisfying. She thought again about printing a ceramic cup with a sipping lid to mimic the feel of a real mug. But every time she thought of the sipper, the face of her long dead son and his little chubby arms reaching for his own plastic sippy cup welled up in front of her. She shuddered and pressed the memory down again.

"Where are the others?' asked Troy.

"Xavier is in the Food Hub. I had to send Jonas and Serena out to the excavation site. It looks like the wall printer might be jammed again."

"Again? That damn thing."

"Did you see the protesters?"

"Sure did. They were quite loud and obnoxious."

"I can see that." Xanthe flicked the comms to show the perimeter. A group of some thirty protesters had found their site. Xanthe was up early when the perimeter alarm went off. She hailed Mission Control immediately, but it would be a couple of hours or so before they could get the security forces over there to remove them. How did they slip though drone surveillance? she wondered. Thirty people were not that easy to hide in the bush. They must have very sophisticated comms jammers for that size group.

The image flickered and went blank. "What the hell?" Xanthe tried to reactivate the camera image, but nothing.

"Troy, you and Dave just checked the perimeter cameras – they were all good, right?" she said in a panic.

"Yes, they were," he said, apprehensive, leaning over the console with her.

The image popped back up. "Ah, thank goodness." Xanthe said. "Must have been a glitch in the transmission." The protesters were there again, chanting away, waving large *One Earth, One Home* banners. A chill crawled up the back of her neck. Something unnerved her about these people.

"Where is Dave, anyway?" she asked.

"He dropped one of his tools. Had to go back to get it."

"That guy is so damn clumsy. He's going to need industrial reinforced velcro in space! We can't go losing tools all over the place."

"You think we'll make it? To space? You think we'll get a shot?" asked Troy.

Xanthe sipped from her bag. "It's pretty close at the moment. We've made up all the food production quotas thanks to Jonas's hacks. And our design is second to none, of course. We just need to get this last section printed and sealed ready for inspection. I think Aryanna is really going to love it." She took another sip and added, "I love it." The thought surprised her. It had all been just a project, an abstraction up to this point. Now that they were getting close, it held more meaning for her. The SimHub was a home, a sanctuary.

"What do you love most about it?" asked Troy.

His voice shifted, quieter. Xanthe felt a warm rush. The intimacy of his tone. She glanced at him, taking in his pale blue eyes. They were crystal pools of ice and light.

"I like the atrium the best. The view to the sky, to the stars, the climb upwards of the plants. Makes me feel big and small at the same time."

"I like that too. Say, I—" he was interrupted by the clamour of Dave arriving back in the SimHub through the airlock.

"There he is!" Xanthe flicked up the security image of Dave removing his suit. "Can you go grab him and we'll do a new-day briefing, now that Serena and Jonas are out dealing with the wall printer?"

"Sure," he smiled with his slow full-mouthed crooked grin. He placed a hand on her shoulder and squeezed before he left to get Dave. Little shards of delight ran down her spine. She took a deep breath and shoved the illicit yearning aside.

She watched the protester holo again and then hailed Jonas and Serena on their helmet comms.

"Jonas here. What's up Commander?"

"Hey, Jonas. What's your sitrep?"

"We sent the drone down to take a look but couldn't see what the problem was. So Serena is gearing up to get eyes on site. She's just about ready to go now." Jonas activated his helmet cam to give Xanthe his perspective. She could see Serena in her abseiling harness over her spacesuit, lowering herself into the excavation shaft.

"I'll get this fixed in a jiffy, Commander. We'll be back in time for morning tea. Tell Xavier I'm counting on fresh tomatoes today!"

"Okay, thanks for that. Serena, be careful. You'll only have line of sight comms down there."

"Roger that."

"Jonas, are the protesters near you?"

"Nah. They're gathered up at the airlock end of the site. We ducked around the back so they wouldn't see us as we came out here."

"Nice work. Okay, well, keep us up to date with your progress."

"Will do."

Troy popped his head back in the comms room. "We're ready. Meet you in the kitchen?"

"Coming now."

She grabbed her bag of tea and joined Troy and Dave at the kitchen table that doubled as ops command and briefing room.

"Where is everybody?" asked Dave as he eased into a chair, limbs stiff after the exertion in the big spacesuit.

"Xavier's in the Food Hub and Jonas and Serena are out on site at the tunnels."

"What? Why?" Alarm sounded in his voice.

"Relax. It's the printer again. It's jammed. I had to send Jonas and Serena out just after you and Troy left for perimeter security check."

"Where are they now?" his face still looked distressed.

"Serena has gone down the shaft to do visual inspection of the machine because the drone couldn't pick anything up."

"She went down the shaft?" Dave was incredulous.

Xanthe was getting annoyed now. "Yes. That's what we do when we can't get things rebooted remotely."

"Where's Jonas? Did he go down, too?" Dave ran his hand through his sweaty helmet hair.

"No he's above ground, as per protocol. What's up with you, Dave?"

"Listen, Xanthe, you need to get Serena out of there. Now."

"Why? What's wrong?"

Dave blinked nervously.

"It's—I've got a…" he searched for words. "I'm worried about those protesters," he blurted.

"They're fine. They're on the other side of the site, far away. I checked in with Jonas and he said they were out of sight."

"Listen, you need to—"

"Command! Command! Come in!" It was Jonas from the comms room, his voice panicked. Xanthe was up like a shot. She ran to the comms room and grabbed the receiver. Troy and Dave followed her in.

"This is Command. Go ahead Jonas."

"Xanthe we've got an emergency situation here!" He turned on the helmet cam. Xanthe, Troy and Dave gasped. A cloud of dust wafted up from the shaft.

"What's going on, Jonas?" Xanthe kept her voice calm.

"Somehow, a protester got in. He snuck up on me when I was watching the tunnel after Serena abseiled down the shaft. He shoved me over and dropped something down the shaft. Then there was an explosion."

"Are you okay? Is Serena okay?"

"I don't know! I can't get Serena on the comms. I can't see anything but dirt down there. Looks like the tunnel is blocked off."

Xanthe's heart raced. She willed it to slow. She took a few deep breaths to calm her thoughts.

"Jonas, did Serena get clear of the shaft and into the tunnel before the explosion?

"I can't be sure," he said. "She was down there a while and might have been heading back to the shaft when that arsehole took me out. She might be in the tunnel, she might be under the debris, or the tunnel might have collapsed on her."

"Where is the intruder now?"

"Not sure. He dashed away. He might still be on site."

"Okay. Stand by." Xanthe looked at Dave and Troy. "I want the two of you to head out pronto with the rescue kit. Wear the lightweight spacesuits for quick response. I want you over there on site in twenty minutes or less.

"Jonas, I'm sending Troy and Dave out to you now. Can you get a look over the edge of the shaft for me? Make sure you clip in," she added. Jonas still disliked heights, even with all the training at the Baths of Caracalla.

His helmet cam wavered over the pit. He turned on the spotlight on his helmet. There was just a mound of earth and remnants of the shaft's reinforcements halfway up the hole.

"Shit!" said Xanthe.

"Commander, I've got to get down there. The guys are going to take ages to get over here. That might be too late for Serena."

"Negative, Jonas. Do NOT attempt this on your own. We don't need you to collapse under there as well."

"Xanthe, time is running out. Serena could be crushed under the debris. Her suit may be compromised, and she'll run out of air, suffocate."

"Negative Jonas, this is not time to play the hero. We don't want to be rescuing two people. Please wait."

She took his silence for compliance and kept his helmet camera view on the holo. She sent a message to Xavier to join her in the comms room. He arrived moments later.

"What warrants interrupting tomato harvest?" asked Xavier as he appeared in the doorway.

She told him and pointed to the camera feed.

"*Putain!*" he exclaimed.

"I want you to do drone surveillance of the site, checking to see if the intruder is still around. Maybe you can see their tracks from the shaft. Check there first."

"Will do." He grabbed the drone case and ran to the airlock.

Xanthe took a moment and then called Mission Control. Claire's voice was dry as usual. Even with the alarming news of a perimeter breach and Serena missing with no comms, Claire remained cold and composed. They would send a chopper. The ground force for dispersing the protesters was already on its way and would arrive within the hour.

Now all she could do was wait.

⟡

Excavation site: Jonas

JONAS MOVED AROUND the edge of the shaft looking for a better angle to see below. He checked his suit watch. Three minutes since the explosion. He thought of Serena gasping for air, unconscious or being crushed.

"Screw it," he said to himself. The abseil rope was still rigged from Serena's descent. He grabbed another harness from the shaft's monitoring shed and slipped it on. He took a deep breath. And then another. The usual fear cinched around his chest. He breathed into it.

"Piece of cake. Only five or so metres," he mumbled to himself. The VR sim was much, much higher. And so were the vertical abseils he did off buildings following the VR training. "You got this," he told himself.

Xanthe's voice belted his eardrums. "Jonas, what the hell are you doing? Stand down immediately!"

350

"No can do, Commander. I won't stand aside while a teammate dies in front of me."

"I said stand down! Stand down, Jonas—"

He switched off the helmet audio comm so he could concentrate. He left the helmet cam on. It was a fair compromise, he thought. Xanthe could at least see what he was doing, and maybe freak out a little less.

He eased himself down into the shaft. It was an easier edge than the descent abseil when he'd gone upside down. He felt that memory seize his body for a moment and he froze. Breathe, you bastard, breathe. His legs trembled but he started moving them again. The mound of dirt appeared under his feet. It didn't look too deep, thank goodness. The shaft walls seemed to be holding as well. Whatever that arsehole had thrown down here wasn't strong enough to blow apart the shaft. It was the first thing they'd printed. Good to know it could withstand blasts like that! Reassuring for the trip to the Moon. If they ever got there. He guided his thoughts back to the task at hand. He dug with his big suit gloves, pushing the earth to the side he thought might be furthest from Serena. He was grateful for the tough fabric of the suit for once. At least it was a bit cooler down the shaft than above ground. The sun was already baking the earth topside when the explosion happened. Sweat saturated the suit lining, pushing the reclaimers past the usual volume. They'd been trained to minimise physical outlay so as not to put pressure on the suit, or themselves. Especially important in space. But this was definitely not space.

The digging seemed to take forever. Six minutes elapsed. If oxygen was compromised, Serena would be starting to experience brain damage. He dug faster, more frantic. There was a buzz nearby. He glanced up and saw the SimHub drone hovering in the shaft. He turned the helmet comms back on. Maybe it could see things he couldn't.

"Commander, the drone see anything I don't?" said Jonas.

"Jonas – thank goodness. I thought you'd lost comms. Xavier's infrared on the drone shows a possible hollow to the right of where you are digging."

He renewed his efforts to the right, desperate now. His glove pushed through a patch of empty space and the dirt collapsed into a hollow. He backed up quickly, in case he fell through. No more dirt moved, so he leant over as far as he dared. He shone his torch into the pit. *There!* He could see a boot. It looked like it was attached to a leg.

"I've got eyes on Serena's boot," he announced. "Serena! Serena! Do you read?" Nothing.

"Jonas stand back, Xavier will send the drone in. It looks like it will fit in that opening."

The drone buzzed past him and slowly hovered through the opening.

"Jonas, looks like the tunnel collapsed on top of Serena. The support struts seemed to have held mostly, but there are some beams down on top of her. You seem to be standing on a pile of dirt blown out from the explosion."

"So, I just need to get in there and move the beams off her?"

"Possibly, though there could be risk of the entire tunnel collapsing if you move anything. It looks very unstable. Stand by. Dave and Troy are ten minutes away."

"It's already been too long, Xanthe! I'm going in." He ignored her protests and eased himself feet first through the hole, earth collapsing a bit more as he pushed himself through the narrow opening. He breathed deeply again. Small spaces didn't bother him. Collapsing ones did. He managed to get his feet on the ground and took a look at the space. No bigger than a crawl space. He could see Serena's full leg now. The rest of her was hidden under dirt and one of the reinforcement beams. He crawled over to her and put his hand on her leg.

"Serena! It's me Jonas! Can you hear me?" He thought he felt a twitch in response. "Good! Good! You can hear me! Listen, the tunnel collapsed, the others are on their way. I'm going to try and clear this earth around you and see if we can get this beam off you." He started scraping the earth off her suit. He managed to free her left leg, but she wasn't responding to his calls or movements. He revealed her torso, with the beam lying across her chest. It didn't seem to be crushing her. Jonas thought it may have fallen and just pinned her down, held up by the collapsed earth. If only he could get to her face! See if she was alive! He couldn't dig over her – that would risk further collapse. He would have to dig under her. He scraped earth from under her body with as much fury and care as he could muster. Something shifted and her upper body dipped below her hip level. Not good, not good! She might have a head injury. He scraped and clawed and swore and sweated. He bargained with whatever deity was listening to save her. Let her be alive! The dread grew heavy and black in his stomach. Her body shifted again. There must be another pocket of space that he'd managed to break into. He reached an arm past her torso and pushed through into – air! There was more space here. If he could keep digging under her, he might be able to drag her out from under the beam.

"I got you, Serena! I'm getting you outta here! Just need to dig a little under you so I can pull you away from the beam." No response.

Xanthe piped equal measure of encouragement and caution. He dared not look at his watch. It felt like an eternity since the explosion. He hoped it wasn't more than a few minutes, but he couldn't look. Wouldn't help anyway. He was aware of Troy and Dave arriving at the top. They were assessing the best way forward. Xanthe cautioned them against joining Jonas lest they cause further collapse.

Jonas felt Serena's upper body fall further into the hole under the beam. It might be enough for him to drag her clear.

"I've got you Serena! Just going to tug you out by the legs.

Hang on!" He shuffled back in the crawl space. There wasn't much room for this manoeuvre. He had maybe a foot from her feet to the wall. He crouched at her feet, gathered them under his arms and leant backwards praying he wasn't going to make it worse. The suit made her light frame heavy. He strained and heaved. He managed to pull her back a few centimetres. Success! He tried again and pulled her feet right back against the wall. He shuffled forward to see his progress. Her head was still under the beam, helmet still on, her arms were bent up against her side. He worked on freeing them so that when he pulled again, they would be clear.

Something shifted above them, and dirt rained down on them. Damn! The crawl space was unstable. Jonas went back to Serena's feet and this time reached under her calves and pulled. He made little progress. He bent her knees to make more room with his back against the crawlspace wall. Thunk! Her helmet was stuck. He scooted over to the beam and dug vigorously under her head to make some more room. He could almost see her face! He went back to her knees and hauled again. The helmet scraped against the beam with an awful screech. At last her head was past the beam.

"Serena!" He wiped at the helmet, clearing the dirt from the visor. It was cracked. He could see her face, a trickle of blood at her temple. "Serena! Can you hear me?" He checked her suit watch for vital signs. Amazingly, they all read green. She was alive!

"Thank God!"

"Jonas, can you check Serena's airflows?" Xanthe's voice came back to his awareness. Had she been talking to him? He wasn't sure. He obeyed her request, found the airflow monitor and O2 levels – secure. She was unconscious and breathing. If the oxygen flow had been pinched or impeded in the sealed suit while Jonas dug her out it would have been a disaster. She might very well have asphyxiated.

He wept quietly to himself. The relief and strain eased a little.

But they were still in serious danger, they had to get out of this crawlspace before it collapsed any further.

"Okay princess, we're getting out of here." He wrapped his arms around her knees and pulled again. She groaned.

"Serena?" He dropped her legs and peered back through the helmet. Her eyes flickered and opened.

"Jonas?" Her voice was muffled through her helmet. Comms not working.

"Yeah, it's me."

"Did you just call me 'princess'?"

He choked a laugh. "Sure did. It is your right and proper title. So good to see you and hear your voice. Are you hurt? Can you tell if you're bleeding anywhere?"

She blinked a few times, trying to focus her eyes. "Give me a moment." She took a sip of water from her suit recycler.

"Try wriggling your toes and work upwards."

She moved her toes, then legs, then fingers and arms.

"My head hurts. But I can't feel any blood or breaks."

"Good news, then! We're going to have to get out of this hole. Troy and Dave are topside with the rescue stretcher. We just need to get you up on that dirt mound through there." He pointed towards the shaft of light behind them. "I'll drag you up there just in case you're injured but can't feel it yet."

Xanthe and the rest of the crew acknowledged the plan. Jonas pulled Serena out a bit further into the crawl space then got behind her. He lifted her under the armpits and heaved backwards.

An almighty crack sounded, and the space collapsed around them. Jonas curled forward to protect Serena as best he could. She screamed.

"My leg!"

Jonas felt a beam pressing down on his back. It had fallen across his shoulders. He guessed another piece of the wall supports had fallen on Serena's leg. They were covered in dirt again from the legs down but there still seemed to be space above their helmets.

"Serena – you okay?"

"No! My motherfucking leg is pinned by something!"

"Jonas – status report." Xanthe's voice said in his helmet comms.

"Crawlspace collapsed," he panted. "I've got a beam against my back. Serena has an injury to her – which leg is it?" he asked.

"My cocksucking right leg! Motherfucker it hurts like a bloody whoreson!"

"Oh, good. At least your swear capacitor seems to be working."

She half laughed at that, then swore some more. She felt like weeping.

"Xanthe, we're stuck. You need to send Troy and Dave. I can't hold this much longer."

"Can you show us anything else on your helmet cam?"

"Negative. I've got a beam pressing me down – can't move or we get crushed."

Xanthe said nothing for a moment.

"Okay. Roger that. Troy and Dave will be down to you soon."

Serena was weeping now.

"Hey. It's not that bad," said Jonas.

"You're a terrible liar, Jonas."

"There are worse things than being buried in a tunnel with me holding your armpits aren't there?"

"Come to think of it, not many."

Jonas started to tremble from the strain.

"You okay?" she asked.

"Not sure how long I can hold this beam up. Can you move forward?"

"No. My leg is really jammed and the rest of me is covered in dirt."

"Serena."

"Yeah?"

"I'm sorry."

"For what?"

"For being an arse."

"What?"

"I'm sorry for being selfish over the food."

"Hey man, that's water under the bridge."

"Maybe." He tried to shift under the weight and felt pain sear through his right arm. His back muscles were taut and cramping. He knew if he folded now, he would crush Serena and he would be pressed down, folded over in two, and would likely suffocate. "I wish I'd been a better man."

"Hey – it's not over, you scum-sucking toad eater! You stay with me, you ballbreaking gonad head!"

"Really? Gonad head?"

"I'm trying. I'm not at my best here."

"Me neither." He felt her body, warm and fragile between their suits. He would have given anything a few months ago to press up against her. What a jerk he'd been! Now he felt something so different for the beautiful woman whose life he sheltered from peril. What was it? Respect? Affection? He admitted he cared for her. She was an esteemed colleague, someone he admired. A friend. He hadn't had many friends in his wild and privileged life. And now it seemed it might all be over. A tear slipped down his cheek and he wobbled under the weight.

"Jonas."

"Yeah."

"I'm sorry, too."

"What the hell for?"

"I'm not the easiest person to be around sometimes. I don't trust people, least of all men. But I trust you."

"You do?" he asked incredulous.

"Sure, I do!" she said. "You've got us out of a jam many times. The food thing wasn't your finest hour, but goddamn it all to fuckery you owned up to it. And you worked your arse off to make up for it. I told Dave that if you can change one thing, you can change anything. And you've done that. You're a good bloke, Jonas." She clunked her helmet back against his and managed to find his leg and give it a squeeze through her gloves. "I trust you with my life. Don't disappoint me now, you swine-snivelling, turd-eating, arse-gobbler!"

"I don't – even know – what that means!" He managed to say between strained pants.

"Me neither. Just don't give up."

Dirt showered down around them and then Jonas felt the blessed respite of the weight of the beam moving off him.

"Hey ho, it's the calvary!" said Troy on the helmet comms.

CHAPTER SIXTY-ONE

"I asked the question, 'Is there anything for which we cannot atone? Cannot forgive?' I thought of the worst crimes: mass murder, torture, rape. I sat with this for a long time. Deep within each of us are monsters twisted and dark; monsters that would ruin worlds. It's just that some of us let them out, and that's what we cannot forgive."

TROY BRUIN,
'PERSON OF THE YEAR' INTERVIEW

SimHub: Xanthe

ONCE TROY AND Dave abseiled down into the shaft, things seemed to happen quickly. They stabilised the beam with ropes, hauled Serena and Jonas from the crawl space and lifted them back to the surface with a very efficient vertical rescue. They returned to the SimHub just as the chopper and the ground crew arrived to secure the protesters and interrogate them. Xavier found the footprints of the intruder, but they led quickly back to the group of agitators and were lost there.

Troy assessed their injuries and determined that none were severe. Mostly bad bruises. They were all shot through with adrenaline and exhausted now that the crisis had passed. Xanthe ordered them all to change and grab a meal while she debriefed with Claire.

Claire was surprisingly calm as Xanthe ran through what had happened. She even gave Xanthe a very rare 'well done'. Unusually, Claire requested permission to listen in to the team debrief even though Xanthe knew she'd do so anyway, without permission.

Xanthe ran through the events herself, reviewing her notes. Something wasn't quite right. How did the intruder get in when they had just done a perimeter check? That security network was very tight. And how did they get out again so easily? Whoever it was must have had insider information about their security system. How? And from whom? And why did Dave get so rattled when she told him Serena and Jonas were out at the excavation site? What was going on there? Her mind skipped ahead to what was next. The explosion had put them well behind schedule. The investigation of the intruder would eat up valuable time. They would have to work around the clock to get back on track.

Xanthe joined the others around the kitchen table, their familiar SimHub crew gathering place. Troy handed out bags of warm beverages. Xavier fussed over Serena and Jonas. So unlike him! Dave sat slumped and sullen at the end of the table. Xanthe was about to check in with him when Xavier rapped the table for attention.

"*Mes amis!* It is my absolute *plaisir* to present our best crop of *tomates!*" He bowed as he presented three perfectly red and ripe tomatoes.

"Xavier, you French devil! You heard my wish and made it come true! You're a prince among men!" said Serena.

"I thought I was your Prince Charming?" said Jonas.

"Puuhhhhleeeezze, darling! You only risked life and limb to save me! Xavier has conjured fresh fruit after nearly a year without any. No comparison." She winked at him.

Xavier sliced up the tomatoes and offered them around, along with some crackers he pulled from the stock cupboards.

As they savoured the tomatoes, Xanthe started the debrief.

"Right, SimHub crew. Time to review where we're up to."

"I'd say we're a little up Shit Creek," said Troy.

"And now's probably a good time to remind you that this meeting is being attended virtually by Mission Control and recorded for review." She gave Troy a reprimanding eyebrow raise.

"Roger that, Commander," he acknowledged, chagrined.

"Let's review what we know," she continued. "06:00 the perimeter alarm goes off. Security cameras showed thirty or so protesters at the edge of the southern end of the site. I send Troy and Dave off on analogue perimeter check to ensure security system is working properly. At 06:15, the tunnel comms show a malfunction on the wall printer. At 06:30, Serena and Jonas depart to investigate."

"Very fast on the suits, by the way!" Xavier said. He was full of praise today. Very unusual.

"We're pros, *mon ami*! We've got the suit change down pat these days. Xanthe – also note that we went the long way around to the western side to avoid the protesters."

Xanthe jotted a note on her data pad and continued.

"07:35, Troy returns to the SimHub."

"Where was Dave?" asked Jonas. "Didn't you stick together?"

"Of course, we did. Dave dropped his wrench and had to go back for it."

Jonas rolled his eyes and Dave shrugged.

"07:50 Dave returns to the SimHub, presumably with the lost wrench." Dave nodded again. "08:12 Dave, Troy and I gather for the morning brief. 08:15, Jonas sounds the alarm. Does that correlate with your suit data records, Jonas?"

"Affirmative. Our timeline is arrival at the shaft at 07:10, sent the drone down at 07:25, pulled it out again at 07:35, Serena abseils at…" he paused to check his data pad with the suit log. "07:50."

"Once down the shaft, I unclipped and went straight to the printer," added Serena. "It was clogged and jammed up. It took me about fifteen minutes to clear it, then I headed back to the shaft when the damn thing blew up in my face."

"That was 08:10. That arsehole intruder knocked me over, then threw something down the shaft."

"Wait – back up a little," Troy said. "At 07:35 I returned to the SimHub and the perimeter was secure. No sign of intrusion at that point. The attack occurred at… what – 08:10? So the intruder must have got through the system between 07:35 and 08:10 at the latest. Dave – you didn't see anything when you went to get your wrench?"

Dave shook his head, his face mottled with red blotches.

"Where was your wrench?" Troy asked.

Dave shifted on the bench. "Around the back."

"Are you sure you didn't see anything?" Dave shook his head.

"When was that comms interruption…?" Xanthe remembered the glitch. She checked the comms records. There it was – a short blackout at 07:45.

"Xavier, the tracks you found – where did they enter or exit?" Xanthe asked.

"Close to the protesters – they go straight from the group out to the excavation site and straight back."

"Troy, how long did it take you to walk past the protesters, from the door of the SimHub?" Xanthe asked.

"About five minutes. They were pretty close."

"Dave, are you sure you didn't see anything? You would have walked right past that site on your way back from picking up the wrench."

He shook his head again and said nothing.

Xanthe stared at him, searching his face. Dave looked away.

"Dave, why did you warn us to get Serena out of the tunnel?" Troy asked, leaning forward.

"What do you mean?" Dave asked, clearing his throat.

"When we met for the day briefing, you were surprised that Jonas and Serena had gone out to the excavation site. You seemed distressed in fact. Why did you want them out of the tunnel?"

All five of them turned to look at Dave.

He shrugged again "Gut feeling, I guess."

There was a pause then Troy added, "You are not a 'gut feeling' kind of guy, Dave."

"Dave, what is it? What do you know?" Jonas pressed.

Dave bit his lip, shook his head.

"You let them in, didn't you?" Serena said. Her voice was flat and quiet.

Dave hung his head, shook it and said nothing.

"Son of a bitch! It *was* you!" Jonas gasped.

They stared at him as he continued to shake his head silently. He rocked backwards and forwards, holding his breath.

The moment stretched between them, heavy and dark.

It was Xanthe who cut the silence. "Why?" she asked gently.

Dave erupted with a choked sob.

"Ahh, fuck! It was me. I did it. I let him in."

"*Putain de merde!*" Xavier exclaimed, jumping to his feet. He rattled off a litany of curses while he paced up and down the length of the table. "*Connard!*" he yelled and strode up to Dave, who cowered below him. He grabbed Dave's shirt and threatened to punch him. Troy leapt up and held Xavier back.

A new awareness fell on Jonas. "You wrecked the air scrubber, too! You knew exactly how to do it. Damn it! I should have guessed!" Jonas cried. "Did you sabotage the waste recycling unit too?"

Dave glanced up at him between sobs. A small nod as he looked away again.

"Jeezzusss freakin' almighty shitsticks! Why in all that's holy would you do this? To us? What the actual fuck?" Serena was livid, her eyes flashing. "Jonas and I could have died down in that tunnel! We nearly did die! Why, for the love of God?"

"I will kill you myself!" Xavier struggled against Troy, trying to leap at Dave.

"Okay, enough. ENOUGH!" They froze as Xanthe slammed the table hard and rose to her feet. "Everyone calm down. Xavier – sit down. We will hear from Dave. Shouting at him won't bring out the truth."

She waited for them to sit down. Xavier, Jonas and Serena continued to throw eye daggers at Dave. Troy placed himself between Dave and Xavier. Troy's face was implacable.

Once they were quiet, Xanthe continued. "David. Explain."

Dave took a deep breath and began. "I disabled the perimeter security when I left Troy to go back for my wrench."

"Why? Why?" interrupted Jonas.

"To let the agent through."

"Agent? What do you mean 'agent'?" Jonas continued.

"I don't know his name. He's an agent for Spaceward Bound, though."

"What?" Troy was flabbergasted.

"Are you working for those Spaceward Bound shit-painting turdballs?" Serena demanded.

"QUIET!" Xanthe commanded. They jumped at her voice. "David, continue."

"I'm not working for them! I signed on to this project, same as you all, to be part of Gaia Enterprises. Then my husband—" Dave sucked in a choking breath as he said the word. "Sven – he got into heavy debt with his gambling. After he stole our daughter's money, he got further into debt, stopped paying the bills, and the bank was about to foreclose and kick him out of our apartment. He's the one who—" Dave took another laboured breath. "He's the one who went to Spaceward Bound and started selling them information about Gaia's Olympus Project. He repeated stuff I told him about the project from our private conversations. I told him about our design plans and project secrets, and he turned around and sold it to them. Then they started to threaten Sven. They told him if he didn't slow Gaia down somehow then they would expose me as a corporate spy."

"They threatened to call you a spy... so you would become a spy?" Serena asked, her eyes wide and incredulous.

"They were putting the screws on Sven. They had records of all their conversations. They put a detective on him and traced all his shady gambling games. They threatened to expose all of that, hold back money so he would be evicted. Sven threatened me: if I didn't do what they asked, he would be forced to call me out as a spy himself."

"Sven and Spaceward Bound both threatened to call you a spy – so you would turn around and do what they wanted?"

"Yes." Dave was dejected, shoulders slumped, his nose running with snot. He wiped it on his sleeve. "I didn't know what to do. Sven was somehow hacking my account so all my wages were going to service his debt – or on more gambling. Sophia was complaining about not having enough food. How he could do that to her I'll never know. He is so... sick. I was worried they would end up on the streets. So, I agreed. At first, it was just to slow things down a little."

"The waste recycler." Jonas said with acid. Dave nodded. "The air scrubber." He nodded again.

"*Ah non! Les tomates!* Was that you too? You put limestone in the plants?" cried Xavier.

"I am so sorry, Xavier," Dave said. Xavier's face was a moving wrinkle of fury.

"All that sleepwalking? Was that just a cover story?" asked Serena.

"I do actually sleepwalk – especially when stressed. Some of those times were real. Some were not. I'd get up, pretend to sleep-walk, and do some adjustments on the project."

"But how? The security cams would have caught you." Xanthe said.

"Troy isn't the only one with a comms jammer," Dave said. He pulled a small disc from his pocket and put it on the table.

"All this time I thought the comms were fritzy! But it was you?" exclaimed Troy.

"And now you've just told Mission Control we have comms jammers. Thanks a lot, dickhead," said Jonas.

"No, actually. I turned the jammer on when we started this meeting. Claire hasn't been able to hear or see anything. She's got a loop of an empty room showing on her display right now."

"Why did you do that?" asked Xanthe.

"If it came out, I wanted to come clean to you, first," Dave said.

"You're a right cunning bastard," said Jonas.

"It just gives us... options," Dave said.

'Hang on a minute. You said you let the Spaceward Bound agent in through the perimeter security," Serena said. "Did you know he was going to blow up the tunnel?"

"I thought it might be something like that. I'd tried plugging up the printer by adding slurry to the print material, but it wasn't slowing the project down for long enough. I couldn't get easy access to the site, given we'd ramped up operations, so they decided to send in an agent with the protesters. They told me they were going to close up the shaft. There was nothing I had on site that could do that to their satisfaction. We picked the day when I knew we had SimHub jobs. Everyone was supposed to be here. Inside. No one was supposed to be in the tunnels." He dropped his head into his hands and sobbed. "I am so sorry, Serena, Jonas. I never thought anyone would get hurt."

"*Salaud!* We could have had Madison instead of you! We let Mad Dog go, the better pilot, and this is how we are rewarded?" Xavier fumed.

Dave flinched at the barb.

"Is Spaceward Bound planning anything else?" asked Troy.

Dave shook his head. "That was it. We are so close to the end of the bid, they just wanted a margin to knock us out of the comp."

They sat in ugly silence. Emotions roiled like a fish swarm in a feeding frenzy. They wallowed in it as Dave sniffed and sobbed quietly.

"Now what the fuck do we do?" Serena said. Their faces were equal measure stunned and angry.

"This is what's going to happen," Xanthe said. "Dave, you're confined to quarters. You will hand over that comms jammer. The rest of us will discuss what our best course of action is."

"We will need to let Mission Control know about the situation," said Xavier. "They will come and arrest this son of a bitch."

"Not yet," Xanthe said. They turned to her with looks of surprise. "Dave is our responsibility. We need to figure this out as SimHub crew, first. Besides, if we let them take Dave away now, the whole project is doomed. We can't finish it without him."

"You can't mean to let him stay?" exclaimed Serena. "Xanthe, we could have died because of this arsehole! How can we trust him now?"

"Look, I don't know," Xanthe replied. "I just want to buy us some time before we give up on the Olympus Project. There's a lot at stake here. For all of us."

"I'm sorry – this is crazy," said Serena. "What makes you think Dave doesn't have something else planned? For all we know there might be another explosion on the cards."

"You're right. We don't know what else he could do or arranged. But we can contain him for now. Jonas, can you and Troy check Dave's room for any other contraband or devices? Also, can you put an external lock on his door?" Xanthe asked.

"Sure can," Jonas said with dark eyes.

"I'm not going anywhere," Dave said. "I have nothing left. I have nowhere to go."

"Forgive us if we don't exactly have confidence in your promises, right now," said Troy.

"Right. Get it done. We will reconvene in thirty minutes. I will report to Mission Control and explain why comms went down again."

∽

Once she knew Dave was secured in his room, Xanthe left the crew and headed to the comms room.

She waited a moment to gather her thoughts before she turned off the jammer. The room lit with hailing signals and Claire's holo jumped up.

"Xanthe! Report! The comms have been down! Is there another crisis?" Claire's tone was distressed this time.

"Negative, Control. Comms went down again as we were about to meet. But we've isolated the issue and have it contained." Not quite a lie.

"What was it?"

"Faulty wiring. Jonas has set up a workaround for the time being. We'll have to do a full repair later." A lie this time. This will cover future comms jams, Xanthe thought.

"And the debrief?"

"Deferred. I've tasked the team with compiling their notes. Xavier will review the drone footage for any further clues."

"Any idea who the intruder was?"

"Negative. At this stage it looks like a coordinated effort between the protesters. They provided a distraction while one of them disabled the perimeter security. No idea how. We are reviewing that too." Strange how the lies came so easily. "Any information from your end?"

"We are interrogating the protesters now. A few seemed to have escaped out into the bush. We are hopeful of tracking them, but it seems unlikely with their comms jamming. We've got forensics out on site now, too, trying to find the source of the explosion. We're clearing debris at the same time and stabilising the site."

"Next steps?"

"Get the site back and ready to finish printing and see if we can get back on track. The team will have to work overtime."

"In that case, we might focus on Jonas getting the comms repair done. He'll need to disconnect the system to do it. We'll be offline for an hour or so. We'll shut it down in ten minutes. Can you have security detail on the perimeter for us?" Hopefully she'll buy that, thought Xanthe.

"Affirmative. We still have crew out there on site. We'll reconvene once you signal comms repairs are done."

"Roger that. SimHub Command out."

Xanthe leant back in the chair and let out a big breath. They had just over an hour to come up with a plan.

CHAPTER SIXTY-TWO

*If we have been injured, punishment makes us feel better in
the short term. For long-term healing, we need atonement.
A chance to make right, to restore good faith, to re-establish
the behaviour we intend to honour moving forward.*

GAIA ENTERPRISES CODE OF CONDUCT

SimHub: Xanthe

AFTER A FEW messages in the Throne Room, they assembled, ready
to cut comms again for the hour.

Serena hobbled in and perched on a seat, elevating her leg with
a grimace of pain. Troy and Xavier were already waiting. At the
designated signal, Troy activated the comms jammer he had in his
pocket. They were free to talk.

The mood was sombre. The issue of trust lay before them, like
a body on a dissection table, a bruised and broken thing.

"We need to decide what to do," Xanthe said. The heaviness
of it made her shoulders ache.

"*Mais non!* Is it not obvious?! Dave has to go! He is full of
treachery. What might he do next?" Xavier's temper seared the
room and he spat his words with gestures for emphasis.

Troy put a hand on Xavier's shoulder.

"I think we all feel betrayed, Xavier. I am personally devastated. We've been through so much together," Troy said. Pain swept his features. "I'm also mindful that we need to stay true to our values. We believe in atonement, not punishment."

"Do you seriously believe Dave can atone for this?" Serena asked, her eyes wide. "How will we ever trust him again?"

"I'm not sure we can," Troy answered. "But I want to believe in redemption. Without redemption we are doomed to be judged forever by our mistakes. There is no room for hope. No room for growth. We all make mistakes. We've all been selfish. But this project," Troy started to choke up. He cleared his throat as the tears welled. "This project is more than just a commercial exercise. It means something. We're betting on humanity here."

"Humanity is living down to expectations rather than up to them right now," said Serena. "I think David shows exactly what we can expect from our fellow humans. Given half a chance, selfishness trumps all."

"Hang on a minute," said Jonas. "I know I'm hardly one to talk. I still wear the guilt for stealing food. That was pure selfishness, even if I rationalised it to myself. But Dave – his motivators were not all self-interested. They were also to protect his family."

"And to cover his own arse!" replied Serena. "He joined forces with Spaceward Bound to protect his reputation from being ruined."

"He is full of *merde!* He makes like he is our best friend, and then all along he is wrecking our project. Who can trust his story now? He is one very good actor. We all believed in him. And look where that led us? Jonas and Serena injured, nearly dead, and now our project bid nearly dead too. I say we give him to Claire and to hell with him," Xavier said.

They fell quiet, each lost in their own thoughts and emotions.

"Xanthe, what do you think?" asked Troy.

She shifted in her seat and put her chin in her hand, elbow

propped on the table. "Well, I've been asking myself, 'What would make me do what Dave did? What would drive me to abandon my professional commitments, abandon my core values, and betray the people I've grown to love?'"

"*Exactement!* No one but a real *trou du cul* would do such a thing!" Xavier's voice lashed the room.

"Xavier, just listen. Let's hear what Xanthe has to say," Troy said, his hand again on Xavier's shoulder.

"I thought about it. There would be one thing that would make me sacrifice everything. If someone said I had to betray my friends, sabotage a project that meant the world to me, literally, and for that I would get a chance to see my little boy – to see *Jack* – one more time… then I would do it."

The mention of the little boy's name pinned their thoughts to that moment in the Stim Room. They all felt it as a turning point in their collective relationship. A moment when their bonds wove together difference, stitched them together as one fabric, weaved them in a web of love and connection. And Dave was there in their memories: bold and crazy and magnificent.

He was all that and the man who betrayed them too. For love.

"For a world worth living in," murmured Troy.

The web of icy pain softened a little in the centre.

"Love and pain are not rational things," Xanthe said. "I think Dave was between a rock and hard place. He made a decision he knew was wrong, but ultimately thought was important to protect this family." Serena started to make a noise and Xanthe added, "And to protect himself. Dave's no perfect martyr, by any means."

"I think we also have to ask why he confessed. He didn't have to. He could have covered his tracks, like he has done so far. It's only because he cared about Serena and Jonas that his whole game was up," Troy pointed out.

"What if we hadn't gone out there that morning? What if the sabotage had happened as he'd planned with Spaceward Bound?

They blow up the tunnel, we fall behind and lose the competition, and we would be none the wiser. Would he ever have confessed?" Serena resisted giving Dave any credit.

"We'll never know," Troy said. "The fact is he saw a danger to us, and he tried to stop it from happening. He's not all good. But he's not all bad either."

"What are you suggesting? We just let him back in, again? *Putain!*" Xavier fumed.

"I can't trust him! I just can't! Every time I'd look at him, I'd feel the tunnel exploding and falling on me. He did that. You don't just get over something like that," Serena said.

"No, you don't just get over it," Xanthe said. "That's what atonement is for. A way of building bridges. Of proving worth. Of proving one's capacity for change. Think about it this way: if something like this happened on the Moon, what would we do then? We can't exactly lock him in his room forever in a sort of space jail. That's impractical and would take too many resources."

"I say shove his arse out the airlock! Let him think about action-consequence while he faced down the dark side of the moon on his own, the *petit con*." said Xavier.

"As much as you are angry right now, Xavier, I know you don't mean you'd send Dave to his death," Xanthe said.

"Ah, *non?*" Xavier raised his eyebrows in a challenge.

"There's another part to this, too," said Troy. "We can't finish the project without him. Even with the forensic team doing clean-up duty, we will be hard-pressed to get the SimHub complete before inspection. If we give Dave up, then we are basically giving up our run at the Olympus Project. All this will have been for nothing."

"*Putain de merde!*" Xavier let out a long line of expletives.

"So, we are going to be forced to trust him?" Serena demanded.

"No – I don't think we'll trust him ever again. At least, not for a long, long time," said Jonas. "I mean, how many of you trust me with food, now?"

No one answered.

"Exactly. You had to lock the food stores to trust me. And I worked the waste recycler for a month until I had shit coming out of my pores." There were a few half-hearted smiles at that. "So it's possible to make it work," Jonas said.

"Sneaking a few snacks and dry crappy breads no one wanted is a little different to blowing up a tunnel and nearly killing us!" exclaimed Serena.

"Yes, it is, you're right Serena," Xanthe said. "If we're going to consider keeping Dave on SimHub crew, it's going to be a long, hard road back for him. And for us. But we don't need trust to make it work."

"How do you mean, Xanthe?"

"We can design around trust – or lack of it," she said. "That's what we do – we're world designers. We design environments that foster development. We can design something to guide Dave's development back to SimHub crew."

"*Bof!* That is crazy. You are too soft-hearted, Xanthe. There is nothing that can bring him back," Xavier said.

"Xavier, are you telling me, that if someone threatened your family – your wife and kids – that you would not do anything – I mean *anything* – to protect them?" Troy asked.

"*Ah, peut-être…*"

"We do not know what we are capable of until our back is against the wall," Xanthe said. "Survival turns us to the shadows we prefer to avoid. But within us lurks all manner of evils. Conditions can push us into the darkness, and just as likely, conditions can bring us back into the light." She paused, then "Here is what I propose," she said.

CHAPTER SIXTY-THREE

*We hold on tightest to what we think is right. We hold
it close, like a shield. The more we think we're right,
the less likely we are to see anything but the back of our
shield, protecting us from someone else's truth.*

ATHENA AI IN WISDOM OF THE AGES

Gaia Desert Base Mission Control Headquarters: Claire

CLAIRE AND MAJA sat in stony silence after Xanthe's briefing.

"Thank you for the report," said Claire to Xanthe's holo. "This
is clearly a serious situation that deserves further consideration. We
will convene the Directors when Huw arrives with Aryanna this
afternoon." She ended the transmission.

Claire turned to Maja and said, "Will you notify the authorities, or shall I?"

"Before we notify anyone, we need to consider this more fully,"
Maja replied.

"I beg your pardon?" Claire was genuinely surprised.

"This is a serious setback to the project, and we do not want to
make hasty decisions right now, especially with Aryanna's arrival."

"I'm sorry, Maja, I'm not following. Do you mean you *agree* to Xanthe's plan? To keep David in SimHub crew until they complete the construction?" Claire felt anxiety crawl across her skin with spidery feet.

"There are merits to this plan." Maja smoothed the creases in her linen trousers. "Without David's contribution, the project will not meet its deadlines and we lose our bid for the Olympus Project."

"But we can always apply to adjust the schedule, make a submission to the Lunar Commission, report on Spaceward Bound's sabotage. We've been betrayed here, Maja! We've had a spy in our midst, colluding with our competitors, and actively destroying our property. His actions are unethical as well as illegal. How can we justify keeping him with SimHub crew?"

Maja reached across the table to pour herself a glass of water. Claire noticed how thin her arms were, these days. The skin of her hands was papery and almost translucent. Like bones wrapped in dry cellophane.

"David was coerced into betrayal by his husband and Spaceward Bound's operatives. We have a case there to prosecute. David should be due his opportunity for atonement, as Xanthe suggests."

"But he broke laws, Maja! His actions nearly led to the death of two of our crew! What are we saying if we let this go unpunished?" The outrage surged through her with an enormous pulse, pushing blood and fury to her face.

"There is a difference between punishment and being held to account. Punishment rarely rectifies behaviour, as well you know. It serves more to assuage the injured than rehabilitate the criminal."

"And what *about* the injured? What if Jonas and Serena had died in that shaft? No punishment, or atonement for that matter, would make up for that. We can't just let selfish, dangerous behaviour go without consequences – serious consequences. Consequences on a par with the transgression." Claire paused to take a deep breath, to channel the tide of her rage. "Maja, David needs to go. What does it say about us if we keep someone who breaks laws and endangers lives?"

Maja's eyes flashed and her mouth hardened. "And what does it say about *us* if we cast someone aside without the opportunity for redemption?" Claire was surprised by the undertone and grit in Maja's voice. "Claire, we are not our actions. We are not our past. The human spirit wants to do good. I agree with Xanthe's assessment that David made poor choices with good intentions. If they redesign the workflow as she suggests, he has the opportunity to make things right. And besides, if they were on the Moon, as we hope they will be, then what would the options be *there*? Not prison. Not banishment. Not execution. Only atonement and rehabilitation."

"Spare me the philosophy lecture, Maja. The case is clear-cut here. David broke the law, sabotaged the project, risked the lives of his comrades, jeopardised a multi-million-dollar, multi-year project. Forgiveness, atonement, it's all superfluous within that context."

"I'm not sure you're seeing the bigger picture, Claire."

Claire's skin prickled at the insult. Not seeing the bigger picture! It was Maja who had tunnel vision. This was too much. She took another breath to keep her anger and frustration from spewing a retort.

Maja continued. "This project is not just a bid for constructing a Moon Base. It's a whole new way of living and being together as human beings. An environment and community precedent that will shape human culture for generations to come. We have to be brave and find new ways of living with one another, especially in confined spaces. We need to face down transgressions, find a way together as a community to help people remain integrated." Maja's tone softened. "We used to execute people when they couldn't follow the laws. Then we put them in prisons. Then we put them in semi-socialised environments with other felons. It doesn't work. We know it doesn't work. The only way is to build links and bonds between people, to build the personal skills to handle the pressures. We break all that if we ostracise someone, if we remove them. We will just be replicating all the old patterns that we know do not work. As a species, we can do better." Maja paused and adjusted her linen jacket as she sat up straighter. "I think we should rally around David. He is a victim of his circumstances as much as he is the villain in this unfortunate incident."

Claire was stunned. Maja was completely blind to the implications of keeping David, a self-confessed traitor, as part of the crew. He could not be trusted. He was a consummate liar! And here Maja was defending him.

"This is just another experiment to you, isn't it?" Claire knew that bitterness coloured her words, but she was beyond caring. "Just like Jonas was. You just want to see what happens. You want to prove your social experiment is right. Are you really willing to risk this after what happened on Terra Blanca?" Maja froze at the mention of the failed project. Claire knew this was Maja's secret shame and biggest regret. "The Olympus Project is Gaia's future, Maja. You are risking it all for this – for this – ego project!"

Maja said nothing. She stared hard at Claire with cold eyes. The silence seeped like a dark and menacing tide between them. Claire's face was a kaleidoscope of colour and emotion.

Maja crossed her hands and rested them on the table in front of her in a sagacious gesture of interminable patience for a less mature, volatile student.

"I see you are overwrought. I suggest we resume this conversation with Huw this afternoon. This will give us both time to reflect on what's at stake, and the best way forward." Maja pushed her chair back from the table and rose, still elegant despite her frailty. "I'll see you then," she said.

Claire watched her go, saying nothing. She felt physically ill.

Maja's condescension and cold rebuke was as unsettling as her narrow-minded attachment to her social 'experiment'. She took a deep breath and focused on releasing the emotional tension. She felt it ease a little.

After a few minutes of quiet breathing, Claire found the clarity she was looking for. Huw would surely back her on this one. He was a pragmatic entrepreneur and commercial betrayals were career-ending. If you crossed Huw, it was game over. Even he could not ignore such an outrageous assault. Claire was sure Huw would defy Maja on this one. This was her opportunity to shore up support and build a deeper connection with him. She would need his support for the succession. Surely, Huw would see how stubborn and narrow Maja was. Claire wondered if the illness was affecting her judgement.

Having regained her composure, Claire turned her mind to building her case, clearly and carefully.

CHAPTER SIXTY-FOUR

*People readily grant power to those who dare to lead. It's easy to
follow a confident idiot; it's hard to follow a humble doubter.
Confidence feels better than doubt. But it's the humble doubter
who makes space for others to lead alongside them. The humble
doubter needs enough conviction to know what's right, but enough
humility to know they are not the only one who has a say about it.*

MAJA GARCIA, THE JOURNALS

Gaia Desert Base Mission Control Headquarters: Claire

CLAIRE WATCHED ARYANNA and Huw step from the chopper. The
whirling blades stirred desert dust and afternoon heat around
them in an angry red cloud. Aryanna wore her signature white
flowing silk suit, its long folds billowing like a parachute. Huw was
beaming, obviously enjoying his role as host to the world's most
enigmatic billionaire.

Maja and Claire greeted them at the entrance to the Mission
Control Headquarters. The heat and dust were pressed back by the
cool air-conditioning as the doors retracted to let them in.

"Maja, Claire, so good to see you!" Huw said. He embraced
them both with genuine affection.

Aryanna removed her enormous eyeshades with perfectly manicured fingers. Her skin was smooth like a china plate. Her eyes were dark globes framed with a brush of long lashes. The effect was disturbing. Claire felt like she was being watched by a creepy life-like doll.

"Aryanna, welcome," Maja said.

"Shall we leave Aryanna to settle in and convene in the conference room?" asked Claire.

"Not yet," answered Maja. "Aryanna, Huw and I have some business to attend to beforehand. That shouldn't take long. We'll meet you there in say, two hours?"

The slight of being excluded sliced at Claire but she covered it well and nodded in acknowledgement. She watched the three of them walk towards the accommodation pods.

I'll be damned if they leave me *out.* She hurried to the comms room and tapped in the private codes she had programmed. The feed to Aryanna's room blinked into view. If she wasn't invited, she'd still be present. There was too much riding on the next few hours.

⤚ᔕ⤙

Aryanna's quarters: Maja

ARYANNA FLOATED INTO the tub chair and gestured for the others to take a seat.

"Maja, it's been a long time," Aryanna said. Her voice flowed like a river over rocks, all long vowels and round edges.

"Yes, my dear old friend. It is good to see you, and so youthful and fresh! You're twenty years my senior but some would mistake you for my daughter."

"Yes, Maja. You look old and wispy. What is the matter with you?" Maja smiled. Aryanna never had time for social niceties and always hit the truth with a cudgel.

"I am ill. I am old. My cells are decaying," she said lifting her emaciated arm as an exhibit.

"Nonsense. I won't hear of it. We can fix that. My company Renaissance has made incredible breakthroughs in cellular rejuvenation. Dr Mohammad Rasheed was very useful in that. I am delighted he is part of this project. I will task Marina to liaise with him and organise a treatment for you at once." Aryanna blinked to activate her Neurolink and sent a message to her AI assistant. "There, done. Marina will send through the details for your program by the end of the hour."

"Aryanna, as much as I appreciate your generosity, I couldn't possibly—"

"Maja, don't be ridiculous. I need you alive. This is a selfish action, as much as it is generous. We have a lot to accomplish, and I want you at the helm."

"We've been working on successors," added Huw. "In case Maja… wanted to take a break."

"A break!" Aryanna scoffed. "Maja Garcia does not take breaks. She is as committed to her work as anyone I have ever met." Neither of them bothered to deny it.

"Though I am curious – tell me about your potential successors. They might fit with some other plans."

Huw glanced at Maja to gain approval to continue. "Claire Edwards is our primary candidate. She has been Gaia's principal trainer for world design for coming on a decade now. She is dedicated, disciplined and thorough." Huw paused and tapped his foot, searching for the right words.

"Well? I sense a 'but' here, Huw. Spit it out," Aryanna said.

"Claire is pedantic and a little obstinate," added Maja. "She is rigid in her perspective and struggles to see the nuances and long-term implications of various scenarios."

"Specifically?" asked Aryanna.

"She came reluctantly to the off-planet project and even now harbours concerns that this is a deviation from Gaia's original intention."

"It *is* a deviation," Aryanna said. "Gaia Enterprises was established to build communities for humans – on Earth. I remember it well. It's one of the reasons I was interested in Gaia tendering for this project. The love of Earth needs to be a primary guide. So, she obviously overcame her scruples on that point. What else is a concern?"

"We've had an incident," Maja said, glancing at Huw. She'd briefed Huw just before the trip here with Aryanna. "One of the crew was being blackmailed to sabotage the project." Aryanna's eyes widened slightly but otherwise her pale plate of a face remained implacable. "Claire wishes to remove the crew member. I do not."

"Interesting development," Aryanna said. Her words washed over them like water pushing debris. "So, Claire wants to remove the offender." Maja nodded. "Sensible in some ways. Clean up the dynamics. Consider it as part of the long-term selection process." Aryanna ran a finger over her lips as she thought. "Why do you wish to keep the offending crew member?"

"I want the crew to manage the process. It is a test of their bonds and ability to resolve conflict," Maja said. "They must manage all crises, no matter how difficult – as they would on the Moon. I think removing the offender is too easy."

"High stakes, Maja," Aryanna said, her voice quiet. "Presumably they need all of them to complete the prototype build. If they cannot complete the project, they lose the Olympus bid."

"And if they cannot resolve this issue, here, now, while there are options, they will fail when there are none." Maja's eyes flashed with a sudden passion. "Their backs are against the wall, but there is still a door to walk through. They either unite and resolve it – together – or they fall apart. That is the stark truth for them, and it is the stark truth for humanity too."

Huw cleared his throat as a tendril of tension crept into the room. "Claire is a rule-follower. She sees this issue as clear-cut. David betrayed them, therefore he must go." Huw's knee bounced as he considered the issue. "I admit, that was my immediate response, too. I was furious! The ingrate! The betrayal! But Maja helped me to see that sometimes what looks like an easy decision has more facets to it."

Aryanna smiled slowly. "Oh, I long for the days when issues were that obvious. It made life much simpler." After allowing a moment of nostalgia, Aryanna resumed her questioning. "And this David – tell me about him." Maja shared what she knew of David's background and the Spaceward Bound blackmail.

"So he's confessed to his crewmates and regrets his actions?" asked Aryanna. Maja confirmed. "A repentant offender… they are often useful. Keen to please. Make up for lost trust and all that. They often work doubly hard to prove their mettle. Yes, it might be beneficial to keep him around. If you can clear up the dramas on the outside. I know Spaceward Bound's founder, Lincoln. I doubt he is aware of this espionage. He would be mortified." Aryanna let a devious smile stretch across her face. "I wouldn't mind discussing the issue with him though. It would take him down a peg or two. And, of course, he would then be in my debt, especially if we do not leak this breach publicly." She seemed resolved on the issue and ready to carry on. "So, Claire is one possible successor but is rather literal and rigid. Are there any other candidates?"

"It's the current SimHub Commander, Xanthe Waters. She has a come a long way over several years. She has come into her own during this project. She has the respect of her crew, and she upholds Gaia's principles of wisdom and compassion. She does tend to stand down and not speak her mind. It will be interesting to see what she decides along with the crew when it comes to David. If she can unite the crew with this breach of trust, she will have what it takes to build communities off-world for the long haul."

"Could she lead Gaia Enterprises as well as run community building?"

"That is the true test," Huw said. "That's why we need Maja to stick around just a little bit longer." He smiled at his old friend.

"With the cell rejuvenation treatment, it will be a lot longer. This talk of succession will be a moot point." Aryanna leant forward to stand, indicating the meeting was closed. "Now if you'll excuse me, I'd like to settle in, and rest until we are due to meet with Claire."

CHAPTER SIXTY-FIVE

*Betrayal is the worst kind of violence. But if the
betrayal is for a good reason, is it still betrayal?*

HUW CHAN, A MEMOIR

Gaia Desert Base Mission Control Headquarters: Claire

HAD THEY ALL *gone mad?* Claire shut down the video link to Aryanna's room. She tried to calm herself with some steady breathing,
but her emotions bucked within her as the sea might crash against
a cliff.

Claire felt Maja's judgement of her as a cold steel knife in her
belly. All these years, a dedicated worker, a trusted trainer of Gaia
Enterprises, and Maja thought her *too rigid?* It was utterly unfair.
She had nothing but Gaia's interests at heart.

But that was the least of it. Claire had been confidante and
sounding board for Maja since Gaia Enterprises began. She worked
hard to measure up to the older woman's ideals. And she'd kept the
secrets of Terra Blanca.

What had gone wrong these past few months? Her quarrels with
Maja had become more frequent. They disagreed more and more

over the direction and governance of the project. Maja was allowing more and more flexibility on this project. She was abandoning the first principles of Gaia Enterprises. Her old obsession for social design experiments was creeping back with far-reaching consequences. Removing David was not only a legal responsibility but a moral one. If this crew was to be the example for the future of humanity, then it needed to act as such. How could Maja not see that?

Claire was more sure now that Maja's physical ailments were affecting her cognitive abilities. She was so dismissive and patronising. Not like her at all.

And how could Maja consider Xanthe as her successor? That insipid frightened mouse? Xanthe was a people-pleaser with no guts to make the tough calls.

Claire stared out the window into the desert. The impenetrable blue of a cloudless sky stretched wordless and waiting. She watched the trees standing bravely, enduring the oppressive heat.

Aryanna was unquestioning of Maja. She accepted her rationale at face value, and Huw, that sycophant, reinforced whatever Maja suggested. They were blind to the slippery slope Maja was leading them down. Experiments in community were volatile and dangerous. Maja knew that, had lived through that, but somehow seemed to have forgotten it. What was it with her? Hubris? Blind ambition? She seemed to have lost her touchpoint of morality. Ethics could be a grey area, she knew that, but threatening the success of a project by betting on less-than-ideal candidates like Jonas was one thing. Retaining someone who had blatantly violated the law was another. What else would Maja allow? Anxiety wrapped the core of her being and tightened. Maja was now a threat. She needed to be stopped before it was too late. It grieved Claire to see her mentor in this light. But if she was to salvage the project from Maja's warped intentions, Aryanna needed to know the truth. She needed to know about Terra Blanca.

Let's see what Aryanna does with that news, she thought.

CHAPTER SIXTY-SIX

*Loyalty and power are jealous mistresses. You can't
serve one without insulting the other.*

HUW CHAN, A MEMOIR

Gaia Desert Base Mission Control Headquarters: Claire

CLAIRE HEARD THE cries just as she was readying for bed.

"Maja! What is the meaning of this!" Aryanna was a silken cloud of white floating down the hall towards Maja's accommodation pod. The black puddles of her eyes sparkled with fury. She commanded the door to open. It remained shut. She pressed the door comm.

"Maja! Let me in at once. We need to discuss this matter urgently." There was no response. "Maja!"

Huw appeared at the entrance to his pod.

"What is it, Aryanna?" he asked and hurried over.

"Huw Chan. Did you know?"

"Did I know what?"

"About *Terra Blanca*." Aryanna's white smooth face creased with anger.

Huw stepped back in alarm. "What about Terra Blanca?"

"Did you know, and were you part of, the deliberate instigation of community disharmony – of rebellion – at Terra Blanca?"

"Ah, what do you mean?"

She stared into his mottled face and knew. "You did," she said bitterly. "Were you party to it? Did you encourage Maja? Or was this project all her own?"

"I – ah—" Huw struggled to find words.

"Goddamn it, Huw! You deceived me! Where the hell is Maja?" She spun and pressed the door comm again.

"What's the matter?" Claire came flying down the hall. "I heard shouts."

"Where is Maja? I need to see her immediately!"

"As far as I know she is in her pod. I saw her there not ten minutes ago. We had our usual evening cup of tea and debrief." Claire stepped over to the door. "Maja? Are you there? Door: open." There was no response to her command. She activated her wrist control and said, "Emergency entrance protocol: door, open." The door slid open.

Maja was lying on her bed, still. Claire rushed over to her, her face dark with concern.

"Maja?" she grabbed the older woman's hands and squeezed, then pinched her shoulders. No response. She checked her breathing. There was a soft tickle of breath along her cheek.

"She's breathing!" Claire said. "But unresponsive. Huw, call Dr Mohammad." Claire rolled Maja on to her side to manage her airway better. Maja's wrist comm was removed and on the side table, so she took her pulse and read the results into her own wrist comm. "She's stable," Claire said to Aryanna and Huw who had stepped away briefly to alert the medic on the room comm display.

The three of them stood staring at Maja's still form. She was a sunken skeleton, tiny and frail on the enormous bed. Dr Mohammad arrived and asked them to step out of the way. He was a flurry of medical efficiency. Within minutes he had Maja attached to monitoring machines and a saline drip administered.

Mohammad turned to the three of them while removing his gloves. "She's unconscious but stable. All her vitals seem fine."

"What's the problem, then?" demanded Aryanna.

Mohammad shrugged. "She has been unwell for some time. It could be fatigue, dehydration. I'll run tests to determine the cause of her collapse. In the meantime, I'll get one of my team to monitor her while we assess what is going on."

"Thank you, Dr Rasheed. We will leave you now. If anything in her condition changes, alert me immediately – day or night. I want a report as soon as you've found anything." Claire ushered Aryanna and Huw from the room.

Huw was rattled and stood uncertain in the hallway.

"Huw, I want to speak with you immediately. In the conference room, now," Aryanna whirled, and her white silk flourished around her. She paused for a moment and spun to face Claire.

"Claire, be on hand. I will wish to speak with you after I am finished with Huw." The word 'finished' hissed on her lips.

Claire acknowledged her command and watched Huw trail behind Aryanna. His shoulders slumped. She forced herself to walk calmly to the comms room. She slid behind the command controls and dialled up the conference room to listen in.

⤐

Conference Room: Huw

HUW CONFESSED ALL to Aryanna. The early Terra Blanca experiment, Maja's zealous social experiment designs. He assured Aryanna they'd left all that behind. They'd learnt the limits of human depravity when coerced and goaded. They focused instead on designing environments that invited humanity's better nature.

"I should have known about this, Huw! I'm an entrepreneur

and a scientist. I understand and appreciate human experiments. I am a human experiment myself with all the rejuvenation procedures I've had. But you've deceived me. What else are you hiding from me?"

Huw's old charm re-emerged. He was a consummate businessman, used to spin. The sudden confrontation on a long-buried secret had flummoxed him temporarily but now he was back in the saddle, riding the earnest horse for all it was worth.

"Aryanna, I can assure you, we have been up-front and frank about everything. Terra Blanca was our biggest mistake, and our biggest lesson. We have learnt from it and resolved never to repeat those same mistakes again. If Maja was here and able to speak for herself, you'd realise I speak the truth."

"But she isn't here, now. She is incapacitated. And frankly, I don't trust you to lead the organisation while my suspicion is on high alert. As of this instant, I am assuming control of Gaia Enterprises until we can assess the full extent of your deception."

"You can't do that!" gasped Huw.

"I most certainly can. Check Article 17.2 of the funding arrangements. It says, 'if there are any risks to the viability of the project, be it financial, operational, or other existential threat, then Aryanna Industries assumes full control of the project – and its management entity.' The management entity being Gaia Enterprises." Her black eyes were cold and blank like chunks of coal. She blinked to send Marina a message. "My team will be here shortly to detain you and to seize management. The authorities will be notified immediately."

"Aryanna – you can't! Be reasonable! The project is near completion! Terra Blanca is history!"

"Enough." She waved her long, graceful fingers at him as if brushing away dust. We will discuss the particulars later once the project is under control once more."

Huw was dumbfounded and shuffled his feet at the door,

uncertain if he should exit or try a new angle of persuasion. He recalled the anguish of the Terra Blanca incident. Huw had supported Maja's decision to run the experiment in the first place. He trusted her. She was brilliant. Her bets on human behaviour had been spot-on until then. When it all went sideways, he'd decided to stick with her. There was no way they could have anticipated the turn of events. It was not really Maja's fault. Somewhere deep within, Huw felt a tingle of guilt. If he'd abandoned Maja, he would have lost his investments, and the whole Gaia Enterprises would have been suspect. He had doubled down, they had buried the incident, and had continued on from strength to strength. Until now. Huw decided to tackle the argument with Aryanna.

The decision was taken from him as Aryanna's personal guard arrived and directed him to return to his quarters where he would be kept under supervision. Huw protested and begged to explain himself, but Aryanna ignored him. The guards stepped between them. All seemed lost.

❧

Conference Room: Claire

ARYANNA ACTIVATED THE room comms and summoned Claire. She arrived within moments, working hard to suppress her surprise at the conversation she had just seen unfold on the spy cam.

Aryanna stood at the huge window overlooking the desert. A late afternoon wind was whisking small tornadoes of dust around the trees which swayed and rustled with the gusts. Claire thought back to an earlier moment with Maja, at the same window, before it all went to Hell.

"How long have you known about Terra Blanca?" asked Aryanna.

"I only just discovered it," she lied. Claire was grateful Aryanna was facing the window, unsure if her lie would pass muster. "I was looking for guidance over the incident with David. I thought that the Terra Blanca files might have something that could help in dealing with difficult community decisions." The lies came more easily than she thought. "When I saw that authorisation – from Maja no less – I was shocked. And concerned."

Aryanna turned to consider Claire. Her smooth white face was a true mask. No movement at all to indicate whether she believed Claire or not. Now was the time to drive home her point, thought Claire. "Maja has been unusually obstinate and edgy with some of her decisions. I have felt all along she was treating this project as more of a social experiment than a commercial enterprise. Then to find that order, from Maja, well, I was terrified to see history repeating itself." That was true. Mostly.

Aryanna stepped a little closer and her big dark eyes roved all over Claire's face. The heavy silence was punctuated by the rise and swirl of the desert wind stirring the trees and sand beyond the glass.

"One never knows, with a whistleblower, if they are a traitor or a hero. Are you running a personal agenda or an altruistic one, I wonder?" she mused. Her voice rippled like a brook. Claire held her tongue, resisting the urge to defend herself.

"I don't know which it is, but I will find out. In the meantime, Claire Edwards, I need you to finish this project. I want you to respond to the crew when they call in as planned. Let them know Maja is indisposed and you have assumed management of Gaia Enterprises under my directive." Claire's spirit soared with delight.

Aryanna paused to brush an invisible stray hair from her forehead with a graceful finger.

"Thank you, Aryanna. I am honoured and will do my best, even under such difficult circumstances." She feigned a suitable amount of humility.

"See that you do. I want a full status report of the project, personnel and any other matter that might affect this project by 19:00 this evening." Aryanna left in a blur of silk.

Claire moved to the window to calm her whirling brain. The

wind gusts rattled the window and shook the trees, dry leaves waving as in salute.

It had taken all her resolve to break the long-held secrecy and reveal the truth of Terra Blanca to Aryanna. She'd composed a few lines of text and forwarded the signed authorisation that proved her story.

With Terra Blanca, everyone knew what had happened. It was one of the first world design projects with a select community of people. But something had gone wrong – terribly wrong – with the governance. It descended into tribal warfare and a whole section of the community had been brutally executed – murdered. Everyone assumed the tragedy was due to poor structure and weak rules.

What no one knew, except for a very few, was that it had been orchestrated by *Maja*. Maja had sent a troublemaker into the community as an experiment, to see how the leaders responded. The troublemaker had been tasked with amplifying competition and rivalry among the different sections of the community. Maja's secret plant led a rebellion on Terra Blanca. But it turned out the troublemaker did his job a little too well. He captured rival factions and imprisoned them, encouraged his followers to 'show them who's boss' and to use fear as a discipline tool. The movement got out of hand and prisoners were tortured. Meanwhile the governing faction moved in to quash the rebellion and executed its leaders – including Maja's hired troublemaker. The community was disbanded once the national authorities got wind of the executions, a practice long outlawed by all civilised societies. The leaders and rebels were tried and found guilty of multiple crimes – including murder. Terra Blanca was confined to history as a lesson of the dangers of unstructured communities left to fend for themselves, to invent laws as they saw fit.

No one knew it was Maja who had been the catalyst for the disaster. Maja – the Chief Executive Officer, the epitome of grace and compassion. No one would have believed it now. Except for the matter of the signed contract with the details of the assignment. Maja had told Claire of this experiment early in her career at Gaia Enterprises, as part of her education of what not to do. She'd brought Claire into her confidence to indicate how completely she trusted her and to emphasise the serious nature of their work in building safe and successful communities. Claire had trouble believing Maja herself until she went investigating all the material affiliated with the project and found the contract Maja had signed, buried in layers of encryptions. For some unknown reason at the time, she'd kept this discovery to herself instead of destroying it. Was it foresight?

But how could she have known her mentor, beautiful and wise Maja, would end up twisted and blind to her own ambitions. Claire's grief left her feeling adrift, floating like detritus carried by the desert wind.

She turned her focus to the present. She was at the helm of Gaia Enterprises, on the cusp of securing the biggest project they had ever tendered for, and the chance to make human history. This needed all her attention and resolve.

The battle is won. Now to win the war.

CHAPTER SIXTY-SEVEN

When we design a world, we design a future. We anticipate
a world worth living in. That doesn't happen by accident.
We can design an environment that encourages trust
and cooperation. The rest is up to the inhabitants.

THE WORLD DESIGNERS' MANIFESTO

SimHub: Xanthe

XANTHE NEEDED SOME thinking space. She left the comms room and headed to the atrium. She sat on the bench and stared up at the skylight. The patch of blue was implacable, unfathomable. Earth sky. She wondered what the sky would look like through such a window on the Moon. Or on Mars.

But that was a long way away now, she thought. They had to deal with Dave's betrayal and somehow get the project back on track before the inspection. In just three days time. The pressure was taking its toll and she rolled her shoulders to release some of the tension that had been building there.

Dave. When she thought about all their interactions, she felt sickened. All this time, hiding and lying, working against them.

But then she thought about why he was doing it: pushed to it by the transgressions of his husband. Dave was trying to protect his daughter and his husband, as well as his own reputation. It was a no-win situation. He must have known what he was risking, not least of which was his chance to be part of the Olympus Project!

Could they really continue working with him? She thought of Serena and Jonas buried under debris. What if they had died? The thought was terrible and dark. How could they ever trust him? Could they forgive him?

Maybe they couldn't right now. The shock and pain were all too recent. But could he be redeemed? Was he genuine in his contrition? Could he prove somehow that his intentions were good even if his choices had bad outcomes?

There was still one question that needed answering. She left the atrium and went to find Dave. This would make the decision for her.

᷍

Xanthe paused outside Dave's room where the door was ajar. She could see Xavier sitting on the bed next to him.

"All I want to know is – why," said Xavier.

Dave leant against the wall and studied the ceiling.

"Xavier, I'm not sure anything I say will truly explain it, no? I was trying to protect my little girl. I was trying to protect my husband. I thought that if slowing down our project a little would do that, then it was worth the price." He looked at Xavier and said earnestly, "I never, ever meant harm to come to anyone."

"Given the chance, would you do it differently?"

"Of course, I would want to do it differently! I'd give anything to go back in time and make different decisions. But I can't. I did what I did at the time, thinking it was the best option from what I had in front of me."

"Why did you not ask us for help?" They looked up at Xanthe in the doorway.

Dave shrugged and sighed. "Shame. I was so ashamed of my husband, his gambling, stealing from our daughter. Then threatening me. Ashamed of how I've let it go on and on, covering for him." Dave hid his face in his hands. "I am so ashamed. I have let everyone down." A sob rattled his chest.

Xanthe entered the room and sat down next to the two of them. "Didn't you trust us?" she asked.

Dave dropped his hands and his red eyes stared at Xanthe. "I'd trust you with my life. I *have* trusted you with my life."

"Then, why not tell us?" Xavier prompted.

"I don't know. I don't know." Dave searched the ceiling for answers. "I wish I did."

"How will you make it up to us? To Serena and Jonas in particular?" Xanthe asked.

Dave blew out a huge sigh. "Put me to work. I'll do anything I can to finish the project."

"How can we trust you?" Xavier said.

"I don't know. I wouldn't trust me after this if I were you. All I can do is to work hard and follow through."

They were quiet for a while, as they came to terms with the uncomfortable loss of something precious: trust.

"What are you prepared to sacrifice, Dave?" asked Xanthe. This was what she really wanted to know.

"What do you mean?"

"What are you prepared to give up?"

"Hang on a minute, I want to hear this!" Serena crowded into the room with Jonas and Troy behind her.

"I'd give anything to make things right," Dave said.

Xanthe tried again, choosing her words carefully. "Dave, are you prepared to let go of your husband? Are you prepared to hand him over to the authorities?"

Dave's face went pale. He looked at the faces of each of his team members. A tear rolled down his cheek.

"I think, perhaps, it's time," he said in a whisper.

∽

SimHub: Dave

THEY STAYED A little while longer in Dave's room. Serena, surprisingly, said very little. She studied Dave's every move, every word. Jonas interrogated Dave with the ins and outs of his sabotage, how he used the comms jammer to hide his actions. Troy wanted to know about his contacts at Spaceward Bound and how the bribery worked, who handled the transactions, who fed the information back to the leaders there. Xavier asked about Dave's husband, how he accessed the funds from Spaceward Bound, how he stole their daughter's money, how Dave thought Sven would react when Dave cut ties.

They took Dave's story apart, piece by piece. They analysed all the vulnerabilities of his world, his thinking, his feelings. At the end of it, Dave was utterly exhausted. He was laid bare, with all his failings for them to see.

Yet strangely, he felt not so much like an empty shell, but a cup, beginning to fill. His colleagues held him in that room, held his spirit, and leant into all the rough and broken bits of him. They reached through their own despair and frustration and anger and found him, searched him out, trying to understand. Though he did not feel forgiven – not yet – he did feel understood. From Xanthe and Xavier and Troy he felt waves of compassion. From Jonas he felt an understanding of someone else who has failed, and tried hard to come back and prove his worth. From Serena, he felt only wariness and suspicion, but the anger was gone. Or, at least, faded to an ember, smouldering quietly.

❧

SimHub: Xanthe

THEY MET AS planned around their kitchen conference room table, minus Dave, who was still locked in his room.

"So. What do we do?" asked Xanthe.

No one spoke. The air was heavy and rippled with anxiety.

"Basically, it comes down to this," said Xanthe. "We either oust him now from the project and make do on our own to get the work done – which will be crazy tough. Or we keep him and finish the project with him." She looked around the table, trying to gauge the sentiment in the room. "All of us know that this is not just about Olympus. All of us want to win the comp and get it done. But I don't think keeping Dave just for that reason is the right thing. If we keep him just to get the project finished this will be another form of bribery. It will breed resentment. And I don't want that in our team." She let that float between them. "This is about trust and how we can work with someone who has broken it. This is about our commitment to the Gaia Principles – specifically the principle of atonement. Of our own commitment to create a world worth living in. That's what we're really deciding now." She felt the words move something – hope – like a snake shifting sand.

"Xavier, what are your thoughts?" she asked.

The big man rocked back in his chair, arms crossed, considering the question. "I think what the man did was *vraiment merde.*" Disgust pinched his lips together. "But I have been thinking very deeply on this. He did it because he loved his family. I understand that completely. I do not agree with his actions, and I think he is one big *salaud* for what he did to us. But I want him to stay. I want him to prove he is not such a *trou du cul.* Plus, he owes us. We work him hard."

"Troy?" Xanthe asked.

"There but by the grace of God go I," he said. "My sense is that there is genuine contrition. He desperately regrets what he has done. There's no one who will work harder than someone who has something to prove. In my mind, he stays."

"Jonas?"

"I can't very well advocate for kicking him out when the team kept me around after what I did." Jonas rolled his shoulders and thought about the issue. At last, he said, "It sucks donkey's balls to lose the trust of the team. I can imagine Dave will go through all seven hells to earn it back."

"So... stay or go?" Xanthe nudged.

"I think... stay. I want to see what the little rotter will do to make it up to us."

"That leaves you, Serena. What are you thinking?"

Serena pulled her hair back from her face. A scowl had parked itself firmly across her features since she had left Dave's room.

"I am absolutely furious with that son of a bitch! Lying to us, pretending to be our friend, and all the while working against us, against the most important project of our careers. All to protect some limp-dicked tragic arsehole who stole from his own daughter? He put that creep ahead of *us*, ahead of SimHub crew, and the Olympus Project. He let those dickheads from Spaceward Bound run rings around us and sent a freakin' terrorist in to blow up the last bit of our hab, nearly killing me and Jonas in the process. And now you want to let him carry on, as if nothing happened. I'm sorry if I do not share your benevolence when it comes to Mr David Traitor Eriksson." Her fury billowed across them, and her colleagues shifted uneasily in their seats.

Xanthe broke the silence. "What would it take for you to consider atonement?"

"Oh, I considered it. I just don't think there is anything he might do that would make up for the betrayal."

"Likely that's true," said Troy. "How do you put back together the pieces of a shattered vase? You can't, no matter how carefully you try. There will always be something out of place, something missing, a little chip here, a dent there." He rubbed the stubble on his chin. "Our choice is to throw it all away or build something new with the pieces. It won't have the beauty and form of what we had before, but it will have something new. An intention. A commitment to take our bond more seriously. Not take it for granted. To look after it. To ask more of each other."

"And if he's just acting now? If he's just putting on another bloody good show?" Serena snapped. "For all we know he is still in cahoots with Spaceward Bound and scheming an eleventh-hour sabotage as we speak."

"That too is entirely possible," replied Troy. "If we offer the chance of atonement and redemption, we don't just fling the doors open and say, 'you're forgiven'. That would be stupid, no matter how much we want to believe in him. We would have to put conditions and limitations on all his activity to ensure his compliance."

"If we do that, is he really proving trustworthiness? Aren't we just making it impossible for him to cheat? That's not the same thing as allowing someone the ability to prove themselves." Serena said.

"I agree," said Xanthe. "It's putting a muzzle on a dog. There's no guarantee that if we ease restrictions, he won't upend the project again."

"If I were him," said Jonas, "I'd be thinking, 'what would be the point now?' We're three days from inspection, we know about his sabotage and so we'll be watching every little thing he does. He's done everything – as far as we know – that Spaceward Bound wanted him to. He's delayed the project significantly and we are at risk of not finishing and losing the bid. We could still expose the bribery and oust them from the comp. If Dave was truly committed to Spaceward Bound, he would let himself get kicked out, arrested, or whatever. Not help us. He knows that we can't finish the project without him. So, if he was still really the bad guy, his job is done. He can go. But he's offering to stay. He's offering to turn in his own husband, after years of protecting him, covering for him. That, I think, is a sign he's changed his tune."

Serena glowered but said nothing.

"If you're right about Dave," Xanthe said to Serena, "and we kick him out, what do you see happening for us?"

Serena looked uncomfortable. At last she said, "We expose Spaceward Bound's espionage and sabotage to the Lunar Commission, apply for an extension, then we work like crazy to get it done."

Xavier spoke next. "I like that as a strategy, mostly. Straightforward, clean. We cut out the cancer and staunch the bleeding. But, one problem: we have no proof. Dave was clear on that point. There is no way to trace the communication with the Spaceward Bound people. All we have is Dave's confession. For an outsider it could look like we are making up stories to cover up our own bungles."

"That rotten little turd has us over a barrel!" said Serena. "If we hand him over to authorities without any proof, we might not get an extension and we fail. If we keep him and he backstabs us again, we fail."

"Or," Troy added, "we keep him, he atones and we deliver."

"This is it," Xanthe said. "Which future do you want to bet on?"

CHAPTER SIXTY-EIGHT

"Defiance is a sexy thing. It's a human being stepping into their power and owning their corner of the world."

TROY BRUIN, PSYCHOLOGY TODAY, INTERVIEW

Gaia Desert Base Mission Control Headquarters: Claire

CLAIRE WAITED IN the comms room for Xanthe to report in. It had been a busy afternoon preparing contingencies, checking Maja's status and responding to Aryanna's sporadic questions. Aryanna had gone to interrogate Huw for another hour. No doubt he'd worked out Claire had been the one to let the cat out of the bag. She'd worry about that later. In any case, truth trumped loyalty.

Claire stretched her arms overhead to release some of the tension in her neck and shoulders. With Maja incapacitated and Aryanna in a rage, she had breathing room now to get the Olympus Project back on track. She could save it from Maja's reckless experimentation. She could pin down Xanthe and expose her incompetence. No way that namby-pamby upstart would take the reins of Gaia Enterprises while Claire had worked so damned hard for too damn long guiding it to its present glory.

Xanthe's holo jumped to life and shut down Claire's reverie. To the matter at hand, she thought.

"Commander Waters, report." No time for niceties now. Keep it straight and official.

"Good evening, Control," Xanthe said, responding to the formal tone. "Pardon me, but I was expecting all the Directors for this brief. Will Huw and Maja be attending?"

"Maja has had a medical emergency and is currently unconscious and being monitored. Huw is... attending to her," Claire lied.

"Oh my God! Is she alright?"

"She is receiving the best of care. Cause of the collapse is unknown, though likely it is fatigue or dehydration." It's astonishing how easily the lies came now, thought Claire. "In any case, we need to keep focused on the project. I have been placed in charge of Gaia Enterprises, reporting directly to Aryanna. We are already behind schedule and have this issue of sabotage and illegal activity to address. What is the SimHub crew determination?"

"SimHub crew has met and considered our path forward." Xanthe pushed her emotions aside and her face drew serious. This is new for her, thought Claire. "We are agreed that David Eriksson will be retained under strict supervision for the completion of the project. We recommend Gaia Enterprises takes steps with the Lunar Commission to address Spaceward Bound's sabotage with respect to the security breach and explosion in the Hub's extension. For our part, we will assist David with securing his daughter's finances and placing a restraining order on his husband."

Claire considered this development carefully. If they kept the traitor working on the project, it could serve two purposes: complete the project as per spec and still be in the race for the Moon. It would also give her time to build her case against Xanthe as an incompetent leader. There were the endless project delays, the subterfuge with their silly comms jammer they thought she didn't know about, and the team dynamic was under threat. Claire had watched the last SimHub crew meeting and knew that Serena was furious at the outcome. They could probably hold it together to complete the build, but after that? Unlikely they would unite once out of the SimHub. Claire could suggest it was Xanthe's poor leadership that let the sabotage go undetected for so long. Yes, this decision could work to her advantage. But she still had one more card to play.

"Commander, you will hand over David for arrest and prosecution."

"Pardon? The SimHub crew agreed to manage the situation ourselves so we can finish the SimHub."

"I heard you. Nonetheless, you will hand over the traitor," Claire insisted.

Claire watched Xanthe buckle, then steel herself for a response.

"I will not. David stays with us until the project is complete."

Claire stared with a menacing look. "Are you defying me, Commander?"

"I am defying an order that contravenes the agreement we have about SimHub governance. As a crew, we assessed the situation, designed a course of action, and now we will follow that through." Xanthe glared back at Claire.

"Your insubordination is noted, Commander Waters."

Xanthe raised her chin in defiance.

"David will be handed over to Gaia Enterprises officials following the completion of the SimHub. Your role as Commander will be reviewed immediately after that. Is that understood?"

Xanthe nodded, her pixie face alive with fury.

"Now, let's go over the detail of the project work and how you propose to manage the traitor through it all."

CHAPTER SIXTY-NINE

*The best things we build are the things we
build together, with love, for love.*

WORLD DESIGNERS' MANIFESTO

SimHub: Xanthe

THEY WORKED AROUND the clock, stealing sleep in snatches. Debris from the blast was cleared by the investigators who were now busy with forensics. SimHub crew moved quickly to set up the wall printer to finish the job, along with the wiring and the other design features. They worked in pairs and never left Dave alone.

Xanthe attended the call between Dave and his husband Sven. She noted the genuine shock and surprise on Sven's face as Dave told the love of his life that it was over, that he had called the gambling authorities and that he would have no access to their daughter until the stolen money was repaid. Xanthe watched the heartbreak as Sven swung between pleading, emotional bribery and direct threats. Dave trembled through the whole thing but held his ground. When he turned off the holo, he held his head in his hands for a long time. Xanthe put her arm around his shoulders, said nothing and waited. At last, he lifted his head. His face was pale and drawn.

"I've tried for twenty years to do that," he said.

"What made you be able to do it now?" asked Xanthe.

"Family. My SimHub crew family."

Xanthe sat with Dave in silence. She thought of Simon, their life together, their son. She felt her grief recede. It was an ebb that left her heart wounded but still beating. She knew now that their time together was also drawing to a close. She knew she would miss Simon. She already did. Already grieved the end of their marriage. But it was time for an ending.

"Dave," she said quietly. "Will you sit with me while I call Simon?"

❧

SimHub Inspection: Xanthe

THE LUNAR COMMISSION sent their inspectors in private helicopters. Aryanna and Claire briefed them first at Mission Control, then joined them on the flight to the SimHub. As directed, SimHub crew waited outside the Hub in full space gear. It was mid-morning and the heat was up.

"My balls are chafing in this suit," said Jonas over the helmet comms.

"I have a swimming pool of sweat running down my arse," said Xavier.

"You boys are going to be stink-town when we get out of this get-up! Make sure you wipe yourselves off carefully when we take our guests through the SimHub. Don't want them choking to death on your pong!" said Serena.

"You too, Troy," added Dave. "You have some sort of King Kong Pong."

They all stopped and turned to look at Dave. It was his first joke of any sort since the incident.

Troy's smile spread wide, and he said, "Call me Kong, then Dave!" and slapped him on the back. "Or better yet, King!"

"Pong will do, I think," he replied shyly. He was pleased they'd laughed. All except Serena who continued to scowl at him.

"Here they come!" Xanthe said.

The helicopter landed and the party hurried over while ducking the rotor blades. Xanthe noticed how clean they looked, how fresh. She suddenly felt very tired, the past few days hitting her in the chest. A year's worth of work was about be tested and assessed. This was it.

Xanthe met the party and led them to the airlock. They all crammed inside and waited for the system to go through its cycles. The airlock opened into the SimHub suit room, and the guests waited patiently as the crew stripped out of their suits, talking through the finer details of the entrance design and functions as they did so. Xanthe was out of her suit first and guided the guests into the atrium while the rest of SimHub crew had a chance to wipe themselves down before following quickly behind.

The atrium was Xanthe's pride and joy. The dome allowed a view to the sky and was populated by a forest of plants that reached skyward, while some hung from the ceiling, drawing the eye upward.

"The vertical lift of the plants to the sky reminds the viewer of their origins. As a dweller on Olympus, we can look up through the veil of plants to the endless black sky of the Universe and feel connected still to the Earth. It simultaneously reminds us of home, while reaching for the stars. For me, it's like a green womb, helping humanity birth its next evolution." She smiled, enjoying the sense of awe she always felt in this room looking up, and knew the others were moved too. The room had a functional aspect to it as well. It helped provide a type of bellows to the whole Hub, expanding and contracting slightly with the outside temperature while the plants absorbed any excess CO_2 and gave back oxygen.

Serena led the next part of the tour to the comms room, where they had the map of the completed SimHub, along with the extensions that would be made on future missions. She described the excavation process and the 3D wall printing that formed the interior of the unit.

Dave, Serena and Jonas took turns guiding the group though the practical aspects of life management of the SimHub: air purification and filtering, waste management and repurposing, water recycling, and all the electronics and AI networks that were fitted throughout.

Xavier was practically bursting at the seams by the time they made it to the Food Hub. His enthusiasm was infectious, and the inspectors grinned through his passionate explanation of vegetable plant stimulation, tomato and cucumber harvests, potatoes grown in human waste compost, the 3D food printer and lab meat that was all operating in a self-contained and self-supporting system.

"We have even produced a genetic copy of milk molecules! So now I can have real milk in my *café*! Which I can tell you is much needed, because the coffee otherwise is *merde*. But we have work to do in this department, *mes amis*, before we can say we have the perfect Parisian espresso!"

Claire winced at his obscenity. Troy was aware of her sensitivity to language and quickly interrupted to show them to the Stim Room. This was Troy's particular project and he was keen to showcase the range of its experiences. He had the inspectors don Virtual Reality suits, Scent Stim nosepieces and the VR headsets. The rest of the crew waited in the kitchen as the guests laughed and hooted through Troy's pleasure palace. They emerged an hour later, red-faced and beaming.

"That was extraordinary! I've been to the Maldives, I've been to Nepal, I've been to Antarctica. And I swear I was right back there again in that get-up! Troy, that was remarkable. Thank you!" Troy bowed at the compliment.

They gave the inspectors refreshments in the kitchen where they sampled all of Xavier's culinary wizardry. They were particularly impressed with the protein extracted from excess CO_2 in the atrium and mixed with the algae flour to produce crunchy green bread.

"Almost as good as cricket protein," Troy whispered to Jonas, who stifled a laugh.

They came at last to the SimHub's latest extension, the rebuilt tunnel.

"The idea here," said Xanthe, "is to add visual interest to a very functional part of the Hub. Being in a self-contained bubble with limited space can be challenging for space-farers. We wanted to make sure they will never get bored of their environment, and have full sensory variety and interest throughout the Hub. Now, as you can see, this section looks like one long tunnel with rooms branching off it. Much like a dormitory or hotel corridor." The inspectors nodded. It was a dull, windowless space. "So, we added a bit of interest. Apollo, bring up the jungle vista."

The corridor erupted in sound and colour. The walls and ceiling were moving with jungle vines, the floor was littered and crowded with plants, or the illusion of plants. The air smelled earthy and moist. The inspectors gasped.

"There are interconnected rooms off the main corridor." Xanthe slid a door back to reveal a room still bursting with illusory jungle life. "Apollo, change this to bedroom, please." The room changed instantly to a cosy space. Xanthe pulled a handle on the wall and a bed folded down. She pulled two more handles and a desk came down. She pulled a felt cube from inside the wall and placed it before the desk. "Each room can be accommodation, or a workspace, or a social space, as the community requires, giving it more flexibility in design and function. Or it can remain as a passageway for a particular theme. Apollo, bring up the art gallery vista." The room faded to a stunning display of classic paintings. Monet, Van Gogh, Picasso. As they went through a sliding door to the adjoining room, they saw old masters, then Renaissance art, then modern sculptures. "There is a full menu of all the art galleries on Earth. Your choice." Xanthe was pleased by their enthusiastic response. "But we don't go to the Moon – or to Mars, or to any other planet – just to wish we were back on Earth. We go to explore. Apollo, bring up the rover." The room changed again. It was as if they were standing on the Moon's surface, barren and stark against the blackness of space. "Let's take a walk on the Moon," she said. They followed her out into the corridor. The tunnel was now the lunar landscape. They walked slowly down its length, all the while feeling they were taking steps on the Moon's surface. "Or perhaps you'd like to take a look at Saturn? Apollo, bring up Saturn's satellite vista please." Then they were floating with the perspective of a satellite, and before them the surface of Saturn and all its colourful swirls displayed before them. "We get live feeds from the rover and the satellite, so the view is always different."

The tour continued with detailed explanations of daily life in the Hub, the effects on their mental and physical health of being in a contained environment for a year, the supplies required for the first Hub construction.

"Aside from the sensory stimulation, we have also developed learning programs to fast-track adult development for greater leadership maturity."

"And how do you do that?" one of the inspectors asked.

"The name Olympus is an ancient one, meant to be home of the gods. Many mountains are named for their imposing height on Earth and even on Mars. The idea of Olympus – a home for the gods – for humanity now on the Moon, gave us the idea of elevating human consciousness. Our training programs focus on developing heart, head and gut connection as a starting point. We come to know ourselves deeply, our foibles, our strengths. We offer programs that throw people together and challenge them to solve problems in the difficult lunar environment, where consequences of actions are vivid and real. And then we challenge perspective in exercises of compassion and complex values exploration, in simulated rock-and-a-hard-place scenarios. The objective is to accelerate people's wisdom and compassion. When they see more, they lead better."

They arrived back at the atrium. "Apollo, bring up the Olympus Project message."

The room dimmed and the holo projection created the illusion of standing on a mountain top with an enormous marble pillar. Statues of various gods towered above them all the way to the ceiling. Across the dark window to the sky, the words appeared in silver writing: *"Memento Mori"*.

"What does that mean?" another inspector asked.

"It's what Roman generals used to ask their slaves to whisper to them as they rode in triumph through the streets of Rome. It means, 'Remember you are mortal'."

The small group looked quietly around them, marvelling at the view.

"What's been your favourite part of this experience?" one of the inspectors asked Xanthe.

She thought for a moment and said, "Learning who we are when all we have is each other." The inspector smiled at that and asked no more questions.

CHAPTER SEVENTY

No dawn ever sees a dusk. It's only day and night that
see the sky painted twice. Dawn to day to dusk to night.
But where does it begin? Where does it end?

MAJA GARCIA, THE JOURNALS

SimHub: Xanthe

AT LAST, THEY left. Xanthe accompanied the visitors to the airlock and cycled them out. She watched them re-board the helicopter and return to Mission Control for further interviews with Claire and Aryanna. Huw was apparently still looking after Maja, who remained unconscious.

Maja would be devastated she missed the guests. The culmination of a life's work! Xanthe felt a twinge of regret for her mentor.

She headed back to the kitchen, where the rest of the crew was waiting.

"Well?" asked Serena.

"Well… we did it. Congratulations, SimHub crew! Our Olympus Project inspection is done."

They hooted and hugged. Even Dave got a back slap or two. Serena ignored him and hugged the others.

"When do we get out of isolation?" Xavier asked. "I've been so focused on getting to this point, I have no idea when we are meant to shut down or get out. Are we free yet?"

"Claire told me the inspectors are making their decision in a day or two. We are the last prototype on the inspection list, and they know we have been locked down for a very long time. Claire wants us to keep up our routines and protocols until they make a decision, in case they want to do a secondary inspection. So I'm afraid it's business as usual for the next two days. We might start by getting some rest! You all look dead on your feet."

"I'm going for a shower. I want to be more King than Pong," Troy said.

"Thank goodness," Serena said. "My eyes are watering around you."

"Mine too," said Dave and he wiped his eyes. "Hey, SimHub crew," he croaked. The quaver in his voice pulled them up short. "Thank you. I'm not sure I deserved a second chance. But I do know that I'm grateful for you all. Whether you keep me or ditch me in the end, you've saved me." They were awkward with each other, unsure of the new tenets of the relationship.

At last Jonas broke the weirdness. "Well, that's all a bit biblical," he said. "You're still in the shit, Dave. And by my count, you have a month's worth of my underpants to wash. You can start with today's. There's a bucket of sweat to wring from them since the water-re-claimer on my suit was doing overtime and couldn't keep up."

"It would be my honour to wring and wash your underpants, Mr Seaborn," Dave said with a courtier's bow. "Let us to it."

※

Xanthe lay on one of the bean bags in the Stim Room, with the star vista projected on the walls and Vivaldi playing softly. She was too wired to find sleep just yet. Her body craved it, but her mind was still raking over the inspection, checking they hadn't missed anything essential, hoping they'd made the correct impression.

Troy entered and asked if he could join her. She nodded and he climbed on the bag next to her, their legs touching. Xanthe noted how warm his skin felt against hers.

"Hey, Xanthe, I want to run something past you," he said. He clicked something in his pocket and then pulled out the comms jammer. Alarmed that Troy would need a confidential conversation, Xanthe sat up.

"What is it?"

"When you told me about Maja, I called up Dr Mohammad to check on her test results."

"And?"

"Something is troubling me about it. Maja has been unwell. Mohammad is calling it cellular degeneration. Apparently, she has not responded to any of the rejuvenation treatments."

"Do you mean she's… dying?" asked Xanthe.

"Yes, slowly. Like the rest of us. It's called ageing."

"So what's bothering you?"

"Her initial test results show no indication of dehydration or fatigue, like Mohammad initially suspected. There's no sign of brain aneurism or cardiac distress. She's just… sleeping."

"What? That doesn't make sense."

"The only thing I know of that would cause someone to go into a deep sleep without any kind of chemical or biological trace is a special tea tincture that I manufacture privately."

"You and your tea tinctures! Did you give some to Maja?"

"No. But I did give some to Claire. Back at selection."

Of course! That's what was in the package Xanthe saw Troy give Claire. Along with the giant kiss.

"Are you and Claire… ?" Xanthe raised her eyebrows.

"Not anymore. We had a thing when we trained together. I let it go. She kind of held on a bit. Anyway, after selection she was struggling to sleep and asked me for something. I gave her the tea, along with its dosages. Too much, and she could be out for days."

"Do you think Claire gave Maja the tea? On purpose? An overdose?" Xanthe sat up in alarm. "But why?"

"I don't know. It's almost too horrible to consider. But I do know Claire has always wanted to run Gaia Enterprises after Maja. And now she's got her chance."

Xanthe looked at Troy, startled by this revelation. "Oh my God, Troy. Maja asked me to consider succeeding her at Gaia. After the Olympus Project. She flew out to find me, in person, in Sydney, just before they announced the selection for this project. She told me I was her preferred candidate, that she would back me when the time came. Do you think Claire found out? Do you think she could drug Maja?"

"I don't know. I truly hope not. But when it comes to power and ambition, even the most noble twist their ideals to justify their actions. Power is a deadly drug, best sipped and never swallowed. I fear Claire's got a taste for it, and is lining up to drink her fill."

"This is serious, Troy. What should we do?"

"I'll get Mohammad to check for traces of the tea. If Claire is administering it, it would have to be orally. There might be some dribbled out on her pillow or bedclothes."

"And if she is?"

Troy looked at Xanthe, his blue eyes clouded with concern. "There will be a storm of epic proportions. Let's hope Gaia can survive it."

SimHub crew crowded into the comms room. Aryanna's holo popped into view with Claire beside her. They'd had news that Spaceward Bound was disqualified pending investigation of unspecified 'irregularities'. That left Gaia and Human Habs in the running. There was no news about the Human Habs project – they had been incredibly secretive.

"SimHub crew I am delighted to announce that the Lunar Commission has named Gaia Enterprises as the successful candidate for the Olympus Project. Congratulations – you are going to the Moon!"

The room erupted in shouts of joy. The hugged each other and clapped.

It took Aryanna a few minutes to regain their attention.

"Apparently, Human Habs had a very strong submission. Their life support systems were miles ahead of ours." Serena bristled at that. Life support tech was her specialty, and she did not appreciate the implied criticism. "We may have to modify our specs and purchase their technology for the design and build. Or we may end up in a collaboration with them. We are currently in negotiation with them and the Lunar Commission over this. Regardless, the rest of our design and build was a clear winner. Congratulations!"

Aryanna briefed them on next steps, the timeline for closing the SimHub and other logistics. They listened with due respect until the end of the transmission.

Xanthe signed off once they were done and said, "Our quarantine is over. Who is up for some fresh air?"

Gaia Desert Base Mission Control Headquarters: Claire

CLAIRE RETREATED TO her own accommodation pod for some solitude once the announcement was communicated to the SimHub crew. She felt a deep river of satisfaction course through her veins. They'd won the Olympus Project and she was at the helm of Gaia Enterprises. Huw was under investigation, as was Maja.

Claire thought about the past twelve months and the years before that. Everything she did was to serve Gaia. She had been dedicated and loyal. She had long admired Maja and believed strongly in what Gaia stood for. But this last project had twisted something in Maja, Claire thought. She was experimenting with

Jonas. And the others too. Maja had pushed for potential over skill in the final SimHub crew selection. Not to mention referencing Xanthe as her successor. It was all too much.

It was up to her now, Claire decided. She had to save Gaia from the founder's delusions of grandeur. It happened all the time. Power had a way of untethering people from what was right. Claire wouldn't let Gaia fall prey to Maja's mistakes. She had stopped it now. She had Maja and Huw restrained and the project saved and back on track.

It was time now for Maja to face the music and account for Terra Blanca and all her decisions since. Claire was secure enough in her position after having delivered the Olympus Project. They needed her to steer it on its next step. Hopefully, minus Xanthe and that traitor David. There would be a reckoning.

Yes, the future was bright.

⸙

Nearby the SimHub: Xanthe

IT WAS EARLY evening and the sun lingered over the hills like a red mistress trailing her shawl.

Xanthe and Troy sat on a rocky escarpment, breathing in the warm, fine air, enjoying the desert sounds and smells. The others walked in the gully below, savouring each other's company and the space around them. Even Serena seemed to tolerate Dave's presence. This was a step up from seething resentment, Xanthe figured.

"What now?" asked Troy.

Xanthe breathed out. She closed her eyes feeling the vastness of the desert, the smallness of them. "We go forward. We build worlds," she said.

Troy took her hand in his.

This time, she let him.

END

LIST OF CHARACTERS

Aryanna Sharif – founder of Earth Alliance, founder and owner of Aryanna Industries

Claire Edwards – Chief Operating Officer for Gaia Enterprises

David Eriksson – pilot of world design business Archello in Helsinki

Dr Jade Mandez – life support medical technician

Dr Mohammad Rasheed – personal physical to the Sultan of Dubai and life extension specialist

Dr Pierre Martin – a Canadian surgeon involved in various genetic modification research projects for human adaptation in low gravity; Surgeon at Humanité Plus

Eli Heltay – spokesperson for the Earth Alliance

Gina Casellatti – mechanic for Space Adventures

Huw Chan – co-founder of Gaia Enterprises

James Gregoire – medical technician

Jonas Seaborn – graduate in land reclamation design, ship engineering and waste management. Son of famous world designers, Don and Jenny Seaborn.

Lincoln Ellison – founder of Surf Tech, a conglomerate of startup tech companies in the Metaverse. Surf Tech was rebranded as Spaceward Bound.

Madison Floyd – decorated pilot and contract air force trainer for Spaceward Bound

Maja Garcia – co-founder and Chief Executive Officer of Gaia Enterprises

Max King – life support technician and Everest adventurer, specialist in oxygen adaptation technology

Pabi Gupta – Singaporean Air Force pilot

Serena Fox – underground world designer, salvage diver, life support expert

Simon – world designer, Earth First advocate

Sophia – daughter of David Eriksson

Sven – husband of David Eriksson

Tony Boss – world designer for Gaia Enterprises

Troy Bruin – world designer for Gaia Enterprises, three-time winner of Sexiest Human Alive, founder and designer of the New Baths of Caracalla

Xanthe Waters – world designer for Damier Designs, former paramedic and ex-Gaia Enterprises world designer

Xavier Consus – world designer for Gaia Enterprises, designer and founder of Terra Verdi

Earth Alliance – advocacy group for Green Economy and the Earth First movement

Earth Rise Tours: low-orbit space tourism operator

Gaia Enterprises – one of the original world design companies

Human Habs – space medicine research and operator of Earth Rise Tours

Lunar Commission – international cooperative agency to establish the first public Moon Base

Sea Rover – the first floating world designed by Don and Jenny Seaborn

Space Adventures – low-orbit space tourism operator

Spaceward Bound – contender for the Olympus Project, previously named Surf Tech, founded by Lincoln Ellison, backed by tech giant Metasyn

Terra Blanca – failed social human experiment in one of the first built worlds

AUTHOR'S NOTE

Thanks so much for sharing the Gaia journey on the Olympus Project!

This book came about as I finished reading Ursula K. Le Guin's marvellous Earthsea series. The themes and imagery haunted me for ages.

As I basked in the afterglow of those wonderful books, I wondered if fiction might be a more powerful way to explore important leadership themes. If a story gets under our skin, might it have the potential to change us from the inside out?

I asked myself:

- How might a novel explore important leadership questions that we face as Earth's inhabitants?

- What kind of world are we moving towards?

- What kind of leadership might we need to deal with it effectively?

- How does leadership maturity affect our approach to survival questions?

- Can we overcome the downsides of earlier stages of leadership maturity when the stakes are high?

- How does trust work? Can it be rebuilt once broken?

- Can we design environments and learning programs that accelerate leadership maturity so we are better able to handle the complex challenges ahead of us?

- What is our relationship to power?

- How does power create blind spots?

- What if we made human development central to our world and community designs?

And then the characters and world took hold of me and we were off on an adventure.

Some readers may be interested in exploring the leadership themes further. As a leadership educator, I host a community of senior leaders in an advanced leadership development program called *Amplifiers*. I also work with leaders and teams in getting equipped for the leadership challenges ahead. If you're interested in navigating the adventures and perils ahead with like-minded leadership explorers, then check us out at www.zoerouth.com

I have also created accompanying leadership resources for the book. You can access these for free at www.TheOlympusProject-book.com

I wish you well on your leadership adventures!

In the meantime, I would like to give deep appreciation to all those who helped bring this book to life.

Thanks goes first to my editor, Darren Nash, who was patient and encouraged me as a first-time novelist. Your feedback helped uncover the potential in my first clumsy pages. I am grateful also to copyeditor and proofreader, Natalie Sweet, and her laser-sharp eyes. Thanks for saving us from sinking in a sea of errors!

I am deeply grateful too for my father-in-law Paul Routh's suggestion I reach out to geologist Ross Fardon, who gave me a fabulous, in-depth and highly entertaining account of how a tsunami might hit the east coast of Australia and wreak all the destruction I've described in The Olympus Project. This established the setting of the book nicely. Thanks Ross!

Thank you also to DD who spent an hour with me sharing all the nitty gritty about pigs and their curious behaviour. I always wondered if pigs really could eat a human. Now I know.

To my cover designers at Damonza – you guys are great! It was love at first sight.

To my beta readers, Alex Ogg and Victoria Walker, thanks for your generous appraisal of the story. It's terrifying to share a draft with all its wobbly bits, and you were gentle and gracious with me – thank you!

Thanks to my team, Louise Dalglish Smith, Abby Lastimosa, Jules Smith and Chris Ashmore who kept the ship running as I buried myself from time to time in the Gaia world.

My husband Rob gets all my love and gratitude for cooking dinners, keeping me grounded and encouraging my writing life. Thanks, honey!

Lastly, to you, my dear reader, thank you for sharing your attention and imagination with this story. Without you, it's just ink and pixels.

Zoë Routh

June 2022.

ABOUT THE AUTHOR

Zoë Routh is a leadership expert, speaker and multiple award-winning author specialising in teams and people stuff. She shows leaders and teams struggling with office politics and silos how to work better together.

She has worked with individuals and teams internationally and in Australia since 1987. From the wild rivers of northern Ontario to the remote regions of Australia, Zoë guides teams to navigate the wilderness of leadership.

Her flagship program *Amplifiers* is a proven and popular national advanced leadership development program for CEOs, Managing Directors, General Managers and Senior Executives from across different sectors.

Zoë is the author of four leadership books. Her fourth book, *People Stuff – Beyond Personality Problems: An advanced handbook for leadership*, won 'Book of the Year' at the Australian Business Book Awards 2020.

Zoë is the producer of the Zoë Routh Leadership Podcast, a show about all things people stuff in leadership.

Zoë is an outdoor adventurist and enjoys telemark skiing, has run six marathons, is a one-time belly dancer, has survived cancer and loves hiking in the high country. She is married to a gorgeous Aussie and is a self-confessed dark chocolate addict. She is English-born, Canadian-raised, Australian-adopted, Outdoor Adventurist and Experiential Educator, Truth Teller, Learner, One-Time Belly Dancer, Slayer of Dragons, and (former) Mother of Chickens.

Connect with Zoë here:

https://www.zoerouth.com

https://www.facebook.com/zoe.routh

https://twitter.com/zoerouth

https://au.linkedin.com/in/zoerouth

https://www.instagram.com/zoerouth/